CRUEL ENFORCER

MAFIA WARS - BOOK THREE

MAGGIE COLE

PULSE PRESS

PROLOGUE

Sergey Ivanov

BEFORE ZAMIR DESTROYED OUR LIVES, MY MOTHER ALWAYS claimed when one door closes, another one opens. She would say it when we were down on our luck and barely had enough food or the lights would flicker off from an unpaid bill.

Somehow, she and my father always found a way to open the next door. Things in our home would get good again until the subsequent chain of events, so I always took new doors opening as a positive scenario.

Until Zamir showed me reality.

Ever since my father's death, I've seen how the door swings open but isn't full of light or ways to solve problems. All the new entryway represents is another path into some new situation, which seems to create more issues swirling with deeper pain.

Tonight, a new door opens. The feeling of dread washes over me when my phone rings. "Eloise, are you almost through security?" I've been in the airport waiting for her for over an hour. My driver parked in the car lot. According to the arrival screen, her flight landed, but she hasn't responded to my messages. It's not the first time she forgot to notify me when she got off the plane. And it's not always easy for her to get through the terminal, but this is the longest I've ever waited for her.

Over the last few months, Eloise's modeling career has significantly taken off. People recognize her wherever she goes and ask for autographs. While she won't admit it, she loves the attention. She will stop whatever she's doing and sign. I wanted to add a bodyguard to keep her safe, but she refused.

Her thick, French accent comes through the line. "Darling, I'm so sorry. I forgot to call you earlier today. I'm not coming to Chicago this weekend."

The pit in my stomach grows. "Is this a joke?"

Her voice turns to annoyance. "No. There's a new nightclub opening my agency wants me to attend."

I move to the side of the airport, toward the corner where there aren't any people. My delivery is calm, but I'm boiling inside. "I'm in the airport right now."

"Sorry. I got swamped, and it slipped my mind," she snaps.

Meaning, she wasn't thinking about me.

Does she ever?

"My brother's rehearsal dinner starts in an hour. The wedding is tomorrow," I bark.

Eloise groans. "Don't be dramatic. I'll see you next weekend."

My jaw twitches. I run my hand through my hair. "Don't bother coming. We're finished."

"What? Don't be silly. I'll fly in next weekend," she states, as if missing my brother's wedding weekend isn't a big deal.

I've said a lot of things to Eloise over the years. Never once have I told her I'm through with her. I breathe through my nose and close my eyes. "I told you months ago to plan on being here this weekend. It's a big event for my family. You've bailed the last two times, and this time, you didn't even bother to tell me you aren't coming."

"I flew in and surprised you to make up for it."

"Yeah, because you were horny as fuck, and only stayed four hours to get off," I spit out.

She rattles off something in French then says in English, "Stop being a baby. I'll see you next weekend."

"No. You won't. Have a nice life, Eloise." I hang up, text my driver to pull up, and storm outside into the snow. Out of all the nasty things Eloise has ever done, this I'm taking personally.

She's never committed to me. We only see each other when she's in Chicago. But she knows what my brothers mean to me.

I'm already agitated enough. My brothers and I intentionally created a war between the two most powerful crime families. The evidence we planted to set up one of Zamir Petrov's thugs was finally discovered. It linked him to the death of Lorenzo Rossi.

For months, we waited for the evidence to show up. It took all the patience I had to not obsess over it. If anything went wrong, the deal Boris made with Zamir for our freedom would be in jeopardy.

My mother created a debt with Zamir when my father died. My brothers and I were ignorant of it. Then Boris found out. I was twelve when Zamir kidnapped her. He made us learn to torture and kill men in order to save her. I don't remember which night with Zamir it was when my mother could no longer look at me. When he allowed her to return home, she couldn't bear to be in the same room as me.

We didn't get my mother back. We saved the shell of the woman who used to be her. The woman who returned to our home barely spoke to my brothers, but she completely ignored me. Shortly after, she killed herself. I came home and water was seeping under the bathroom door. I broke it down and found my mother in a bloody tub.

For five years, I barely slept. I never knew when Zamir would call. Nightmares haunted me. Men's voices, the smell of their decay, and visions of their agonizing faces filled my every thought day and night. None of it ever went away. Anxiety plagued me. If I fell asleep and missed his call, there would be consequences to pay. I learned the night of my mother's funeral what happens when you don't act on Zamir's wishes. My brothers got a front-row seat to watch.

Then, when I was seventeen, Boris negotiated a deal for our freedom. We aren't really free. Once a year, Zamir still owns Boris. That means he still owns us. Part of the deal is all Ivanovs are off-limits. So far, Zamir has held up his end of the bargain. I don't believe it will last forever. You can't mix with the devil and expect him to keep his word.

I'm always waiting for the other shoe to drop. Whenever Boris gets the text from him, warning he's going to require him to do whatever sadistic thing he has planned, my fixation on killing Zamir and destroying everything he's a part of intensifies. My insomnia can last weeks. Sometimes it'll stretch past a month. Screwing Eloise was the one thing to calm me. Except for the last few months. The few times I've seen her, the spark I usually feel for her isn't there. She begs me for my dick as she always has when we're together. In some ways, she's more desperate than ever for what I give her.

The problem is, her confidence, which I usually admire, has morphed into ego and snobbery. The remarks she usually reserves for others have found their way to me. While I control her in the bedroom, I would never want her to be a doormat in public or private. Somehow, she's under the impression it's okay to treat me like one. I'm not sure when it changed. So much is going on, I didn't notice it until recently.

When Boris called a meeting and told us the war had started, a calm went through me. You would think a war would do the opposite, but I could have just had a mind-blowing orgasm and smoked a joint after, I felt so much peace. Then he dropped another bomb. And the ticking in my jaw and tightening of my chest started all over again.

The head of the Polish mafia, Bruno Zielinski, visited Giovanni Rossi in prison. Giovanni is Lorenzo's father and the head of the Italian mafia. It makes me uneasy. If they form an alliance against the Petrovs, it will be harder to keep things in equilibrium between each side. The war could backfire on us.

My mother's words, "When one door closes, another opens," ring in my ears, but I'm not sure I like what I see on the other side. One thing I've learned is you need to choose your door wisely. Eloise standing me up for an hour at the airport during my brother's wedding weekend is just the icing on the cake.

Selfish woman.

Everything about our relationship is about her. I should have ended things with her a long time ago. I kept thinking we were too good together for her not to eventually drop her *I don't do relationships* act and commit to me.

All she wants is my cock.

Sure, everyone close to me thinks she's a bitch. She's a strong woman. I like that about her. She can stand up for herself and doesn't let others take advantage of her. In public, she's a piranha. She'll eat you up and spit you out just for looking at her the wrong way. It's a quality I wish my mother would have had. Maybe then she wouldn't have fallen prey to Zamir.

I never reprimand Eloise for her actions. It turns me on watching her alpha attitude with others. Not the times she is nasty for no reason but the ones where others underestimate her. One time, someone commented on us being together since she's Black and I'm white. It was a woman, so I couldn't show her my wrath like I would have had she been a man, but Eloise put her right in her place.

Alone in the bedroom, she can't do anything without asking for my permission. Usually, it's while she begs. She's submissive. I'm the opposite and demand full control. Experiencing her morph from the powerful, take-charge woman she shows the world to one who fully trusts me to determine her every move is something I get off on. The first time I showed her who was in charge confused her. She wasn't used to it. No one had made her succumb to their every wish or made her give up her control. She didn't understand how she could love it so much. It created an addiction within her for more. I saw it. It's a side of her no one else gets to see.

Well, not many.

I know she dates other men when she's not in Chicago. I'm free to see other women, too. I rarely take advantage of my freedom and don't ask Eloise details about the times we aren't together. I did once, and it ruined our weekend. So I stay away from the topic, pretending it's not happening.

But it is. She admitted it to me drunk one night. She also confessed she loves me, how I'm the only man who truly gives her what she needs, and how she wanted to only be with me.

Then she woke up sober the next morning and conveniently forgot everything she blurted out. She hopped on the first plane out of Chicago, and when I tried to discuss getting serious again, she told me she was drunk and didn't mean a word she said.

Things were tense between us for a while. I decided to stay away from her and tell her we were through. Then Boris pursued Nora in secret, we started getting pulled into the O'Malley's issues with the Rossis, and Zamir texted him. When he disappeared, I felt like my skin was crawling. Then Eloise showed up at my door. So I spent twelve hours controlling and fucking her until it was time for my workout with my brothers. I went to it, came home, then woke her up. I repeated tormenting her until she lost her voice from all the pleasure I gave her.

She left for her flight, and I felt calm again. It's then I decided to once more overlook her inability to commit to me.

The next time I saw her, I took her to a grand opening for a restaurant my brothers and I invested in. At first, I couldn't put my finger on it. Then it hit me. She was annoyed to be with my family. She didn't want me to take her out to a nice dinner or spend the evening with people in my life. She was only here for my cock.

Her bitchy attitude was getting to me when an altercation with Lorenzo Rossi occurred. So she got her wish. I took her home and gave her what she wanted. But it didn't calm me how it usually did. That was the last time I saw her.

Now I get to be at all the events on my own this weekend.

I get in the car and light up a bowl. I need to calm down. I can't go into Anna and Dmitri's rehearsal dinner anything but happy for them. This is one of the rare times my brothers and I get to celebrate. I'll be damned if I let Eloise spoil it.

The ride to the restaurant isn't long. I pop a mint, rub lemon hand sanitizer on my palms, and try to cover up the scent of my weed as best as possible. My insides are still in turmoil but not as bad as at the airport.

I arrive and go through the motions. When Maksim turns up by himself, I'm surprised. I don't ask him where Aspen is, and I'm grateful no one asks me why Eloise isn't with me.

They're probably relieved.

It's not a secret my brothers don't like her. They've never said anything, but I'm not stupid.

I do my best to forget about Eloise and enjoy my family. At the end of the night, Maksim swiftly comes over to me and growls, "I need you to come with me."

"Where to?"

"Cat's Meow."

I raise my eyebrows. "Seriously?" The Cat's Meow is a co-ed stripper nightclub. It has everything you could ever want for a night of trouble.

"Yep."

"This your way of trying to get over whatever is going on with you and Aspen?"

"Not funny," he barks.

I hold up my hands. "Easy there. All right. I'm not doing anything exciting. Guess it's a night at the Cat's Meow. But do you want to tell me why we are going there?"

He scowls. "To get my woman."

My anxiety only gets higher when he tells me Aspen and her friends are in Wes Petrov's VIP suite.

When we bust through the door, Zamir's son, Wes, and his three thug friends each have a woman on their laps. Adrian headlocks their guy on the door right away. I only glance at Aspen and can see she's drunk and not overly excited to be on Wes's lap. Her fear from the current scenario of us barging in with guns and knives pulled is evident in her expression.

I ignore the other women. All I see are a room full of Petrovs I want to slice and dice and toss to the lions to enjoy.

After throwing out some threats, we get the women out of the room. Adrian and I are left. We slowly back out and hightail it out of the club. Maksim is standing outside his car, and relief fills his face. Adrian and I get into the back of the other vehicle with three of Aspen's friends.

Like Aspen, they're all beautiful women. One has magenta hair and slides on top of Adrian the minute he sits. "Thanks for saving us," she says.

He stares at her.

The blonde woman twists her fingers and winces. "Thank you. Sorry about that."

I'm about to respond to her when the woman next to me slides her hand on my thigh. Electricity races straight to my cock. I turn and remind myself to breathe.

She's stunning. Her dark skin glows against the dim light in the car. Her hazel eyes pierce me. They swirl with confidence, but it's different than Eloise's. Hers has a warmth and coldness to them. It's a polarity I've never seen before. Her lips are lush and pouty. I think of a dozen different things I want to do with her mouth.

She puts her face right next to mine. "You're the youngest Ivanov brother?"

"Yes."

"Thirty-three, right?"

"Last time I checked."

She looks me up and down, and a stirring in my belly ignites. She tousles the top of my hair. "So you're a young silver fox?"

"Kora!" her blonde friend mutters.

I don't respond. Out of all my brothers, I started getting gray hair the soonest. I only have a little mixing into my black locks. Maksim's hair is the closest to mine out of all my brothers. Boris has only a few strands of silver. Dmitri shaves his head. When I made a comment about my hair, Maksim told me not to worry about it, claiming it's made women even more attracted to him.

Kora ignores her friends and leans even closer. The scents of tequila and flowers mix in my nostrils and send heat down my spine. Her eyes focus on my lips then she slyly drills her eyes into mine. "What do you think of cougars?"

"Kora!" the woman reprimands again while putting her hand over her mouth and laughing.

I lick my lips, studying her, and she inches her hand closer to my groin. I reach for her hair. I almost groan at how soft it is with just a hint of coarseness to it. I twirl it tight around my fist. I grip her hand on my thigh, move it to her other hand and secure my fingers around her wrists. "It depends on what the cougar can handle."

1

Kora Kilborn

ADRENALINE SHOOTS THROUGH ME. THE INCIDENT IN THE VIP room should make me run from Sergey. All it did was give me wet panties.

My decision-making process might be off a tad. I've been drinking—a lot. Aspen adamantly kept ordering shots, and we all participated with her. I had a bad feeling about the VIP room, but it happened quickly. I tried to get off the thug's lap I was on, but he wasn't releasing me. The fear building in my chest was growing when the Ivanovs busted through the door.

I didn't know who Sergey was. I had never met him before tonight. Aspen only told us about Maksim's brothers. However, she lied about Sergey. She said he was good-looking.

He's not.

Sergey is a bad boy of sexy sin, tempting you to toss all your morals and respect out the door so he can touch you. He's wearing a suit coat over a form-fitting designer T-shirt. Every inch of fabric hugs his ripped body perfectly. His face is an angel of innocence mixed with the devil. Piercing brown eyes, rough full lips, and a beard frames his slightly crooked nose. It's a bend a man gets from fighting, not a natural imperfection. And I'm sure he knows how to scratch a woman just enough to drive her mad with his beard. Making him even sexier are the tiny strands of silver in his dark hair. They are barely visible and add to his broody expression.

His looks aren't really fair. Looking at him puts me on edge. It's an orgasm waiting to happen yet never comes. So Aspen severely downplayed Sergey's looks in our discussions.

The gun he has lodged in his pants should make me keep my distance. I'm an attorney. My job requires me to stay away from anything criminal. He just pulled a gun on a room full of men and never flinched once. Instead of using my head, all I can think about is giving him some. That was before he spoke and his sexy Russian accent came out.

It's not as thick as Maksim's, Adrian's, or the other man who was in the room. I think his name was Bogden, but I didn't pay close attention.

I'm a naturally confident person. Being an attorney suits me. I can be as assertive as I want, and no one questions it. It's something other women, and some men, tend to find intimidating. It's why I love my friends so much. They understand and appreciate me for who I am. I don't have to tone it down or hide with them. I usually spend most of my time on dates keeping myself in check. It's probably why I've not found "the one" yet. Hailee claims I'm setting myself up for failure, since I'm pretending to be softer than I am. She says if a guy can't handle me how I am, I shouldn't be with him. I keep thinking if I tone it down, they will see the good parts of me and learn to understand and appreciate the traits that usually scare men off. So far, it hasn't worked out very well.

Due to my alcohol consumption, I don't think about how I shouldn't be as forward or hide my personality. I'm not the only one making decisions I might regret. Skylar is now straddling Adrian and has his shirt half unbuttoned. I try to not gape at his abs and don't miss Hailee's mouth hanging open to the floor.

Instead, I focus on Sergey. "What do you think of cougars?"

I'm thirty-eight, five years older than Sergey. I've been with younger guys before. They've always wanted me to show them what I've got. It's fun for a while. I guess it fits my dominant side.

He surprises me, creating a zing in my body I've not felt before when he secures his long fingers around my wrists and tightly winds my hair around his other fist. I gasp as he tugs my hair back. Fire lights in his eyes so hot, I wonder if hell could burn any brighter. In a low growl, he replies, "It depends on what the cougar can handle."

The car stops, the door opens, and I shut my gaping mouth. The throbbing in my lower body intensifies. I swallow hard then mutter, "This is me."

He releases my hair, dragging his finger down my neck, and rubs his thumb on my arm before releasing my wrists. He gets out and reaches in for me.

I'm confused by his gentleman's action. Most men I've dated don't hold the door open for me or attempt to help me do anything. I think they assume I can do it for myself, so why bother. Deep down, it's always upset me. I want a man to do for me what they do for others. I may be independent, but chivalry doesn't need to be dead.

He helps me out of the car and guides me toward the building.

"What are you doing?"

"Making sure you get inside your home safely."

My heart beats faster. The alcohol wears off. I straighten up. "It's okay. You don't have to do that."

He grunts. Is he amused by my statement? He continues leading me to the elevator and punches the button. It opens immediately, and he guides me in. Another couple follows. Sergey puts his arm around my waist, tugs me into his body, and splays his palm on my stomach.

Another wave of buzzing makes my knees turn to jelly. I try to maintain my composure.

"Sorry, I drank a lot," I mumble, wondering why my body is reacting like this. I just met him. A quiver sets off low in my belly, and he tightens his arm around me.

The elevator stops on my floor, and the other couple steps aside. Sergey leads me to my place. I fumble with the key, and he puts his hand over mine. I stand straighter, take a deep breath, and allow him to turn my hand so the door opens.

He motions for me to go through, and he steps in and shuts the door. His eyebrow arches, and his piercing gaze meets mine. "Do you always play in cougar town?"

I'm not sure how to respond. I've suddenly lost all my courage. I had plenty of it in the car, but it's now hiding somewhere in the ocean of flutters swirling inside me.

When I don't respond, he moves toward me. I retreat until I'm up against a wall. He secures my wrists, pins them to the wall with one hand above my head, and holds my chin. His body presses against mine. Heat emanates from his muscular frame and mouth, penetrating into me. In a low voice, he states, "It's too bad you've had so many drinks tonight."

"Hmmm?" I arch my sex into his body then swallow the lump in my throat.

He tilts his head, strokes my jaw with his thumb while still holding my chin, and studies me. He glances down, but our bodies are too close together to see anything, except my cleavage.

He puts his thigh between my legs then his mouth near my ear. "Are you always in control?" Wet warmth flicks against my lobe.

I whimper.

He shimmies his thigh between my legs, adding sweet friction to my clit. "Answer me."

"Yes," I breathe before I can think.

He keeps moving his leg, exciting me more and more. His erection pushes into the side of my waist. "Do you think you could handle me?" His lips and teeth move along my neck and jaw, leaving tingles in their wake.

"Mmm," is all I can get out. Every pulsing sensation I could have terrorizes me. It's like riding on the O train and not knowing when to get off or if you should get off.

He holds my arms higher and places his lips next to mine.

I move forward to kiss him, but he doesn't allow me.

"Be a good girl and say please." He drags his hand from my chin to my head until he has my hair wrapped around his fist, taking any power left away from me.

There's no thinking about anything. His leg continues to rub against me, and desperation to have him consumes me. I whisper, "Please."

"Say it again, louder." His expression is the same he wore when he demanded the thugs in the club release us. There's no room to argue or disobey. His thigh slows.

"Please," I cry out.

Approval fills his eyes. His leg moves faster, his lips and tongue slide against mine so quickly, I get dizzy. He kisses me deeper and deeper, controlling every aspect of my mouth.

And then I start coming. An earthquake of endorphins hits me, and I moan in his mouth while vibrating between him and the wall.

I'm unsure how long it lasts. But when he finally pulls back from my lips, his cocky expression only heats my blood more.

He slowly releases my wrists, sliding his hands down my arms, then stepping back. "It was nice meeting you, Kora."

I blink, trying to regain my balance. I reach for his shirt and yank him into me. "Where are you going?"

He glances at my lips again then back to my eyes. "What I'll do with you requires consent. You've drunk a lot tonight."

My pulse intensifies, and my mouth goes dry. "What would you do to me?"

He smirks. "Maybe some other time you'll find out."

"What?" I barely whisper.

He winks, spins, and walks out of my condo. I stand against the wall, inhaling lemons, a touch of weed, and sandalwood.

The door opens back up. Sergey pops his head inside. "You need to lock your door, Kora."

It confuses me further. "Oh, right."

He shuts the door. I stumble to it and turn the locks in place then peep out the eyehole.

As if he knows I'm watching him, another cocky expression appears, and he nods. He turns and leaves, and I slide down the door until I'm on my butt.

I don't know where that man came from. He's not like my typical little cubs. All I know is I don't *want* more, I *need* more.

2

Sergey

Kissing Kora and leaving is the equivalent of giving a kid a present on Christmas and telling them not to open it.

She's had too much to drink.

I leave and wait to hear the locks click. When I stick my head back inside, she hasn't moved from the wall. Her breasts are still rising and falling quickly. She gazes over at me, and I internally fight with my cock not to go any farther into the condo. If I do, I'm staying. I'll hate myself in the morning. She can't give me her full consent in her current condition, and one thing I can't stand is men who prey on women in any way. So, I tell her to lock her doors, leave again, and wait until I hear the click.

When I get in the car, the pink-haired girl is straddling Adrian, and he's holding her hands so she can't move. The blonde is wincing and shaking her head.

"Stop touching my cock," Adrian tells her.

"Skylar," the blonde says.

The pink-haired girl leans into his ear and says something. Adrian's face hardens, and he gives me a blank stare.

I'm not sure what happened in the club when he was supposed to be watching Aspen, but I know Adrian well enough to know this girl did something to piss him off. But he also must like her; otherwise, he wouldn't be letting her straddle him or look so upset.

I turn to the blonde. "I'm Sergey, by the way."

"Oh, sorry! I'm so rude. I'm Hailee." She shakes my hand, and the car pulls out. "Sorry for..." She cringes. "Everything."

I grunt. "You're good. I glance at Skylar. She's whispering something else to Adrian. He clenches his jaw, staring at the floor. I turn back to Hailee. "You're the good one, aren't you?"

Her face turns beet red. "No. Yes. Maybe?" She bites her lip.

I laugh. The car stops, and she says, "Skylar, you're home."

Adrian moves his head to the side, away from Skylar's mouth, and lifts her off him. He gets out then reaches in for her, but she's unsteady on her feet and throws her arms around his neck, giggling.

I turn back to Hailee. "How much did you all drink?" I take my pipe out and crack the window.

Hailee bites her lip so hard, I worry blood might seep out. She scrunches her forehead.

I light up my bowl, take an inhale, and hold it out to her. "You don't have to answer that. Want a hit?"

Her eyes widen slightly, and she shakes her head. "No. I don't umm..."

"Sorry. Is this offending you?"

"No. I tried it once. I was in high school, and my friend dared me. But I didn't feel anything. So..." She shrugs.

"You must not have inhaled."

"I did. I coughed," she claims.

I snort. "Doesn't mean you inhaled."

"Isn't that a lie presidents claim?"

"Yep. But guarantee you didn't."

"Why do you do it? What does it make you feel like?"

I find it amusing in today's environment, I'm sitting in a car, explaining weed to a thirty-some-year-old woman. I blurt out, "It's one of the rare things that helps me relax."

"Why can't you relax?"

I glance out the window. "Life."

"What else relaxes you?"

"Huh?"

"You said one of the rare things. That means there are more."

Fucking Eloise. But I have a feeling your friend Kora would do wonders for my nerves, too.

"Working out."

"I always want to do more after a workout," she absentmindedly says.

I smile. I like Hailee. She's easy to talk to. Way too innocent for my taste but a nice woman. I admit, "Sometimes it does that, too." I lean closer to her. "What do you do for a living?"

"I'm a kindergarten teacher."

So cliché.

"And Skylar, the pink-haired girl. What does she do?"

"She works with a fashion designer. Her boss is an ass."

"Such a naughty word for a teacher," I tease and take another drag off the bowl.

"Ha ha!"

I casually ask, "And what's Kora's story?"

"You've probably heard of her."

I raise my eyebrows. "Oh? Why would I have?"

"She's always getting awards and press. She's *the* Kora Kilborn. Chicago's top divorce attorney."

"I've never heard of her. Of course, I've never been married, so I haven't had the need to get a divorce."

"All the uber-wealthy women hire her."

"So she takes men to the cleaners then cuts their balls off, huh?"

Hailee laughs. "Guess that's one way to describe it."

The door opens, and Adrian gets in the car. In Russian, I say, "Did your princess get inside all right?"

His face hardens, and he grabs my bowl. He inhales a large amount of smoke and holds it in.

"Easy, this shit's strong," I warn him. Adrian doesn't usually smoke, which is how I know Skylar got under his skin.

He turns toward the window and slowly lets it out. Then he looks down, realizes his shirt is still unbuttoned, and fastens it.

Hailee blurts out, "Sorry. Skylar drank a lot."

"I know. I was there," Adrian barks.

"Easy," I reprimand him.

He sighs. "Sorry, Hailee."

She quietly replies, "It's okay. I'm sorry we caused so much trouble for you. I hope we didn't get you in trouble with your boss."

Adrian and I both snort at the same time.

"What's so funny?" she asks.

"Adrian isn't in trouble. And we're cousins, so no matter how much he failed at controlling the four of you, it's impossible for him to get fired."

"Don't be a dick. If you were there on your own, you wouldn't have stood a chance, either." He points at Hailee. "You and your friends need to be more careful."

Her face reddens again. "I know."

"Lay off her. She's the innocent one."

"I'm not innocent," she claims.

Adrian and I exchange a glance. He says, "Sure. Whatever you say."

The car stops.

"This is me." She picks her purse off her lap. "I truly am sorry. Thank you again for getting us out of that room."

Adrian leans forward. "A woman like you doesn't belong anywhere near those types of men. Please make sure you're more careful next time."

Her face drains of color, and she nods.

I step out then reach in to help her out.

She smiles big. "Thank you. Have a nice night."

I grip her elbow and lead her into the building. "What's your floor?"

"Three. I can make it from here."

I smirk. "I'm sure you can. However, until you're in your apartment with the doors locked, I'm not leaving."

"Oh. Okay," she says and steps into the elevator.

I walk her to her door, wait until she's inside, then go back to the car.

"Jesus, those women," Adrian groans when I slide onto the seat. "Talk about a bad night at work."

I point at his shirt. "I don't know. It looks like you had a bit of fun. You missed a button."

He scowls and reaches for my bowl then takes another hit.

"How did they end up in Wes Petrov's suite?"

He shakes his head then releases the smoke. "I'm done talking about this. I don't want to hear it from you or Maksim tonight."

"Fair enough." I grab a bottle of water and down half of it.

"I thought Eloise was coming into town today?"

"Nope. She decided to call me after I waited for over an hour inside the airport for her like a pathetic loser. She forgot to call me earlier and isn't coming. She's going to a nightclub opening instead."

Adrian's head jerks back. "Shit, that's...fuck, that's harsh."

"Yep. I told her to have a nice life."

He whistles. "Are you going to let her come crawling back?"

"Nope."

"Really? Even if she showed up at your doorstep, groveling?"

I scoff. "Eloise and groveling. What a concept. Will never happen. She's always right."

"Dude, you have to admit she's a bit of a bitch most of the time."

"Watch it," I warn. I told her we're through, but I still won't let anyone disrespect her.

The car stops. I slap Adrian's hand. "See you tomorrow at the wedding."

"Yeah, tell Maksim to think before he comes at me. I'm not backing down on this one. Those women are out of control, and there is no way anyone could be responsible for all four of them."

"Maksim's going to tell you he gave you directions to protect Aspen."

Adrian scowls. "I did exactly what he would have done. What any Ivanov would do."

"Still his woman he wanted protected."

"Who sat on Wes Petrov's lap," Adrian says with disgust. My brothers and I may hate the Petrovs, but Adrian and his brother, Obrecht, may have a deeper level of abhorrence toward them.

"Good luck with convincing Maksim," I reply and step out. I go into my penthouse.

All night, I toss and turn. I replay my kiss with Kora, wishing she hadn't been intoxicated so I could have stayed and shown her what I wanted to do to her. I think of Eloise. I'm angry and hurt. I feel betrayed by her actions, but it's the last straw. No matter what our past is, I don't want anything to do with her. I refuse to be her doormat any longer.

My mind spirals to the war between the Rossis and Petrovs. I try to figure out any other reason Bruno Zielinski would visit Giovanni in prison, but I can't come up with anything feasible.

I think again about Kora, then Eloise, then the war. It becomes a vicious circle. I don't sleep. My insomnia never gives in. When the dark of night begins to turn into morning, I leave and meet my brothers at the gym.

We have a heated conversation about the previous night's events but put it aside. It's Dmitri's wedding day, and we all want there to be nothing but happiness for him and Anna today.

I shower, put on my tux, and freeze when I get in my living room.

In her French accent, Eloise says, "That tux was made for you." Black silk cascades around her body, accentuating every curve and stopping mid-thigh.

My heart thumps harder. She's perfect, as if she's about to walk the runway. I keep the emotion out of my voice. "What are you doing here?"

She steps forward and slides her hands under my jacket. "Since when don't you kiss me when you see me?"

My jaw twitches. It's something that started after my first night with Zamir. I can't control it, and every time it spasms, I hate myself more. It's a reminder of all the things I've done but didn't want to. The tiny vibrations continue, but I say nothing.

Eloise drags her finger over my jaw, and I jerk my head away from her. She quickly laces her fingers around my neck and puts her lips an inch from mine. "I'm sorry I missed last night."

My silence continues, but this time, it's from shock. Eloise has never apologized to me before. She doesn't believe in sorries.

Her eyes glisten, which throws me for another loop. "Do you want me to leave?"

I'm unsure what I want. Last night, I was clear we were through. Maybe she has realized the error of her ways?

Her face scrunches, and she nods. She spins to leave, but I stop her.

"Why are you fucking with me like this, Eloise?"

"I'm not."

"Then tell me honestly why you are here."

She hesitates. "I promised you I would come to your brother's wedding. I should have been here last night. You were right to be angry."

Her words seem sincere. She steps forward again. Her hand goes to my cheek. "Do you want me to go with you or leave?"

Spending the wedding on my own doesn't appeal to me. I cave. "I want you to come with me."

She smiles. "Good. Now kiss me. I've missed you."

I kiss her, but it doesn't light me up the way it usually does. All I can think while she kisses me is it isn't anything like the kiss I shared with Kora.

I take Eloise to the wedding, but we aren't there very long before she returns to her typical self. When she sticks her nose up and makes rude comments about what Anna designed for the wedding, it hits me. Eloise is a nasty person. No matter how long we've been together, I don't think I want her anymore.

The entire night, I keep wishing I knew more about Kora. I wonder what it would be like if she were here with me. Every time Eloise makes a snide remark, it's a slap to my face. Things are off between us all night. When the wedding is over and we get back to my penthouse, I pick up her bag.

"What are you doing?" she asks.

"I've booked you a room at a hotel. Let's go."

Her eyes widen. "Sergey, what are you talking about?"

"It's time we ended this."

"Don't be silly." She reaches for my dick, and I grab her wrist.

"It's over between us. I wish you well, but find someone else's cock to use."

"Why would you say something so crude?"

I snort. "It's true. All you want from me is sex. You didn't come to be part of my family's event or my life. You came to get laid."

She doesn't deny or admit anything.

I nod. "That's what I thought. Let's go." I spend the car ride pushing her off me, reiterating her attempts to seduce me aren't going to work, and I finally get her into her hotel room.

She makes one final effort to get me to stay, but it doesn't work.

I've had enough of Eloise. From now on, I'll just have to work out or smoke more weed to relax. She's had me for years but never truly wanted me. I won't be hers to use any longer.

3

Kora

ALL WEEKEND, MY BRAIN IS A VIDEO ON REPEAT. I REPLAY everything about Sergey. He owned every part of me. No man had ever taken control of me the way he did. I was putty against his body, and he knew exactly how to touch me.

I got off from his thigh.

My face heats thinking about it. His kiss was enough to make my knees turn to jelly, but no man had ever made me orgasm through clothes or during a first kiss.

I need to get my mind off him. He's everything my mother warned me to stay away from, including the ease with which he carried a gun.

It was hot.

He's trouble.

I go back and forth about whether I should ask Aspen where he'll be next so I can "run into him."

Get a grip. It was a night of fun. Move on.

He's so alpha, he won't like me once he sees my true personality.

"You need a man who is opposite you, Kora. Someone strong but who can be more of a pleaser. Someone who is okay letting you lead. You can't have two alphas in the same house," my mother's voice rings loud and clear in my head. Whenever I broke up with anyone who didn't fit this mold, she would remind me I'm outspoken, and yang needs the yin, not more yang. It's part of her speech about how I'm a male personality wrapped in a woman's body. The girls told me she was cruel to say such a thing, and just because I'm a go-getter with an opinion doesn't mean I'm masculine.

I've tried dating guys who are more passive. It drives me up the wall. I make decisions all day long. I fight for clients and take bullet after bullet from other attorneys. Sometimes it gets personal. I've learned to have a thick skin. However, it would be nice to have someone take care of me for once. No matter what my mother believes, I don't need to make all the decisions outside of work. It would be a relief not to have to and give the reins to someone else.

I'd have to find a man not intimidated by me, who doesn't think I'm a bitch.

I've been wrong about men like him before. They can be the biggest alpha in the world but can't handle a woman who shows any sign of strength.

Something about Sergey strikes me as different. I can't put my finger on it, but he seemed to be into my outgoing onslaught of forward comments.

I was drunk. Do I even know what I said? I probably read every-thing wrong.

I'm still struggling with whether to ask Aspen about Sergey and secretly pursue him to see if anything else would happen between us when she calls. I'm at work, knee-deep in an asset discovery for one of my new clients.

I answer, "You can't just have your badass boyfriend, his stud brother cub—who kisses like a porn star...or what I think one would kiss like—and their muscle men bodyguards wave their guns and knives around in a club, then not talk to us all weekend."

Her voice sounds nervous. "Kora, I can't talk about this right now. There's another reason I'm calling."

Worry fills me. "Are you okay?"

"Ummm...yes. I need something from you ASAP."

"Sure. What is it?"

She hesitates then asks, "Can you write up papers for Peter to sign off on alimony?"

What is she talking about? I just finalized their divorce. Her piece of shit ex will never agree to sign off.

"Hello?" she asks.

My gut flips. I clear my throat. "What's going on, Aspen?"

"I can't get into it right now. But how quickly could I get a document for him to sign?"

"I can create it in fifteen minutes. But you'll need two witnesses and a notary. When are you meeting him?"

"Today at some point. I need it as soon as possible."

The hairs on my neck rise. "Aspen, where are you?"

She lowers her voice. "I'm at Maksim's."

"Send me his address. I'll bring the forms."

"It's okay. Just email it."

"No."

"Kora—"

"I'm your attorney. I'm not sure what's going on, but text me the address, or I'm not writing up the document."

She takes a deep breath. "Can you just do it?"

"Send me the address," I repeat. I don't know what is happening, but I'm not going to let her do something that could come back and haunt her. I don't know anything about Maksim Ivanov, her boyfriend, other than Skylar and I negotiated with him in Vegas so he could sleep with Aspen. It was a crazy night. After witnessing the Ivanovs storm into the VIP room, threaten the Petrovs, a prominent Russian crime family, and all of us walked out of the room unscarred, I'm smart enough to know he's into things that can't be good. I wonder if Skylar and I got Aspen into something terrible.

Maksim's dangerous, just like his brother, Sergey.

I can't believe we were sitting on Petrov laps. I shudder about what could have happened.

"Kora—"

"Aspen, let me talk to Kora," Maksim's muffled voice comes through the phone.

I stand straighter and stare out at the crashing waves on Lake Michigan.

Yeah, put him on. I'll make it clear whose rules we're following. No matter what, I'm not letting Aspen do anything with Peter unless I'm there to represent her.

She sighs and puts it on speaker.

"Kora, it's Maksim."

"What's going on, Maksim? Why the secrecy?"

His voice stays deadpan. I can tell he's used to negotiating, too. "Peter has agreed not to take another penny from Aspen. Are you able to quickly draw up the paperwork?"

He's not going to get one past me. "I can. But as Aspen's attorney, I won't give her the form unless I witness him signing."

"Why? Is there a legal reason you need to be there?"

"It's not required, but I don't put anything past the weasel. I prefer to witness it all," I state.

"He won't be giving Aspen any trouble again. We'll be fine with the paperwork on our own," Maksim insists.

"Sorry, no can do."

"Kora, just send it," Aspen says.

At least they are on speakerphone.

"Aspen, I'm your attorney and friend. I'm not budging on this."

Maksim quietly laughs. "I can see we're going to waste a lot of time fighting, which I prefer to avoid. Draw the papers up. Are we able to meet at your office in an hour?"

I'm surprised he caved so quickly. I smile, happy to not have to continue arguing. It's part of my job, but I prefer not to have to fight all the time. "And Peter will be able to make it, too?"

"Yes."

"Great. An hour works. I'll see you then." I hang up and intercom my para-legal. I tell her what I need and sit at my desk.

Why would Peter ever agree to sign off on something like this?

I don't have a good feeling about this. Peter is a mooching waste of space. I negotiated his alimony to ten percent of what he could have gotten. It pains me Aspen has to pay anything, but I couldn't get it eliminated.

Whatever is going on, I need to make sure Aspen crosses her t's and dots her i's. The last thing I want is for her to get hurt. I want to believe Maksim has her best interest at heart, but I can't fully trust him yet.

The documents are drawn up, and my assistant brings them into my office. I double-check they are correct then stroll into the conference room. The uneasiness I have around this doesn't go away. Aspen is one of my closest friends. I would do this for any client, but this has a personal element to it. Plus, I hate Peter and everything he's done to Aspen.

I'm lost in thought when my assistant announces, "Kora, Mr. Ivanov and Ms. Albright are here."

They step into the conference room. I spin, walk over to Aspen, and hug her. Maksim leans down and kisses my cheek. I smile, try to be friendly, and remind myself he doesn't have any reason to hurt Aspen. I motion for them to sit. "Where is Peter?"

Maksim smiles. "Sergey will be here with him soon."

"Sergey?" My face heats, and my stomach quivers.

"Yes."

I sit straighter. "Why is he with Peter?" I'm sure he's not friends with him nor has he met him before Aspen.

Maksim puts his arm around Aspen's shoulder and smiles. In a friendly but no-nonsense tone, he replies, "Kora, we won't be discussing any of the details. He will come in, sign, then he will leave with Sergey. You are a smart woman and saw what I am capable of in the club. There are things you should not ask and questions I will never answer. This is one of them."

Oh no you don't. I will ask any question I want when it comes to Aspen and her divorce. I sit back, cross my legs, and pin my gaze on Maksim. "Aspen is not only my friend but my client. If you are having Peter sign something and he is coerced, it could come back and hurt Aspen."

Maksim nods. "Yes. I'm sure you understand I will go to extreme lengths to protect my krasotka. She will not be in any danger now or in the future due to that man. If she ever is, I will take care of it."

I doubt he's talking about legal methods.

For several minutes, I stare at Maksim, giving him the expression I've mastered over the years. It says I won't be intimidated, and I'm also not dumb.

Aspen clears her throat then waves between us. "I'm here. In the room."

I glance at her. "I think we should talk alone."

"No. Whatever you want to discuss, you can say it in front of Maksim. I will not hide information from him."

"I'm your attorney. This—"

"Mr. Albright and Mr. Ivanov are here," my assistant interrupts. I look up. Peter steps into the room. He looks like he hasn't slept in days. His blue eyes are bloodshot. His hair is wet and there is a dried spot of blood on his cheek. It could be from shaving, but given the fact Sergey is standing behind him, nudging him to move forward, I highly doubt it.

"Kora. Good to see you again." Sergey towers over Peter. He cockily licks his lips while checking me out. His black T-shirt and jeans fit just right, hugging his muscles.

I pull my eyes away from his thigh, reprimanding myself for the memories of how it got me off during our kiss. I try to control my racing heartbeat and the heat rising through my body and up my cheeks.

"Sergey. Peter," I coolly reply. "Have a seat."

Great. Now Sergey gets to see me at my most masculine.

There goes any possibility of him wanting anything else to do with me.

Time to get over it. Aspen needs me.

Tone it down.

Peter sits between Sergey and me, focused on the table.

A few moments pass, and Aspen slams her hand on the table. She seethes, "Look at me."

That's my girl. About time you got pissed. Throughout her divorce, she kept calm and civil with Peter. I'm glad to see her finally showing some hostility toward him.

He's such a weasel.

Peter takes a nervous breath and slowly meets her eyes.

"How could you steal from me? And you took the only thing I have left of my mother's."

My gut drops.

He says nothing. His lips quiver.

"Answer me," Aspen demands.

"He took your mom's rings?" I ask in disgust.

Aspen glances at me and nods. "And my laptop and a box of new checks. The ones with only my name on them."

Oh, now you're going to pay, Peter. I rip up the agreement I planned on having Aspen sign.

"What are you doing?" Aspen asks.

"I'll be back in a moment." I rise.

"Kora—"

"I will be right back." I leave the room. My pulse is beating in my neck like a jackhammer. All Peter has ever done is take

39

from Aspen. She's supported him since she was eighteen, and now he stole the only material possession she cares about.

I bet it's not even worth more than a few hundred dollars.

My paralegal types all my documents. I don't even talk to her about this one. I storm into my office, rage consuming me, and type quickly. I instruct three of my staff members, "Follow me. I need witnesses."

I return to the conference room with them, sit, and spin in my chair toward Peter. I try to ignore Sergey's eyes and twitching lips when I cross my legs.

I put a piece of paper and a pen in front of Peter, set my phone on the table so it faces him, and hit the button. "You are being recorded. Please state you agree to be on video."

Peter furrows his eyebrows.

Sergey gets another cocky expression on his face and states, "I agree. Don't you, Peter?"

I'm sure the Ivanov brothers are coercing Peter. I'm not stupid. However, my only concern is I cover Aspen's ass. Peter deserves whatever the Ivanovs want to dish out, plus some.

Peter reluctantly states, "Yes."

"Please state your name," I instruct.

Sergey's jaw twitches.

Great. I've gone all alpha, and he's front and center to see it.

"Peter Albright."

"And do you admit you broke into your ex-wife's home on..." I look to Aspen for the date.

She replies, "Saturday."

"This past Saturday and stole Aspen Albright's property? The contents were her deceased mother's wedding rings, laptop, and a box of checks for her personal bank account. An account you are not on? Is this correct?"

Peter's face reddens, and his jaw clenches.

I sternly demand, "Please answer the question, Peter."

"Yes," he admits.

I nod. "And you agree to sign this form, giving up all rights to any alimony payments from your ex-wife in exchange for Aspen not pressing charges?"

His hand trembles. He stares at the form and clenches his fist.

Yep, you're not here on your own accord.

Serves you right.

I may be an attorney and took an oath to uphold the law, but I still grew up on the south side of Chicago. As my sister says, "You can take the girl out of the ghetto, but you can't take the ghetto out of the girl." There are times I find it appropriate to claim ignorance or look the other way. Anytime you try to hurt one of my friends is one of them.

"Answer the question. Yes, you agree? Or no, you do not agree?" I bark.

He clears his throat. "I agree."

"Please sign the form."

He closes his eyes, squeezing them, but then picks up the pen and quickly signs.

I point. "Please date it as well."

He obeys and puts the pen down.

I slide the paper to Aspen. "Please sign you agree to these conditions."

She doesn't read it, signs, dates, and shoves it back to me while glaring at Peter.

I rise and take it to my coworkers. "Please sign as witnesses." I address my assistant, "Please notarize."

They sign and notarize, and I motion for them to leave the room. Once they are gone, and the door is shut, I turn off the video and glare at Peter. "You've always been a mooching piece of shit. I never thought you'd do something so hurtful to the only woman who's ever supported you no matter how awful you treated her. I hope you rot in hell."

Peter scowls at me, his eyes in flames. "Shut the f—"

Sergey's hand flies to his throat. He squeezes it until Peter is red and choking. Sergey leans into Peter's ear. In a low, controlled voice, he says, "You need to learn your manners in front of ladies. When I remove my hand, you're going to apologize. And if it isn't sincere, my hand isn't going to be any nicer the second time around." He releases him.

Holy hotness.

I think I need a new pair of panties.

Peter holds his throat. His eyes are wet.

"Now," Maksim growls.

Peter looks at me. "I'm sorry."

I shake my head. *What a pathetic loser.*

"Are we done here?" Aspen asks.

I smile at her. "Yes."

She returns the gesture. "Thank you."

I wink.

She rises and puts her hands on the table. "You were only shown mercy today because of me. I will never require it again. If you attempt to contact me, or steal from me, or break the terms you agreed to with the Ivanovs, I will lift any protection I have given you. Don't forget it."

"Aspen—"

"No. Don't you speak to me. We're done." She hugs me. "Thank you." She spins to Maksim. "Ready?"

His lips twitch. He dips down and kisses her. I'm happy for my friend, but I get uncomfortable. Maksim holds her possessively, as if she's his everything, and all I can think about is how Sergey took control of my body during our kiss. I avoid looking at him but then get sucked back into Maksim and Aspen's hot mouths all over each other.

What is with these Ivanovs? Are they all alpha, possessive studs?

Maksim keeps his lips near her but says loud enough for us to hear, "You sure you don't want my brother to give him what he deserves? Hmmm?"

Against my will, I lock eyes with Sergey. They are cold and hopeful. I realize he wants Aspen to permit him to hurt Peter. He also doesn't seem to care about hiding from me what he's capable of.

Because he isn't interested. He just saw me be my most aggressive. The part of me that isn't attractive to men.

Aspen glances at Peter then back at Maksim. "No. Your brother has better things to do with his time today than stew with trash. Let's go."

Maksim grunts, puts his hand on her ass, and leads her out the door.

Sergey rises and yanks Peter out of his chair. He scowls. "Let's go."

I rise, dying for Sergey to give me any indication he may still be interested in me.

His arrogant expression fills his face. He nods at me. "Good to see you again, Kora. Have a nice day."

"You, too." If I didn't put the nail in the coffin, what I can't stop from coming out of my mouth next, surely does. "Peter, I hope you burn in hell and burn some more."

Peter scowls. Sergey raises his eyebrows then says nothing and leaves.

I sit back down and put my hands over my face. Out of all the meetings I could have had, why did Sergey have to come to this one?

4

MC

Sergey

MAINTAINING MY ROLE AROUND KORA IS HARD. SHE'S A piranha, and it's making my cock harder than a rock.

Eloise is a piranha.

She's not Eloise.

What if she is?

Kora's pencil skirt is going to be the death of me. She's crossed her long legs several times. All it makes me want to do is dive between her thighs.

Maksim kisses Aspen, and I stare at Kora. She's avoiding me. Probably for the best, since all I keep wondering is, *How pink is her pussy?*

Fuck. I bet it's a beautiful, soft pink.

I wonder if she'd let me tie her up and eat it.

I could throw her on the table and shove my face between her thighs and—

My brother's voice rips me out of my thoughts. He and Aspen leave.

Time to get this piece of shit out of Chicago.

I yank Peter up. "Good to see you again, Kora. Have a nice day."

"You, too." She turns to Peter. In a razor-sharp voice, she says, "Peter, I hope you burn in hell and burn some more."

Jesus, she's a piranha.

Sexy as fuck.

I raise my eyebrows, sizing her up one last time and wishing there was more room in my pants, which suddenly feel restricted. I leave the conference room and snag her card before leaving her office. When I get to the bus station, I warn Peter one final time and remind him he's never to step foot in Chicago again.

Maksim should have let me kill the prick.

Several days pass. I try to get Kora out of my head. I stop myself several times from calling her or going to her house. I just got out of a messed-up situation with Eloise, and I don't want to make the same mistake.

Plus, Kora saw me in two very undesirable situations. The first time, I pulled a gun on the Petrovs. She was drunk, so I can't know if she would have hit on me if she were sober. The second time, I was in her office, and she didn't give me any clues she was still interested. Her blush when I walked in could have been embarrassment from the other night.

She probably thinks I'm a thug, since I was manhandling Peter.

It's been three days since our encounter at her office. I'm tired of staring at her business card. It's almost eleven at night, I'm antsy from issues going on at work, and I've smoked a bit more than I should have. I cave and text her.

Me: *What are you wearing, lapa?*

Kora: *Who is this?*

Me: *Your cub.*

There's a long pause. My pulse quickens.

Maybe she's seeing too many younger guys to know it's me.

Dots appear on the phone but then disappear. I light another joint and make myself wait.

Kora: *What does lapa mean?*

Me: *It's a Russian term of endearment. Guys call their girlfriends it, but it means paw. I thought since you wanted to be my cougar, it was appropriate.*

Kora: *Interesting.*

Me: *What color are your panties?*

Kora: *I'm not wearing any.*

I groan and once again think pink thoughts.

Me: *Have you and your friends stayed out of trouble?*

Kora: *Yep. Nothing but boring stuff going on right now.*

Me: *Staying away from thugs, huh?*

Kora: *Current status: thug free.*

Crap. Why did I write that?

She just confirmed why she should stay away from me. I can't really deny I've got some thug in me. It's not something I'm proud of, but I'm a violent person who does criminal things. Kora is smart. I'm sure she can see it. I try to figure out what to write next.

Kora: *So, did our friend get out of the city?*

Me: *Yep.*

Kora: *Good.*

Me: *Hailee said you were a big shot. I can see why.*

Kora: *Hailee?*

Me: *After I dropped you off. You're quite the ball buster.*

Several minutes pass. I'm not sure if she's doing something else or if I said something wrong.

Me: *You still there?*

Kora: *Yes.*

Me: *That was a compliment, btw.*

Kora: *Thanks.*

This is why I shouldn't get high and text women.

Me: *What were you doing before I texted you?*

Kora: *Preparing for court tomorrow.*

Me: *Do you always work this late?*

Kora: *Sometimes. This is a complicated case, so...*

Me: *What time do you get up?*

Kora: *Five.*

Me: *Why so early?*

Kora: *I have to work out.*

Me: *That's what I'll be doing but not till six.*

Although I'd rather be working you out.

Jeez, I really know how to have a stimulating conversation.

I need to end this before I embarrass myself any further.

Me: *Get some sleep, lapa. Good luck in court.*

Kora: *Thanks. Night.*

Me: *Night.*

My insomnia is on overdrive, and I don't sleep. I leave earlier than usual for the gym. When my brothers show up, I've run six miles and am covered in sweat. No matter how much I work out, I can't get Kora out of my mind. She's becoming an obsession. Eloise was one, too. I'm trying to avoid falling into the same situation where I get hung up on a woman who isn't capable of committing and doesn't want more than sex from me.

I remind myself again Kora isn't Eloise.

Don't make the same mistake.

All day, I push Kora out of my mind while visiting our job sites. It's important we reiterate to our employees there will be no layoffs, and we will move directly into the next project. We can't risk any of our men falling prey to Zamir.

At least I have the fight tonight to take my mind off Kora.

When I finish, there's an hour for me to shower then get to the gym. Boris is fighting. My brothers and I always attend, so it'll be nice to do something besides fixate on Kora.

I get off the elevator, step into my living room, and freeze. My chest tightens. "Eloise. What are you doing here?"

She's sitting on my couch with her legs crossed. Her miniskirt is barely covering her privates. The black form-fitting top she wears accentuates her cleavage. Her makeup is perfect, and not a hair is out of place. She sits back like she owns the place—*my place.* Her thick French accent, which used to turn me on, now annoys me. "Darling, we need to talk."

"About what?"

"Us."

Let me guess, she wants my cock.

"What about us?" I ask.

"I miss you. We should be together."

I walk over to her and hold my hand out.

She smiles, takes it, and when I pull her up, I don't need to ask her. I already know why she's here and what she wants. She doesn't want me. "So you want to make a go at this? Commit to one another?"

She does what she always does and avoids my question. Her lips come toward mine. I turn my cheek then fist her hair and tug it back.

She gasps. It's one I've heard too many times, full of excitement and anticipation. She reaches for my belt, but I hold her wrists.

I put my lips next to hers. "What did you miss about me?"

"Stop playing games. Let's do what we do."

And there's the truth.

Anger spins in my gut. "I'm going to say this for the last time. We're done. Find someone else to get you off, Eloise. It's never going to be me again."

Her face falls. "Why are you acting so impulsive?"

I snort. "Get out of my house. Don't come back, or I'll call the police and have you arrested for trespassing and stalking."

She gapes. "You wouldn't."

"Try me. Might not be too marketable for your career."

She doesn't move. I put my arm around her back, snatch her purse off the table, and lead her to the elevator. She tries to argue with me all the way to the lobby. I guide her to the security desk.

"Frank, I want Eloise removed. Take her access away."

Eloise's mouth hangs open.

Frank nods and types.

"Sergey—"

"We're done. Don't come back. I'm warning you." I leave, go back to my penthouse, and take a few hits from my bowl to settle my nerves before I jump in the shower.

The last week, since seeing Kora again, I've barely thought about Eloise. I've tried to stop myself anytime I compared the two women. It's not fair for me to hold Eloise's short-comings against Kora because they have some of the same traits. I don't want another Eloise, but the things that attracted me to Eloise, I also see in Kora. I can't deny it. They are both total piranhas. I'm not sure if Kora is too much like Eloise or if she's different. I want to say she's the good of Eloise without the bad. But I can't be certain, so it makes me cautious.

Seeing Eloise makes my blood boil. It's a reminder I lack something for her to want anything from me besides my dick.

She's the only woman who's ever helped calm my insomnia.

As much insomnia as I've had lately, I wonder if I should have taken Eloise up on her offer. It's always worked in the past.

I don't want her anymore.

Based on our kiss, I want to believe Kora would let me domi-nate her, yet I'm not sure about that, either. I've been with enough women to understand that not all women are okay with my methods. I can respect their preferences, but it's a deal breaker for me.

I take a shower, get dressed, and leave. When I walk through the lobby, I'm relieved Eloise is nowhere to be seen. On the way to the gym, we pass Kora's building.

It would be so easy to stop by on my way home.

Don't be a psycho. She probably has numerous guys taking her out all the time.

I think about her all the way to the gym. When I get inside, I go into the office and make some phone calls. I'm in the middle of a call with one of our foremen when Aspen walks in, followed by her three friends.

My dick twitches when I see Kora. Her high cheekbones glow, her pouty lips are a muted red, and her hair is in a perfect, sleek ponytail.

Perfect for taking control of her.

She's wearing black leather pants and a white fuzzy sweater. It's cropped to her waist and hanging off one shoulder.

I end my call and beeline toward the group, which now also includes Anna, Nora, and her brothers.

"I have to use the restroom. Can you point me where I go?" Kora asks.

"I'll show you," I reply.

She spins, her face slightly flushes, and she purses her lips. In her confident tone, she replies, "Lead the way."

I put my hand on her back, and her breath hitches.

I lean into her ear, "Did my cougar miss me?"

Her lips twitch. "I don't know. Did my cubby miss me?"

I check her out, lick my lips, then open the door and motion for her to pass.

I wait out in the hall, and when she comes out, I steer her the opposite way of the fighting area.

"Where are you taking me?" There's a slight nervousness in her voice, which surprises me. She didn't show anything but surety any other time I've been around her.

"You'll see."

I open another door and lead her in then lock the door behind me. The moonlight shines through the window, creating a faint aura around her face. I leave the lights off.

Her breathing quickens. "Where are we?"

"A private training room." I drag my finger over her cheekbone. The smell of gin mixes with her floral scent. "Have you been drinking tonight?"

She swallows hard. "Yes. I had a martini at Skylar's before we came."

Only one. Good.

I inhale deeply. I lower my mouth to her neck, kissing it, then murmuring in her ear, "Are you sober enough to make decisions and not be upset tomorrow?"

"Yes." Her heart beats faster against my chest.

I circle my arm around her waist and move one foot at a time. She moves with me, letting me guide her to the wall. "Good girl. First test passed."

"Test?"

"Mmhmm. I want to see if we should go out."

She smirks. "And what does this entail?"

I press my body into her, kiss the pulse beating in her neck, and she shudders. "I think two people should be physically"— I scrape my teeth on her shoulder, and she whimpers —"compatible."

She stays quiet.

"I bet you're a busy woman with lots of pressure. Hmm? Did I get it right?"

"Yes. You're correct." Her hands lace through my hair.

I kiss her jaw then stop next to her lips. "And you're the one always in control?"

She takes a deep breath.

I softly laugh when she doesn't answer. Then I hold her face, pinning my gaze to her big hazel eyes. "I don't ask permission, Kora. The only word I listen to is stop. Some people need code words. I don't see the need."

"Like a safe word?"

I reach behind me and grasp her wrists. "Yes. Have you used one before?"

"N..." She clears her throat. "No."

My lips twitch. My ego's digging she never needed one with any other guy before. The other part of me is cautious. She might not be able to handle what I'm into.

Best to start slow. See if she can handle the basics.

I move her hands over her head. "Don't move." I slide my palms down her arms, bunch her sweater, then pull it off her. I enclose my palm around her wrists, keeping them high above her head.

A cloud moves over the moon, and the room darkens. Her skin radiates with a bronze glow. Her chest rises and falls faster. I drag my finger over her strapless, lace bra, and her nipples pucker underneath. Goose bumps break out on her arms.

She puts her mouth near mine, but I move my head away. "Not yet, my little lapa."

"Do you call all women lapa?"

I snort. "No. Don't move your hands."

I reach for the jump rope hanging on the wall, throw it over the bar, then quickly wrap it around her wrists. I get rid of all tension and close her fist around the rope.

"Does this make you nervous?" I brush my lips quickly against hers. She flicks her tongue against my lips as I retreat.

"Should I be?"

I don't answer and reach behind her and unclasp her bra. I toss it on the bench several feet away. "Your breasts are amazing." I trace my fingers around the fullness then lick and suck each nipple until her breath is labored.

Someone tries to come into the room. The knob clicks, and there's a knock.

Kora tenses.

I shout out, "Go away."

"Ummm...maybe we should—"

"It's my gym. Relax." I kiss her, hungrily sliding my tongue against hers until her body goes limp and she's moaning. In several seconds, I have her leather pants and soaked underwear down to her ankles. I reach around her and palm her ass, stepping as close to her as possible so she can feel my erection. "I'm hard for you, lapa. I have been since I last touched you. Then you kept torturing me in your office. You're a real piranha. You know that?"

She closes her eyes then tries to move her legs around my thigh.

"You want my cock or my thigh?" I tease.

She opens her eyes. They blaze with a desperate fire. She murmurs, "Your cock. Please."

I rub my cock between her legs and lean into her ear. "You can't have it right now."

She freezes.

"I'm hungry, lapa." I want to see if she'll surrender to me or tell me to untie her. It's happened before. I even dated a woman once who wouldn't let me go down on her. It was another deal breaker for me. If I can't feast on every part of my woman, then what's the point of being with her?

I make my way down her body with my hands and mouth, licking and gnawing, until she's sweating and trembling. When I finally throw her thighs over my shoulders, I pause and inhale her scent for a moment. She bucks her hips toward me, and I grip them. "Stop moving. Those who have patience get rewarded."

To my delight, she obeys.

The clouds move past the moon, and light shines on her, creating a gorgeous silhouette of lips, breasts, and a glimpse of her pink paradise.

A calm washes over me. I kiss the inside of her thigh, continue to inhale her, and blow on her pussy.

She jerks back and gasps.

One long stroke of my digit over her slit is all it takes to make her cry out. "Please."

"Please, what? Finger fuck you?" I glide two fingers into her, inching farther with each thrust, then adding a third.

She rocks on my hand, clenching her walls around me. "Oh God!"

"Or do you want my mouth on your pretty little cunt?" I maintain my current position and bite her clit.

"Holy..."

"There isn't anything holy about me," I growl then increase the speed I'm pumping my digits into her.

The moment my mouth hits her pussy, I groan. She's succulent, sweet and salty, and everything I assumed about how she tastes, or sounds, or feels was wrong.

I thought she'd be similar to Eloise. It's an ignorant assumption. Every part of her is a thousand times more potent, and I'm officially in trouble.

"Sergey," she breathes, barely audible.

I tease her with my lips, tongue, and teeth until she's shaking hard, urgently thrusting her hips into my face, and screaming my name.

My cock's hard and throbbing. But the bell rings for round one. I shimmy up her limp body and release her wrists. Her hands fall around my shoulders. She's still trembling.

"Good girl. You passed." I kiss her, hungry, desperate, wanting all of her. I almost ask her to come to my place for the night.

Then Eloise's face pops into my mind. All the mistakes I made with her, I don't need to make with Kora. It includes giving in to my temptation and spending all night with her. If I do, my addiction for her is going to spiral.

Better to wait until I take her out, and I can figure out if she's the same as Eloise or different.

If I did this to Eloise, she'd want to go back out to the gym and pretend nothing happened.

Eloise would never come to a boxing match.

Still, Kora is a piranha and so is Eloise.

I pull her pants up, secure her bra, and help her into her top. "Enjoy the fight." I spin and walk out, leaving her in the dark, and joining my brothers.

When she comes out, I avoid looking at her. She leaves without saying goodbye. Once I'm home, I smell her scent on my fingers and jack off, but nothing does anything to make me stop obsessing over her.

5

Kora

NOTHING TAKES MY MIND OFF SERGEY. OUR TIME TOGETHER before the fight leaves me with mixed feelings. The longer he ignores me, the more pissed I become.

Everything about him is hot and possessive. He's a dangerous bad boy of ripped muscles, dominant behavior, and a touch so electric, it instantly lights me on fire.

I've never allowed a man to tie me up before. Maybe it's because I usually date the betas. My mother taught me they are reliable, trustworthy, and supportive. She claims it's what a woman like me needs.

All those traits are correct about the men I've dated the longest. However, my mother failed to mention they would bore me to hell in bed and require me to continue making all the decisions in life.

My most exciting sex has always been with alphas, but once we get past the physical attraction, my personality doesn't keep them around. It's rare I even get in a position to have sex with domineering men. The few times I have, all but one didn't attempt to do anything borderline close to what Sergey did. The one who did wanted to tie me up; I freaked and said no. Something in my gut told me not to trust him. He was a business banker and probably never even had a speeding ticket. There was no reason besides the red flags in my brain telling me to stop.

I didn't question anything Sergey did. The moment he put his hand on my back and led me into the room, I was his to possess. Why I felt comfortable fully trusting him perplexes me. He's violent. I can feel it. Whatever he's involved in, I don't doubt is against the law. I still couldn't resist him. Anything he wanted to do, I would have done.

The most vulnerable I've ever been during any intimate moment was with him. I had no control over anything. I didn't even know I screamed out until my voice became raspy. When he kissed me after, I felt his hunger. I wanted all of him. He saw it then walked out.

He's left me feeling cheap.

I don't expect him to announce to the gym what happened or give me a lifelong commitment. I've had plenty of one-night stands and crazy sexual moments. I'm no saint, but the way he leaves me in the dark, to stagger out on my own, surprises me.

Round two is starting when I come out to the ring. Hailee and Skylar raise their eyebrows with smirks on their faces. I hold my head high, put on my confident facade, and return their smirks.

Thank God I went into the bathroom and pulled myself together.

Throughout the fight, I keep sneaking glances at Sergey. He's with his brothers, Anna, and Aspen, and doesn't once look my way.

All I want is one peek. I'm only five feet from him. We could be strangers. It's making me feel like a desperate schoolgirl looking for attention. It's everything I despise. I'm Kora Kilborn. I don't beg men. They beg me.

It sounds egotistical, but it's true. The men I'm typically in relationships with beg me for everything—my time, their O's, and everything in between.

Instead of acknowledging my existence, he acts like I'm no one to him. It's as if he didn't just get me naked and make me come on his face so many times, I got dizzy.

He thinks I'm a piranha.

I cringe, sneak another glance at the back of his hard body, and wonder if it makes me a challenge for him—someone to break and control for fun. Is he the crocodile ready to swoop in and swallow me whole?

He said I passed the test. What does that mean?

I can't inhale his scent without my knees turning to Jell-O. Staring at him makes my insides quiver. Recalling how his body pressed against mine only makes me feel desperate to experience every part of him.

Get a grip.

As soon as the fight is over, I go outside. I need air. If I continue to be in the same room as him, I'm going to say something. He'll see all my cards. It'll expose all the emotions I'm feeling. And I'm not a woman who allows others to know what hurts me. Not unless you're my close friend, and rarely do I admit pain. It's easier for me to offer comfort to others and help solve their problems.

When I step outside, the bouncer, Leo, is there. He asks, "Who won?"

I force a smile. "Boris."

He nods. His thick neck barely moves. His Russian accent is more pronounced than Sergey's. "You shouldn't be out here. It's not safe."

I snort then point across the street, several buildings down. "You see the light on in that building?"

"Yeah."

"I grew up in that apartment. My sister and mother still live there. They refuse to move even though I told them I'd pay for a new home near where I live." It's something I'm not happy about, but I can't force them to move. It's hard for me to understand how they would rather live in run-down government housing than accept my help. I know it has to do with their pride. Regardless, it angers me they can't swallow it and put themselves in a safer situation. It hurts me they've only seen my condo once and declared I'm too fancy for them now. If I didn't still visit them, I would never see them, since they refuse to come to what they declared as my "uppity" building.

He raises his eyebrows. "No shit?"

I motion to the street corner where two men in black hoodies are standing against the brick building. "See those thugs?"

His eyes turn to slits. "Watch who you're calling a thug."

It takes me by surprise. I assumed he would use the term without batting an eye. "You know them?"

"Enough. They may be dealing, but they keep order around here."

"Yeah, they do. They're my cousins, DeAndre and Terrell." I avoid telling him my brother used to stand with them every night until he got shot in a drive-by shooting. I don't mention I've lost track of how many times DeAndre and Terrell have been in and out of jail. I'm not a fan of their life choices. It wasn't easy to pull myself out of my environment. In some ways, I did the impossible. Maybe it's why I'm such a control freak. Growing up, nothing was ever in order. Food was scarce toward the end of the month until my mother's food stamps arrived. All my clothes were hand-me-downs from my sister. They often had holes or were worn out. She got to pick them out from the second-hand store, but nothing was ever my choice. My mother had multiple boyfriends. Some of them were nice. Some, not so much. Power outages from unpaid electric bills were a normal part of life. I got good at reading in the dark near the window so I could do my homework.

I'm not sure why I worked so hard in school. No one told me I could make something of myself. If anything, the exact opposite occurred. My mother drilled into my, and my siblings' heads, this was life and to accept reality. She didn't understand why I studied so hard. There was this urgency inside me to be the best at whatever I did. So I poured myself into my studies and got a full ride to college.

My mother couldn't understand why I wanted to go to college, either.

Leo glances at the corner again then me. "You've done well then. You've escaped the hood."

"My point in telling you this is if anyone in this neighborhood tried to hurt me, they wouldn't live to tell about it. And I'm still around enough they know who I belong to."

"Ah, but you should never get cocky," Leo warns.

"Sure," I say, pull my phone out, and text the girls I've left. I pat Leo on the shoulder. "Have a good night." I stroll across the street and pull out the key to my mother's house. I planned on coming later in the week, but since I'm here, there's no time like the present.

When I walk through the door, she turns down the TV. "Kora, what are you doing here?"

"I was watching a boxing match across the street."

Her eyes turn to slits. "What business you got with those Russians?"

I feel my body tense and refrain from lecturing her.

It's not worth it.

My mother disagrees about everything in my life. She doesn't like I'm an attorney. She sees lawyers as overpaid ambulance chasers. No matter how well I do, or what recognition I get, her distaste for my profession doesn't change. She also doesn't understand why I won't represent my cousins when they get into legal trouble. It doesn't matter how many times I try to explain I'm not a criminal attorney. In her mind, I'm selfish and have forgotten my roots.

"Aspen is dating the brother of the boxer who fought tonight." I don't dare mention Sergey. She would disprove of everything about him, and I'm definitely not admitting I just let him tie me up in his training room.

She purses her lips in disapproval. Years ago, when the gym across the street opened, many people in the neighborhood didn't approve. They didn't like that the men outside it typically spoke Russian. It didn't matter the new tenants bought the building or crime on the street went down since Leo is stationed there almost all hours of the night and day. The community saw it as foreigners who were invading their space.

I should have put two and two together when Aspen said we were going to a fight. When we pulled up to the gym, I didn't say anything to the girls or Maksim. And I've never brought my friends to my mother's house. It's not safe for them. They met her when she visited my condo. My sister and mother were both rude to my friends. It was embarrassing, and I've not attempted to mix the two parties together again.

I bend down and kiss her cheek. "Are you doing okay?"

She huffs. "Money is getting low, but I'll survive."

It's the same answer she always gives me. While she won't move, she's more than happy to accept my cash.

I pull an envelope out of my purse. I give my mother money once a month. If it were just for her well-being, I wouldn't care.

I hate that my lazy sister, who refuses to get a job and is always nasty to me, gets to live off my hard work. She's two years older than me and hasn't worked since she was twenty-two. But the situation is what it is. I can't change it, and I don't want my mom to struggle. No matter how much she does or doesn't approve of my choices, she's still my mom. My father didn't leave her in a good position with three children to feed all on her own, so I give her more slack than some people might.

I set the envelope on the table next to her. She pretends it doesn't exist, but she complains she has no money, every time I visit.

"Jamal came by today."

My gut clenches. "Oh?" Jamal and I dated for several years when I was younger. My mother thinks he's perfect for me. He has a cell phone business in the neighborhood. He's a nice man, but there was never a spark. He has no backbone when it comes to me, either. Anything I'd say he would agree with, which only annoyed me.

It's one thing to always want to get your way at work. It's another to have your man never have an opinion or question anything. To this day, Jamal, nor my mother or sister, can understand why I'm not with him.

"My sink was leaking. You know how long the landlord takes to repair anything. He came right over when I called and fixed it."

"It's another reason you should let me get you a new place," I try again.

My mother blows air out of her lips. "Jamal asked about you. I think if you stopped in the store to see how he's doing, he'd take you back."

"I've told you, I'm not interested in Jamal. There's no chemistry between us. He's a nice guy but not for me."

Her eyes turn to slits. "Then who is, Kora? Hmm?"

Why do I even bother coming here?

"Where's Neicy?" I ask.

"On a date."

"With who?"

My mother shrugs. "You know Neicy."

I sure do. Somehow, my mother thinks it's okay for Neicy to never settle down, but I'm supposed to be unhappy and tether myself to Jamal for life.

"Jamal's a nice man with a good business," my mother reiterates for the thousandth time.

I walk to the window and gaze out. Sergey steps out of the gym, and my heart flips. He talks to Leo for a moment then his car pulls up.

"Kora, you need to get your head out of the clouds. When a good, decent man shows interest in you and continues to years after you've torn his heart out of his chest, it's time to realize what you're passing up. Women would throw themselves at Jamal for a chance for him to take care of them."

I watch Sergey get into his car. It takes off and drives down the street and out of sight. I spin to my mother. "I don't need a man. I can take care of myself."

My mother rolls her eyes. "Yes, Ms. Moneybags. You can pay your bills. Do you want to end up all by yourself? I'll fill you in on a secret. It's not fun."

Guilt my mother is by herself, and some fear I'll end up just like her, consumes me. She's never had a man who truly loved her. A few years ago, she stopped trying to find him. She stated it was too hard for her to find a good man, since she had three kids to support, and now she's too old.

I love my mother, but there isn't anything about her I envy. I don't want to end up like her. She has always been unhappy. I want to share my life with someone, but I won't choose any man just so I don't end up alone.

I'm so tired of this conversation.

"You're going to be forty in less than two years. The window to find someone is almost shut."

I want to tell her she's wrong and mean. The problem is, the voice in my head says, *"Is she right?"*

I don't stay much longer. I order a taxi. When I get home, I shower, then climb into bed. I'm tempted to text Sergey, but I stop myself. No matter how much I want him, it's best if I forget about him.

He's trouble and into playing games. As much as I don't want to admit it, my mother is right about one thing. I'm not getting any younger.

6

Sergey

MAKSIM AND ASPEN WORK TOGETHER AND FIGURE OUT A WAY to rezone the city lot back to residential. It's time to start the cleanup, but Dmitri says, "If it snows, we're screwed. The ground can't be frozen."

"Sam gave us a three-week turnaround time when we did our due diligence. He's always been reliable on estimates. This next week's weather is supposed to be over forty, including overnight. Let's hope we get an early spring and it stays that way," Maksim declares.

"And if it doesn't?" Boris's eyes grow darker.

"We'll figure it out."

He shakes his head. "This is cutting it too close."

There's a clause in our purchase agreement. We only have a small time frame to clean the lot, or it reverts back to the city.

"What other options do we have besides moving forward?" Maksim asks.

"At this point, nothing."

I cross my arms. "What if we do?" I stayed up all night with insomnia, trying to stop myself from texting Kora and thinking about how to make sure nothing happens to cause us to lose the lot. I studied the contract until I couldn't look at it anymore. Then I made a bet with Boris in the elevator on the way up to Maksim's penthouse.

"What are you talking about?" Maksim asks.

"Hear me out."

"We're all ears," Dmitri states.

"We've relocated all the residents on the northern lot. Let's have Sam start there. Then we can begin construction while he's cleaning up the rest. Our guys stay working with no issues."

"Except we have the ninety-day stipulation with the city."

I smile cockily. "We only have to start the process. It doesn't say we have to finish it."

"Maksim, get out the contract," Dmitri says.

Maksim obeys, and I give Boris an arrogant look.

"You set me up," Boris mutters.

Yep. Take that, big brother.

"Well?" Dmitri asks Maksim.

"Sergey is correct. It clearly states we need to commence the cleanup. It says nothing about when we have to finish it."

"The cleanup on the northern lot was estimated only to take five days, correct?"

"Yes."

"So start the cleanup on the old city lot on Monday. Let's demolish the buildings on the northern land, and then we'll pause the cleanup and have Sam move to the other lot if it's going to take longer than anticipated."

Maksim rises and pats me on the back. "Little brother, I think you might have just saved our asses."

I hold my hand out to Boris.

Boris grunts, pulls his wallet out, and slaps a thousand dollars in my hand.

"What's that all about?" Dmitri asks.

"I bet him I could solve our problems today."

"I should've known. How long have you been sitting on this idea?" Boris asks.

I tap my head. "Shower ideas."

"Well, you should shower more often then. Good job."

"Maksim?" Aspen yells.

"In the office," he replies.

Aspen comes in and tells us the city promoted her. We all congratulate her and leave. I get in my car and decide I'm on a roll. I want to see Kora. I'm not sure where she disappeared to after the fight. I looked for her, but she wasn't around her friends. I thought maybe she went to the restroom, but then Aspen announced that Kora texted she left.

"Does she always take off when you are out together?" I asked.

Aspen shrugged. "She has a case that's driving her insane right now. I think it adds a lot more to her plate when she has to go to court, and she's been in it all week."

It's another reason I didn't text Kora last night. I didn't want to disturb her while she was working.

I'm hoping she doesn't have to work all night tonight. I pick up my phone and text her.

Me: *Are you free for dinner tonight?*

Several minutes pass. Dots appear on the screen but then disappear.

My stomach flips, nervously waiting for her response. When several minutes pass, I get antsy.

Me: *Are you in court today?*

Kora: *Yes.*

Me: *Right now?*

Kora: *I'm on a fifteen-minute recess.*

Me: *Let me guess, you're kicking ass and taking names.*

Kora: *What makes you say that?*

Me: *I've seen you in action. You're a piranha.*

I stare at the phone, waiting for a reply, but I get nothing.

Maybe she had to go back inside the courtroom?

I glance at my watch. It's four. I'm several blocks from the courthouse, so I decide to have my driver park in the lot, then make calls to the foremen, telling them what our plans are moving forward on our projects. I instruct them to make sure our workers are aware there won't be any layoffs. Tomorrow I'll make the rounds and reinforce there is enough work for the next two years, and no one needs to worry about paychecks. However, the sooner word gets out, the better. We can't risk any of our guys feeling like they need to lean on Zamir Petrov for support.

It's a nice day, so I get out of the car and wait.

Around five, Kora steps outside. A soft-pink form-fitting dress and matching suit jacket hug her body just right. I groan. She looks as hot as the last three times I've seen her, but the pink reminds me of how much I want her back in my mouth.

Patience.

She's talking to a woman who I assume is her client. The lady looks distraught, and Kora puts her hand on her shoulder.

They speak for a while. Two men come out of the building. One of them says something. Kora spins and steps in front of her client, as if to shield her. I'm too far away to hear what she says, but she steps closer to the man and speaks. The man replies, and Kora addresses the other suit next to her.

He scoffs, and Kora points at the first man. He steps closer to Kora and gets in her face then starts looking over Kora's shoulder at the other woman, barking out something I can't hear.

Kora pushes her client back farther with one hand and stays planted. The man steps so close to her, he's inches from her face. His is red, and the two keep exchanging words.

I don't like what I'm seeing. Without thinking, I rush up the stairs, reach for the back of his suit jacket, and pull the man away from Kora. I growl, "Get away from her!"

He catches his footing and spins. "Who the fuck are you?"

"I'm about to be your worst nightmare."

"Sergey!" Kora cries out.

I glance quickly at Kora. Anger and shock are both evident in her expression. The woman behind her is shaking, and tears are falling down her cheeks.

I step closer to the man. He's close to my height and looks like he keeps in good shape, but I don't doubt I could take him. His eyes blaze with rage, and he scowls.

The second guy steps away from us. He's probably never worked out a day in his life, and fear fills his face. He pushes his glasses up his nose. "Jack, let's go."

"Larry, get your client away from mine. The next time he steps within one hundred yards of her outside of court, I'm filing for the restraining order," Kora threatens.

Jack spins away from me. He points in Kora's face. "Don't you threaten me, you—"

I grab his throat and lift him so high, he stands on his toes. He reaches for my hand, but I'm gripping him too tight. He chokes and turns purple.

"Sergey!"

I lean into his ear. "Listen to me, you piece of shit. I'm going to let go, and you're going to apologize to these ladies. Then you're staying here, and we're leaving. If you come near either of them again, I'll hunt you down and find everything there is to know about you. Don't push me. I guarantee you won't like what I'm capable of." I release his neck, and he bends over, choking.

Larry's eyes are wide. He might have pissed his pants for all I know. Kora is gaping at me while still shielding her scared client behind her.

I yank Jack up by the collar. "Say you are sorry," I order through gritted teeth.

He barely gets it out.

I get back in his face. "Don't forget my warning. I won't repeat it. I'll take action." I release him, put a hand on both Kora and her client's back, and lead them to my car.

"Sergey," Kora mutters.

"Don't talk right now."

I put them both in the car and say, "Hold on a minute." I close the door and jog back to the two men. Jack is still trying to catch his breath. Larry is asking him if he is okay.

I put my arm around Larry and lean into his ear. "You seem levelheaded."

"Y-Yes."

"If you or your clients ever disrespect my woman or anyone she represents again, I'm coming after you, too." I pat him on the shoulder and go back to the car. When I get in, I put the divider window down. I look at Kora's client. "Ma'am. Where can I drop you off?"

Her lip quivers, and she cries harder. "I... I don't know. He'll be home eventually."

My gut drops. "You still live with him?"

She nods, scrunches her face, and looks at Kora.

"Sorry, I'm going to assume since you're Kora's client, you're divorcing him. Is this not true?"

"Yes, but..."

"It's not straightforward," Kora claims.

"What do you mean?"

"This isn't your business. My client's—"

"No. It's okay. You can tell him," the woman says.

Kora's face hardens. She purses her lips.

The woman replies, "When I filed for divorce, he revoked my access to all our assets. I don't have a penny to my name right now. Kora tried to get the judge to make him give me access and force him out of the house, but..." She closes her eyes.

"But what?"

Kora's jaw clenches. "Selena's husband is connected. He's friends with every judge in town. The judge conveniently said he needed the weekend to review the case. It's a stall tactic for Jack to get what he wants."

My stomach knots. I address Selena. "So you have no money and nowhere to go?"

She bites her lip and shakes her head.

"Has he hurt you before?"

Shame fills her face, and she focuses on her hands twisting on her lap.

Kora's face confirms what I assume.

The savage man who resides in me stirs. I take a few deep breaths to calm him. "Do you have family you can stay with?"

"She moved here from Greece. Jack cut communication off with her family years ago," Kora softly informs me.

"I see." I address my driver. "Igor, take us to Serenity Plaza."

"Why are we going there?" Kora asks.

I roll the divider window up. "My brothers and I built it. The units are all sold, and the showroom model is fully furnished. We were going to have the furniture removed Monday, but I'll cancel it. You can stay there as long as you need." I reach into my pocket and take my billfold out. I hold the cash I won from Boris, along with whatever else is in my wallet, out to Selena. "Take this, and I'll get more for you if you need it."

She opens her mouth, and her eyes dart between the money and me.

"Go on. Take it." I push the money at her.

"I-I can't do that."

"Sure, you can." I reach for her hand. "You put your fingers around it like this then move it away from my hand."

I pull my hand away, since she is still frozen.

"I... I... this is a lot of money!" she exclaims.

"Don't worry about it. I won it off my brother this morning."

Her forehead wrinkles.

I gently push her hands toward her so she's not leaning over the seat. "What is your husband's last name?"

Her eyes widen. "Why?"

"Sergey—"

"I want to know the name of the man who has left her vulnerable and is threatening her," I tell Kora in a firm voice.

"It's Christian. Jack Christian."

I snort. *Figures. A holy name for a bastard.*

The car stops. "We're here." I step out.

"I can't—"

"You can. No one else is using the place. I think you'll find it has everything you need." I reach in and hold my hand out for Kora. "Come on. You can put your stamp of approval on it for Selena."

Kora raises her eyebrows. She slowly reaches for my hand. I help her out of the car and tug her into my chest. She inhales sharply.

"You look beautiful, my lapa." I peck her on the lips, wink, then help Selena out of the car.

I guide both women inside and authorize security to give Selena and Kora full access.

We go into the apartment. It's a three-bedroom home, and something occurs to me. I turn to Selena. "Forgive me. Do you have children you need to go get?"

She shakes her head. "No. It's just me."

"Okay. Will you be comfortable here?"

She glances around. "Is that a serious question?"

I chuckle. "Great. I'll leave you my cell. If you need anything, just text me."

She looks at Kora then back at me. "I think I'll be okay. Thank you. You don't know..." She stops, and tears fill her eyes again. When she composes herself, she smiles. "Thank you."

"You're welcome."

Kora turns to me. "Sergey, can you give Selena and me a moment?"

"Sure. I'll meet you in the lobby."

"Thank you."

I open the door, and Selena yells, "Wait!"

I spin.

"Sir, who are you?"

"I'm Sergey Ivanov."

I'm a goddamn cruel enforcer, and if your husband tries anything else, he's going to see my wrath.

"Kora, I'll meet you in the lobby. Take your time." I step into the hallway and shut the door. I call Adrian.

"Sergey, what's up?"

"I need you to find everything you can for me on Jack Christian."

$\mathcal{MC}$

Kora

FOR THIRTEEN YEARS, I'VE BEEN AN ATTORNEY. THERE'S A misconception about high-net-worth divorces. People assume domestic abuse only happens to poor women. It's a big lie. In some ways, it makes the process of divorce even harder.

When one person controls all the assets and has powerful connections, they can make your life a bigger hell than before. I've not taken a dime from Selena. I normally require multiple deposits throughout a case as my time begins to rack up. When women like Selena come to me, it's typically through a friend. They never ask. They believe no one will help them and there is no way out.

Once I hear their story, I work the case for free. I don't even take anything once the divorce is settled and their prick ex-husbands have to pay them. For what these women have gone through, they deserve to keep every penny. The satisfaction of knowing I helped them is better than money for me. Plus, I take on enough standard high-net-worth cases, so I'm not hurting for cash.

Selena's case has many layers to it. She's an immigrant from Greece. Jack is nearing fifty. She's barely thirty. They met while he was on vacation. She fell hard for him, and he convinced her to leave her family and marry him.

Over time, he cut off all her ties to her family. Things got so bad, they made her choose between him or them. She was already living in fear, since Jack was hitting her. Her family disowned her. He's an uber-rich businessman with political and judicial connections. It doesn't help Selena. He also refused to allow her to become a U.S. citizen. Over the years, he renewed her green card, which ensures she doesn't have the same rights he does. One wrong move and she could end up deported. She's petrified she'll end up homeless in Greece or here.

I tried to get her into a shelter, but everywhere is full. I offered to let her stay at my condo, which I shouldn't do, since it's crossing the attorney-client line, but the words were coming out of my mouth before I could stop them.

I need to keep a level head at all times while I'm fighting for her. Getting too close to a client can interrupt my ability to fight for them. Emotions need to be kept out of my negotiations. When I worked on Aspen's divorce, I struggled to maintain my cool. Peter wasn't beating Aspen. He's just a spineless moocher. Before the other week, I never thought I would add thief to the list of his undesirable traits. In Selena's situation, I have a more challenging time not bringing emotion into my battle. Her story hits personal nerves for me.

When I was a child, my mother had an abusive boyfriend. The only reason it stopped was because he died. Rumor has it my cousins took care of him. I pray we never find out. Somehow, prison for killing a man who abuses women doesn't seem to be justified in my eyes. I still see my mother's beaten face and limp body lying on the ground. So, in a lot of ways, it's good Selena refused to move in with me.

There are many women I've helped over the years. Some of their spouses have assets. Some don't. I won't lie and say taking down a rich man who thinks he's above it all because of his connections doesn't feed something in my soul.

Over the years, I've had numerous men get in my face. Sometimes it's other attorneys. When their clients do it, half the time the lawyer pulls them away from me, and the other half they stand by, similar to how Larry didn't step in. It makes my insides shake and takes everything I have to not back down, but no one is going to intimidate my clients or me.

None of them have ever hurt me. I did have to file restraining orders against a few of my clients' exes to stay away from me after several threats. At this point in my career, I consider it part of the job.

Sergey came out of nowhere. I'm not used to anyone fighting my work battles for me. I saw the rage in Jack's eyes, and my gut flipped faster than it usually does in these situations. I can't help but wonder if he would have hit me if Sergey hadn't stepped in. Larry wouldn't have stopped him. My body turned from quivering fear to the throbbing I always feel when I'm around Sergey. It's the same feeling I had when he took charge in my office and threatened Peter. I shouldn't feel excited when he displays his power over other men, but something about it turns me on.

The thoughts I have are mixed about how he stepped in. I'm grateful he gave Selena a place to stay, but I'm used to fighting these issues on my own. My gut tells me Sergey isn't going to forget about Jack, either. The last thing I need is this case to get more complicated if Jack decides to talk to his friends in high places about Sergey's threats.

"Kora, I'll meet you in the lobby. Take your time," he says in his deep Russian accent.

When the door shuts, I turn to Selena. "Are you okay?"

She nods and sweetly smiles. "Yes. Is Sergey your boyfriend?"

"No."

I want him to be.

That isn't a smart idea for so many reasons.

He's emotionally unavailable. It won't happen, so stop worrying about it.

She furrows her eyebrows. "Really? Why not?"

"I just met him," I blurt out.

Her grin widens. "He seems pretty enthralled with you."

Time to move this conversation away from Sergey and me.

"I think it's best if you stay in the apartment as much as possible. The security guard said your code for the elevator works for the roof as well. It might be best if you utilize it for fresh air but keep out of sight. I don't trust Jack not to look for you."

Her face falls. She nods. "Okay."

"I have an older laptop. I'll bring it by and set up an account for groceries to be delivered. Clothes, too. You'll need some things."

"It's too much."

I put my hand on her shoulder. "Selena, this isn't the time to not accept help."

She closes her eyes and takes a deep breath. Her lids flutter open, and her eyes glass over. "You're already doing so much for me."

I snort. "You forgot how fun it is for me to take Jack down."

She bites her lip.

"What size are you?"

"Medium to large, depending on the brand."

"I'll have some clothes sent over tonight. Do you have the burner phone I gave you?"

"Yes."

"Good. I'll call you tomorrow. If you need anything in the meantime, call me."

"Okay. Thank you." She hugs me, and I return her embrace. I leave, and when I step into the lobby, heat courses through me. The pulsing in my body begins. Sergey's talking with the security officer. His T-shirt stretches over his back muscles. I have to refrain from reaching out and touching him.

He's speaking Russian. The security guard glances over Sergey's shoulder at me.

Sergey stops talking and spins. He eyes me up slowly, intentionally pausing on different parts of my body and licking his lips while staring at my sex. When he drags his smoldering eyes back to mine, I can't seem to think anymore.

"Selena okay?"

"Yes."

He nods, puts his arm around my waist, and says something in Russian to the guard. He leads me out to the car.

I shouldn't let him touch me. He's a dangerous bad boy.

He's the most unselfish man I've ever come across, based on what he just did for Selena.

Nothing good can come from being around him. He already thinks I'm a piranha and only wants to play games with me.

Once again, I'm putty in his hands. I fall into his body, fitting perfectly, unable to retreat from his arm. He's quicksand, and I'm the girl trapped and unable to get out. The more I tell myself he's not a good idea, the further I fall into his muscular frame.

His scent of sandalwood, lemon, and a hint of weed isn't helping the current state of my panties.

As soon as we get into the car, he surprises me and straddles me. He grabs my wrists and pins them behind my head. His mouth comes inches from mine. "Why did you leave last night without saying goodbye?"

My heart beats faster. The air thickens in my lungs. I attempt to move my hands, but he holds them secure.

"Stop moving, Kora."

I instantly obey him.

His lips twitch. "You've been a bad girl. Haven't you?" He arches an eyebrow.

"What?"

He leans into my ear and flicks his tongue behind it. His lips suck on my lobe. "I don't like it when my lapa disappears. It makes me think about all kinds of things."

"Like what?" I whisper.

His other hand unbuttons my suit jacket and slides under my shirt, stroking the curve of my waist. He doesn't answer my question. "I think you've been working too hard. And while I like you in pink, I prefer you to not wear anything."

My belly flutters, and my lower body squirms, but there isn't much room. His erection presses into me, and his lips come near mine again. He drills his gorgeous brown gaze into mine. "Why didn't you answer me about dinner?"

"I..." I look at his lips.

"Tell me why, lapa."

I swallow hard, trying to remember the reasons I should tell him it's best if we stay away from each other.

Something passes in his eyes. His jaw twitches. "You don't want me to take you out?"

"No—" I clear my throat as his face falls. "I didn't say that."

He just gave me the perfect out, and I fumbled.

I don't want an out.

I'm playing with fire with him.

"Then answer my question, Kora. Do you want to go with me to dinner tonight?"

I blurt out, "I don't know, are you going to leave me in a dark room and ignore me the rest of the night?"

Shit. Why did I just say that?

I turn toward the window. Heat blazes in my cheeks. My insides shake.

Where is my ability to shut my mouth?

He releases my wrists and puts his hands on my cheeks, forcing me to look at him. Surprise fills his eyes. "I hurt you?"

I attempt to look away, but he holds me firmly in place. I can't avoid his eyes but say nothing.

In a stern voice, he orders, "Tell me how I hurt you, lapa."

"You didn't," I lie.

His eyes turn to slits. "Don't ever lie to me, Kora. I won't do it to you, so don't do it to me."

"Sorry."

He kisses me. It's soft and gentle, the opposite of any of his previous kisses. It leaves me wanting more, just like his other ones. When he pulls back, he says, "You're forgiven. Now tell me how I hurt you."

"You made me feel cheap."

His eyes widen. "Because of what we did?"

"No. Because of how you left me and ignored me all night." As I say it, I hate myself for admitting it. It makes me sound like a schoolgirl, desperate for his attention.

"Ah. I see." He takes a deep breath. "I'm an idiot and assumed something. I'm sorry."

"What did you assume?"

The spasm in his jaw intensifies. "The wrong thing."

"What—"

"Are you going to hold it against me or accept my apology, lapa?" Worry laces with his confidence.

"I'll forgive you," I say without even considering whether I should or not.

He rolls off me and tugs me onto his lap, pushing my skirt up, so I'm straddling him. His long fingers lace into my hair, and his other hand glides under my jacket then shirt. He splays his palm on my spine.

Tingles break out in all my nerves. My sex sits on top of his erection, pulsing. I want to unzip his pants, push my panties to the side, and sink on top of it.

He kisses me, rough, hungry, as if I'm a drug he can't get enough of and needs more. Between kisses, he mumbles, "Dinner? Tonight?"

"Mmhmm." I slide my tongue back in his delicious mouth.

The car stops, and Sergey hits the locks. We continue kissing for several minutes then he steps out and escorts me to my door.

"Are you coming in?" I ask when I get inside.

His cocky expression mixes with heat. "No, lapa. If I come inside, I'm not leaving and you'll be my only dinner. I'll be back at seven to pick you up for our date."

8

Sergey

ELOISE HAS ALWAYS MESSED WITH MY HEAD. I'M PISSED AT myself for letting her get between Kora and me. I hurt Kora, and I'm kicking myself for it.

I go home and change. I put on a dark pair of jeans, a black T-shirt, and a blazer. The sleeves are ruched to my elbows and display my arm tattoos. It's tailored to fit me perfectly and has several seams designed in it.

When I pick Kora up, the blood pounds between my ears harder. She's wearing a hot-pink, cold-shoulder top. It has rhinestone straps. Her black skinny jeans show off her long legs and ass perfectly.

I hand her a dozen long-stemmed pink roses and lean down to kiss her cheek. "You're stunning, my lapa."

She reaches out and traces one of the seams on my jacket. "So are you. I love this."

I slide my hand around her and palm her ass. "Are you hungry?"

She nods. "Mmhmm. Where are we going?"

"That depends."

"Please don't tell me I have it wrong, and you're one of those guys who makes me choose where we go."

I chuckle. "No. I can make a choice."

She smiles. "Good."

"You don't like to pick?"

She shrugs. "I make decisions all day long. It's kind of nice not to have to figure out every detail of my life."

"Are you picky?"

"No. I was raised to be grateful for whatever is in front of me."

I grunt. "You and me both." I drag my index finger over her jawbone. Her sculpted features take my breath away every time I see her.

She briefly closes her eyes and takes a deep breath.

I steal a quick kiss. "We should go."

"Let me put these in water. And thank you. They're beautiful. Pink's my favorite color."

My pulse increases, and I lick my lips. "It's quickly becoming mine, too."

"Really?" She seems surprised. I can't fault her for it. I'm not a guy who would be into pink normally.

"Yep."

She bites on an amused smile. "Okay, give me a minute?"

"Sure." I release her.

She goes into the kitchen, finds a vase, and fills it with water. Then she cuts the stems and sticks them in the glass. The scent of roses fills the air. "Thank you again."

"You're welcome. By the way, you have a nice place. Have you been here long?"

Pride crosses her face. "A few years."

"It's nice." I hold her jacket out. She turns and slides in. I wrap my arms around her and button it. The scent of flowers and sugar fills my nose. I murmur in her ear, "You smell good."

Kora turns her face toward me. I splay my palm on her thigh, and her breath hitches. I press my lips to hers for another quick kiss. "Do you have work to do tonight?"

She sinks into me. "No."

It would be so easy to stay here and order in.

"Good." I kiss her neck, spin her, and lead her out to the car. As soon as we're both inside, my phone buzzes. "Sorry. Let me turn—" There's a text message.

Dmitri: *Maksim took Aspen to the hospital. Call me ASAP.*

I hit the button.

He answers immediately.

"Dmitri, I didn't see your text. What's wrong?"

"Wes sent Aspen a poisonous snake, and it bit her."

Rage cyclones through my body. "That mother..." I take a hard breath through my nose then glance at Kora. "Is she okay?"

"She's still unconscious. We just got here. Boris is trying to calm Maksim down."

I put my hand on Kora's thigh. "I'll be there soon." I hang up and shake my head.

"What's wrong?" she asks.

"Aspen got bit by a poisonous snake."

She gapes at me for a brief moment then recovers. "How would that happen?"

Disgust and hatred fill every particle of my being. "Wes Petrov."

"What does that mean?"

"Dmitri said he sent her a gift."

Worry explodes in Kora's expression. "Where is she?"

"They just arrived at the hospital."

"Is she okay?"

I pull her into me. "I hope so." I roll the divider window down. "Change of plans. Northwestern Memorial." My hand balls into a fist. I take controlled breaths, trying to calm myself. My jaw spasms, and it only infuriates me more.

Kora wraps her hand over my knuckles. "Sergey, are you all right?"

"Yep."

She quietly says, "I need to ask you something."

I raise my eyebrows.

"What's the deal between your family and the Petrovs?"

My stomach drops. "Nothing."

She angrily states, "Something has to be. After everything that happened in the VIP room and now Aspen—"

"The Petrovs are the scum of the earth."

"Sergey, I don't want to be rude, but I'm also not stupid. The Petrovs are mafia. I know I was intoxicated, so things are a bit fuzzy, but I remember Maksim saying something in the VIP room to Wes about Ivanovs being off-limits. Then Wes said something about inciting a war between Ivanovs and Petrovs. What did that mean?"

I should have known she would eventually ask questions. Kora is intelligent. She can put two and two together. My world with the Petrovs has never crossed into any of my personal relationships before. I'm unprepared.

All the time I've not been able to sleep, I could have been thinking about how to respond to this.

My chest tightens. I firmly respond. "We have a history, and it's not good. That's all I'm saying about it."

She turns to stare out the window.

I sigh and lower my voice. "I'm sorry. That came out harsh, and I didn't mean it to."

She turns to look at me, and I cringe inside. She's grappling. I assume she is debating whether she should even be in this car with me, much less on a date.

I will not let the Petrovs destroy any more good in my life.

I reach for her face and cup her cheeks. "I'm sorry, my lapa. Some things are better not discussed. The Petrovs unfortunately were part of my childhood. My mother got involved with them. It's messed-up family stuff, and I don't want to discuss it, but please don't be angry with me."

She hesitates then smiles. "Okay. You're forgiven."

I'm only partially relieved. Kora's too smart to drop this and let it go. It is only a matter of time before she asks again. I need to figure out what I'll tell her.

I pick up her hand and kiss it. "This is screwing up the night I had planned for us."

She tilts her head. "You still didn't tell me where you were taking me."

"I'm not telling you. Maybe we won't need to stay at the hospital long, and we'll still get to go."

We pull up to the hospital entrance. The car stops. I open the door and step out, reach in for Kora, then guide her inside.

We get to the waiting room, and my brothers and Adrian are there. Maksim is aggressively speaking in Russian, and everyone is huddled around them. Nora and Anna are several feet away.

I release my hand from Kora's back. "Excuse me for a minute." I join my brothers.

Maksim says, "I don't care what the consequences are. I want him found and taken to the garage immediately."

Dmitri puts his hand on Maksim's shoulder. "You need to calm down, or they will throw you out of here. We will handle this. Right now, you need to focus on Aspen."

Maksim's eyes turn to slits. He barks, "She could die!"

Adrian's phone rings. He says, "It's Obrecht. Let me find out where he says we're at."

Maksim holds his hand out. "Let me—"

"Mr. Ivanov," a nurse says.

Maksim spins. "Yes."

"The doctor said you can go in now. She's trying to wake up."

"Is she okay?" I ask.

The nurse smiles. "I think we caught it in time. Come with me."

"Thank you." Maksim follows her down the hall.

"Ladies," Dmitri says.

Kora asks, "Do you know if Hailee or Skylar know about this?"

"I'm not sure, but I don't think so. We don't have their numbers, and Maksim's been..." Nora glances down the hall.

"Okay. Will you excuse me so I can call them? I'll be in after."

"Sure," Nora replies.

"You want me to wait with you?" I ask.

She smiles and shakes her head. "No, you go in."

"Okay."

We go into the room. Maksim is still seething, and we try to keep him quiet. Aspen finally wakes up, but the doctor comes in, and we all leave.

I stroll down several halls and find Kora. Her back is to me. She looks agitated and leans against the wall then shakes her head, focusing on the ceiling.

In an annoyed voice, she snaps, "How much do you want, Neicy?"

Who's Neicy?

She repeats in a firm voice, "How much, Neicy?"

I almost turn to walk away and give her privacy, but she exclaims, "Twenty thousand!"

My red flags go up, and I stand paralyzed, unable to stop eavesdropping.

"What do you need twenty thousand dollars for?"

Why is this woman asking her for money?

Kora snorts. "If you expect me to give you twenty grand without knowing what it's for, you must have lost your marbles."

Who is this person?

Kora's voice changes to worry. "What's wrong?"

For the next few minutes, Kora goes back and forth with whoever this Neicy person is, begging her to tell her what is wrong. "No! Don't hang up!"

I get angry. Whoever is on the other end of the line is playing games with Kora. I can see it without knowing the entire situation.

They must have hung up. Kora calls her right back and begs, "Please tell me what's wrong."

A long pause takes place, and Kora holds the phone away from her ear. I can hear a woman's muffled voice even though I'm several feet away.

Kora finally says, "I'll have to move some things around. I'll bring the money over in the next few days."

I don't like any part of this conversation. This Neicy person gives me bad vibes.

"Okay. Will you at least tell me if you're going to be all right?"

More silence.

"Neicy, please tell me what you're having done."

More loud shouting. Kora cringes and holds the phone away from her ear again.

Where's my piranha? Why's she letting this woman treat her like this?

"Okay. I'll see you in a few days, then?" There's a brief silence, and Kora hangs up. She puts her hand over her face and gently bangs her head into the wall.

I slide my arms around her and murmur in her ear, "Who were you arguing with?"

She jumps then leans into me. "My sister."

"What's wrong?"

She hesitates then shakes her head. "Nothing." She spins. "Is Aspen doing any better? Can I see her?"

I cross my arms. "Kora, what's wrong?"

She looks away. "My family is complicated. I don't want to get into it."

I stay silent, debating whether to push her or not. I don't like what I heard, and my gut is telling me something isn't right.

I just made her stop pressuring me about my family situation.

"Can I see Aspen?" she asks again.

"She just woke up. The doctor is examining her."

"Kora!"

We turn. Skylar and Hailee are trotting down the hall. Hailee is wiping her face.

"Is she okay?" Hailee frets.

"Yes. The doctor is with them now," I assure them.

"How did—" Skylar's cheeks heat. "I need to go to the restroom." She quickly turns and walks down the hall.

That was strange.

"Ladies. Aspen is passed out again. They expect her to sleep a long time because of her pain meds," Adrian says behind me.

Did Skylar run away because of Adrian?

I need to ask him what's up between them.

"What did the doctor say?" Hailee asks.

"The doctor said it was shallow and doesn't think she'll have any long-term issues. It's going to take a few weeks, possibly months for her to be back to normal, or know for sure," I reply.

"Months!" Hailee shrieks.

Adrian winces. "Easy there, killer. I'd like to keep my hearing."

"Sorry."

Adrian cracks his neck. "Dmitri and Anna are staying with Maksim. He said to have the rest of us leave."

"I'll go get Skylar and tell her," Kora volunteers.

Adrian walks past us. "No. I'll relay the message."

Hailee's eyes widen, and she focuses on Kora.

Yep. Something is definitely going on.

"We'll meet you in the lobby." I escort Hailee and Kora through the hospital with a hand on their backs.

"We should wait for Skylar," Hailee insists when we get on the elevator.

I snort. "Adrian will bring her to us. Unless there's something you're worried about?" I arch my eyebrows.

Hailee's face turns red. "No."

"Okay. Have you been working out?"

"No. Why do you ask that?"

"You seem like you have tons of energy."

"Ha ha! Funny!"

"Did I miss a joke somewhere?" Kora asks.

"Just facts I learned about Hailee regarding her pot-smoking skills."

"Hailee doesn't smoke weed," Kora informs me.

"I did once," she claims.

"Mmm... I think we went over this?" I tease.

Hailee rolls her eyes. "I inhaled."

I grunt. "No, you didn't."

Kora bites on her lip. I've not asked her what she thinks of my pot habit, but I'm pretty sure she's aware I smoke. In my experience, most attorneys are closet smokers, but I'm not sure what her opinions are or if she ever does.

"I did," Hailee quietly mutters. Then she says, "I guess it's good Aspen is sleeping. I've got a ton of paper umbrellas to finish making."

"What for?" I ask.

"For my students to decorate. The theme for our bulletin board outside our classroom is *April showers bring May flowers*."

My lips twitch. "How very teacher-ish of you."

"Are you making fun of my profession?"

"No. I loved kindergarten. My teacher got mad when I sniffed the glue though."

Hailee groans. "You weren't one of those kids."

"My friend dared me. I couldn't back down."

She shakes her head in disapproval. "Do you know how bad that is for you?"

I snort. "It's not as bad as what I made my friend do."

"What's that?" she asks.

"I dared him to eat it. After I sniffed it, he couldn't say no."

Hailee puts her hand over her face and shakes it. She opens her two fingers, revealing her blue eyes. "You were one of those kids."

I proudly smile. "Yep."

"Your teacher must have been happy when the year was over."

"Ms. Ebony? Nope. She loved me. Cried when I graduated to first grade." She did. She was my favorite teacher, too.

"Probably tears of relief," Kora points out.

"Doubt it. She used to bake cookies and sneak me a few, up until I was out of elementary school." I rarely think anything happy about my childhood. Until I was twelve and Zamir broke me, I didn't know any evil. Sniffing glue was the worst thing I ever did. After Zamir, it became hard to remember anything before it.

Hailee smirks. "My guess is she wanted to make sure you didn't eat more glue."

"I only sniffed it. I wasn't dumb enough to put it past my lips." I glance at Kora, checking her out like a pervert, then cockily claim, "I reserve my mouth for the finer things in life."

9

Kora

"Wow. This is amazing!" The restaurant Sergey brings me to is a Russian pop-up concept. It's outside, and the overall idea is you're in an ice dome. It's not frozen, but it feels like you're inside an igloo with heat. There's a table and plush, circular seating.

The server brings me a glass of cabernet and Sergey a vodka. In a thick, Russian accent, the server asks, "Do you want to order appetizers?"

Sergey rattles off several things in Russian, and the server replies. I don't know what he's saying, but there's something sexy about the way the words roll out of his mouth. He leaves and shuts our door flap.

Sergey puts his arm around me and takes a sip of his vodka. "Do you know what's going on between Adrian and Skylar?"

"Nope. I hoped you would have the details."

"Hmm." An amused expression appears on his face. "Hailee's interesting."

"How so?" I take a sip of my wine.

He shrugs. "She's a good sport. I like her. She's pretty innocent, isn't she?"

I can't deny it. "Is that your way of saying I'm not?"

He puts his head closer to mine. "God, I hope not."

"Why not?"

He arches an eyebrow. "I need a woman who can handle me. Not a naive, frail thing. Plus, innocence is boring, don't you think?"

"Hailee isn't boring or frail."

"I didn't say she was. I was making a point. Don't put words in my mouth." His hand slips lower, so it's around my waist, and he slides it in my pants. "Besides, I think it takes a more cultured woman to be okay with sitting in public and letting me do this, don't you?" His finger slides through my slit, and he slowly circles my clit.

I open my mouth.

A smug expression fills his face.

I quickly survey our surroundings and clench my crossed legs tighter.

No one can see in here.

Until the waiter comes.

Screw the waiter.

Nope, I only want to screw Sergey.

Or, he can just keep doing this.

He pulls my chin toward him so I'm inches from his mouth. His eyes are golden flames, studying my reaction. "What is the situation with your sister, my lapa?" His finger swipes me faster.

I swallow hard. Heat oozes through my cells. My breathing becomes shallow. I don't want to tell him about how my family doesn't like me but uses me for money. It's the truth. I've known it for a long time. My friends don't understand why I put up with it. I don't understand, either. The only reason I have to give is that they're my family.

He slows his finger and brushes his lips against mine. I try to continue kissing him, but he pulls back. His finger moves faster. "Tell me."

"Why?" I barely get out and close my eyes. He has me on edge. I'm a ticking time bomb ready to explode, but he hasn't pulled the pin.

He kisses my neck then licks behind my ear. "I want to know."

Tremors start in my toes and climb up my legs. "Oh God," I breathe.

"You seemed stressed on your call," he murmurs and tugs my hair so I'm looking at the top of the dome.

Pellets of sweat break out on my skin. I whimper.

"Did I get it right? Hmm?" He slides his finger into my sex, and his thumb takes over, circling me. "Tell me, lapa."

I nod.

He drags his finger down my neck, and shivers run down my spine, mixing with the adrenaline building in my veins. "You want me to release some of your stress? Hmm?"

"Please," I whisper, desperate, and not caring that the waiter could come in at any moment, or someone will walk by and peek closer through the thick plastic.

He nips me on the ear then repositions my head next to his. He speaks quietly but firmly in Russian, studying my eyes and playing my lower body like I'm a violin and he's the musician.

I'm clueless what his words mean, but they increase the flutters in my stomach. My whimpers get louder. He slides his tongue into my mouth and makes me erupt into thousands of pieces while muffling my cries.

He slowly glides his hand out of my pants and slides it up my shirt. His warm palm stretches across my naked stomach. His lips twitch against mine. "Feel better?"

"Mmhmm."

He strokes the side of my head. "Tell me what your call was about."

I close my eyes. "My sister has something wrong with her health and needs an operation. She won't tell me what is wrong."

He teases, "That wasn't hard, was it?"

"No," I admit.

"I'm sorry to hear she's sick. I hope she'll be okay and tell you soon."

I open my eyes. "Can we change the subject? It's—"

He flicks his tongue back in my mouth and caresses my stomach with his thumb. He holds my head possessively, as if I'm his and there's no question about it.

There's something about Sergey I can't seem to get enough of or resist. I'm not used to it, or a man making demands, or one touching me in public.

I slide my hand in his hair, taking from him everything he gives me, wanting all the parts he hasn't yet. I stroke his cock, which only makes me desire it more. He groans into my mouth. We continue kissing until the server clears his throat.

I jump, unaware he came into our dome.

He sets down several dishes. He and Sergey converse in Russian, and he hurries out, shutting the flap.

"What did you say?"

His eyes twinkle. "I ordered some more things and told him to shut the door on the way out." He removes his hands from my body, and I instantly miss his skin on mine.

"What is this?"

"Are you going to remember the names?"

I wince. "I'll try."

He points to the table. "Say zakuski."

"Zakuski."

His eyes light up in approval. "Very good, lapa."

"What does it mean?"

"Think of it as a spread of Russian appetizers."

"Kind of like tapas?"

He picks up each item and feeds me then himself, telling me different names of food and making me repeat them back.

"Impressive," he praises me.

"What's that?"

"Your Russian."

"Really?"

"Yes." He takes a drink of his vodka, and I take one of my wine. "So why won't your sister tell you what's wrong?"

"You heard my conversation?"

Guilt crosses his face. "I might have eavesdropped. So why is she withholding information from you?"

I try to avoid answering him. It's too embarrassing to admit my sister has something medical going on. She needs twenty thousand dollars for an operation and won't tell me what kind or her diagnosis. I snap, "Do you always listen to conversations that aren't your business?"

He cringes. "Ouch. Sounds so harsh when you say it like that."

Crap. There goes my alpha aggressive personality. I need to tone it down. "Sorry."

"Why would you be sorry? I didn't have a right to listen in."

My chest tightens. I blurt out, "For being a piranha, as you call it." I instantly regret it and avert my eyes to my wine-glass. I swirl the wine in it, wondering why I can't seem to keep control of anything around him. In a normal conversation, I would never admit any of my insecurities.

He pins his gaze on me. I can feel the intensity. My cheeks heat, and I take another sip of wine to avoid him.

"Have I insulted you?"

I turn toward him and put on my attorney's face. "No."

"Are you sure? I feel like I may have."

I'm not getting out of this.

I sigh. "I'm aware I can come across a little too strong at times."

"When would you consider it the wrong time to be strong?"

"What do you mean?"

"Tell me when you think you should have to back down on what you know is right or your opinion."

"I-I... You know what I'm saying."

Sergey grunts. "No, I don't. Explain it to me."

I look away. *This is so embarrassing. How am I supposed to answer him? Am I supposed to admit guys run from me?*

He turns my chin toward him.

I hate feeling anxious. I'm usually not. All day, I'm confident about who I am and what I do. Dates are one of the few things I always feel unsure about how to act or what to say. Over the years, it's gotten worse, as more men have rejected me. I take a nervous breath.

He traces my jawline. "You know what drives me insane?"

Tingles compete with my nervous flutters. "What?"

"Women who have no backbone. Ones who can't stand up for themselves or what's right."

I don't say anything.

"When I call you a piranha, I mean it as a compliment. You didn't get where you are by sitting back and letting other people run all over you or hiding who you are. I like that no one messes with you."

"If that were true, you wouldn't have threatened Jack today." *And I wouldn't let my family run all over me.*

His eyes turn to slits. His voice turns so cold, I get a chill down my spine. "If he, or anyone, ever lays a finger on you, I'll kill them."

My heart pounds faster. "You shouldn't get involved in my work issues."

His face hardens. "He was in your face."

"Yes. But it's nothing I haven't handled before."

Sergey shakes his head. "No one is going to get in your face, or they'll deal with me."

"You can't threaten every man who tries to intimidate me."

He snorts. "Watch me."

"Sergey—"

"What do you want me to do, Kora? Not do anything when someone tries to harm you?" he barks.

I tilt my head and put my hand on his cheek. "I didn't say that. And what you did for Selena today was incredibly kind. Honestly."

His jaw spasms under my fingers. Darkness swirls in his ordinarily warm eyes. "What do you know about her husband?"

"I can't disclose anything to you. It's confidential."

"How many times has he threatened you?"

"He hasn't before."

"Don't lie to me, Kora."

"I'm not. Things got out of hand today."

"He doesn't seem like the type of man who is going to lose quietly."

"Let's change the subject," I suggest. Sergey's assumption is mine, but I'm not going to discuss her case with him. It's not professional and won't lead anywhere good. I need Sergey to cool off regarding Jack.

He lets out a long breath. "Okay. Are you from Chicago?"

I shift. "Yeah. You know my neighborhood well."

"Oh?"

I'm not sure why I'm worried about telling Sergey where I'm from, but the voice in my head says maybe I shouldn't.

He waits for me to answer.

I finally admit, "It's where your gym is."

Shock fills his face.

"You can pick your jaw up off the floor now."

"Sorry. You grew up in a rough neighborhood. I didn't expect..."

"What? You thought I was a Michigan Avenue girl?"

His face stays serious. "Most people never escape that neighborhood."

"Yeah. My mom and sister still live there. They won't let me relocate them."

Something shifts in his expression.

"Why do you have that look on your face?"

He finishes his vodka and taps his glass.

"Sergey?"

His eyes meet mine. "They won't have a choice soon."

"What do you mean?"

"The state put the entire block of their buildings up on auction. It's a private bid. My brothers and I put ours in. Those buildings are so outdated, it's an electrical fire waiting to happen. Whoever gets the bid has to knock them down and build new government housing."

Goose bumps pop out on my skin. "Where will all the residents move to while construction is going on?"

"The state plans on relocating them to the north side in several complexes they have set aside."

"What? My mother won't go to the north side."

"She won't have a choice."

"When is this happening?"

"The state moves slower than private companies do. But within the next twelve months is my estimate."

My heart beats hard. I want my mother and sister out of the neighborhood and moving somewhere nicer. I assume the north end government housing is just as dangerous, only a different community of people they don't know.

Maybe this will be the catalyst they need to move closer to me.

"Will you tell me when you find out what is happening?"

Sergey nods. "Sure."

"What about your building? Is that being torn down, too?"

"No. We own it and have updated it already. It's not government housing."

"Oh, right." I take a long drink of wine. "Why did you buy your gym in my old neighborhood?"

"When my brothers started buying property, I was still in high school. They put everything back into the business. We didn't have extra funds growing up, but Aleksei's boxed since he was in Russia. He was my dad's best friend. He saw Boris's talent and trained him for free as well. But he didn't have a gym or a ring. Boris is best friends with Nora's brother, Killian. He boxes, too. For a while, Killian's trainer, his uncle Patrick, let Aleksei train Boris in their gym. Patrick got a lot of grief from the O'Malleys since we aren't Irish. When everything..." Sergey stops, and pain fills his eyes. His jaw spasms. He takes a drink and clears his throat.

What was he going to say? Why does he look so haunted?

"Boris and Aleksei thought it would be good for me to learn to box. But it created more issues in the O'Malley's gym. They made constant comments about the Russians taking over. So Maksim and Dmitri surprised Boris on his birthday with the gym. It was what we could afford at the time. We've never seen the point of moving it."

"Why did they want you to learn to box?"

"They just did."

That's not really an answer.

He flips the conversation back to me. "You never answered me. What's the situation between you and your sister?"

"Tell me why they wanted you to learn to box first," I try to negotiate.

His face hardens. "It's a good way to destress. And I'm not as good as Boris. Now tell me why."

"You should be an attorney."

A line forms between his eyebrows. "Why?"

"You avoid going deep and shift the subject away from you."

He taps his fingers on his glass.

The server unzips the flap and says something in Russian. Sergey responds then asks me, "Do you want anything else, lapa?"

"No, thank you."

He replies to the server and pulls out his wallet. The server hands him the bill, and he slaps cash into the check holder and gives it to him. They exchange final words, and Sergey downs the rest of his vodka. I finish the last sip of my wine.

Sergey helps me out of the booth and guides me to his car. He pulls me onto his lap. "What are you doing Sunday?"

"Sunday?"

His cocky expression appears. "Yeah, Sunday. Around four."

I shrug. "Probably reviewing Selena's case for Monday."

His face falls. "Can you do it earlier in the day?"

I try to contain my smile. "It depends. I usually go to yoga then brunch with the girls. We missed last weekend. But I might be able to fit it in somewhere else during the weekend if there was a good enough reason."

"Are front row Bulls tickets a good enough reason?"

"You have courtside tickets?" I'm a huge Bulls fan and have never been in those seats.

"Yep."

"How did you get those?"

He grunts. "I've had them for five years."

"You like basketball?"

He scrunches his face. "Why do you seem surprised?"

"Not sure. Russian boxer and basketball don't seem to mix."

He snorts. "I love all sports."

I'm not sure if I'm more excited about spending more time with Sergey or going to the game. "I'm a huge Bulls fan."

His arrogant expression grows. "I figured you were."

"How did you know?"

"You've got a signed basketball in your house. I saw it the first night I dropped you off."

He pays attention.

"So, do you want to go?"

I casually say, "I guess I could rearrange my schedule."

"Great. I'll pick you up at four. We'll grab an early dinner at the stadium before the game."

My insides do a happy dance at the thought of another date with him. I lace my hands behind his head. "Thank you for dinner."

He smirks. "Don't forget the exciting trip to the hospital. I deserve extra points for that one."

I softly laugh. "Noted."

He drags his fingers up the side of my torso, and I shudder. He mutters something in Russian then licks his lips.

"What did you just say?"

He hesitates. "I want to take you somewhere."

"Where?"

His eyes search mine. "Have you ever gone to an underground club?"

My heart beats faster. I already know the answer before I ask it. "You mean like a rave?"

He grunts. "No."

Blood pumps hard through my veins. I wait for him to explain more.

"Do you want to go?"

"What happens at this club?"

He strokes my cheekbone. "Lots of things."

"With other people?"

He arches his eyebrow. "Some are into that. I'm not. If anyone touches you, I'd kill them. But you don't have to worry about that. Consent is required for everything."

"What kind of things?"

He leans into my ear. His tongue flicks on my lobe. He murmurs, "Things I would never want to do with an innocent woman."

I don't bother telling him I'm pretty sure I've never done whatever it is he's alluding to, so that makes me innocent. I'm too curious to give him any reason not to take me. I want to see whatever this is, and I also don't want our night to end. My stomach flips in nerves.

He kisses my neck. "It's members only. I'll keep you safe. What's your answer, my lapa?"

I hesitate.

He holds my head so my lips are an inch from his. "It'll make the Cat's Meow seem tame. You in or out?"

I swallow the lump in my throat. "Okay."

The corners of his lips turn up. "Good. Just remember, the only word I listen to is stop."

10

Sergey

I'M A MAN OF MANY FAULTS. I DON'T PRETEND THEY DON'T exist. One of them is my tendency to obsess over the woman I'm dating. It's what makes the arrangement I tolerated with Eloise ironic.

I'm possessive. I don't want any other man's hands on my woman. I don't like to date multiple people at once, which is why I rarely did, except when I was trying to get past Eloise. Some guys have no problem managing multiple women, but all it does is stress me out. Each time I tried, the exact opposite of what I was trying to achieve occurred. My addiction to Eloise grew deeper. Then I'd convince myself if I stayed in her life long enough, she would eventually commit to me. If I just gave her what she needed, showed her how much she meant to me, and displayed patience, she would finally see I was worth it.

Foolish is the only word to describe me. I wasted years of my life loving Eloise while she destroyed my heart piece by piece. Repeating my mistake is something I'm trying to avoid, but I feel my obsession with Kora growing.

If I take her to my place, I'll keep her with me all weekend. When I wake up each morning and see her next to me, I'll get more attached. It's a mistake I made with Eloise when I met her. Since my feelings for Kora feel more intense than when I first got together with Eloise, every warning bell is going off in my head to not give in to my obsession too soon.

Kora already told me she has work to do over the weekend. I want to take her to the game. Eloise would never go with me. I'm excited Kora's a fan. It gives me an excuse to take her out again and something to look forward to once I drop her off at her house, but I'm not ready to end our date.

I have to have her.

The club. If I take her there, I can drop her off after, then have a day to distance myself.

She might not be into it.

There's only one way to find out.

I might as well use it before my membership runs out. I paid enough for it.

It's safer for our relationship if there are other people around to keep me in check.

I don't want to hurt her again.

Kora agrees to go to the club with me. I tell my driver the address. It's not far, and when the car stops in front of the building the underground club is in, I hold Kora's face in my hands. I don't think she has what I would consider prudish notions, but I don't want to make assumptions. I'm confident she hasn't done anything like what could possibly happen in the club. "Don't read into whatever we do tonight."

She nervously asks, "What are we going to do?"

"I don't know yet." It's true.

"What do you mean?"

"I don't have a set plan. Let's go in and see where the night leads us."

She glances out the window then back at me. "Okay. I'm game."

"Promise me, when I drop you off, you won't feel cheap again. Otherwise, we aren't going in."

"Are you going to leave me in a dark room to fend for myself and find my way home?"

"No. I'm not letting you out of my sight."

"Then why would I feel cheap? I told you why I felt that way."

I give her one last chance to back out. "When I said this makes the Cat's Meow look tame, I wasn't exaggerating. I don't know all your beliefs."

"If it makes you feel better, I'm the one who suggested we go to the Cat's Meow. Not a lot shocks me."

"This might."

She smiles. "Well, shock me, then."

I kiss her then mumble, "Tell me again what I listen to."

"Stop."

"Good girl." I get out and reach in for her. Kora steps out, and I guide her into the building. In some ways, it's strange coming here with Kora. Eloise introduced me to the club. It was the first night we did anything together, and she brought me here, thinking she was going to dominate me. At first, I played her game. When I switched roles on her, I took her by surprise. Afterward, I took her to my house. For days we stayed together until she had to fly out for work.

Eloise wanted me to become a member, so I did, but we hadn't been here in a long time. I've never come by myself. My membership runs out in a month. I don't plan to renew it, but it seems like the perfect way to spend more time with Kora without fully embracing my obsession with her.

When we leave, I'm dropping her off at her front door. I need to do things differently than with Eloise.

I bypass security, enter the elevator code, and when it reaches the top level, we step out into the room. Seductive music plays but not too loud. I tug Kora closer to me as we walk through the bright-red, foggy air and step into the bar.

Plush seating areas, along with small tables, fill the open space. Like the Cat's Meow, there are male and female strippers. The difference is everything is extremely high-end. Membership dues are one hundred thousand dollars a year. Women, as well as men, are vetted before they are approved. Strippers wear real jewels around their nipples or other body parts. Each piece of lingerie is handmade and more expensive than most people's rent. Unlike the Cat's Meow, they aren't there to give lap dances or pick up bills off the floor. They are on salary and there to add to the atmosphere.

Guests can be touched if granted permission. Strippers cannot. It's a very clear rule. No tips of any form are allowed to any employee. The madame, and her husband, enforce all policies.

It's early, so the bar isn't full, yet several members are already engaged in sexual activities. I study Kora as she glances around the room. Her cheeks heat, and I lean into her ear. I stroke the curve of her waist with my thumb. "There are more rooms, and this is tame compared to those. Should we stay, or should I take you home?"

For a split second, I think she's going to tell me to take her home. But she pins her hazel eyes on me and straightens her shoulders. "Let's stay."

I peck her lips, relieved I don't have to drop her off yet. I'm not ready to let her go, but I'm not going back on my word to myself not to take her to my house. "Let's get a drink."

We go to the bar. "What do you want, my lapa?"

She hesitates then says, "Tequila and a water."

"A shot?"

"Yeah."

"Shot of tequila, a water, and a double Beluga," I tell the bartender.

He replies, "Go sit, and I'll have Shelly drop them off."

"Four fifty-eight. Ivanov," I say. Everything runs to your account, complete with thirty percent tips. There is no signing or cash.

He nods, and I guide Kora to a dark corner, away from anyone else. I sit in the oversized chair and pull her onto my lap.

"Do you come here a lot?" she asks.

"No. I haven't been here in close to a year."

"Why not?"

"I don't come by myself."

"Who do you normally come with?"

My chest tightens. "A woman I used to see."

"But you don't anymore?"

"No."

The waitress comes over with our drinks and sets them on the table. I nod to her, and she smiles and leaves.

Kora glances around, and her cheeks heat again. I slide my finger over one side. She closes her eyes and takes a deep breath.

"Does it embarrass you?"

She leans an inch from my lips. Her eyes drill into mine with a confidence few women have. "Being in a room where others are having sex?"

"Yeah."

127

"No." She slowly licks her wrist, picks up the salt shaker, and adds the white grains to her skin. She reaches over and grabs her shot and tosses it back then sucks on the lime.

My heart rate increases. She's so damn sexy and doesn't know it. Her ability to attempt to make me believe she isn't nervous is making me harder. My dick twitches against her ass, and she cockily arches an eyebrow. I spin her so she's straddling me. Her breasts are inches from my face. They rise and fall faster, and she stares at me in surprise.

I fist her hair and move her face closer to mine. "Do you want another drink?"

"No," she breathes.

"Do you know why I like pink all of a sudden?"

"Why?"

"Because all I think about is your pussy and how much I want it in my mouth again."

She swallows hard.

I lean into her ear. "And that pink tongue and mouth of yours, you're going to beg me to fuck." I drag my finger down her neck, and she shudders.

She turns her head, and I slide my tongue past her lips. The taste of tequila and limes circle my mouth. The scent of her floral perfume flares in my nostrils. Her fingertips are electric jolts to my skin.

I deepen our kiss, slip my hand up her shirt and under her bra, then roll her nipple between my fingers. It puckers and hardens, and I want my mouth on it. I lift her shirt, pop her breast out of the cup, and suck it.

Kora moans softly, grinding herself against my cock, and rubbing her thumbs on my ears.

Her breasts become my smorgasbord. I tighten my arms around her, licking and sucking her until she trembles.

I find her mouth again. She kisses me, and I place my palm between her legs. It's hot and damp, and the aching between my legs grows.

"If this doesn't faze you out here, then let's go back," I suggest then kiss her some more.

"Mmhmm." She lightly drags her nails down the back of my neck. Zings rush down my spine. "You aren't going to get me naked out here?"

I hold her face in front of mine. "No. I'm taking you to a more intimate space."

She nods and breathes, "Okay."

I move her off me, rise, and help her up. I guide her through the door. We enter a hallway. Instead of walls, it's floor-to-ceiling glass. I bypass it all, not interested in the people taking part in different acts in each themed room. I'm only interested in one place.

The members call it the dungeon. It's darker than the other rooms. Almost everything is black, whether it be leather or metal. A few silver items dot the room but not many. It's the only area in the club where members can control the music, heat, and lights.

I don't call it a dungeon. To me, that's not what it is. I am a master of torture, and this room is another chamber. It's a playground for me to utilize pain to give pleasure instead of my normal blood and death.

Before Eloise, I only knew how to use punishment to get what I wanted before I would kill a man. She stirred something in me. It's like I knew exactly how to take the skills I had acquired from Zamir and focus them on her. It only took one time and she was hooked. She craved the pain that led to the pleasure. And I was at a point in my life I needed an outlet to do something with my skills besides create bloody outcomes.

At first, Eloise couldn't understand why I didn't want to spend all our time at the club. She didn't know my secrets and assumed I wouldn't be able to give her the same attention outside of the dungeon. She would never have fathomed she was sleeping with a cold-blooded killer.

I can kill anywhere, just like I can break a woman anywhere. And maybe that's the difference between the men who come here and me. I understand the art of torture. Patience is something Zamir taught me. Too many men to count have begged me for their last breath. Numerous women have begged me to do things they never dreamed they would want or would be so desperate to need.

I joined the club for Eloise. It was a waste of money. I did the same things to her at my house I've done here. And the more I fed her addiction, the more she begged me to hurt her. Sometimes it got to the point I had to stop. We would fight when that happened. But I had my limit and wasn't going to pass it.

But now, I wonder if it's better I break Kora here instead of at my house. Here, women seem to understand something they never experienced before will happen. Maybe it's better and easier to have an open mind that one can't have if you aren't in this environment. Then, when you crave what you don't understand afterward, and you're so desperate you're willing to do it anywhere, you don't have to deal with any confusion about what will happen—although you will still have mixed feelings about why you want it.

I lead Kora into the dungeon. When I step in, I feel a calm wash over me. It's the same peace I feel before I torture a man.

"What is that?" Kora asks.

I don't need to see what she's looking at. It's an iron wall, with over one hundred places to restrain a person. No matter your preference, cuffs, rope, wire, silk, it's all here, ready to be utilized at your discretion. There are intricate places for body parts to fit through—hands, feet, heads, elbows, knees, cocks, it doesn't matter. Flat metal mixes with round metal. To the average person, it would look like a beautiful metal piece of abstract art, with a black wall behind it. A sadist like me sees it as my playground of opportunity.

There's enough room for several people to be restrained at once and at some point in the night, others typically come in. Tonight, they won't. Eloise always required the show and sounds of others experiencing what she was going through. I never cared for the voyeurs or to watch the others receive similar punishments as Eloise. I want Kora to myself. Unless she tells me she needs it, I'm not letting anyone in and already hit the button so it's clear to anyone who comes near the door.

I caress her jaw with my thumb and study her nervous eyes. "It's what I'm going to tether you to for hours unless you say stop."

Her breath hitches.

I unbutton her jeans and slide my hand in her pants. "You're getting wetter at the thought, aren't you?"

She nods.

I slide two fingers in her and fist all of her hair. I tilt her head so she can't move, and murmur in her ear, "If you say stop, at any time, I'll stop. It'll be over and I'll take you home. We won't do anything like this again. So think about what you want before you speak."

She furrows her eyebrows then tries to hide the fear in her eyes, but anyone who is a master at torture wouldn't miss it.

I keep playing with her, utilizing my thumb to circle her clit, and kiss her taut neck. "Do you want me to stop, or should we keep going?"

She shuts her eyes. Her breath becomes shallow. Heat rises into her face. "Don't stop. Oh God...oh...oh..."

I pull my hand out of her pants.

Her eyes fly open. Confusion appears in her hazel orbs.

"Orgasms are earned, my lapa. And from here on out, you don't come unless I permit you. Every time you don't surrender to me and give me whatever I want, there will be consequences."

"Like what?" Her voice comes out raspy.

"It depends on what I choose to do." I palm her ass, tug her as close to me as possible, and shove her hand in my pants. I refrain from groaning. Her warm fingers coil around my cock, and she rubs the tip with her thumb.

I give her one last out. "As you can see, I'm ready to get started. Are you, or do you want to stop?"

She takes a deep breath, straightens her shoulders, and looks me in the eye. In her confident voice, she proclaims, "I'm ready."

I assess her one final time, kiss her until she's breathless, then step back.

"Strip."

She obeys.

I light up my bowl and take a hit. I hold it out to her, she takes it, inhales a deep breath of smoke, holds it in her lungs, then tilts her head to the ceiling, and slowly releases it.

I hand her a glass of water. "Drink."

She takes several sips then stares at me.

"Finish it."

"Why?"

Because you need fluids for how much sweat is going to flow out of your body.

I step closer to her, reach around her, and slap her ass hard.

She jumps into my chest.

I rub her cheek and fist her hair so her head tilts back. She inhales sharply. "Don't question me. Ever."

Her forehead creases.

"Are you sure you want me, or do you want me to stop?" I arch an eyebrow and drag my fingers up her spine.

"I want you," she whispers.

I lean down, and she moves to kiss me, but I avoid her lips. I murmur in her ear, "Good girls get rewarded. Bad girls get punished. Decide who you want to be. In my experience, there's only room for one of us to be bad. It's not you." I pause for a moment, letting her absorb my statement. "Now be a good girl and get on your knees."

11

Kora

CURIOSITY LACED WITH AROUSAL AND FEAR TAKES OVER. I'VE never done anything like this. I'm not sure what Sergey will do to me or what I agreed to. Something pulls me to him. He's iron. I'm the magnet, unable to stop myself from wanting and needing him. It's not the fear of the unknown racing through my blood. It's the possibility I may say stop and not have whatever this is again. I saw and heard the finality in his voice. He's not threatening. His requirement for me to submit to him isn't something he will bend on. If I don't, my instinct tells me it will be over between us.

Desperation to please him and keep him wars with my normal stance to be the one in control. I'm not used to feeling like I have to keep a man. There are other men I liked. When things ended between us, I was disappointed, but everything about Sergey is different. Every touch he gives me lights a need within me I didn't know I had. I've not even had him yet, and the craving for all of him is so intense, I've never felt so desperate for someone. It confuses me.

What am I doing?

This isn't like me.

Nothing felt right in the past. This does. How can it be?

It's him. He feels right.

I haven't smoked weed in years. It's something I stay away from most of the time. There's always so much work to do. If I indulge, I relax and can't concentrate on my work. But when Sergey offers me his bowl, I don't hesitate. I need to turn off my mind and obey his every command without analyzing things. The combination of the tequila shot and weed hits me. I lose my inhibitions and forget I'm Kora Kilborn. I stop thinking about how he's a man who has violent tendencies, possible ties to the mob, and how I shouldn't be here with him. I allow the essence of the dungeon and all it may represent to swallow me whole.

The voice in my head that is always in charge tells me to run, but a new woman fights her and wins. She shuts my bossy self up and takes over.

Naked, I drop to my knees, automatically focusing on his feet. I'm unsure why I do. I've never submitted to anyone before to know the protocol.

Sergey steps forward and tilts my chin up. The heady scents of sandalwood, lemons, and weed intoxicate me further. His eyes flare with power and sin, but there's a calmness I didn't expect to see. I assumed a man in his position would have agitation in his expression. The depth of his composure is striking. It's something beyond what you get from a hit of weed or alcohol. Only experience can produce the level of serenity he displays.

It gives me confidence in him and the power I'm handing over to him.

His thumb brushes my lips. "When we leave here, don't forget you belong to me."

"You're the one who left me in the dark and ignored me last time," I remind him.

His face hardens. "Kora—"

I put my hands in the air. "Hey, you brought it up!"

He releases a breath, tilts his head, then traces my cheekbone. "I won't ever make that mistake again. I need your full trust from here on out."

"What are you—"

"Shh." He puts his fingers over my mouth. "Do you trust me, or should we stop?"

I don't answer. His words make me wonder what I'm getting involved in.

He tucks a lock of my hair behind my ear. His eyes turn to slits. "I think we should go."

"I do trust you," I blurt out.

I shouldn't. He's a bad man in so many ways, with good sprinkled around the corners. It's the crumbs of his goodness I'm betting on won't allow anything horrible to happen to me.

He sniffs hard through his nose then slowly releases it. He studies me until I'm uncomfortable.

"Why are you staring at me?"

"A sculptor could have created your face." He traces my cheek and jawbone. "I do have one question for you."

"What?"

He leans down to my ear. "What's a beautiful, successful woman like you doing here with someone like me?"

The air becomes thick in my lungs. I freeze, unsure how to answer him.

"I know you see the devil in me. Why aren't you running?"

I stay silent.

"Look at me," he growls.

I meet his eyes, and he pins his steely gaze on me. "When the time comes, and the fear inside you grows, remember the devil is on your side. His obsession with you isn't going to wither. It doesn't die unless you cross him. It grows more powerful with time, and when you give in to his temptation, he will reward you in ways you didn't anticipate."

A nervous flutter increases in my gut. I bite my lip.

"Ah. There it is."

"What?"

The corners of his lips turn up. If fire erupted behind him, I might think he is Satan himself. It ignites a strange feeling inside me. I'm not sure what to make of it. My conscience says to run, but an overpowering sense I need to make him mine consumes me.

He pulls me up and guides me to the wall so I'm looking at the iron. He positions me so my face is against the metal opening. "Don't move." He slides his fingers over the sides of my breasts. He steps back. The sound of metal hitting the floor echoes in my ear.

My heart pounds faster. I concentrate on my breathing, staring at the dark wall.

He steps against me, skin to skin, with his warm, hard frame and erection pressing into me.

I whimper from the force of the hum in my blood accelerating. I move my hands to touch him, but he stops me and stretches my arms as far away from me as possible, with his over them. His hot breath hits my ear, and I shudder. His deep voice murmurs, "Have you ever not had the ability to grasp anything?"

"No."

His dick pulses against my spine. His middle finger strokes over mine. "Have you ever not been able to talk?"

I swallow hard. "No."

"Have you ever allowed someone to manipulate your body so you have no control over it?"

"No."

"Why not?"

"I-I don't know."

"Yes, you do. Tell me. Admit to me why you're letting me do this but no one else." His tongue slides behind my ear, and he flicks it on my lobe.

I squirm between the iron and him.

He demands, "Don't overthink it. Tell me, lapa."

It rolls out of my mouth. "I want you. So badly."

He groans. "Close your eyes."

I obey even though he can't see me.

He speaks Russian, between kissing and biting the curve of my neck, pulling my hands higher until they are flat against cold metal. He splays his hands over mine then takes his foot and moves my ankles farther apart, until I'm slightly uncomfortable and don't want to stretch any farther.

I gasp.

He swiftly clasps something around my wrists, and another piece of cold metal replaces where his hands were, taking away my ability to move my fingers. I'm the filling in a sandwich, and my pulse beats harder with anxiety.

Tingles of fire erupt from where his fingertips and lips caress me, slowly moving over my spine and sides of my torso to my right leg. He restrains my ankle, moves back up my leg, pausing over my ass, and inhaling. A soft groan echoes in my ears then he continues to torment my left leg until he locks the cuff around it.

The air hits my skin. My breath calms as I get used to the position he locked me in. The music changes. The sound of whines and cries fills the room.

He's listening to Afghan Whigs?

I got into the band when I was in college. Most people haven't heard of them. It was the first time I heard anything that wasn't hip-hop or pop. The gritty voice of the singer rings in my ears.

"Sweet Son of a Bitch" plays and moves into "66." Sergey steps behind me and slides something smooth over my pussy, rolling it on my clit, then dipping it in and out of me, twirling it against my walls.

Heat flies through me. I arch into the iron but can't go very far. I'm too tightly restrained.

He reaches around the iron. His forearm slides on my nipple while his fingers twist my other one. Whatever he has in his other hand, he pulls out of me and slowly circles it on my clit.

"Oh God," I whisper, already shaking, wanting to grip anything but unable to bend my fingers.

"Relax, my little lapa. Don't fight what you can't win."

"Sergey," I whisper, on the verge of falling but not only over the cliff of pleasure but into whatever he and this world of his represents.

His lips are sparks on my neck. "Good girls get rewarded," he reminds me, removes whatever was in my lower body, then slides his arm up. He sticks his hand through the iron and pushes it into my mouth. "Suck."

I obey. Sugar and my salty arousal mix on my tongue. A strap tightens against my cheeks.

He gagged me.

Something about it freaks me out. I begin to panic, but I can barely budge an inch.

Sergey's hand palms the back of my head. He barks, "Stop moving and be quiet."

I still.

He lowers his voice, and his warm torso covers my back, calming me. "Do you taste how fucking sweet you are?"

I stay silent, not sure how to respond.

He tugs my hair, and my face comes away from the iron enough to see him in my peripheral vision. His lips move to my cheek. "This is what I thought about all day. My mouth on your sweet, throbbing pussy."

Every part of my body pulses, remembering how he drove me to insanity the last time he took control of me.

He repositions my head against the iron, drags his hand through the metal, and fingers me, putting me back on the peak of the mountain, ready to fall. "You'll suck all of it until it's gone. Otherwise, we'll stop. Do you want me to stop?" His hand freezes.

I can't speak, so I stay silent, continuing to hold the sucker in my mouth so I don't drool. I couldn't release it if I tried anyway. It's securely fastened. Something about not letting anything escape out of my mouth becomes a challenge.

He moves his hand again, and I moan. He stops. "I assume you want me to keep going?"

I whimper, desperate for him to continue.

"Good girl." He slowly resumes his movement, never letting me come, torturing me until my skin is slick with sweat.

He palms my sex and slaps my ass. It's hard. Then he slides his fingers back in me and rubs the sting on my cheek. He pinches my nipple until it's painful while shimmying his forearm against my other. Then he switches his hands and repeats the process, creating a new sensation in my tender breast.

I love and hate him all at once. It's cruel then almost pleasurable until he continues to refuse to send me soaring. I don't understand why he's keeping me this way. His erection is hard as steel against my spine. I'm shaking when the gag falls out of my mouth from sucking it down to nothing. "Please...oh...please," my raspy voice cries out in a desperate voice I've never heard before.

He groans and sniffs the crook of my neck. "I'm so hard for you, Kora."

"Please, Sergey," I beg.

"Surrender to me, lapa."

"I am... I have."

"You haven't."

"Please," I try again, not sure what else I'm supposed to do.

"When I slide my cock in your tight, pretty cunt, I want you as mine, Kora."

"I am...please."

His lips hit my ear. "You're still fighting me, my lapa."

"How," I whimper. "Tell me."

A new song comes on. It's something about the devil and sin. He takes some sort of tool, and little electric jolts prick my spine. Tears begin to stream down my cheeks. It's too intense, yet I miss it when he removes it.

"You can tell me to stop," he suggests, as if to test me.

For a sliver of a second, I consider it. "Don't stop. Please, I need you."

He tugs my hair again. "Is it just my cock you need, Kora? Hmm?" he quietly says, studying my eyes.

My thoughts aren't logical at this point. I hardly know the man. I should stay away from him, but every cell in my body craves him. "No. I need all of you. Please."

He speaks in Russian, speeds up his fingers, and puts the tool on my belly button.

"I can't...oh fuck!" I scream as an intense surge of endorphins explodes through my body. It's a strange thing, not being able to move. Spasms filled with adrenaline consume every fiber of my being. When I cross the line and fully surrender, I realize how much I didn't understand. It becomes clear why Sergey tortured me like this.

The high is more powerful than anything I've ever experienced. It goes on and on. He continues to keep his arms wrapped around me. The tool falls out of his hands. He manipulates my breasts and sex while growling Russian in my ear.

I don't know what he says. I have no control over anything. The power of his body against mine, wrapped around me, is the safest I've ever felt— even during the hurricane of intense pleasure that's so excruciatingly good, it might destroy me.

The instant it's over, he unlocks my wrists and ankles. He spins me so my back is against the iron then reattaches my wrists and sandwiches them with metal again.

It happens quickly. He drops to his knees and throws my thighs over his shoulders then devours me with his mouth.

I'm sensitive from everything he already did. The instant his tongue and lips hit me, the tremors reignite. My cries compete with the music. I surrender to him and every sensation he gives me.

He slowly rises to his feet, sliding along my shaking body on his way, then ravishes my mouth with the same intensity he just bestowed upon my pussy. His hands glide up my arms, and he releases them. They fall over his shoulders, limp and exhausted.

He circles his arms around me and carries me to a bed I didn't even know was in the room.

I sink into the mattress, my skin humming against his, new need racing through my veins.

The head of his cock presses into me. It's warm and wet, and I spread my legs wider.

"Are you on the pill?" he murmurs between kisses.

I barely come up for air. "Yes."

He freezes, and his gaze pierces mine. "I'm clean. Do you want me to get a condom?"

"No. I'm yours." Not once in my entire life have I ever told a man not to wear a condom. The need to not have anything between us digs into my soul.

He doesn't wait. He thrusts his hips, and I cry out.

"Shhh." He strokes my damp hair. He speaks in Russian and begins moving.

Holy shit...oh God...

He's not all the way in, and I'm clenching against him. The girth of him feels as if he might split me in two.

"Relax, my lapa." He takes my wrists, puts them over my head, then pins them with one hand. His other arm slides under me, and he palms my head.

The weight of his body is heaven. I'm used to being on top. The men I'm with usually want me to ride them. I like it, but this feels incredible. He's a blanket of zings, and I want him to stay wrapped around me forever.

He thrusts harder, inching deeper and deeper in me until our hip bones meet. Our chests heave against one another. He retreats from kissing me and pauses, letting me adjust to all of him. His eyes study me. "No more pain tonight. Relax so I can take care of you."

I'm not sure how to take what he means, but I don't respond or argue. I surrender fully to him.

"Good girl," he praises then pushes my arms tauter, returns to kissing me, and thrusts in and out of me, faster and faster.

My moans become too loud to silence. He buries his face in my neck and grunts while sucking on my skin. He slides his other hand up my arm then laces his fingers through mine, resting them on the bed next to my head.

The warmth of his skin creates torturous friction on my walls. He pounds harder, and I spiral. A new type of high pulses within me. Fluids soak the sheets. I continue quivering. He says something else in Russian. His erection pumps hard in me, spurting his hot seed deep, and I soar once more. A low, throaty groan escapes him.

In our aftermath, he lies on top of me. His chest heaves against mine. His hot breath in the curve of my neck gives me goose bumps. I shudder under him, trying to understand everything he just did to me.

He lifts his head, releases his hands from mine, then rolls off me.

Did I seriously tell him not to use a condom?

What was I thinking?

Our fluids soak the mattress. Everything is wet and sticky, and I slowly sit up. I focus on the mess we made and then turn. "Sergey."

He raises his eyebrows.

"I haven't ever...umm..." I swallow hard.

He closes his eyes. "Please don't tell me I made you feel cheap again."

"No. That's not it."

His eyes open. "Then what is it?"

"I've always used a condom. You're clean though? You've had a test?"

Anger fills his face. "You think I would lie to you about that?"

"No. I just..." I put my hand on my stomach. I flip it on him. "Why didn't you ask me if I was clean?"

"If you had something, I trust you would tell me so we could talk about it."

"You're right. I would, but I don't."

"Yeah. That's the difference between you and me. I already know you would."

"I'm sorry."

He shakes his head, turning away from me. His back is an artwork of tattoos. I've never seen anything like it. Even in the dark, its brilliance is stunning.

I crawl on my knees, press my body to his back, and put my arms around him. "I'm sorry."

He freezes, as if something is wrong, then puts his hands over my arms, gripping tightly. He turns. "I would never hurt you or do something to damage you, Kora."

"I know. I'm sorry. I had a freak-out moment. You know I'm a control freak, right?" I tease.

His lips twitch. "Not always."

"So you forgive me then?"

He reaches around me and rises, holding the side of my hips. "Yep. I think it's time to show you what a real shower is like."

"There's a shower here?"

"Mmhmm." He glances back, drilling his eyes into mine. "Do you still trust me?"

"Yes."

"Good. You'll get rewarded, then."

1 2

Sergey

"I LEFT MY PURSE ON THE CHAIR OUT IN THE BAR," KORA SAYS.

We just finished showering and put our clothes on.

"It'll still be there. Promise," I reply.

She puts her arms around my shoulders, stroking the back of my neck. Nervousness enters her eyes, but she asks, "Do you want to stay over when you drop me off?"

I've told myself a thousand times to keep my distance, not to take her to my house, and to hightail it out of her building after she's secure in her condo. I didn't expect her to ask me to stay. Before I can talk myself out of it, I cave. "Yes."

She smiles, and my heart soars.

I kiss her again. "Let's get out of here."

I lead her out of the club and into the bar. There's a couple where we were sitting, but it's too dark to see who until we get closer. I plan on grabbing Kora's purse and leaving when my gut drops. I protectively step in front of Kora. The blood in my veins heats with rage.

Eloise is on top of the man and turns. In her thick, French accent, she arrogantly says, "Sergey." She's mostly naked, wearing only a thong.

I don't care if Eloise is here, or that she's about to screw another man. What gets me is whose lap she sits on.

Rage fills me when a sinister smile appears on Wes Petrov's face. "I didn't know they let filth in the club." He tilts his head toward Kora, and his expression turns cockier. "You want to join us?"

Eloise scowls at her.

I push Kora farther behind me. I pick up her purse and hand it to her. "Go wait for me by the elevator."

Her eyes widen, but she obeys.

When she's far enough away, I turn to Eloise. "What are you doing?"

Wes grabs the back of her knees and tugs her closer to him. "She likes real Russian cock, don't you?" He runs his finger down her cheek, and she slightly shudders. "Go on and tell him."

Eloise turns her head. She purses her lips. Her eyes swirl as if she's high and pissed. It's a look I've seen too often. It's one I don't miss being at the end of, and as much as I don't have any desire to be with her anymore, my insides shake.

What is she doing with him?

We've run into Wes before. We were at an event. It was one of the rare times she had me escort her to a work party.

She knows who he is and what he is part of.

Wes and I exchanged words at her event. When we left, I warned Eloise he was bad news. I told her he was part of the Russian mafia.

Why would she get involved with him?

How long has this been going on?

I need to get Kora out of the club. His thugs will be here, too.

"I wish you the best, Eloise."

I start to leave but stop when Wes shouts, "Ivanov."

I pause and turn.

"Did your brother and his whore like my gift?"

My fists curl at my thighs. The madame of the club comes up to me and touches my back.

I freeze from the small touch near my spine, and my skin crawls.

"Mr. Ivanov. It's been a while. How are you?" she asks.

"Just leaving," I bark, turn back to Eloise, and say, "I'm not sure what game you're playing, but you chose the wrong pawn." I leave and quickly am at Kora's side. We say nothing and step into the elevator. I hold her tight to my side and text my driver to meet us out front.

Was Eloise seeing him when she was with me?

I need to talk to Obrecht.

I tell my driver to go to Kora's.

She quietly asks me, "Was that Eloise Boucher? The French runway model?"

"Yes," I mumble and focus on texting Obrecht.

Me: *I'm calling you in the next ten minutes. Pick up when I do.*

Obrecht: *You all right?*

Me: *Just pick up when I call.*

I can't wait to kill Wes.

Zamir is next.

"Is she your ex?" Kora asks.

I snort and turn toward her. "If you can call it that." My chest tightens.

I need a hit.

I grab my pipe and light it, taking a deep inhale. I offer it to Kora and crack the window, slowly releasing the smoke.

She shakes her head. "No, thanks."

I fire off a text to Adrian.

Me: *Are you home?*

Adrian: *Yeah.*

Me: *At your house?*

Adrian: *Yep.*

Me: *I'll be over soon.*

"Eloise is who you used to go to the club with?" Kora quietly asks.

"Unfortunately," I mumble.

"How long did you date?"

"Too many years."

Silence fills the car, and I focus on the passing buildings, trying to calm my insides.

"When did you break up?"

I toss my phone on the seat. "Not too long ago. Can we not talk about Eloise?"

"She was with Wes Petrov," she quietly states.

"In the flesh."

I take another hit, trying to calm my rage. All I can think about is making sure Wes Petrov pays for almost killing Aspen and all the other years I've dealt with him. Seeing Eloise on his lap, practically naked, makes me worry about what their alliance could be.

Was she playing me this entire time?

Did she only come to the wedding with me to spy on me?

Was I sticking my dick in her while Wes was, too?

Is Zamir a part of this?

Paranoia sets in, and my mind spirals. The car stops in front of Kora's building. I get out and reach for her.

We say nothing on the way to her condo. When she gets in, I kiss her on the cheek. "Have a nice night. Lock your door."

Her eyes widen. She quietly asks, "You aren't staying?"

"I'm sorry, I can't. I'll pick you up Sunday at four for the game."

"O-Okay." Hurt fills her face.

What am I doing?

I step forward, firmly hold her cheeks, and kiss her, flicking my tongue in her mouth until my dick's hard again. I press my forehead to hers and close my eyes. "Don't hold this against me. Please."

"Will you tell me why you can't stay?"

"I think you know why."

"Because of her?"

My eyes fly open. "No. I don't have any feelings left for her."

She doesn't look convinced.

"It's because of him. I thought you would understand this after he almost killed Aspen."

Worry fills her expression. She reaches for my cheek. "Sergey, what are you going to do?"

Instead of answering her, I kiss her again. "I have to go. I'll see you Sunday."

"Sergey—"

"Don't ask me questions about this, Kora." I peck her on the lips one last time and release her. "Lock your door."

I step into the hall, wait until I hear clicking, then leave. As soon as I get in my car, I call Obrecht.

"I know where he's at," I say in Russian.

He replies in Russian, too. "How?"

"Don't ask. I'll text you the address, but there's something else you should know."

"What?"

"Eloise is with him."

The line goes quiet.

Obrecht finally asks, "You want me to pick her up, too?"

"We need to know how long she's been seeing him. What if—"

"Sergey, don't jump to conclusions. I'll handle it. Let me talk to her, and I'll find out what she knows."

"Maybe I should—"

He grunts. "No. She'll respond to me. I'll handle it," he repeats.

"Okay. But if—"

"Sergey, don't spin out about this. I'm the right person to take care of this. You aren't, and you know it."

I sigh. "You're right."

"You tell Maksim you saw him?"

"No, not yet. Get the fucker to the garage before you tell Maksim. He's too hot right now."

"Got it. Send me the address."

I hang up, take another hit of my pipe, and go to Adrian's. My brothers are all with their women, and I don't want to disturb them. I hit the code for the penthouse and get out of the elevator. I knock on his door. He's in only a pair of shorts.

"Sorry. I don't even know what time it is. Were you asleep?"

A cocky expression appears. "No. I wasn't sleeping." He crosses his arms. "It's after two. What's going on?"

"I just talked to Obrecht."

"And?"

"Wes was at the club."

Adrian's eyes turn to slits. He scratches his cheek. "Are you still going there?"

Adrian is the only one who knows about the club. I took him there one time. We were on a double date with one of Eloise's model friends. I've never even told my brothers about my membership.

"No. I haven't been in almost a year. I have a month left and...well, it's a long story. But guess who was on Wes's lap?"

"Who?"

"Eloise."

Adrian's jaw clenches. "Tell me you're lying."

"No. Hey, can I come in and grab a water?"

He steps back. "Sorry. Come in." He turns to walk toward the kitchen.

"Jesus. What the fuck happened to you?" Fresh blood is welling in long scratches from his shoulder blades to the middle of his back.

Adrian glances at me with a smirk on his face. He licks his lips. He nods at the purse on his table.

I scan the room, but no one else is with us. I lower my voice and switch to Russian. "Shit. I'm sorry. You should have told me not to come over."

He hands me a bottle of water and continues in Russian, "It's fine. She needed a break."

"Might want to have her put some antiseptic on those scratches." I down half the bottle of water then peer closer. I tease, "Those might leave scars."

Adrian raises his eyebrows and purses his lips. "No offense, this is a nice visit and all, but break time's almost over. Is Obrecht taking care of Eloise, or do you want me to pick her up?"

"He said he'd handle it."

"Well, if anyone should talk to her, it should be him. He'll make her sing like a canary. I doubt she'll talk to me."

Obrecht has something about him women can't resist. He can get them to disclose their deepest secrets without ever breaking a sweat. And they all think he's their friend after. Since Eloise is female, we can't use our standard torture tactics.

"I'll talk to you tomorrow." I toss the empty bottle of water in the trash.

Adrian follows me to the door. "Kora went with you, didn't she?"

I don't reply.

"Tell me Wes and Eloise didn't walk in on you two in the dungeon."

"No. I didn't let anyone in. I kept the closed-session light on."

"Good. Those women are wild, but I don't think you should put her in the same boat as Eloise."

"I'm not."

"Are you sure about that?"

"What are you implying?"

"Kora doesn't seem to me to be the type of woman who would be okay with a roomful of people watching her get tortured."

"I know you don't like what Eloise and I were into—"

He holds out his hands. "I don't judge. You know me. I'm just telling you, Eloise fucked with your head. So don't let all her crazy shit make you think it's okay for Kora. I guarantee you it isn't."

I don't want to discuss anything I did with Kora with Adrian or even reminisce about Eloise. I nod to the purse. "Have fun."

Adrian's cocky smile appears. "Don't call me too early tomorrow."

I fist-bump him and leave. When I get in the car, my mind begins to spiral over Adrian's comment.

Kora seemed to like what we did tonight.

I didn't even touch the surface of what Eloise used to make me do to her.

Something in me didn't allow me to push past what we did tonight. I couldn't. I had resisted Kora long enough. All I wanted was to wrap around her and make her mine.

With Eloise, I would have had to wait. I would have had to spend hours utilizing more advanced tools and techniques to make her happy.

Insomnia plagues me all night. I draw and write all my random thoughts about Kora, Eloise, and Wes. By the time the sun comes up, I have a notebook full of gibberish. If one saw it, they might think I was a comic artist.

It should be therapeutic, but it's done nothing for my hatred toward Wes, his father, or even the growing disgust I have for Eloise.

My obsession with Kora builds, but I worry I'm making all the wrong moves with her. Adrian's comment sticks in my head. My past haunts me, swirling into my future. It's nothing new. Every day I breathe is about trying to escape the ghosts, but nothing ever works.

I throw on my workout clothes and go to the gym. When I step out, it's around noon. I talk to Leo for several moments and then I glance across the street. Kora steps out of the building and approaches two men on the corner.

My heart beats harder. I didn't leave things the best with her last night. It's another thing I regret. The Petrovs create a craziness inside me. It makes me unable to think clearly. "I'll talk to you later. I'm going to go say hi to Kora."

"That's not her," Leo says.

"Sure it is—"

"Look at her clothes. Your girl doesn't dress that way."

I've never been with Kora in front of Leo for him to know we're together. But nothing ever seems to get past him. Instead of asking him how he knows, I study the other woman.

Leo's right. The woman across the street is in pajama bottoms and a jacket. I was so happy to see Kora, I didn't notice what she was wearing. The woman's features are strikingly similar to Kora's. She's smoking a cigarette with two men, and one puts his arm around her. She holds the cigarette up to his lips, and he inhales.

"It must be her sister," I comment.

Leo points. "That's her mother's place. She doesn't like Russians though."

"Why do you say that?"

Leo snorts. "Her mother tells me every time she walks over here to get her lotto tickets." He references the convenience store next to our gym then motions to Kora's sister. "That sister over there is trouble. If your girl is related, watch out."

"Why? What has she done?"

"Nothing to report. It's the vibe I get. But mark my words, she's trouble."

Kora's sister stumps out her cigarette, the man pats her ass and kisses her, and she goes inside.

I survey the street. The boarded-up windows and bars over glass aren't a new sight for me. I'm in this neighborhood daily. It's rougher than the one I grew up in. When Dmitri discovered the bid for the new government housing contract, my brothers and I were all happy about the neighborhood revitalization. The buildings are a fire hazard waiting to happen. My brothers and I all believe no matter your economic status, you deserve safe housing. It's a short-term inconvenience for the residents.

My parents did everything they could to make sure we had a safe home. A group of men in our community would make sure repairs were made on others' homes when needed. My brothers helped, but I was too young to do much. They also reiterated my father's rule that we stayed out of trouble and concentrated on school. Getting out of our situation was hard enough. I can only imagine what life was like for Kora growing up in this environment. The hurdles she had to overcome to get where she's at are next to impossible. It makes me respect her more.

What is her sister going to do with twenty thousand dollars?

Why wouldn't she tell Kora why she needs it?

Family is complicated. I know this too well. It's not my place to get involved with Kora's personal matters, but something doesn't feel right about the phone call she took at the hospital. Leo's words that her sister is trouble doesn't help the bad feeling in my gut.

"See you tomorrow," I tell Leo and get in my car. I smoke a joint on the way home. When I get inside my penthouse, I force myself to make a healthy breakfast. I begin doodling again until the several nights of not sleeping suddenly hit me. I pull the shades, shed my clothes, crawl into bed, and crash.

My insomnia creates vicious cycles for me. For days, I don't sleep, then when I do, my dreams are vivid. Sometimes they haunt me. Sometimes I have happy ones. Either way, I'm so deep in them, I can't escape. Nothing wakes me up until I get through whatever my mind is trying to torment me with.

My nightmares always end with Zamir. It's right after my mother's funeral. I'm a kid, and he's teaching me the lesson for ignoring his call and not coming to the empty warehouse. Four chairs face me. My brothers sit tied so they can't get out. Agony streaks through their faces, watching Zamir torture me. The fourth seat is for Zamir's son Wes to watch.

Zamir has me restrained by ropes at the ankles and wrists. I'm standing on my tip-toes, which is how he has us torture most men.

Zamir takes hours, cutting the skin on my back, then placing pieces of hot metal over it. He takes his time, slicing my skin first, then pressing the hot iron on it.

The pain almost makes me pass out, but I don't. Every time it becomes possible, Zamir knows to back off. I beg him to kill me and end it all. My brothers' screams echo in my ears, matching Wes's laugh. When Zamir finally finishes, he takes off his shirt and stands in front of me. In Russian, he says, "Let me show you what now marks you forever."

He turns. His back is a perfect tattoo of five-pointed stars and a circle around them. He yells with his arms in the air, "I am the devil. So are you. There is no escaping it. I own you, and when I call you, do not disobey."

It's always the part where I wake up. I don't remember the weeks following that event. All I know is what my brothers tell me they did to take care of me.

I'm full of sweat, shaking, with tears streaming down my face. It takes me several minutes to realize I'm awake. I go into the bathroom and shower. To torture myself further, I take a mirror and hold it out, looking at my back. Then I reach around and touch it.

My brothers made me get tattoos over the scars. The guy we all use is talented. He covered my entire back so the scars look like part of the design. It's abstract. It allows me not to wear a shirt. I get compliments instead of horrified looks, but nothing can fix the feel of the bumpy destroyed flesh.

It's why I prefer to restrain women. They can't trace the outlines or ask me about it. I didn't think when I sat on the edge of the bed in the dungeon. When Kora pressed her torso to it then put her warm arms around me, I freaked inside.

Once we got in the shower, I used the restraints on the ceiling and restricted her from touching me.

Eloise traced my scars once. It was one morning after a long night. I was still sleeping. When I woke up, I told her I was in a knife fight as a kid, then I flipped her on her back and did everything I could to make her think about her instead of me.

She never asked again. It shouldn't surprise me. Eloise is into Eloise. Something tells me Kora won't be as dismissive as Eloise, so I need to remember to keep her in front of me.

I throw the mirror in the drawer and change. I pick up the phone to text Kora and see how she's doing, but my phone says it's past three in the morning.

Figures. Just my luck. Another boring night to myself.

I grab my weed and papers and roll a joint. I take a puff when the phone rings.

"Boris, what's going on?" I answer.

"Sergey. Meet at Maksim's. We need to go to the garage." The line goes dead, which isn't unusual. He doesn't have to say anything else.

Obrecht picked up Wes. My night suddenly got a lot more interesting.

13

Kora

"NEICY, PLEASE TELL ME WHAT YOU NEED THIS FOR," I BEG, handing her the envelope. I spent the morning at the bank, arguing with the manager who told me I needed to wait a week for that much cash. After threatening to pull all my accounts, he finally gave me the money.

It's one of the rare occasions my mother isn't home. She went to my aunt's house, who also lives in her apartment building.

Neicy tucks the large envelope in her oversized purse. "Don't worry about it."

"Neicy! Tell me!"

She huffs and lights up a cigarette. After she inhales and blows it out, she annoyingly glares at me. "My health is my business."

"Are you at least going to be okay?"

"Yes. Once I get the operation, I'll be fine."

Her lack of disclosure only worries me further. "Let me go with you."

"No. Darnell is going to take me."

"Who's Darnell?"

"The guy I'm seeing. He has a car."

"Are you sure—"

"I don't want to discuss this any further." She exhales another long breath of smoke.

"Will you at least tell me when you're having the surgery so I can come help you?"

"I'm going to stay with Darnell. I don't want to be a burden to Mom."

"So Mom knows what is going on?" I ask, hurt she told her but not me.

Neicy shakes her head and points to me. "No, and you aren't going to tell her, either. I don't want her fussing over me or worrying. I'm going to tell her Darnell is taking me away for a vacation."

I try one more time. "Will you please tell me what's going on? I won't tell Mom."

She butts her cigarette out in the ashtray. "No. Darnell is picking me up soon. I need to get ready."

I take my cue to leave and rise. I try to hug my sister, but she doesn't return my embrace. "I hope you're okay. Would you have Darnell let me know when you're out of surgery? And tell him I'm here to help, too."

"He won't need it," she snaps.

I hold my hands in the air. "Okay. Will you at least have him text me when you're out of surgery?"

"Sure. Fine. I'll see you later." Neicy leaves the room with her purse.

My first thought is she's going into her bedroom to count it and make sure I didn't give her a dollar less than her request.

I'm such a bitch. She's sick, and I'm nasty.

What is wrong with her?

I feel lost about how to find out her medical situation. My stomach is a nervous wreck over whatever is happening with her.

I leave and get in my taxi. For the hundredth time, I consider texting Sergey to see if he's okay but talk myself out of it.

After he dropped me off, I barely slept. Learning he dated Eloise Boucher for years and she was the woman he used to take to the club was hard enough. Seeing her perfect body, practically naked, and how Sergey went right into texting when we got in the car didn't do anything for my self-esteem.

Was he texting her?

Eloise isn't just a runway model with a killer body—she's a gorgeous Black woman with a sexy French accent. Lately, you can't go into a store without seeing her face on a magazine or tabloid cover.

He did the things he did with me, with her, in the same room.

How many times did she get restrained against the iron wall?

I didn't have an issue knowing Sergey used to go to the club with other women. We both have pasts, but I didn't have a face to put with his. Now I have a visual, and one as gorgeous as Eloise's in my mind somehow makes me a bit crazy.

She's a supermodel.

Witnessing Sergey's reaction when he saw her and how he ran from me after he dropped me off doesn't help my insecurities. Now I'm questioning if he even enjoyed what we did. For all I know, he might be regretting bringing me to the club and taking me into the dungeon instead of her.

I shouldn't have asked him to stay. He blamed his distraction on Wes Petrov. I know he hates Wes. I didn't like him from the Cat's Meow and understand all he represents. I have a deeper repulsion for him after what he did to Aspen.

I wish I could get the voice in my head to shut up about Eloise and stop imagining Sergey doing everything he did to me to her. The nastiness in her eyes directed at me tells me she wants him back. She may have been on Wes's lap, but you don't look at another woman with hatred unless you still want her man.

What am I saying? He's not my man. He may have texted Eloise and gone straight to her last night.

He said not to hold it against him. He was going after Wes.

I decide not to text Sergey. I tell the cab driver to go to Serenity Plaza so I can check on Selena and give her my extra laptop. I'm also looking forward to getting my mind off Sergey, even if it's only for a little while.

I text her burner phone I'm coming up, get through security, and knock on her door. She lets me in, and we sit down in the family room.

"Thank you for the clothes. You're so generous to me," she says.

"Did they all fit?"

"Yes. And the groceries came, too." She smiles appreciatively.

"Great. Here's my laptop so you aren't cut off from the world. Don't go on any of your social media accounts."

"I won't."

I hand her the laptop and a piece of paper. "That's the account I set up for you for groceries."

"Thank you. I really can't tell you how touched I am."

"You're welcome." I glance around the apartment, still shocked Sergey is letting her stay here. Everything is high-end and new. "And you're comfortable here?"

She snorts. "Is that a question?"

I hesitate then gently say, "You didn't want to file the restraining order because of your housing situation. After what happened Friday, I think it's time."

She takes a deep breath. "Is there any way he can find me?"

"I'm not going to lie to you. There's always going to be a chance of him discovering where you are, and you should always be cautious. I hope once some time passes, he moves on, but some men don't."

Fear fills her face.

"Let's not jump the gun. The important thing is you're safe right now. One step at a time, remember?"

She bravely nods. "Right." She glances around. "Kora, how long can I realistically stay here? Sergey said as long as I need, but it seems..."

"Once again, I won't lie to you. I don't know him very well, but he and his brothers all seem like men of their word."

Unless he tells you he's going to stay the night with you. I push the thought to the back of my head.

"Can you talk to him for me? I don't want to overstay my welcome and have any surprises. You understand timelines better than I do regarding my type of divorce. If I don't get a spot in the shelter, and he needs me to move out, I need to figure something else out."

"Sure. I'll be very clear what your situation is and how long you may need housing."

"Thank you."

"What are you going to do to stay busy?"

She shrugs. "I'm not sure. It looks sunny out. I was planning on checking the roof out today."

"That's good. After we see what happens in court this week, it might be okay for you to venture out a bit. Do you have any friends you want me to contact so they can visit you?"

Red fills her cheeks. She twists her fingers in her lap and focuses on them. "I umm..." She looks up. "Jack didn't make it easy for me to build any relationships. The only reason Sister Amaltheia knew me was from before he stopped me from going to church. I don't think he liked me associating with other Greeks."

"Men like Jack are known for cutting off all their wife's ties to others. Don't be embarrassed."

She bites on her lip.

"Tell you what, my friends and I normally go to yoga and then brunch after on Sundays. I would like you not to leave the apartment this weekend since things are heated, but why don't I bring them here? I think you'd like them, and I know they would love to meet you."

"Really?"

"Yes. The only reason I might not be able to bring them here is if my friend Aspen is up for company. She got bitten by a snake and is recovering, but I know she's going to be sleeping a lot from her pain medication." Maksim sent everyone a group text message last night.

"Is she okay?"

"She got lucky, and the doctor thinks she won't have any long-term issues, but only time will tell."

"I hope she recovers quickly."

"Thanks. Let me talk to the girls and see what we're doing tomorrow. I'll text you."

Selena's face brightens. "I could cook a traditional Greek brunch for you if you want. I would need to order some more groceries today, but they deliver fast."

"Sounds delicious. If it's not a hassle for you."

Selena laughs. "It would give me something to do."

I rise. "I'll find out what the plans are and let you know right away."

"Perfect." She walks me to the door and hugs me. "Thank you again...for everything."

"You're welcome." I leave and go home. When I get inside, I call Maksim.

His Russian accent is more pronounced than Sergey's, and I have to listen more closely. "Kora."

"Hey, how's Aspen?"

"Still sleeping. The doctor said it's normal and it's good for her recovery."

"Do you think she'll be up for visitors tomorrow?"

"Honestly, I'm not sure, but I wouldn't plan on it."

"Okay. I'll touch base tomorrow."

"Thanks, Kora."

"Sure. Let me know if you need anything."

"I will."

"Bye." I hang up and text Hailee and Skylar.

Me: *Maksim doesn't think Aspen is up for visitors tomorrow. I have a friend who wants to cook us an authentic meal. Are you okay if we change plans?*

Hailee: *Maksim told me the same thing earlier. I'm in.*

Skylar: *Sure!*

Me: *Hailee and I want deets tomorrow, Skylar.*

Hailee: *Yeah, time to fess up.*

Skylar: *About what?*

Hailee: *Your disappearing act would be a good start.*

Me: *I'm more interested in Skylar's O town experience with Mr. Bend Me Over.*

Skylar hasn't told me anything has happened between her and Adrian, but it's obvious something has by the way she took off and our brief call when I told her about Aspen.

I asked her when we were at the hospital, "Are you going to tell me what happened last night?"

"Not here," she replied. Then she proceeded to get flustered and disappear when she saw him.

Dots appear next to Skylar's name, then disappear, then reappear again. It goes on for several minutes.

Hailee: *What about you and Mr. Glue Sniffer?*

Me: *At least he didn't eat it.*

Skylar: *Who ate what? Were any body parts included in this?*

Hailee: *Eww.*

Skylar: *Seriously. Who are we talking about?*

Hailee: *Kora's Mr. Bad Boy in a Suit, Russian cubby.*

Skylar: *When did he get that nickname? And did you make that up, Hailee?*

Hailee: *Yes. It seems appropriate.*

Skylar: *Well done.*

Me: *Can we get back to your Mr. Bend Me Over?*

Skylar: *I'll tell you tomorrow. But I want full deets on your Russian cubby.*

Me: *See you tomorrow at yoga.*

I have no idea what I should tell my friends about last night with Sergey. I'm confused about how I feel about everything that occurred. Before Eloise entered the picture, I didn't think twice about anything. Now I'm not sure what to make of all the things I allowed Sergey to do to me or how much I liked it.

Hailee: *Are we all still going to the art exhibit tonight?*

Skylar: *I'm in.*

I groan. I forgot about it. I've wanted to see the exhibit for months, and we finally snagged tickets. It immediately sold out. If I'm going to brunch, then the basketball game, I have to spend the rest of the night working on Selena's court case.

Me: *I'm so sorry, but I have to get caught up on work.*

Hailee: *For reals?*

Skylar: *You wanted the tickets more than we did.*

Me: *I know, but I can't get around this. I'm sorry.*

Hailee: *Guess it's you and me, Skylar. Lots of time to give me the lowdown first about you and Mr. Bend Me Over.*

Me: *Not fair!*

Skylar: *We'll miss you but see you tomorrow.*

Hailee: *Don't work too hard.*

Me: *Have fun. See you tomorrow.*

I spend the rest of the night working and trying not to read into what happened the previous night. I remind myself there's bad blood between Sergey and Wes. By the time I go to bed, I've convinced myself he was shaken up over seeing Wes and maybe his ex as well, but it's understandable. I really like him and haven't ever wanted anyone as much as I want him.

The next day, I go to yoga, then brunch with my friends at Selena's. I try to focus on the girls and not the exciting flutters I have about seeing Sergey again. I don't tell them about the club or what we did. I focus on the restaurant he took me to and admit I like him. Then I tell them about our date tonight. I get home, spend an hour getting ready for the game, and wait.

Four o'clock comes and goes. Around four thirty, I text him.

Me: *Hey, did I get the time wrong? Did you say four?*

I wait, but there's no response. Hours pass. He never arrives, or calls, or texts. Anger and hurt engulf me.

He stood me up. In all the years of dating, no man has ever done this to me before. It's cruel.

Any insecurities I have about what we did flood me. All I can see is him and Eloise in the dungeon. I wonder if he got back together with her. Did she go to the game with him?

A part of me wonders if something happened between him and Wes.

He can't be stupid enough to go after the son of the head of the mafia.

He has to be with her.

When I wake up Monday, I try to cover up my swollen eyes. Court gets canceled. The judge claims he's sick, but I know it's another tactic Jack arranged.

All day and night, I keep looking at my phone, checking to see if he's responded or I somehow missed something from him.

There's nothing.

When I wake up on Tuesday, I decide I can't keep doing this. I'm not a desperate schoolgirl. I refuse to become one, waiting for a man to give me attention.

I block his number so he can't contact me, but it's really to make sure I don't spend any more time staring at his name and looking for messages that will never arrive.

No matter what I do, I can't escape the memories of my night with him. If only there were a block button for my mind.

Sergey

Wes, his three thugs who were with him at the Cat's Meow, and the bodyguard Adrian had by the throat, all hang in the air naked, upside down.

I take a chair and put it directly in front of Wes. I grab a fifth of vodka and a shot glass. For hours, I focus solely on Wes as Maksim tortures him. Every time Wes cries out, I laugh or take another shot. It's the same as he did the night his father tortured me. Something about it seems justified. The only problem is I wasn't even thirteen. Wes is closer to Maksim's age. So he would have been around twenty-four when his father branded the devil's symbol on me.

No matter how many men I've tortured and killed, two things are always off-limits: women and children.

The Petrovs have no boundaries. It's a deeper level of evil to watch a boy get tortured and find humor in it. While my brothers, Adrian, and Obrecht work on Wes's thugs, I wait for Maksim to get his wrath out of him enough to comprehend I'm waiting. One thing about Maksim and Dmitri, they don't have the patience Boris and I do. So I tap into every ounce I have, telling myself when I do get my turn at Wes, it'll be worth the wait.

It could be afternoon or nighttime the next day before Maksim finally realizes I'm due a turn.

I've had half the fifth of vodka, but I don't feel it. I've put my rage on simmer. I'm about to bring it to a boil and let it overflow.

There's only one thing I want to do to Wes. The devil resides in a burning pit of flames. It's only appropriate he gets a glimpse of the rest of his eternity.

"I have been selfish. You've been patient," Maksim says.

I take a hit of my joint and hand it to Maksim. "You might want to sit back and chill out for a while."

To my surprise, Maksim takes the joint, inhales, and sits. He doesn't usually smoke.

I pat his shoulder and grab the gas can and flame extinguisher. "Adrian. Obrecht."

They step away from the thugs who had Skylar and Kora on their laps and join me. "Help me rotate him."

We turn Wes so he's no longer hanging upside down. His head falls forward. If I didn't know better, I would think he was dead. I'm not sure if Adrian, Obrecht, Maksim, or I hate Wes more.

Adrian takes the flat blade of his knife and holds it to Wes's chin so he's looking him in the eye. In Russian, he states, "Your father kidnapped our Natalia. He threw her in his whorehouse and gave her to you as a gift. Once Sergey is done with you, we will have our turn."

Obrecht nods to me.

I dip my knife in the gasoline and begin carving the sign of the devil on his back. Every slice is with precision. I make sure it's enough gasoline to get on his skin but doesn't roll down his back. My cuts are shallow enough to cause pain but not enough to put him in shock or make him lose too much blood.

Obrecht and Adrian cross their arms. Scowls fill their faces. Wes cries out and screams for me to kill him.

Obrecht steps forward and holds his knife to his balls. In Russian, he says, "This is tame compared to what my brother and I will do to you."

Tears fall down Wes's face as I continue to slice his back. When I finish, I nod to Maksim.

"Boris, Dmitri!" he yells, comes over, and hands the joint to Adrian.

Dmitri picks up the fire extinguisher.

Boris grabs the lighter.

Maksim steps in front of Wes and leans into his ear. In Russian, he murmurs, "You watched my brother get tortured and laughed. Nothing will ever make up for it. We're going to light you on fire and brand you. Then we're putting it out so my cousins can slice your balls into pieces. When you pass out, we're going to wake you up and feed them to you. It still won't make up for what your family has done to ours. When you take your last breath, you better be ready. We're coming for you in hell. Your true punishment will be far worse than anything we can do to you on this earth." Maksim sniffs hard, steps back, and motions to Boris.

Boris flicks the lighter, and the symbol I perfectly outlined erupts in flames.

Wes screams, and after twenty seconds, I say to Dmitri, "Put it out."

Everyone steps back, and Dmitri releases the fire extinguisher on him. White foam covers his back, and Wes's cries become whimpers.

I look at Obrecht and Adrian. "Cut off his balls."

Wes doesn't last too much longer. When he takes his last breath, I go up to the man who wouldn't release Kora from his lap at the Cat's Meow. I have my brothers help me put him on his feet as well.

"Remember me?"

He pisses, but it isn't the first time of the night. There's already a large puddle on the ground.

"Shh," I murmur in his ear and stroke his cheek.

He shakes harder. "Let me go," he barely gets out in Russian.

"That's what my woman asked you to do. Since you wouldn't let her go, I'm not letting you go, either."

The next few hours, I take my time torturing him. All I keep thinking of is him holding my lapa against her will.

When all the men are no longer breathing, I'm not sure what day it is. I'm still in my killing trance. I help Obrecht and Adrian incinerate the bodies until there's nothing left but ashes. Adrian and I dispose of them in Lake Michigan, which isn't far from the garage.

I only begin to snap back into reality when we're back and I've showered. I stare at my back in the mirror.

Wes is dead. Zamir is still alive.

I step out of the bathroom. Obrecht and Adrian are sitting at the desk in the garage.

"The balance is off. The Rossis will have more power now," Obrecht states. He said it days ago when we first got to the garage.

I sit in the other chair. "I told Boris we need to bleed Zamir out. Slowly kill him, find out about every part of his operation, and take it over. If we run it, we can slowly destroy it all. If we only kill Zamir, it won't ever fully die."

"Boris go crazy on you?" Obrecht asks.

I shrug. "He didn't like it."

"What did Maksim say?"

I snort. "Boris didn't tell him. You know what Maksim and Dmitri would both say. I thought Boris would have my back so we could approach them, but he didn't."

"That's because you're talking crazy. We let this Rossi/Petrov war play out. One by one, each side gets smaller. Then we kill Zamir. Nothing will be left at that point," Adrian insists.

"It sounds too easy to me," I claim.

"I hope it is." Obrecht rises. "Let's get out of here."

We leave and go home. I walk into my penthouse, go into the kitchen to grab a water, and pull out my phone. I turn it on, and while I'm waiting for the screen to light up, my gut drops.

The basketball tickets are on the counter.

"Fuck," I growl and close my eyes. I didn't think about it. The only thing I thought about the last few days was the task at hand.

Fuck, I'm an idiot.

My phone turns on. The screen reads, *Tuesday*. I quickly pull up my text messages and read the one dated Sunday at four thirty.

Kora: *Hey, did I get the time wrong? Did you say four?*

I hit the call button, but the ringtone pattern sounds off. She doesn't answer, and it doesn't go to voicemail. I try again, but I get the same results.

I text her.

Me: *Kora, something happened. Please let me explain. I tried calling, and it just rings. I don't think your voicemail is on. Please call me.*

I send the message, but it never says delivered. I send several more, but nothing happens. Then it hits me.

She blocked me.

My chest tightens, and I text my driver to meet me downstairs. I get in the car and go to her place, but no one answers when I ring her bell. I glance at my watch and realize it's only two and a workday.

Where will she be?

I get back in the car and call her office. Her assistant tells me she isn't available.

"Is she in court?" I ask.

"I'm sorry, sir, but I don't disclose Ms. Kilborn's schedule."

I hang up, unsure of what to do.

Selena. She would be in court with her.

I decide it's quicker to go several blocks to the apartment and see if Selena is there. If she isn't, then there is a good chance Kora's in court, and I can wait for her outside.

I go to Serenity Plaza and bypass security. I knock on Selena's door, and she opens it. Her face is a mix of curiosity and fear. "Sergey. Come in." She opens the door wider.

My heart sinks, knowing Kora won't be in court, and I'm not sure where to find her. I step inside. "Hey, Selena. Are you doing okay?"

She nods and smiles. "Yes. We were just discussing you. I'm- I'm glad you're here."

"We?"

"Kora and me."

"You were talking to her?"

"Yes. She's here."

My pulse beats so hard, I almost get dizzy. "What were you discussing me for?"

"Come in," Selena says and motions for me to follow her.

I take a deep breath and go farther inside.

Kora is standing at the window with her back toward me, talking on the phone. She's in a black suit. Her hair is in a sleek bun, showcasing her long neck and sculpted cheekbones. The hot-pink collar of her blouse matches her heels. Her hand is on her waist, and she says, "I need it taken care of before five."

Please don't hate me, my lapa.

I need you to forgive me.

"Thank you." She hangs up, spins, and when she sees me, her face pales.

"Since Sergey is here, we can ask him all my questions now," Selena says.

Kora regains her color. Her cheeks turn red, and her face hardens. Her tone is curt when she says, "Yes. Let's all get clear on what the situation is so we don't assume one thing when reality is another."

I love everything about Kora's piranha ways, but as I imagined, and quickly confirm, being on the receiving end sucks.

Kora

IT'S NOT FAIR. SERGEY LOOKS JUST AS DELICIOUS AS USUAL. HIS brown doe eyes pierce mine, tugging at my heartstrings, making me want to forget about everything he did and pretend it never happened.

I wish I could.

I can't.

"Kora—"

"Selena is in a dire situation. She can't risk to be told one thing and have anything else happen. We would appreciate it if we can clarify things about her living arrangement."

Keep it professional. Selena can't afford to be homeless.

I wish I could trust Sergey and his promise, but I can't.

"What is there confusion over?" Sergey asks.

I motion to the couches. "Please. Let's all sit, and we can discuss it."

Selena perches on the end of the couch, nervously twisting her fingers.

I take the armchair and cross my legs.

Sergey's eyes dart to them then back to my face.

You're never getting between them again. As I tell myself this, a needy throb begins between my legs, and I curse myself.

He cautiously sits on the other end of the couch. He twists to face Selena. "What are you concerned about, Selena?"

"She needs to know how long you and your brothers will allow her to live here."

"As long as she needs to. I already told both of you this. Nothing has changed, and I won't go back on my promise to you."

"Yes, well, verbal agreements and reality are two different things, aren't they?"

Sergey's eyes turn to slits. "My word is good. However, if it makes you sleep better at night, I'm more than happy to put this in writing."

Selena blurts out, "You don't have—"

"Yes, we would feel better if you did. These types of divorces can sometimes go on for years. As you are aware, there are security issues Selena has to deal with involving her husband."

"Did he do something else?" Sergey growls.

"No!" Selena assures him.

"How long are you willing to allow her to stay?" I ask again.

"I just told you, as long as she needs to," Sergey firmly states.

"Great. So if I put an agreement together stating Selena can stay until her divorce is final and the court awards her assets, you and your brothers will have no issues signing?"

"I am capable of signing any agreement regarding this apartment. You don't need my brothers to sign off," he states, as if I insulted him.

I shift in my seat and uncross my legs then recross them.

His eyes trail my body. He licks his lips and takes a deep breath.

I continue, "The LLC owns the property."

"You researched my property?" Sergey asks.

I can't tell if he's upset or impressed. "Yes. As I stated, I can't have my client homeless."

"She isn't going to be," Sergey reiterates.

"Great. You and your brothers won't mind signing an agreement then, so Selena and I have peace of mind?" I force a smile.

Sergey leans forward. "As I just told you, the only signature you need is mine. Any of my brothers, including myself, can sign at any time to sell or rent the apartment. I don't need permission."

"What would you base that on?"

Now I'm just being bitchy.

This isn't going to help Selena. Keep your personal stabs out of it.

Sergey shakes his head and scowls. "Can I speak with you alone, please?"

"Anything you need to say, my client is privy to. This is her life after all."

Sergey turns to Selena. "Would you please give Kora and me a few minutes?"

Her eyes widen. "Sure."

"That isn't necessary," I firmly state.

Sergey rises then pulls me up off the chair.

"Stop. What are you doing!"

He grips my elbow and says in my ear, "We're going into the bedroom to talk. Stop causing a scene."

"I'm not—"

"Kora, you should go," Selena blurts out.

Surprised, I turn my head toward her.

She nervously gazes between us. "I'm fine out here. Go talk."

What the heck am I doing? She's my client, and this is so unprofessional.

I shouldn't have dug at him.

Sergey's hand slides over my waist. He guides me down the hall.

I should push away from him, but I sink into his body. I hate myself for still wanting and responding to him.

The moment I step into the bedroom, Sergey shuts the door and spins me against it. His body presses into mine, and my heart beats faster. His sandalwood, lemon, and weed scent consumes my senses. He puts his elbows on the door next to my head. "You blocked me."

"That's all you have to say?"

"No. I have a lot to say, but I don't think you're ready to hear it."

Anger rears up inside me. "You have a lot of—"

His lips roughly press into mine, and he slides his tongue in my mouth, flicking so urgently, I can't help it and kiss him back.

What am I doing?

He stood me up.

I push his chest to get away from him, but he steps even closer and doesn't let me move.

"Stop fighting me, Kora," he demands in the same voice he used in the dungeon.

I freeze. I shouldn't. I'm not sure why I do. But I suddenly can't seem to move.

He puts his hands on my cheeks. His voice softens. "Do you honestly believe I would stand you up?"

"What would you call it?"

"Something happened. I'm sorry I caused you to question my feelings for you, but I didn't have a choice. I wasn't even aware of how much time passed."

My stomach lurches. I blink hard. "You were with her, weren't you?"

His head jerks back, and his eyes widen. "You think I was with Eloise?"

I say nothing, willing myself not to shed a tear.

"I told you I don't have any feelings left for her."

I focus on the ceiling, my insides shaking.

"Goddamnit. Look at me," he barks.

I meet his gaze.

"I will only say this once, so listen closely. I do not now, nor will I in the future, ever want any part of Eloise. Since I met you, I've not wanted her. You're the one I obsess about, *not her*. The only interaction I had with her since I dropped you off at your house was at the club when I was with you. Something came up Saturday night. I couldn't avoid it. I wasn't thinking about anything besides what I needed to do. I just got home about an hour ago. I didn't even know what day it was until I saw the tickets on my counter and turned on my phone."

My lips tremble. I want to believe him, but I don't want to be a stupid woman. "If you weren't with her, where were you? What was so important you couldn't text or call me?"

His jaw spasms. "I can't tell you, Kora. You have to trust me."

"Blindly?"

"Yes."

I try to stop my tears again and look away.

"Kora."

I shut my eyes. I'm not someone who handles being in the dark. My sister's situation is killing me enough. I don't need it with my man. I whisper, "I can't."

He turns my chin. "I was not with her, my lapa."

Hearing him call me his lapa only tears me up inside. I want to be his, but how can I?

In a firm voice, he orders, "Tell me you believe me."

"If you weren't with her, who were you with?"

He sniffs hard. His jaw tics faster. "You're the most intelligent woman I've ever come across. I won't pretend you don't see what I'm capable of doing to other men. So stop making this about her. Think about what happened and who I would need to take care of. Take her out of the equation. For the last time, she doesn't have anything to do with this, my lapa."

What is he...

My chest tightens.

His voice from Friday night fills my head. *"It's because of him. I thought you would understand this after he almost killed Aspen."*

I've been so stupid. He told me he was going after him, but I've been so jealous and insecure, I convinced myself it was about Eloise.

A new fear fills me. Not that Sergey would hurt me but what he may have done. My blood runs cold.

"Ah. I see you understand now." His warm-brown eyes are dark, swirling with evil but also pain.

It strikes me, and I reach for his face, putting my hand over his twitching skin. I swallow hard. "Did you..."

"Don't ask, Kora."

I stare at him, not sure what to do or say, unable to get the right amount of oxygen in my lungs.

He puts his head on my forehead. His voice is gravelly. "Don't run from me."

His jaw spasms more, and I stroke my thumb over it. He closes his eyes, as if in pain.

It hits me how much I don't know about Sergey. "I need to know who you are."

"You know who I am...with you."

"Who are you when you aren't with me? I can't be with someone if I don't know who they are. It's not something I can bend on. I don't operate that way."

He freezes then takes a deep breath. Something passes in his eyes, and I don't know what to make of it. He kisses me and steps back. "I'm the devil. And I don't want you to know him."

"Sergey—"

"Draw up a contract that says Selena can stay for as long as she wants rent-free, and I'll sign it."

"I—"

"It's okay, Kora. I should have known better. I'm sorry about Sunday. I really am. I never meant to hurt you, and you're right. No matter how much I try not to be him, he's in me. And I don't want you subjected to any part of him." He walks out, leaving me more confused than before, wondering how we got here.

I woke up wanting to hate Sergey for the assumptions I made about him and Eloise. His unspoken words told me he's a murderer. No part of me should want him. But the loss I feel at him walking away tears me up.

As the day progresses, the need for him grows and spirals. All my red flags are up, telling me to stay away from him, but I can't get his eyes out of my mind. They swirled with hurt, and not something surface level but something deep and scarring. By the time darkness sets in, I'm obsessing over him. I want to fix all the broken pieces within him.

He murdered Wes. I need to stay away.

Wes was a horrible man. He hurt a lot of people.

I'm an attorney. I can't be with a killer.

I unblock his number and text him.

Me: *I'm sorry I blocked you and for assuming you were with her.*

Sergey: *You're forgiven. I'm sorry again about Sunday.*

Me: *I have the contract. Can you give me your address, and I can stop by and have you sign it?*

Sergey: *Tonight?*

Me: *Yes. If you aren't doing anything.*

He sends me his address. My heart races.

Me: *I'll be there in an hour or so, if you're flexible on the time?*

Sergey: *No problem.*

I shower, spend the next hour fixing myself up, and debate about what to put on. I decide on a pink set of lingerie. The mesh bra is delicate and showcases my nipples. The panties are crotchless, and I add a garter belt and stockings, then put a sweater dress over them. I lie and tell myself I'm just going to have him sign the agreement and then I'll leave.

My drive to go after what I want got me where I am in life. It's usually a good thing. Sometimes, it gets me in trouble.

Tonight, I've passed the point of playing with fire. I know enough about Sergey to stay away, but my desire for him won't let me.

Even the devil has a temptress. I just never thought it would be me.

16

Sergey

My brain is telling me not to let Kora come over. Our situation is clear. She's a successful attorney who worked hard to get where she's at and escape the bad in her life. I don't need to put her in any possible harmful situation.

What was I thinking?

Wanting Kora as mine and thinking we could have a life together was foolish. It's not possible to change who I am. My brothers and I are in the middle of a war between two powerful mafia families. Boris is marrying into the O'Malleys, a prominent Irish crime family. His child will be an Ivanov/O'Malley. Our bloodlines will cross as well as our alliance. Only so much time can pass before the Rossis or Petrovs figure out we set them up. If it happens before they do enough damage to each other, everyone we love will be at risk.

Kora doesn't need to be close to any of this.

She knows I'm a murderer.

She already knows too much. If I get any closer to her, I'm going to tell her things I shouldn't—details too risky for her to be privy to. It could destroy her career and put her in a dangerous situation.

I thought she was the one.

The truth slaps me in the face. No matter how much I obsessed over Kora, I didn't admit it. Everything about her is what I want. She's smart, beyond beautiful, and strong.

She even likes basketball. I've never dated any woman who wanted to go with me. I usually go with Boris, since he bets on all types of sports.

Fuck. I wish I could have taken her to the game.

How could I ever take care of her? She deserves a man who doesn't have any of the demons that haunt me.

Part of me wants to beg her to forget about our conversation earlier today, but I know it's impossible.

Sign the paperwork and get her out of here as soon as possible.

I pace my penthouse, staring out into the early evening sky, watching the waves crash against the shore. The longer I stare, the more frustrated I get. I try to figure out how we can be together and what it could look like, but all I see is an ending where Kora gets hurt.

I'm a killer. I saw the awareness in her eyes. Shock, fear, and disappointment swirled in her hazel orbs. There is no escaping it. I'm a bad man, and she's a good woman. The two don't mix.

My buzzer knocks me out of my anxious thoughts, and I hit the button. "Hello."

"Mr. Ivanov, Kora Kilborn is here."

"Give her the code for the elevator." Most guests get escorted up so they don't know how to enter my home. I don't think twice about Kora knowing the four digits.

I take several deep breaths, trying to calm my nerves.

Sign and get her out of here. It's for the best.

I go to the elevator and wait. The lift dings, and the doors open. My heart races.

Why does she have to look so amazing every time I see her?

She steps out, and her floral scent drifts to my nostrils. I internally groan.

Her voice is sweet, filled with confidence and a hint of nervousness. A tiny smile appears. "Hi."

I reach to kiss her but freeze. "Hi."

An awkward silence fills the air.

Her cheeks flush pink, torturing me further.

"Sorry. Come in." I motion for her to go first. It's a mistake. Her dress hugs her round ass in perfection. It lifts slightly as she walks, revealing the top of her thigh-highs and a clasp.

She's wearing a garter belt.

My mouth goes dry, and blood pounds hard between my ears.

She spins. "Wow! Your view is amazing!"

Yeah, it's even better since you walked in.

"Thanks."

"Have you lived here long?"

"A little over a year. It took some time to do the remodel."

"You gutted it?"

"Yes."

She studies each side of the penthouse then turns toward me, smiling bigger. "It's great, Sergey. Really stunning."

I don't respond to her. Being in the same room and trying not to touch her is torture. My eyes seem to have a life of their own. I can't control the way they drift over her body, taking in every curve. "You look beautiful."

Why did I say that?

She steps toward me, stopping less than an arm's length away. She lifts her head, but I can't help noticing how her breasts rise and fall faster. Her fingers graze the tattoo on my biceps.

Zings race down my spine.

"Your tattoos are really intricate. They have meaning."

I gaze at the ink on my arm of a sharp-pointed knife. A serpent sheds its skin and wraps its body around it.

"A snake shedding its skin represents transformation, immortality, and healing. It's the form of rebirth."

The twitch I hate so much begins. I clench my jaw, trying to stop it, but like usual, it doesn't do anything to turn it off.

Her nails trace the knife.

Unable to tear myself away, I focus on her expression, looking for any sign of what she thinks. I'm unprepared for what she says next.

A line between her brows forms. She slowly inhales. Her hazel eyes pin mine. "What you do with your knife gives you life. In others' deaths, you were reborn." It's a statement, not a question.

A chill runs down my spine. I should have known she would put two and two together. No one ever has. Many have asked, but I've never told them the truth. My answer is always the same. I tell them it's a design my tattoo artist drew, and I thought it looked cool.

It's a lie. He didn't design it. I did. I assumed no one but my brothers or I would ever understand.

She traces the infinity symbols which make up the scales of the snake. Her expression turns to sympathy. "You want to heal with each new death but can't."

Kora's ability to decipher the true meaning only makes my craving for her multiply. The need I've been trying to extinguish all day since I left her at Selena's slices my heart.

"Now you know how fucked up I am. Did you bring the papers for me to sign?" I mumble, in a trance and unable to pull my eyes from hers.

"Yes. I'm-I'm sorry about insinuating you needed your brothers' permission today."

"Can we skip the apologies? Otherwise, we're going to be here all night while I tell you again how much I regret not thinking before I left."

She raises her eyebrows. "What should you have thought before you left?" She bites her plump, pink lip.

Sign the form and be done. This is only extending the inevitable.

I move my hand toward her cheek then catch myself and pull it back.

Do not touch her.

"I should have known I would be gone for days. Thinking about you sitting around, waiting for me, believing I stood you up..." I let out a long breath. "I'm sorry. You didn't deserve that."

She nods and palms my chest, sliding her hands up so one cups my neck. The other hand moves to my face, and she presses her thumb where my jaw spasms.

"I should sign your form," I attempt again.

"Did you sleep when you were gone?"

"No. Why do you ask?"

"You said you didn't know what day it was."

My stomach twists. Discussing anything with her is a slippery slope. Something about Kora makes me want to tell her every bad thing I've ever done, as if she could somehow wrap her goodness around me and make it all better.

She would hate me forever.

"You know what I've done and what I am capable of continuing to do. Let me sign the papers and then it's best if you leave." My stomach flips as I say it.

Her nails lightly scrape my neck. She steps so close, I feel her heartbeat. It's racing like mine. "What if I don't want to leave?"

The presence of her body touching mine is too much. I slide my hand to the back of her head and fist her hair. "Don't tempt me, Kora."

She doesn't flinch and stares at my lips. "You don't want me to be your lapa anymore?"

I lean closer to her hot mouth. Our breaths merge. It takes all the strength I have, but I try to warn her and be the man she deserves, instead of the selfish one who's yelling at me to make her mine. "I think we were clear about what we wanted. You require disclosure about who I am, and I won't give it to you. The things you already know only scrape the surface of what I do. If you were privy to the depths of what I'm capable of, you would run. It's not a world I want you in, and you should steer far away from me, Kora."

"Should and reality are two different things most of the time," she murmurs then slides her hand through my hair, tugging me so close, our lips almost touch.

"I'm trying to do the right thing for you," I admit and palm my hand on her ass.

She closes her eyes briefly and shudders. Her voice is raspy when she says, "Are you tired?"

Is she ignoring what I'm telling her?

"No. I have severe insomnia." I circle my thumb on her ass. "Hardly anything destresses me enough so I can sleep."

She drags her hand along my jaw, down my torso, and strokes my cock. "What do you usually do to relieve your stress?"

My dick pulses. She's a vixen. I try one more time. "I think I've been a gentleman and told you I can't give you what you need, Kora."

"What do *you* need?"

Is she playing with me?

"Kora, this isn't—"

"What gets rid of your insomnia, Sergey? I want to know."

I bunch her dress up until my hand is on her naked ass.

She makes a tiny gasp.

I knew she had on a thong. I bet her ass looks perfect in it.

"Sometimes lots of weed."

"Okay. What else?" she asks in a breathy voice.

I lick my lips, and my jaw twitches faster. "Fucking. Lots of fucking where I'm in control, all night and into the next day."

Flames dance in her eyes. "I can clear my schedule tomorrow."

I groan inside. *What is she saying?* "I won't allow you to know him."

She seems to understand I'm talking about the devil inside me. Her hands hold my cheeks. "Then I'll have to be okay with only knowing who you are with me."

A low, heavy sigh comes out of me. "Don't say things you'll regret, Kora. I don't want to be toyed with."

"Okay. I don't want to play games." She releases me and attempts to step back, but I still have her in my grasp. I assume she's come to her senses, and my heart sinks. No matter how many times I attempted to get her to make this decision, I still want her to throw caution to the wind and be mine.

I remove my hands from her. Her hazel eyes pierce mine as she backs away. She slowly pulls her dress over her head and tosses it on my couch.

Blood boils and surges with lust so potent, I ball my fists next to my thighs to steady myself. The devil may wear red, but she's wearing pink. My erection gets so hard, it aches against the fabric of my pants.

For several moments, I check every inch of her out. I don't miss the way her nipples are already hard and poking against the thin mesh. Or the way her panties split into two thin lines, begging me to dine on her. If it were only about her hot little body in her lingerie, I could handle it.

It's her eyes causing the most chaos in my veins. There's a deep need I haven't seen before swirled within her confident stature.

"I said I could clear my schedule tomorrow. Do you want me to?" she asks and arches an eyebrow.

It's a stupid question from the smartest woman I know. I

couldn't resist her offer if my life depended on it. My mind has already broken through the last barrier of reason and fallen back into the obsession zone.

I step forward quickly, tug her hair, and she gasps in surprise. The moment my lips meet hers, our tongues collide in a desperate desire for the other. I deepen it until she's gripping my shirt and whimpering.

I pull out of the kiss. "The devil doesn't come and go, my lapa. You're about to make a deal with him, and this is your last out. If you stay, we aren't going to keep discussing this and going in circles. Not tonight, or tomorrow, or anytime in the future. You're accepting what you told me earlier today you can't. Do you understand me?"

She nods.

"I need to hear a response from you."

"Yes."

Relief washes through me. I sniff hard then command, "Kneel."

17

Kora

SERGEY COMMANDS ME ALL NIGHT. AT TIMES HE EDGES ME, pushing me past the brink of where I think I can go. Sometimes he spanks me. It makes me wet. I don't understand why, but it does. He always praises me for it while dipping his fingers in my sex and rubbing the sore skin on my ass until I come.

He puts nipple clamps on my breasts then takes a flogger to me. When he releases the clamps, all of my skin is on fire. He sucks on each sensitive nipple, and a sensation I've never felt before assails me with pleasure.

I don't understand why I like what he does to me. It confuses me, but I'm an addict who can't get enough. Everything he does is with expertise, as if he knows my body better than I do.

Several times, we have intercourse. I'm not sure if it's the insomnia or just him, but he's always hard. Within minutes of releasing inside me, he's erect again.

We're in a room similar to the dungeon. Some of the items hanging on the wall or placed on the shelf look scary. Sergey leaves the room to get more water. There's a stocked refrigerator in the room, but we've gone through several bottles. I don't want the juice in the fridge, and he has a thing about keeping me hydrated. As soon as he leaves, my curiosity gets the best of me. I go to the wall and pick a few of the toys, not understanding how they could be pleasurable or fun.

When he comes back into the room, I'm touching the points of a tool. They're sharp, and a chill crawls down my bones.

Sergey wraps his arms around me then takes the item out of my hand. He hangs it back on the wall. "I don't think this is for you."

I sink into him and turn my head. "Did you use this on her?"

He stays quiet and keeps his gaze pinned on mine.

"Is this something you need?" I asked, and for a brief moment considered letting him use it on me.

In a stern voice, he replies, "No. She needed it. You don't."

"But you enjoyed using it on her?"

"Honestly?"

"Yes."

"No."

Surprised by his answer, I asked, "Why didn't you enjoy it?"

His jaw spasms. "You really want to know this?"

"Yes."

"Why?"

I reach for his jaw and put my hand over his tics. "I want to know about you. Not the parts everyone else sees but these pieces."

He hesitates. Nerves enter his expression. He finally replies, "It's too close to the thing I'm most talented at."

"What's that?"

"Not anything I'm going to disclose to you."

I stand straighter. "I'm not going to judge—"

"It's not about your thoughts on the matter. You agreed to accept not knowing about parts of my life."

The truth of our verbal contract hangs in the air. He's right. I hate not knowing everything about him, but I did accept his terms.

Silence fills the room, and he doesn't move, as if he's ready for me to argue or bolt away from him.

I decide to try a different angle. "If you didn't like using that on her, then why did you?"

Something dark flares in his eyes. "People need different things, lapa."

"How do you know I don't need it?"

Why am I asking him this?

"You aren't a masochist."

I take a deep breath. "But I like when you...the pain..."

A smile plays on his lips. "Yes." He palms my pussy.

I shudder.

He kisses my cheek and murmurs in my ear, "You like a bit of pain, but you don't need it to come."

My insecurities spin in my mind. *He was with her for years. What if he does need a masochist?*

He seems to know my thoughts and squashes my worries. "I prefer to get you off anywhere we are. Don't you?" He moves his thumb over my mound.

I think back to our dinner date and can't stop my smile. "Yes."

"Good." He gives me a chaste kiss on the lips then guides me to the bed. "It's rest time."

"Rest?"

"You need some sleep. Don't worry though. I'll wake you up." He winks.

I laugh, and we slide into bed. He puts his arm around me and strokes my thigh and hip. He's warm and makes me feel safe. I quickly fall asleep until little flutters erupt on the back of my body.

"Mmm." I don't open my eyes. I'm still in a sleepy state. Sergey's scent and warm flesh consume my senses. His lips travel down my spine, and his hands follow.

I attempt to move, but my wrists are bound again. *They're still under the pillow. How did he restrain me while I was sleeping?*

Probably because he exhausted me.

I'm not sure what time it is or if it's the next day already.

"On your knees, lapa," he commands. "Keep your head on the pillow."

I don't think and assume the position, pulling my knees toward my breasts. My insides pulse.

He inhales deeply. His hot breath is on my exposed privates, and the throbbing intensifies. His warm hands palm my ass, and he kisses each cheek.

In a quick move, he slides his hands between my thighs and spreads my legs apart.

I gasp from the surprise.

His mouth hits my pussy, and I arch into the bed.

I grip the top of the mattress. "Oh God!"

He grunts, splays his hand on my back, and caresses me while teasing my clit until I'm sweating and begging him.

His tongue moves faster and faster until I'm shaking and screaming out his name.

When I'm coming down, he drags his teeth across my marbled nub. It sends another shot of adrenaline through me, and I jerk my arms, but there's nowhere for them to go.

He lurches over me. His muscular frame hums against my back. "Morning," he mumbles near my ear then slides his tongue behind it.

"Morning," I pant, aroused and pressing my ass into his erection.

"Are you relaxed?"

"Is that a question?"

"Good. I need you to stay that way and trust me."

I freeze.

His voice turns to amusement. "You already failed."

I fill my lungs with as much oxygen as possible and slowly exhale. "Sorry."

"I'm going to make you feel really good, my lapa." It's a statement with no room to question.

I nod, not sure how anything can feel better than what he just did to me.

"Clasp your hands together if they aren't."

I let go of the mattress and lace them together.

He strokes my hair. "Squeeze your hands together but nothing else if you need to."

"What are you—?"

"Shh. Look at me."

I turn.

His smoldering eyes are more intense than usual and drill into mine. The smell of my orgasms flares in my nostrils. His finger circles the tight opening of my ass. It's wet and slightly cold but quickly warms.

I take a deep breath.

"Stay relaxed, lapa."

I nod. I don't do ass play. It's one of those things where I've been curious about the hype but never trusted anyone I dated. I could say stop, and he would, but I trust him.

"My guess is no one has taken this pretty ass before?"

"No," I admit and swallow hard.

A satisfied, cocky smile appears. "You know the code word." His eyes never leave mine.

A moment passes, as if he's waiting for me to say stop.

I don't tear my gaze from him.

He finally nods. "Submit to me, lapa."

"I—"

"You're thinking. Feel. Don't analyze. Let me control your body." He raises his eyebrows, as if in a challenge. "Unless you want to say the code word?" His finger inches in and out of me, and a new sensation I've not experienced before takes hold.

I pant out a, "No."

He kisses me. I stick my tongue out of my mouth, but he pulls away, then refocuses on my eyes. He removes his finger, and I feel the loss.

It surprises me when I instantly want it back in me.

His lips twitch, and something bigger replaces his finger. I focus on breathing and briefly close my eyes.

"That's it, my lapa. You like it, don't you?"

"Yes," I say, and my cheeks scorch.

"Why are you blushing, gorgeous?"

I don't reply. I've never considered myself a prude, but something about admitting I like him playing with my ass feels taboo.

He pushes it farther in me and then twists it while pulling it back out. Each time it passes my barrier, a whimper flies out of my mouth. Heat courses through my veins, and drops of sweat slide down my skin.

His lips brush against mine. "I want all of you, Kora. All the things you never let anyone else do to you, I want to do."

"Yes. Please," I whisper, not worrying about anything I ever have in the past but wanting to experience this with him.

He plays with me for a few more minutes. His cock is hard, and pre-cum drips on my leg.

I beg him again. "Please. I want you." Everything Sergey does to me, I enjoy. Many things I've never done before. As good as he makes me feel, I love it the best when he's inside me. I want to see what it's like with him in every part of me.

He glides his tongue in my mouth. I attack it with mine and moan as my body continues to throb.

His warm palm flattens against my ass with whatever he put in me fully lodged. He pulls out of our kiss, readjusts his body over mine, and leans on his elbow. His arm slides under my torso, and he pulls me up close to him.

I misunderstood what he was going to do. The tip of his cock hits my sex. His deep voice murmurs in my ear, "Your beautiful pussy needs some attention, don't you think?"

I'm so full. I'm not sure how it's possible, but I shimmy my hips to try and sink over him.

"Greedy girl. Stay still."

I freeze.

"Relax." His tongue flicks my lobe.

I inhale a slow, shaky breath.

His cock begins to slide in me, and my mouth becomes an uncontrollable O. Every thrust is slow. The friction from his shaft seems more intense than ever before. I don't know how he fits inside me. Every inch feels as if I've reached the maximum capacity, but he keeps moving farther in until his pelvis is flat against my ass cheeks.

His hot breath hits my face. "Okay, lapa?"

"Yes."

"Feel how hard I am for you?"

"Yes." My insides slowly spasm on him.

He quietly groans. "Are you squeezing your hands together?"

"Yes."

He kisses my cheekbone and begins to thrust. "Now you can move."

I meet his movements, matching his lazy speed.

"Fuuuuck," he grunts.

"Sergey...oh God..." I barely get out. My body tries to clench him, and tremors move from my toes up through my body.

His arm under me tightens, holding me so I can't fall away from him and into the mattress.

I squeeze my hands, bringing them closer to my head, but the silk's tension is already at its maximum. Adrenaline teases me, giving me pleasure and hinting at a tidal wave of chaos. Our sweat merges. His chest heaves against my spine. Tingles race down my neck from his kisses.

"Everything about you is good, Kora," he mumbles into the curve of my neck.

The typhoon hits me. I grip my hands, and white light consumes me. I lose any control I have left of my body. It shakes uncontrollably into his hard flesh. Sergey pounds harder and deeper, keeping me spinning through orgasms and crying out incoherent things.

His low, throaty groan hits my ear. Right before he detonates inside me, he pulls whatever is in my ass out.

"Oh God!" I scream as his erection stretches me so full, the white light turns black, then white again, from the additional surge of endorphins.

In our aftermath, I lay in a heap of fluids. Sergey collapses on top of me, kissing the back of my neck with his forehead pressed to my head. His heart beats into my shoulder in a rapid rhythm. He moves so he's on his knees and slides his arms over mine then releases me from the silk ties. He rolls off me, rises, then picks me up.

I'm still breathing hard. I slide my hand around his neck. "What are you doing?"

He pecks me on the lips. "I'm ready to get out of this room."

"Oh?"

His lips twitch. He carries me through his penthouse and into his bedroom suite. He sets me on his bed and puts a throw over me. "I'll be back." He reaches for the wall switch and flips it. The fireplace on the opposite wall lights up.

"Where are you going?" I ask.

He puts both elbows near my head. "Have you always asked tons of questions, or did they teach you that in law school?"

I wince. "Always."

He chuckles. "It's a quality I love about you. Don't change it, and don't go anywhere." He winks, and my insides flutter.

I curl into the pillow, appreciating his muscular frame and wondering about the ink on his back.

Several minutes pass, and he scoops me back up, then takes me to the bathroom. He said it was morning, but I'm not sure if it is. Blackout shades cover the windows. Candles light the room. He sets me in a bubble bath and slides in behind me.

I lie in his arms, happy, content, feeling a connection I can't explain. I don't know him very well. He's a mystery and hasn't hidden the fact there are things about himself he won't tell me. I know he's capable of bad things, but I only feel safe when I'm with him.

I tilt my head and circle my arm up, gliding my hand in his hair. "Tell me about your back tattoo. It's beautiful. I've never seen anything like it.

His body stiffens, and his jaw tics. Hatred fills his eyes. In a flat voice, he replies, "My guy knows what he's doing with ink."

I pull my hand from behind his head and over his jaw.

He closes his eyes.

Why doesn't he want to talk about his tattoo?

"Sergey, did I—"

"Did you tell your work you wouldn't be in today?"

"No. Not yet. What time is it?"

"Close to seven."

I roll closer to him. "Are you going to sleep at all?"

"Maybe after this bath, I might get a few hours."

"So, will you eventually crash for a long time?"

"Typically. It's why I wasn't thinking clearly when I left Saturday night."

"What do you mean?"

"I had just woken up. It was the first time I slept in days. When I got the call, I just bolted."

"What call?"

He stares at me. His face hardens.

Right. I don't get to know.

I signed up for this.

Why can't he tell me?

It's best if I don't know.

"How long have you had insomnia?"

He turns to the window, focusing on the drawn shades. "Since I was twelve."

"Did something happen that you can link it to?"

The spasm in his jaw intensifies. He closes his eyes.

I suddenly wonder if he's asleep. I whisper, "Sergey?"

"Hmm?" He opens his eyes, and they're glassy. But he also looks tired.

"Do you want to try and sleep?"

"Yeah. Let's get out and lie down."

"Okay." I get out of the tub and reach for the towel. I dry off and secure it around my body.

Sergey rises.

I grab the other towel before he does. I hold it out and wiggle my eyebrows. "Spin, and I'll dry you off."

A cocky expression appears.

I softly laugh. "Don't be too eager."

He grunts.

I dry off the front of his body, kissing his cock, torso, and chest. "Spin."

He reaches down and picks me up.

"Hey!" I cry out.

"You're making me hard again."

"What are you going to do about it?" I taunt him.

He carries me into the bedroom then sets me on my feet. He removes my towel. "Get in bed."

I obey.

He dries his back off then tosses the towel on the floor. "It's my turn to rest."

"We should try to sleep."

A smirk appears. "Not what I had in mind."

"No?"

"No. Get on your knees."

I do as he says.

He wiggles his finger, and I move my legs until I'm at the end of the bed. His arms circle my waist, and he palms my ass. He spins, taking me with him so he's sitting on the edge of the bed, and I'm straddling him.

I reach around his neck and start to slip my hands down his back, and he grabs my hands and repositions them behind me.

He opens the drawer of his nightstand, picks something up, and quickly ties my hands behind my back. He leans into my ear. "You ever ridden a guy while tied up?"

"No," I admit.

He moves his hands to my hips and slides me over his erection. "Good."

All my years of riding men during sex doesn't compare. I could say it's the restraints, but it isn't just that. It's Sergey.

He may have said he wanted to rest, but he gives the same attention to me as any other time we've done anything. When we're done, he slides under the covers, tugs me into his arms, and kisses my head.

He lights a bowl, takes a puff, and offers it to me. I take one and realize it's the first time he lit up since I arrived.

"Turn on your side," he instructs.

I follow his orders, and he wraps his body around mine.

"Didn't know you were a spooner," I tease.

He kisses the spot where my jaw meets my neck. "I'm not. You're special." His voice is teasing, but every part of me wants it to be true.

We both fall asleep. I wake up in a panic. I forgot to tell my office I was skipping work.

I creep out to the family room and pull my phone out of my purse. I call my assistant and tell her I'm fine and sorry for not giving her a heads-up I wouldn't be in today. I breathe a sigh of relief. I didn't have appointments and planned on doing paperwork and research.

When I walk back into the room, Sergey is on his stomach, with the sheets down to his waist. The fireplace creates a warm glow, and I stare at his toned upper body.

He's delicious.

I sit on the edge of the bed, in awe of the beautiful abstract piece of art on his back. I can't help myself and lightly trace over the pattern then freeze when I discover bumpy skin.

I glance at Sergey, but he hasn't moved and appears to still be asleep. I inspect his ink further and cautiously touch spots all over his back that have damaged skin.

What happened to him?

Is this why he wouldn't let me dry his back?

Who did this to him?

Anger fills me. Someone hurt him. There isn't any way his skin would be destroyed without it being intentional. The scarred tissue is in a pattern with perfectly pointed stars which can't be the cause of an accident.

I can't help myself and kiss his back. Each star, I press my lips to, as if it could somehow make it better.

It won't. I'm not stupid, but emotion overcomes me, thinking about what could have caused this.

He's been hiding his back from me.

It's a realization that slaps me in the face. Besides the one time he angrily sat on the edge of the bed at the club, he's never turned his back toward me. And he froze when I hugged him. This beautiful, strong man hides his agony. If it weren't painful, Sergey wouldn't have covered it up with tattoos. He wouldn't hide his back from me.

My heart wants to slide behind him and hold him, but I'm worried he may wake up and be angry. I finally go to my side of the bed and get under the covers. The minute I do, he pulls me into him.

"You're awake?" I whisper.

He tightens his hold around me but never answers. His lips rest on my head, and his heart beats faster into my shoulder. I don't move or speak again.

How do I get him to trust me enough to tell me what happened?

How do I help him?

It takes me a long time to fall back asleep. The voice in my head keeps saying *he won't,* and *this is what you agreed to.*

Sergey

KORA KNOWS ABOUT MY SCARS.

She didn't just feel a few lines like Eloise did. She traced every part of them. Each star, the circle surrounding it, and the intricate little marks Zamir made, she caressed and kissed.

I should have flipped over and stopped her, but something kept me paralyzed. I couldn't move and pretended to be asleep. It was so different from when Eloise ran her nails over my skin, as if my scars were dirt she had to remove.

Kora did the exact opposite. Her fingertips were gentle. Her lips touched them as if they were something to be worthy of her kiss instead of disgusting scars. Besides the tattoo artist and my brothers, no one except Eloise has ever touched my back since Zamir branded me, and definitely not anyone's lips. Eloise only felt it the one time. I told her never to touch it again, and she obeyed.

I'm not sure why I didn't tell Kora to stop. Maybe it's because every time she touches me anywhere, I want more of her. Minutes pass without her fingers or lips on me. Her body heat still warms me. Every passing second increases my paranoia.

Is she disgusted? Maybe she's going to leave and go home.

Why didn't I flip over?

She rises off the mattress, and I squeeze my eyes shut. *She's going to leave.*

When she slides next to me, I take a deep, quiet breath to calm myself and reach for her. I need to feel her skin on mine.

"You're awake?" she whispers.

I can't answer her. Something about her feeling my back, kissing it, then still wanting to be near me chokes me up. I don't trust myself to speak. And my lapa will surely ask me questions.

I don't allow myself to fall back asleep until she's softly breathing next to me. When I wake up, she's facing me and tracing my jaw. Her beautiful face lights up, and a tiny smile appears. "Hey."

I reach up and stroke her hair. "Morning."

She laughs. "It's evening."

"What time?"

"Almost seven." Her stomach growls.

My lips twitch. "Want to go to dinner?"

She pecks me on the lips. "Yes, but can I take a raincheck? I have to try and make up for not going in to work today, or I'm going to have consequences tomorrow."

Disappointment she has to leave fills me, but I can't expect her to stay with me forever.

Not yet.

She already has her clothes on. Shit, she's leaving.

I sit up. "Did I create a work headache for you, keeping you here?"

"No. I'd rather stay in your bed, but if I don't leave soon, I'm going to have a big one tomorrow."

Guilt replaces my disappointment. She called off work because of me. "I'm sor—"

She puts her fingers over my lips. "Don't ever be sorry about our time together." She pins her hazel orbs on me.

I lick my lips. My mouth is dry. *I need some water.* "Can I do anything to help?"

That's a dumb question. She's an attorney. What could I possibly do?

A sweet expression appears. "No. Thank you for asking. Unfortunately, I need to go home and face the music."

I reach for my phone. "Let me text my driver."

"I'll take a cab."

I sternly shake my head and say, "No." I text Igor. "Let me throw on some clothes."

"But I prefer you naked," she teases.

"Then you should have stayed undressed." I wink and go into my bathroom. I swish with mouthwash, brush my teeth, then put a T-shirt and joggers on. I step out of the closet, but Kora isn't in the bedroom. I go out to the family room and find her.

She's on the phone, staring out the window. Her voice sounds worried and stressed. "Another twenty? Neicy, please tell me what's going on. I'm worried about you."

She holds the phone away from her ear and cringes. A shrieky voice comes through the phone.

"No. Of course I want you to get better. I'll get you the money, but please, tell me what's wrong."

More yelling from her sister and wincing from Kora.

"Okay. I'll bring it by as soon as possible. It's going to take me a few days. I need to cash some things out."

My red flags rise. I don't want to get between Kora and her family, but I don't like how she's giving her sister large sums of cash without knowing what is going on.

"Neicy, I already gave you all the cash I keep liquid. I'm not sure how long it will take, I've never cashed anything out."

I step toward her and put my arm around her waist.

Kora shuts her eyes and sinks into me. "As soon as I can get it, I'll bring it over. I promise. Bye." She hangs up and sighs.

"Is everything all right?" I ask but already know it's not.

She straightens and nods. "Yeah." She turns and forces a smile. "How long will it take for the driver? I really can take a cab."

"No, you won't," I firmly say. My phone buzzes, and I look at the screen. "Igor's out front."

She attempts to appear as if everything is okay again, but she's distracted. "Thanks...um..." She scrunches her forehead. "I'll see you soon?"

I cock an eyebrow.

Her face flushes.

I pull her into me and kiss her deeply until her body relaxes and she's returning my hunger. "Thanks for coming over and staying."

Her lips twitch. "It was fun."

"Yeah, it was. We should do it again sometime. Maybe on the weekend so I don't mess up your work schedule."

Her blush deepens.

"Come on." I guide her to the door and into the elevator and push the button.

"You don't have to walk me downstairs."

I snort. "I'm not walking you downstairs."

"What would you call this?"

"I'm escorting you home."

"You don't have to go out of your way. Really."

I huff again then lead her through the lobby and into the car.

When the door shuts, I slide my arm around her shoulder. I lean close to her face. My pulse beats harder. "Guess what I have?"

"What?"

"Tickets for next week's game."

She doesn't reply but nervously bites her lip.

"Do I get to redeem myself?"

She hesitates.

"Courtside not nosebleed seats," I tease, but I'm worried she might say no.

"Okay. What time?"

"I'll pick you up at six." I kiss her until the car stops outside her building. I get out and reach in for her then escort her to her unit.

"Thanks. I'll see you next week?" she asks.

It pulls at my heart. No matter how much time we just spent together, I know she's wondering if I'm going to show up.

"Yes." I tug her to me and palm her ass. "Maybe you should pack an overnight bag."

She tries to bite her smile. "Maybe I will."

I pat her ass and kiss her. "Go catch up on your work. I'll see you tomorrow night. Lock your door."

"Yes, sir."

I put my hand to my ear. "Say that again."

She laughs and pushes me away. "Get out of here."

I wink and leave. When I get in the car, I tell my driver to go to the gym.

A text message pops up.

Kora: *I forgot to have you sign the contract.*

I almost text her I'll come back but change my mind.

Me: *I'll stop by your office tomorrow. Noon work?*

A few moments pass.

Kora: *Yes.*

Me: *Do you have more crotchless panties?*

Kora: *Yes.*

Me: *What color?*

Kora: *Black, brown, champagne, purple...should I keep going?*

I groan.

Me: *Champagne as in pinkish or yellowish?*

Kora: *Pale pink.*

Me: *Wear those. See you at noon.*

I know what I'm eating for lunch tomorrow.

I get to the gym and step out of the car. "Leo," I say, and fist-bump him.

"Sergey. You just missed Boris, but Adrian and Obrecht just arrived. Aleksei's staying late if you want to jump in their session."

"I'm sure—"

Loud rap music blares. I turn, and a car comes barreling down the street, then stops in front of Kora's mom's building. Her sister kisses the man behind the wheel then stumbles out of the vehicle. "DeAndre! Terrell!" she screams while waving her hand in the air then begins laughing.

She doesn't look ill.

I refocus on the two drug dealers who hang out on the corner. They exchange words, and one walks toward Neicy as she continues to swagger down the sidewalk.

"That girl's trouble," Leo mutters.

I don't take my eyes off Neicy.

She pulls a wad of money out of her pocket and hands several bills to one of the men. He puts something in her pocket, and they talk for a while longer.

"Amazing how brave she's gotten lately," Leo says.

I turn to him. "What do you mean?"

He shrugs. "She used to hide buying. It only happened every so often, but she's grabbing stuff almost daily."

If it were only pot, I wouldn't be so judgmental. I understand the need for it. But DeAndre and Terrell don't sell weed. They sell crack.

Is that what Kora's money is buying?

The anger I feel bubbles and turns to boiling when Neicy struts across the street and goes into the carryout. She comes out with a fifth of whiskey and cigarettes.

She doesn't look sick, only drunk and high. Still, I don't want to assume something false. I pat Leo. "I'll see you later."

I walk into the gym. It's full of boxers training. I jump in on Adrian and Obrecht's workout. I try to concentrate, but I can't get rid of the bad feelings I have surrounding Neicy. It may be Kora's family, but I'm not going to let her get taken advantage of or stay in the dark any longer.

Aleksei unties my gloves, and I wait for Adrian and Obrecht.

Since Obrecht is in charge of monitoring the war between the Rossis and Petrovs, I address Adrian. "I need medical records and a tail."

Adrian raises his eyebrows. "For Jack Christian?"

I had forgotten all about Jack and the tail I put on him.

"No, but what did you find on him?"

"Still working on the dirt."

"Who's Jack?" Obrecht asks.

"A wife-beating piece of shit," I reply.

Obrecht's face hardens. "Who's his wife?"

If there's one thing an Ivanov can't stand, it's a man who hurts a woman. Obrecht and Adrian might hate it more due to what happened to Natalia.

"No one you know."

"If it's not Jack, then who do you need info on?"

"Neicy Kilborn."

Adrian's blue eyes turn icier. "Isn't Kora's last name Kilborn?"

"Yes, it is."

"What's the relation?"

"Sister."

Adrian crosses his arms. "You have an address?"

"Across the street."

Adrian's eyes widen. "Kora grew up in this neighborhood?"

"Yeah."

"Shit."

"Yeah. But I need her current medical records ASAP."

"You want me to stay on her or Jack? I can put Bogden on the other."

My jaw begins to tic. Both issues need a tail, and both concern Kora.

Her safety is more important than money. Money can be replaced, she can't.

Adrian and Bogden are both competent, but Adrian's a bit more experienced than Bogden, and we're closer, so it probably makes me biased toward him. "You stay on Jack. Put Bogden on her sister. But I want information on both ASAP."

"Done."

We shower and leave. I drive past Kora's old apartment, the dealers on the corner, and I'm once again amazed she escaped her environment.

I get a good night's rest, work out with my brothers in the morning, and keep myself busy all morning visiting our job sites on several new buildings we're in the middle of developing. I stop at the florist, pick up a dozen long-stemmed pink roses, and go to Kora's law firm.

Her assistant escorts me to Kora's office when I get there. She's at her desk, engrossed in work. A concentrated frown is on her face. Two deep lines run across her forehead.

"You said to bring Mr. Ivanov straight back when he arrived," her assistant announces.

She looks up. Her eyes brighten when she sees me. "Come in."

I step in and close then lock the door. I shut the blinds for the glass facing the hall then turn and set the flowers down on the desk.

"These are beau—"

I consume her lips, controlling her tongue, holding her head firmly to mine. I missed her. It hasn't been twenty-four hours, and I already feel rebalanced just being in her presence.

"You look stressed," I murmur then kiss her some more.

"Mmhmm. Little," she admits.

"Did you wear the panties?"

Her face turns crimson. She nods.

She obeys me so well.

My dick twitches. I reach for her zipper and lower it. Her pencil skirt falls to the ground. I swallow hard at her pale-pink crotchless panties.

"Go sit on the edge of your desk, facing the window."

Golden flames ignite in her eyes. Her hips sway as she walks to her desk. I stare at her lush ass, wishing I could take it but knowing this isn't the environment for that kind of activity. She stacks her work in a pile then sets it aside. After she puts her laptop over the files, she props up on the desk, then crosses her legs.

I sit in her chair then adjust the level so it lowers as close to the ground as possible.

Perfect.

She smirks.

My pants become uncomfortably tight from her sassy little look and half-naked body in front of me. "Did I tell you to cross your legs?"

She says nothing. Her lips twitch, and she slowly uncrosses them, pinning her gaze on mine. She puts a leg on either side of my thighs. The heels from her stilettos rest on the seat of the chair.

Naughty, sexy girl.

Pink is definitely my new favorite color.

"Your assistant said you had a 12:30?" I ask, kissing her inner thigh and rolling the chair as close to the desk as possible.

"Mmhmm." Her hands slide into my hair.

I kiss her leg as close to her pussy as possible, sniff hard, and look up at her. "Good thing I know how to eat fast."

Kora

"TEN DAYS? THAT'S RIDICULOUS," I STATE. I SHOULD HAVE come yesterday to the bank, but it was closed by the time I got out of work. The entire day I tried to catch up from taking an unplanned day off, and the only break I had was when Sergey came to sign paperwork.

I shouldn't have let him come to the office and distract me.

My face heats, thinking about his lunchtime visit. Sergey's tongue is an Olympian next to an amateur in a race if I compare him to any of my previous lovers.

Who am I kidding? Everything about him is gold-medal worthy.

I squirm in my seat and refocus. "This isn't acceptable."

The bank manager pushes his hand over his bald head. It's turning redder the longer I argue with him. I'm assuming he isn't used to and doesn't like confrontation. "Ms. Kilborn, the shares have to be sold. It takes trade plus three business days for it to settle. Monday is a bank holiday. The mutual funds sell after the market closes. Friday, the funds will be available to transfer into your checking account. Once that happens, we have to request the cash be available to disperse."

"You're a bank."

"Yes, but large sums of money need to be requested. This is the policy—"

"Do I need to move my accounts?" I threaten.

He sighs. "Ms. Kilborn, we value your business and want to keep it. However, I cannot make any exceptions as I did last time. My boss just verified we cannot do anything to give you funds sooner."

"What if I put my portfolio on margin? You said it was an option versus cashing them out." I'm not a financial guru, and I don't want to put them on margin, but Neicy sent me a text yesterday asking when I would have the funds. She still won't tell me what's wrong, and it kept me up all night. The manager made it clear if the market goes down, I could have a margin call and end up having to add more money into the account. Besides my student loans for my law degree and my condo, I've worked hard to not go into debt. This sounds like a similar risk or gambling with my investments. I paid off my loans before I bought my condo. I only kept ten thousand in my checking for emergencies, another ten thousand in my money market, and all my other funds I invested in stocks, mutual funds, and retirement accounts. I didn't replenish the emergency fund yet. I planned on getting it back to ten thousand over the next few months with my earnings and didn't expect Neicy to need more.

"There is an approval process for the margin account. You're looking at the same time frame, maybe a few days sooner."

I sigh in frustration.

"Ms. Kilborn, this is the second time this month you've needed a large amount of cash. If this is something you think you might need more of in the future, the margin would be a good idea so you can access the funds quicker. It will only take several business days to convert the money into cash if you have the margin account set up."

My heart beats harder. *Will Neicy need more?*

It would help if I knew what was wrong.

Why won't she tell me? I know we aren't close, but I am her sister.

I blink hard, trying to control the emotions squeezing my chest. I rise. "Please submit the paperwork to sell my investments and call me as soon as the cash is ready."

Relief fills his face, and he stands and holds out his hand. "Very well, Ms. Kilborn. Thank you again for your business."

I begrudgingly shake his hand, attempting to not come across as a total bitch. It isn't his fault, but it's irritating I've done what all the financial gurus tell you to do, yet I can't access my money at a moment's notice.

It's not normal to need this amount of cash in today's age.

It's not the first time the thought has plagued me. I text Neicy.

Me: *The bank can't get me the cash for ten days.*

Neicy: *What?*

Me: *If you can take a cashier's check, I can get it to you sooner.*

Neicy: *I need cash. You know I don't have a bank account. Don't throw your upper-class shit on me.*

Me: *Can't I have one made out to your doctor's office or the hospital? I don't understand why they need cash.*

Neicy: *Forget it, Kora. I'll suffer in silence or die and then you can keep your money. I'm sure that will make you happy.*

Me: *Die? Neicy, PLEASE tell me what is wrong. I'm so worried about you. This is tearing me apart.*

Neicy: *You just want me to beg. You're enjoying my bad luck.*

Me: *Of course I'm not. I can't sleep. I'm so worried about you.*

Neicy: *Don't make this about you, Kora!*

I take several deep breaths.

Neicy: *Are you giving me the money or not?*

Me: *Yes. As soon as I get it, I'll bring it over.*

Neicy: *Fine.*

Me: *Please take care of yourself.*

There's no answer. I walk several blocks to my office. I need to find out what is going on with Neicy, but I'm not sure how. My mother may or may not tell me if she knows, but Neicy insisted she hasn't told her. So I can't ask.

I'm deep in thought, not paying attention to anyone around me. The walkway light turns green. I cross to the other side of the street. When I turn, I run straight into a man's chest.

"Just who I was coming to see," a deep voice seethes.

I look up. Jack Christian is scowling at me. I take a step back.

He reaches for my arm so I can't move.

"Let me go," I firmly say, but fear twists in my gut.

He leans close to my face. In a slow, menacing tone, he enunciates, "Where. Is. My. Wife?"

I've had many crazy things happen while representing clients, but no one has caused the cold shiver to run as deep into my spine as Jack.

We're in public. He can't hurt me.

Would he?

His eyes look crazy.

"Let go of me," I repeat, but I don't sound as confident as usual.

He grasps my arm tighter, and I wince.

"You're hurting me." I shove my hand into his chest, but he grabs my wrist.

"Tell me where she is, now."

I'm not sure what to do. My insides shake, and I try to push away but can't.

"Kora, is this man bothering you?" a familiar voice with a Russian accent says.

Jack tears his eyes from mine and looks to the left of us. "Mind your own fucking business."

Adrian grabs his neck, pushes his chin to the sky, and squeezes so hard, he releases me.

The sidewalk clears, and there are a few loud gasps. Jack continues to flail, attempting to fight Adrian off.

"When a woman says to let her go, you let her go," Adrian growls, moving him against the brick wall.

Jack turns purple.

"Adrian!" I call out. As scared as I was, we're in public. Adrian could get arrested.

Adrian says something in his ear I can't hear and finally lets him go.

Jack crouches down, trying to catch his breath.

Adrian puts his hand on my back in a protective manner. Too shocked, I allow him to guide me down the street. He leads me into my building. "Kora, are you okay?"

I should thank him for saving me from whatever the situation could have evolved into, but I blurt out, "How do you know where I work?"

His face hardens. It takes him a moment too long to reply. "You're Kora Kilborn. Famous divorce attorney."

He's lying.

"Are you following me?"

"You should put a restraining order on him."

"Answer my questions, Adrian."

He says nothing.

I grab his arm and lead him closer to the corner, out of the way of traffic. "Adrian, why are you following me?"

More silence, except for his hard sniff and lick of his lips as he doesn't flinch.

"What did he want from you, Kora?"

"Goddamnit, Adrian, answer my question!"

"I'm not following you, Kora."

"No? Then how do you know where I work?"

"I told you—"

"You're lying!"

Blood pounds between my ears. The longer Adrian is silent, the angrier I get. Then it hits me. "Did Sergey have you follow me?"

"I'm not following you, Kora."

Disgusted he's lying to me, I dig into my purse and find my phone. I dial Sergey.

"Lapa. You stressed and need me to swing by your office?" Sergey answers in his cocky voice.

My rage grows while my lower body annoyingly throbs. "Why is Adrian following me?"

The line turns silent and then, "Did something happen?"

"Tell me why Adrian is following me," I repeat in an angrier tone.

"He's not."

"Stop lying," I say, louder than I should.

Sergey exhales slowly. In a controlled voice, he replies, "I'm a block from your office. I'm not lying nor discussing this over the phone." The line goes dead.

I glare at Adrian.

He crosses his arms and arrogantly says, "You could thank me for saving you from that douchebag instead of looking at me like you want to kill me."

"I wish we weren't in public right now."

"Why?"

"I'd slap you," I admit.

He grunts. "Wouldn't be the first woman."

"I bet."

Adrian's smirk grows. From the corner of my eye, I see Sergey walking in. I spin and redirect my glare on him. I try to ignore the butterflies competing with the anger stewing in my belly.

Why does he always look so good?

"What do you think you're doing, having Adrian follow me?"

Adrian groans. "You don't listen."

"You need to stop talking," I instruct then focus on Sergey.

"He's not following you, Kora. We're not lying."

"Then how does he know where I work? Why was he on the street?"

"Calm down. You're drawing attention to us."

"Don't tell me to calm down," I seethe but lower my voice.

Sergey puts his arm where Jack did, and I wince.

He holds his hands in the air. "Whoa. What's wrong with your arm?"

"Jack had her pinned on the sidewalk," Adrian replies.

"Pinned?" Sergey's face turns red, and his eyes flare with rage.

"I'm fine."

"Let me see your arm."

"No. Tell me why Adrian is following me," I repeat for what feels like the hundredth time.

"Still not listening," Adrian mutters.

"He's following Jack. Now let me see your arm," Sergey orders.

I should have put two and two together.

I need to calm down so I can think.

I exhale. "Why is Adrian following Jack?"

Sergey's face hardens just like Adrian's did, but his jaw twitches.

"You aren't going to tell me?"

"You don't need to know."

I step closer to Sergey. "Are you kidding me? It's my client's husband."

"He's not a good man, Kora."

"No kidding! Do you think I'm stupid?"

His eyes turn warmer. "No. You're the smartest woman I know."

My heart skips a beat, but I ignore it. "Then tell me wh—" A cold feeling moves through me. I swallow the thick lump forming in my throat. "Are you going to..." I gaze between Adrian and Sergey, who both have the same expression on their faces.

"I'm going to make sure you're protected, my lapa."

The beating of my heart increases so fast, I feel sick. "You can't do whatever it is you're planning on doing."

"I'm not planning on doing anything," Sergey replies.

"Call it off. Stop following him."

"No."

My stomach twists. *Jack's an asshole, but has he done something to warrant Sergey killing him?*

Not yet.

What am I saying?

Would he kill him for no reason?

"Sergey—"

"It's not up for discussion." He shakes his head, and the darkness reappears in his eyes.

"Excuse me?"

"You heard me."

This is why two alphas should never be together.

"This is my client's—"

"It's for your protection," he barks.

"No—"

"Yes!"

Jack's scum, but it's too close to home. Any harm to him could cause issues for Selena. My job is to protect her. I don't need anything ruining her case.

"Can I talk to you alone?" I ask.

Adrian snorts. "I'll see you outside. And you're welcome."

"Adrian," Sergey warns.

He shakes his head and leaves.

I walk closer to the corner and spin. "I need you to call off whatever this is with Jack. Selena's case could be harmed."

"*You* could be harmed. And let me see your arm. Take your jacket off."

"This isn't about me, Sergey. I have a duty to make sure nothing jeopardizes Selena's divorce."

He steps closer so my back is against the wall and puts his hand on my cheek. "I don't know the details of what happened on a *public* street, but if Adrian had to intervene, I don't need to know anything more. Jack Christian is bad news. I won't lie to you. I'm not calling off anything. Your safety is at risk. Selena's, too."

My quivering insides are conflicted. Sergey's trying to protect me, but I can't have him tailing my clients' exes who make threats. "This isn't anything I can't handle or haven't before."

Anger fills his face. "Really? Your clients' exes have assaulted you on the street before?"

"I wasn't assaulted."

"Your arm is sore from him grabbing you. Adrian had to pull him off you!"

I stay quiet.

"I'm not going to stand by and let you be a sitting duck, Kora."

"This is my career. It doesn't concern you. And I know how to take care of myself. Stay out of my work issues."

"Not negotiable," he states.

My insides shake in anger. He doesn't have a right to get involved and have Adrian follow Jack. "You're overstepping."

"I know you've seen a lot, Kora, but my instincts are rarely wrong about these kinds of things."

"This is my business, not yours."

His jaw spasms faster. "Making sure you're protected is my business."

"No, it's not. Call it off," I demand again.

"Not happening."

I've never had anyone I dated interfere with my work before. Something tells me there is nothing I can say to stop Sergey from whatever it is he's trying to achieve by following Jack. "What are your intentions with this nonsense?"

"It's not nonsense."

"Don't avoid the question."

"Don't ask questions you know I won't answer. And we've already agreed you wouldn't ask questions. Now let me see your arm."

I move my head back an inch, and it touches the wall. *Is this what he thinks?*

"I never agreed to allow you to do anything like this and not ask questions. This involves my client."

His face hardens. He quietly says, "Kora, let me see your arm. This isn't worth fighting about."

The truth is ugly. It hurts, and I can barely get oxygen in my lungs. No matter what I say, he isn't going to listen to me. He thinks my agreement not to ask him questions about what he did to Wes allows him to do whatever he wants and keep me in the dark.

"If you don't tell me, I can't do this."

His eyes turn to slits. "I told you not to toy with me the other night. I've been clear about where I stand. You said you didn't want to play games."

"I'm not. You didn't tell me you were going to require my ignorance on things involving my cases."

"It's one case. One bastard who's already done something to physically harm you," Sergey insists.

"It doesn't make it right."

He takes a step back. "What are you saying, Kora?"

"Call it off or tell me what your intentions are."

"I won't do anything to put you at risk, and it's not in your best interest to know anything."

I shut my eyes and concentrate on breathing.

He can't do this. It's not professional. Selena could be put in a bad situation. My entire career could be destroyed.

"Then I can't be with you."

The expression on Sergey's face is painful. His eyes fill with betrayal and sadness. It mirrors my feelings, but I can't look the other way when my business is concerned.

He shakes his head. "I thought you were different." It's a bullet to my heart. "Have a nice life, Kora."

I want to run after him, tell him I don't mean it and I'm sorry. Instead, I stay plastered to the wall, watching him disappear through the door.

I blink hard, turn toward the wall, and swipe at the tears leaking onto my cheeks. I manage to get to the bathroom without running into anyone I know and pull myself together. The rest of the day, I attempt to concentrate on work, but Sergey's hurt face is all I see. I keep hearing him say, "I thought you were different." Eventually, I shut my door and close the blinds, then break down.

I thought he was different, too.

Sergey

My patience is wearing thin. "How can there be nothing on him?"

Adrian groans. "Chill. I didn't say nothing. I said we haven't found anything yet. There's a big difference, and it's only been a few weeks."

"It's been a month!"

"We're close. I can feel it," Adrian insists.

I scrub my hands over my face. Since I walked out of Kora's office building, I've barely slept. I can't stop thinking about her or smelling the pillow she slept on, which still has her floral scent on it. I sent the tickets for the basketball game to her office with a note for her to take a friend. It only seemed fair since I stood her up the first time. She sent me a text.

Kora: *I just got the tickets.*

Me: *Enjoy.*

Kora: *You don't have to give me your tickets.*

Me: *After what happened the first time, it wouldn't be right for you not to go.*

There was a long pause before she replied.

Kora: *Can I buy them from you?*

Me: *Are you trying to insult me?*

Kora: *Are you sure? They're courtside, not nosebleed.*

My smile was bittersweet at her reference to the joke I previously made when I tried to get her to agree to go.

Me: *Yes, I'm sure.*

Kora: *Okay. Thank you.*

Me: *You're welcome.*

That was several weeks ago. If I can find out what Jack's hiding, Kora will understand why I insisted on doing this. Maybe then she'll understand she needs to trust me, and we can be together.

When I walked away from her, I was mad and hurt. It doesn't compare to the ache I feel all day long without her.

I used to miss Eloise, but I don't remember it feeling anywhere close to how bad this feels.

Adrian slaps a yellow envelope in front of me. It's four inches thick.

"What's this?"

He snorts. "Bogden's findings. I think you'll find it interesting."

Neicy.

I open it and pull out a stack of 8x10 photos. My gut drops as I sort through them. "Jesus."

"She's a piece of work. How is Kora related to her?"

I mutter, "No clue." Every photo I stare at makes my gut churn. I knew Neicy was taking advantage of Kora, but seeing it only makes me sick.

Adrian picks up a picture of Neicy in a jewelry store, paying cash for several items. "Family fucking family over."

The photos range from Neicy going on shopping sprees, to buying crack from her cousins on the corner, to having several nights at luxury hotels with her current boyfriend. Every photo displays her pulling out cash. The ones that break my heart the most are Kora handing her a thick envelope. I have no doubt it's the twenty thousand Neicy requested. Kora gets out of a taxi with an envelope sticking out of her purse in a different outfit, which makes me believe she gave her money more than once since I last saw her. One of the handoffs is on the street. Neicy didn't even have her go up to the apartment. The photos look hostile, and when Kora turns to get in her taxi, she's wiping tears from her eyes.

"What about medical records?" I ask Adrian, wanting to make sure I haven't overlooked anything.

He shakes his head. "Nothing. Bogden tapped into her phone records, too." He pulls out a stack of papers under the photos.

"No traces of calls to anyone, except her boyfriend, mother, and some friends. This is ninety days before we started tailing her up until yesterday."

My heart breaks more for Kora. As much as I hate to wish anything medical on anyone, I know how much this will hurt her.

Adrian separates the paper pile and hands me a stapled packet. "Here's the documentation on everywhere Neicy's gone in the last few weeks. No doctor appointments. All she does is party, shop, or hang out with her boyfriend."

I collect everything and shove it back into the envelope. I don't want to stare at it anymore.

Adrian shifts in his seat. "How much did Kora give her?"

"Too much."

"You want Bogden to stay on her?"

"For now." Until Kora knows the truth, I don't feel right lifting the tail.

My bell dings, signaling I have company coming up in the elevator. "That's my brothers."

Adrian rises. "I need to go."

"Find something on that prick."

Adrian nods. "Don't worry, I will." He pats me on the back and leaves as my brothers walk in.

They all exchange greetings then my brothers take a seat at the table.

"It's confirmed. Three more leaders are dead on the Rossi side," Maksim says.

"Zamir's got more strength right now," Dmitri states.

"We're going about this the wrong way," I blurt out.

"Sergey," Boris warns.

Maksim's eyes turn to slits. "What are you two hiding?"

"Nothing," Boris replies and gives me a look to shut my mouth.

I blurt out, "We need to get in the Petrov organization and destroy it piece by piece until nothing is left."

Boris growls a sigh and shakes his head.

Dmitri turns in his chair next to me and scowls. "Are you crazy?"

"No. If we only kill Zamir, we don't destroy it all. They're still a threat."

Maksim leans over the table and points. "What you're suggesting is suicide. We stick with the plan. We let the Rossis and Petrovs kill each other off. Nothing has changed. Don't get any crazy ideas, little brother."

It doesn't surprise me my brothers won't listen to me. My thoughts are dangerous, but I don't see how to destroy the entire Petrov operation unless we're on the inside. We'll always be watching our backs, waiting for the other shoe to drop.

Dmitri sits back in his chair. "We play this out for now. If anymore Rossis end up dead, we need to intervene."

"Darragh is in agreement. We'll have his blessing," Boris states.

I groan. Darragh is Killian and Nora's uncle. He's the head of the O'Malley crime family. In order for Boris to marry Nora without her family disowning her, my brothers and I had to meet with him and agree to an alliance. The meeting was a few weeks ago, and I'm still a bit uneasy over it.

Boris scowls. "We don't have the power to do this without the O'Malleys."

"Yeah, and your dick made sure we got it, didn't it?" I sarcastically remark. All my brothers and I warned Boris to stay away from Nora. We love her and her brothers like family, but there was no way he could get involved with her without dragging us into O'Malley crap. It ties us for life. The meeting with Darragh was painful. I sat quietly and let Maksim speak for us. He assured Darragh we were all for the alliance but weren't going to take orders from him. All I see is a future of O'Malley headaches, especially since his son, Liam, is now out of prison and always dragged Killian into all his bad decisions.

"Something you want to say?" Boris asks.

"Nope. Already said it," I remind him. Boris and I got into it after the meeting with Darragh. I love my brothers. No matter what, I'll stand by them, but it doesn't mean I have to like all their decisions.

Maksim moves the conversation along. "We should be good to go tomorrow to finish the cleanup on the city lot. The weather is forecasted to cooperate, assuming nothing changes."

We go through several of our projects. When my brothers leave, I take out all the information Adrian gave me on Neicy.

This is going to crush Kora.

I can't keep it from her.

I text her.

Me: *I need to see you.*

Fifteen minutes pass. Dots show up on the screen then go away. I finally get a message.

Kora: *Did you call it off?*

Me: *Nope, and I'm not going to.*

Kora: *Will you tell me your intentions?*

Me: *You already know the answer to this.*

Kora: *Then we don't have any reason to get together.*

Me: *This isn't about what you think.*

Kora: *I don't think it's a good idea.*

Me: *Don't trust yourself around me?*

She doesn't reply, and my heart races faster.

Me: *I'm not texting you for a booty call.*

Kora: *What is this about?*

Me: *I can't discuss this over text.*

Kora: *I'll call you then.*

Me: *No. Trust me. We can't discuss this, except in person.*

Kora: *I'm home for the next hour. Can you come now?*

Me: *I'll be there in fifteen.*

I breathe a sigh of relief she's going to meet me. As much as I'm dying to see her, I've intentionally not contacted her. I don't know how she will react, but I don't want her getting this information alone.

My stomach twists on the way to her place. When I get to her front door, she opens it, and how much I miss her intensifies. She seems to have gotten more beautiful. She's wearing a hot-pink pencil skirt and black top. My mind immediately goes into overdrive, and my pants get tighter in the crotch.

She had to wear pink.

"Come in," she says and opens the door.

I step in, reach to hug her, then freeze.

She doesn't want to be mine right now.

"Have you been good?"

She smiles, and my heart squeezes. "Okay. You?"

"Same." I stare at her, trying to find something in her eyes that will let me back in, but I don't find it.

"What can I do for you?" she asks.

"Straight to business, huh?" I tease, but it comes out accusing.

She sighs, shuts her eyes, then admits, "This isn't easy for me, Sergey."

Good. She still has feelings for me.

"Then why don't you trust me and stop staying away from me?" I didn't intend on getting into this, but it flows out of my mouth. I feel like my soul is gone without her. She filled something in me. I'm not sure what it was, but the ache never goes away.

"I can't."

This conversation isn't going anywhere. Give her the information.

"Sorry to hear that. I miss you." I hold out the envelope toward her.

She doesn't reach for it. Sadness fills her eyes and slices my heart further. "I miss you, too. I wish you would trust me instead of expecting me to be the only one who dishes out the trust."

Ouch.

"I do trust you."

She snorts. "Yeah? How?"

"I clearly stated this was for your protection. It's never been about trust."

She blinks hard and turns her face away. When she turns back, her eyes are glistening, and she takes the envelope. "What is this?"

"Information on Neicy."

Her eyes widen. "What has she done?"

"I think it's better if you open it and see for yourself."

She stares at the package then pins her gaze on me. "Why would you have information on my sister?"

"I told you I would protect you. It includes people hustling you."

A line forms between her eyebrows. "Hustling me?"

I nod to the envelope. "Open it."

She hesitates then slowly removes the contents. As she thumbs through each photo, the color drains from her face.

"I'm sorry to be the one—"

"The one what? To pry into my family life and follow my sister around?" Her voice cracks, and her lips quiver. Tears well in her eyes.

"Lapa—"

"Don't call me your lapa!" she cries, and a tear slips down her cheek. "You didn't have a right to do this."

"She's stealing from you. You don't deserve—"

"Get out!"

"Kora—"

"Leave!" she yells. Her face scrunches, and she looks away. Tears drip off her chin.

I try to put my arms around her, but she shakes out of my grip. "Don't touch me."

"Kora—"

"Get. Out," she enunciates in a dead voice and opens the door.

I stop in the doorway. "I didn't do this to hurt you."

She laughs with more tears falling. "Did your spy tell you how my mother and sister hate me? Or how they only use me for money? Did they fill you in on how ashamed they are of me about who I am and what I've become?"

My chest tightens. I try to hide my anger. Not at her but at her mother and sister who can't see and appreciate the amazing, beautiful person she is. "You have nothing to be ashamed of. If they can't see the exceptional, special woman you are, then they don't deserve you."

"Just leave," she quietly says and turns away from me.

It kills me to leave, but I do. When I get in my car, I call Bogden.

In Russian, he answers, "Sergey. What's up?"

"I want immediate notification if Kora visits her sister."

"Will do."

I hang up, go back to my penthouse, and pace. I want to help Kora, but I'm not sure how. If my brothers did to me what Neicy did to her, I would be a wreck. And what she admitted to me about how her family feels about her angers and hurts me. I can't get her face full of tears out of my mind. An hour passes, and I receive a message.

Bogden: *She's at the apartment.*

I text my driver and sit outside her mother's building. A half hour passes, and Kora steps out of the building, wiping her face.

I jump out of the car and pull her into my arms.

She attempts to push away from me. "What are you doing? Leave me alone."

"No," I say, holding her tighter.

She shoves her arms into my chest again, but it's pointless. I'm a lot stronger than her.

"Stop fighting me. I'm not letting you go," I tell her, and my heart shatters further when she breaks down sobbing.

"Why do they hate me?" she cries as her body heaves against mine.

"Shh."

"I'm so stupid."

"No. You're not. You're generous and kind."

She shakes her head into the curve of my neck.

I manage to get her in the car. I tell Igor her address, and she whispers, "No."

I lift her chin. "Where do you want to go?"

Her tear-filled eyes drill into mine. She doesn't respond.

"My place, Igor."

21

Kora

MY ALARM RINGS, AND I QUICKLY SWIPE THE SCREEN ON MY phone. I turn toward Sergey to see he's still sleeping. The faint hint of morning sun is shining through the window. I'm not sure what time we fell asleep. He didn't take me to his dungeon last night. We stayed the entire time in his bedroom. He kissed all my tears. All night, he repeated how beautiful and special I was, and all the things he thought made me different from other women that turned him on.

I trace the bite mark on his neck that's purple and wince. He restrained my wrists. I came so hard, I bit down on him.

Jesus. I'm turning into a vampire.

I lie still for a few minutes, trying to push the thoughts of what my sister did and my mother's reaction out of my head.

My mother told me I was selfish.

Neicy hustled sixty thousand dollars out of me.

How could I have been so stupid?

I spent too many nights to count not sleeping and worrying about my sister. Nothing is wrong with her. She just scammed me.

And she's smoking crack.

My mother's final words hurt more than anything she's ever said to me before.

Take your uppity ass out of here, and don't come back, you selfish snob.

I replay the confrontation over and over in my head, trying to see if I was in the wrong, but I can't find anything. It's the last straw, but it still hurts.

I didn't talk much to Sergey when we got back. He tried, but I couldn't. Everything turned physical. The ache I had for him all month had grown to the point I couldn't stand it anymore. When he showed up outside my mother's building, I had no more energy to stay away or even think about why I shouldn't be with him.

Sergey lies on his stomach. His back tattoo is even more stunning and beautiful in the morning light. I have to remind myself it's only there to cover up his scars.

I shouldn't touch him when he's sleeping. He has insomnia issues, and I'm unsure how that affects his normal sleep. He seems to be in a deep slumber, so I reach out and trace over the stars. Before I know it, my lips are pressing against them.

"Why do you kiss it?" he mumbles so quietly, I freeze. His eyes are still closed.

Did he ask that, or did I imagine it?

"Do you like grotesque things?"

I kiss the last star and keep my hand on his back, caressing it. I slide down on my side and throw my leg over his. "There's nothing about your body that isn't perfection."

He grunts but doesn't open his eyes.

"What happened?"

"We aren't discussing this, Kora."

And we're back to this.

"You just learned ugly, horrible things about my life, yet I don't get to know your secrets?"

"It's not the same."

"How is it not?"

"It's not." His voice is sharp with finality.

My second alarm reminder blares out. I quickly pick it up and silence it.

He's never going to let me in. No matter what he knows about me, he's never going to trust me.

I roll away from him, but he pulls me back. "Where are you going?" His eyes fly open, and his gaze drills into mine.

"I have to go to work."

He pins his body over me. My heartbeat quickens. He strokes the side of my head. "Are you doing better?"

Why does he have to be so sweet yet such a hypocrite?

"I'm fine. If I don't go, I'm going to be late."

He gives me a chaste kiss, then stares at me, kisses me again, then returns to scanning my face.

"I have to go," I quietly state.

"Are you going to cut me off again?"

"Cut you off?" I ask, amused at his choice of words.

"Yeah."

"You walked away from me," I remind him.

He raises his eyebrows. Hurt appears. "Your exact words were you couldn't be with me."

"Why can't you tell me what you plan on doing or stop following Jack?"

"He's a piece of shit."

"Yeah, I know."

"Why can't you trust me, Kora? I would never do anything to hurt you."

"It's not me I'm worried about." Jack has gotten worse over the last month with his threats. There's always something coming up where the judge extends our court date. Jack has called my cell and office, threatening me to tell him where Selena is. I can't say I'm not disturbed by it, and knowing Sergey has someone following Jack does give me comfort.

Part of me wonders if I'm more concerned about what Sergey will do to Jack or if it's stubborn pride. Then I remind myself Sergey is a killer. It's too big of a wild card for Selena's case. If Sergey would let me in, I could possibly understand his thought process and not be so opposed to whatever he's planning. But all this morning has done is show me he's still an arm's length away.

He's always going to be. He hasn't lied.

I should stay away from him, but this past month was torture. I felt off without him. Too many times to count, I started to text him or almost called him and stopped myself. A few times, I got into a taxi and stopped in front of his building. I chickened out and didn't come inside.

"Can we go back to the night you promised to know us and accept that?" Sergey asks.

"It didn't include you interfering with my client cases," I softly say.

"Your safety and protection aren't negotiable, my lapa. Can we get past this?"

My heart skips a beat when he says things that make me believe I'm his. I want to be. I've never had a man want to protect me. I'm the one to always take care of me and everyone around me. For that reason alone, I should tell him yes and stick my head in the sand. He didn't have to make the effort to find out what was going on with Neicy. Shame about how my family sees me and what she did stabbed me in the heart, so I lashed out at him. But I'm grateful he discovered the truth even though it's left me drowning in an ocean of hurt. It was so much better staying here with him than going back to my condo by myself. I know Sergey is trying to take care of me. When I'm with him, a hole in my heart fills. I can't explain it and don't understand it. I want to figure out how to accept this part of him he won't let me know.

"I'm trying. You're asking a lot. I want to trust you and feel like I can't."

"Anything I do is to protect you, my lapa."

"I believe you. It doesn't make it easier for me."

He swallows hard. "You'll try though?"

I take a deep breath. "Okay. But you have to get off of me, or I'm going to be late."

His mouth twitches. He moves his hips so his erection presses against my wet heat, and I automatically open my legs wider. "Igor can drive fast."

I mentally go over my morning schedule and decide arriving a few minutes late won't screw up my day then lift my hips.

Forty minutes later, several orgasms in bed and in the shower, and we leave.

"You don't have to escort me home every time I stay at your house."

He snorts. "You should keep some stuff at my place."

He won't tell me about his past or other things I want to know, but he wants me to keep my personal items at his house?

I quickly throw on work clothes, and he escorts me back to the car. It's another thing no man has ever done for me. Sergey may be a dirty bad boy, but being a gentleman seems ingrained in him. When we get to my work, he steps out and reaches in for me.

I put my arms over his shoulders, and he circles his around my waist. Flutters fill my belly. "I'm going to admit something."

He cocks an eyebrow, and my panties twist. His expression is a mix of cocky and amused. Flecks of gold speckle in his warm-brown orbs, and I could get lost in them.

"I secretly love your alpha-gentleman-protection-escort service."

He laughs. "My what?"

Heat creeps into my face. "You know what I'm saying."

His face turns serious. "What's the but, Kora?"

I wince and say, "I think if you drop me off in my office, my employees are all going to know I was up all night in cougar town."

"I see. And is it the fact I'm younger, or that I kept you up all night that's bothering you?"

"I never think about our ages, but I can do without the office gossip today, that's all." It's true. Sergey's more of a man than anyone I've ever dated. He may be younger, but I don't feel like I'm with a younger guy, except for his endless hard-ons, which I have no complaints over.

His lips twitch. "Okay."

I touch the bite mark I left on him. "Sorry about this."

He grunts. "I'm not." His hand slides up, and he fists my hair. "I think we're better together than apart."

My heart skips a beat. I nod.

He kisses me, deep and hungry, turning my insides to Jell-O and holding me firmly to his growing erection.

"This is illegal," I mutter as he flicks his tongue back in my mouth.

"What? Getting you wet before you walk into the office?"

He's such a dirty cub.

It's so hot.

I slightly move my hips, and a groan rumbles in his chest. In his ear, I whisper, "I'm not the only one with a problem."

He grunts and squeezes my ass. "Go to work."

I kiss him one last time and am about to go in when I freeze. "Hey, umm..."

He strokes my cheekbone with his thumb. "What is it, my lapa?"

"Thank you."

He raises his eyebrows.

My heart races. "For finding out about my sister and being there for me."

He winks and gives me a chaste kiss. "Go to work."

My day goes by fast. I've got several client meetings and paperwork. It's near four when I get a text.

Aspen: *Don't forget about the pub reopening tonight.*

Hailee: *What should I wear?*

Skylar: *I'm ready!*

Aspen: *Casual. It's a pub.*

Hailee: *Is Nora going to try and push Killian on me?*

Me: *I forgot but glad you reminded me.*

Skylar: *You don't like Killian? He's pure-grade Irish butter, ready to be slathered all over you.*

I laugh out loud.

Me: *Irish butter?*

Skylar: *Yeah, top-notch dairy, not the fake stuff made from plastic.*

Aspen: *Do we need to have the butter vs. margarine conversation again? You really shouldn't be a hater.*

Me: *Let's get back to Hailee. What's wrong with Killian?*

Hailee: *Nothing. He's a nice guy.*

Skylar: *And hot with a boxer's body.*

Hailee: *Yes, but I don't think he's interested, and honestly, I get the friend vibe only with him. Nora keeps pushing him on me, and it's embarrassing.*

Me: *Operation Save Hailee from the Irish butter will be in full effect tonight.*

Hailee: *Thank you.*

Skylar: *Is there anyone else going to be at this shindig we can push on Hailee?*

Hailee: *Me? What about you?*

Skylar: *I don't have a problem getting laid. You do.*

Hailee: *No, I don't.*

Skylar: *Yeah, you overthink everything and miss all the super dirty, hot opportunities.*

Hailee: *I do not!*

Skylar: *What's the dirtiest thing a man has done to you lately?*

The text chain goes quiet. I can only imagine Hailee racking her brain, trying to come up with something.

Aspen: *I'll see all of you tonight. I need to finish and get out of here.*

We all text our goodbyes.

I wonder if Sergey will be there.

I finish my project and pack up to leave. When I get in my taxi, I text him.

Me: *Are you going to be at Nora's reopening?*

Sergey: *I forgot all about it. My brother just reminded me. Are you?*

Me: *Yes.*

Sergey: *Want me to pick you up?*

Me: *I already made plans to ride with Skylar and Hailee.*

A few minutes pass.

Sergey: *Wear a loose skirt and crotchless panties.*

22

Sergey

"How do dozens of steel pallets get stolen without it being an inside job?" I bark at Dmitri, pissed about the money we're losing but more at the fact we've got a traitor in our employment.

"It's nearly impossible," he agrees.

I stare at the list I made of who has keys to our machinery. "More long-term employees. It's starting to make trusting anyone in our employment harder."

Dmitri sighs. "I suppose the more we grow, the bigger the possibility is of this happening."

Both Dmitri's and my phone buzzes.

Maksim: *Meeting at my place. Get here as soon as you can.*

"Shit," I mumble at the same time Dmitri does. Messages from Maksim like that are never anything good. We're already sitting in my car, so I tell Igor to go to Maksim's. "What do you think this is about?"

"No idea." Dmitri glances nervously at me.

When we get inside Maksim's penthouse, Boris is pacing. Obrecht and Adrian are there.

My gut flips, and my jaw spasms. I will it to stop, but like always, I can't control it.

"What's going on?" Dmitri asks.

Boris spins. I've never seen him look so freaked out. "Zamir planted bones from men he had me torture and kill, on the city lot."

"How do you know they're yours?" I ask.

"He made me brand their bones while they were still alive."

"With what?"

"His symbol."

My stomach twists so fast, I get queasy. *His symbol.* The sign of the devil. The mark he signed on my back.

"I'll get with my contacts in the coroner and D.A.'s office," Obrecht states.

"Do you think there is a connection to the stolen steel?" Dmitri asks.

"Zamir is fucking with us. It's time to take him out," I growl.

"Sergey, enough!" Maksim barks. "Get it out of your head, little brother. We have a plan, and we're sticking with it."

"Our plan is flawed. He's more powerful than the O'Malleys and us combined. If we don't eliminate him now, we're asking for more trouble."

Adrian throws a rubber band he was fidgeting with on the table. "Sergey's right. I'm tired of waiting."

"Patience, my brother," Obrecht says.

"Enough with the patience," I state.

Maksim slams his hand on the table. "You two need to cool it. Obrecht, get with your contacts. The minute you find out anything, let us know. We discuss nothing over text or calls. Adrian, go with him. The rest of us keep our cool and continue to implement the plan we have in place *patiently*. When we get new information, then we'll reassess."

"It's time," I insist.

Maksim steps quickly to me and puts his hands on my cheeks. His thumb presses over my twitching jaw, and his icy blue eyes pierce into mine. "You will have your day. We will all step back and watch you destroy him, but you cannot act in haste."

My day with Zamir.

It's never going to come.

It is. I have to be patient.

"I have to go and get ready for the reopening," Boris says.

I forgot about Nora's reopening. I glance at the time. If I'm going to shower and not be late for her surprise entrance, I need to go as well.

We all part, and Maksim reiterates we need to keep things moving until we know more details. I get in my car, and my phone buzzes. Kora asks if I'm going, and we go back and forth.

At least she'll be there, and I can try and take my mind off how bad this day has been. I don't know who stole our steel, but I'm going to find out. I'm not sure what Zamir is trying to do by putting the bones in the lot, but it's flipping me out.

I light up my bowl, take a deep drag, and hold the smoke in my lungs. I slowly exhale. I take several more hits then get out of the car, go into my penthouse, and shower. After I towel off, I pull the handheld mirror out of my drawer and turn. For several minutes, I stare at my back, focusing on the stars, which look like they are part of a brilliant piece of art.

The memory of Kora's fingers and lips touching them this morning sends a wave of emotion crashing through me.

I need to lay off the weed the rest of the night. Too much is going on today, and I'm getting soft.

I put the mirror away and get dressed. I get to the pub a minute before Nora and Boris walk in. I'm not sure if Kora is already here or not, but my brothers and the O'Malleys surround me.

After I congratulate Nora, I glance around and spot Kora, Aspen, Hailee, and Skylar sitting in one of the new round booths. I could pull up a chair, but instead, I slide into the booth next to Kora right as Hailee says, "He said he wanted to lick my furry pussy."

"Well, guess I arrived at the right time," I say, trying to keep a straight face.

Hailee's cheeks turn crimson.

"Hailee, do you have shaving issues?" I ask and slide my hand on Kora's inner thigh.

"No! I'm very well-groomed, thank you very much!" She covers her face with her hands.

Aspen puts her arm around Hailee's shoulders. "Aww, you shouldn't have to defend your furry pussy."

"I do not have a furry pussy!" she says, a little louder than she probably meant to.

"Chill, Hailee! We know your wax schedule." Skylar takes a drink of her martini.

Kora turns to me. "Hailee was on a new dating site."

I slide my hand higher up the inside of Kora's bare thigh. "Did you swipe right, Hailee?" I tease, figuring Hailee's probably never even had a one-night stand.

"It's not that kind of site," she says.

I'm sure it isn't.

"Sergey, we need to know your thoughts," Skylar says.

Aspen groans then holds her drink up and makes a circular motion with her finger to the server.

Skylar's face turns serious. "Can a clit be erect?"

I glance at Hailee. "Hailee, what do you think?"

Hailee tosses a peanut at me. "Stop teasing me!"

I lean forward and curl my pinky so it strokes the top of Kora's slit. She squirms in her seat. "Swollen, marbled, hard, and lickable, yeah. Erect? Mmmm, not sure about that."

"Can a guy have a beefy penis?"

I chuckle. "Do the four of you sit around and make these questions up?"

"Nope! These are legitimate words our previous lovers have whispered in our ears," Skylar claims.

"No shit? Give me a context."

"Kora, it was your man, you tell it."

"Skylar," she groans.

I turn to Kora and grin. "Please. Do tell, Kora."

She rolls her eyes. "Maybe Skylar should tell about the guy who asked if she could come over and blow his impressive member."

"Did you do it?" I ask.

Skylar stirs her drink. "I asked him to send a dick pic first. Then when I got the photo, I told him it was cruel to set a woman up with those types of expectations."

"Ouch!"

She shrugs. "He set himself up."

I ask Aspen, "And what kind of stories do you have?"

She shakes her head. "None. I was married for eighteen years, remember?"

"Kind of sad you met Maksim and missed all this, huh?"

She laughs. "Nope. But you really should hear Kora's story."

"Aspen!" Kora reprimands.

I trace the seam of Kora's panties, and she leans forward, moves her butt closer to the edge of the seat, and puts her elbows on the table.

That's my girl. She wore crotchless panties as I instructed her. I slip my digit on her clit. I barely move it, but she takes a deep breath. I pin her with my eyes. "Did he ask to lick your erect clit?"

"Nope. That would be my date," Skylar admits and drinks several mouthfuls.

"You get all the winners, huh?"

"Yes, she does!" Hailee chirps.

I point at her. "I don't know if you should be talking, furry pussy girl."

"Don't call me that!" Hailee says.

I laugh and turn back to Kora.

She stays quiet.

"Come on. Tell me," I urge.

"He asked what she thought about his beefy penis going in her forbidden zone," Hailee blurts out.

I cock an eyebrow, Kora's face flushes, and I glance at Hailee. "What's a forbidden zone, Hailee?"

Hailee's face returns to purple.

I pull my hand out of Kora's pants and rise. "I need a drink. Nice conversing with you, ladies." I leave then talk to Nora's brothers, Nolan and Declan, at the bar for a good ten minutes. There's a piece of ribbon on the counter. It's kelly green with four-leaf clovers and says congratulations on it. I wrap it around my hand and pretend to fidget with it. I refrain from looking at Kora's table and head through the hallway and into the new break room Nora added for the employees. I text Kora.

Me: *Excuse yourself to the bathroom—second door on your right.*

I wait for several minutes, and Kora finally walks in. I shut the door and attempt to lock it but realize there isn't one.

Oh well. I'll just have to make her come quickly.

"What's wrong?" she asks.

I tug her close to me then fuck her mouth with my tongue, pushing it in and out, until she's shuddering and moaning. I murmur in her ear, "I want to make sure you understand what a real beefy cock and erect clit feel like."

She chokes out a laugh, but I cover her mouth.

"Shh." I spin her in front of the table, hold her neck, and guide her head to the table. I take her wrists and tie them together with the four-leaf clover ribbon. It takes seconds for me to drop my pants to the middle of my ass and lift her skirt. I enter her in one thrust, and she arches her back.

"Oh God!"

"That's my girl. Always wet for me, aren't you?"

"Yes! Oh!" She moves her hips perfectly in sync with my thrusts.

"That's it, lapa." I reach around her and strum her clit.

"Sergey!"

In Russian, I growl, "Your sweet, tight pussy needs my Russian cock, doesn't it?" I hold both of her wrists with my right hand. I push them to the side of her body, and her inner walls clutch my shaft. I thrust harder and circle my fingers faster.

"Oh God... I'm coming...oh God," she shrieks and arches off the wood.

I move her wrists to her back and splay my palm over them, holding them flat so she can't grip anything. I keep her body pressed to the table.

"Sergey," she cries out.

I need to come so she doesn't let the entire bar know we're in here.

I plunge deeper in her, and her body becomes an earthquake tormenting mine. I thrust faster and faster until I spurt my hot seed deep inside her, groaning and falling over her body.

We stay still for several minutes, catching our breath. I kiss the back of her neck. "Come home with me tonight. I'll lick your furry pussy," I tease.

She laughs, and I untie her hands. I spin her around.

"I rode with Hailee and Skylar."

"I'll give them a ride."

"Okay."

I grab some napkins out of the holder and help clean Kora up. I toss them then cup her face in my hands. "We should stop at your place so you can pack a bag for the weekend."

She bites her lip.

My pulse quickens. "Is that a no?"

"I have work to do. I can't ignore it."

"So? Bring it with you." I lean into her ear. "I'll even give you my Wi-Fi code."

She tilts her head and smiles. "Wow! An Ivanov internet secret! You must really like me!"

I run the pad of my thumb over her lips. "I do."

Her hazel eyes bore into mine. "I'm super boring when I work."

"I have some things to do for work, too." I wiggle my eyebrows. "But I'll keep you destressed on our breaks."

Her grin gets wider. "Okay. We'll stop at my place."

I give her one last peck on the lips. "I'll go first. The bathroom is across the hall."

"Thanks."

I leave the room, and Boris is waiting just outside. "Having fun?"

I smirk. *You have no idea, big brother.*

He nods toward the alley. "We have business to discuss."

"I'll be out in a minute." I step into the bathroom, feeling relaxed, and clean up. It doesn't last long. My anxiety builds in my chest within a few minutes during the conversation in the alley.

My brothers, Adrian, and Obrecht are outside.

Obrecht crosses his arms and leans against the brick wall. "Kacper and Franciszek Zielinski just got arrested. The examiner found their DNA all over the bones. Since it's already in the system for their prior convictions, it popped right up."

Boris blurts out, "Zamir planted this on Bruno's sons?"

Obrecht's voice is deadpan. "No. The O'Malleys did."

Fuck! I barely hear the rest of the conversation. I should be happy there's no more risk of linking the bones to Boris, but he hasn't even married Nora yet, and we already owe Darragh.

"Zamir isn't going to be happy his plan for the bones didn't go according to his wishes. We need to strike before he does again," I insist.

After some more conversation, I finally hear the words from Maksim's lips I've waited years for. "Sergey's right. It's our only opportunity. If we're all prepared with a plan, we can take him out."

I'm going to get my chance to show Zamir who he created.

Darragh and Liam join us, and my anxiety only increases further. I light up my pipe and inhale a significant stream of smoke into my lungs, holding it there before slowly releasing it.

Liam was part of making this happen. Now, we also owe him. As much as I like Liam, he's always acted before he thinks.

Boris asks, "Why did you plant evidence regarding the bones against the Zielinskis?"

"How did you know?" Liam replies.

Boris ignores him.

Darragh steps closer in our circle. "The head of the Polish mob visits the head of the Italian mob in prison. Why do you think that is?"

"We aren't sure yet," Boris admits.

Darragh points to my brothers and me. "You've recruited his people, given them enough to feed their families and not turn to him. Instead of staying in your community, you've crossed the line into his. You've put another target on your backs."

Maksim addresses Liam. "What do you know about this?"

"I was in the laundry room on my shift. Two of Rossi's top guys were talking. They didn't say Ivanov, but there was enough to put two and two together. Giovanni agreed to come after you to help put you out of business if Bruno aligned with him against Zamir."

"And you are only telling us this information now?" I seethe, stepping toward him.

Once again, Liam doesn't think.

Liam gets in my face. "I had to verify I was correct. It's the same thing my father would do. I'm not the same hothead who acts without thinking anymore."

I stand speechless, not sure how to respond. That isn't the Liam answer I expected.

"You should have told me," Boris states.

Liam spins and barks, "So you could start a war with the Zielinskis without absolute certainty? And what if I was wrong? Then you'd have another family coming after you, putting Nora and the baby in more danger. Sorry, but I'm not putting my family at any risk unless it's necessary."

The alley goes quiet. *Has Liam changed?*

Darragh clears his throat several times then takes another drag of his pipe. He slowly exhales the smoke. "Bruno's sons will go to prison. Our men inside will kill them. But Rossi has the power of the Poles behind him now, too. And that's a problem for all of us." He steps toward Maksim. "Your family has done well. You've made a lot of enemies in the process. What I'm teaching the O'Malley men is to look at all angles where you may be vulnerable. Do not overlook anyone in the process. I've made the same mistake in the past. I will never do it again. Lead your family wisely because we are now connected."

Joined to the O'Malleys for life. I try my hardest not to scowl at Boris for his actions. Those actions got us here.

We couldn't have started this war between Rossi and Petrov without them.

For life. I take another hit of weed.

Maksim's ice blue eyes pierce Darragh. He finally nods. "We will need to take into consideration the power of them together. The balance will be thrown off considerably."

"Yes. And Bruno will not take it lightly that the bones have been planted against his sons. He will assume you did it. I suggest you move swiftly to handle this issue. The wrath of two men who have lost their sons becomes more powerful," Darragh warns.

"Understood," Maksim replies, but all I feel is a new sense of dread.

No matter what we do, we can't escape mafia life. I hate the thug I've become. My father would roll over in his grave if he knew his sons were masters of torture, killers, and involved with all these mafia families.

There's no doubt in my mind. The false hope I've carried bursts into flames. We're never getting out.

23

Kora

LAST NIGHT, SERGEY AND I WENT TO A BASKETBALL GAME then stayed at my place. We had a great night. It was late when I fell asleep, and like always, he didn't close his eyes until I passed out. When I wake up, he's lying on his stomach with his arms under his pillow.

I've not gotten bored looking at his sexy body. It's chiseled perfection, inked with beautiful designs. His back intrigues me like always, and I stare at the unique and stunning artwork.

I wish he would tell me what happened.

I should give him a massage. I bet he's never let anyone give him one.

I can't help myself. I grab my massage oil, slide on top of him, and start working the knots out of his shoulders.

"Kora, what are you doing?" His voice is firm.

I lean over and press my naked chest over his flesh. I glide my hands over his shoulders. "I'm giving you a massage."

"I'm good. Roll over, and I'll give you one."

I kiss his cheek. "No. I'm giving you one." I move my hand down his back and find a knot in his deltoid. My fingers graze the tip of one of his stars, and he flips me over so fast, it freaks me out.

"Sergey!"

His eyes are lit with anger. The scowl on his face is a mix of hatred and sadness. It tears at my soul. His pecs move up and down faster than they should be after just waking up.

"Sergey." I reach for his face, and he jerks his head toward the window. The tic in his jaw pulses.

Within seconds, he gets off me and goes into the bathroom. He shuts the door.

I sit up in bed, cursing myself for touching his back.

What was I thinking?

I should be allowed to touch my man's back.

He should tell me what happened to him. Maybe I could help him.

He's never going to let me.

I go into my closet and put on my robe. The sound of the shower fills my ears. I sit on the edge of the bed, waiting for him.

Twenty minutes pass. The door opens, and I jump off the mattress. "Sergey, I'm sorry."

A towel is around his waist. He stays positioned so only the front of his body faces me. "You're fine. I need to go."

"It's five thirty."

"I have a workout with my brothers." He throws his shirt on from the night before then steps into his pants.

"Your workouts are at seven."

He freezes, closes his eyes, then releases a stress-filled breath. "I need to go, Kora."

"I'm sorry. I didn't—"

"Don't be sorry. You're fine." He fastens his belt and slides his feet into his shoes. He steps toward me and kisses me. "I'll call you later."

I hold his cheeks. "I'm sorry."

He gives me another chaste kiss. "I have to go."

I stare at him with my insides churning and kicking myself for creating this type of reaction. I've triggered him, and I'm not sure where it puts our relationship.

He leaves. I work out, shower, then meet the girls at the bridal shop. Nora invited my friends and me to her dress fitting, and we all agreed to take the day off work.

At least I have my friends.

All goes well until Hailee gets a call and doesn't take it. Skylar wrestles her for her phone to see who it is then tosses it to me and tells me the code. I open her missed calls.

"Ohh, Liam. You should call him back." Hailee met Nora's cousin, Liam, at the reopening. He's got the hots for Hailee. She won't admit it, but she's dying to go out with him. He's an Irish bad-boy, with gorgeous blue eyes, strawberry-blond hair, and tattoos covering his rock-hard body. The chemistry was sizzling between them, but she's always scared of the bad boys and chickens out for the safe, boring guys.

Hailee goes back and forth, telling us to give her the phone back, and when Liam texts her, asking if she will go to the wedding with him, I reply for her.

Hailee: *I'd love to.*

I smirk and hand the phone to Hailee. "Here. You can thank me later after your trip to O town."

Hailee snatches the phone and sits up. She reads the text. "I can't believe you did this."

"Oh, come on. Live a little for once. You were totally into him. And you gave him your phone number, so you obviously want to go out with him. All these prim and proper guys aren't doing anything for you," I claim.

"You shouldn't interfere with other people's business. You don't know a thing about him."

"Okay, tell us what's wrong with him."

Hailee stares at her phone. My stomach drops. I sit up straighter.

Crap. Maybe I shouldn't have replied.

Nora quietly asks, "Liam told you, didn't he?"

Hailee glances up, and guilt fills her face. She winces. "No. I did an online search on him last night."

The color drains in Nora's face. "Are you scared of him?"

Why would Nora ask that?

What did Hailee discover online?

Hailee's expression turns red from distress. "Should I be?"

Nora confidently states, "No. Liam is a lot of things, but he would never hurt you or any woman."

In the next few minutes, Nora informs us about Liam's long stint in prison for killing the murderer of her father.

The guilt I feel consumes me.

I'm seriously messing up big-time today.

Dmitri's wife, Anna, softly says, "I really like Liam. I don't get any bad vibes from him. Maybe you should give him a chance, Hailee."

Nora blinks back tears and spins. She says to the sales lady, who looks super uncomfortable, "Can you add my veil, please?"

She nervously nods and adds it.

"Can you give us some privacy?" Nora asks.

"Sure." She leaves the room and shuts the door.

I want to tell Nora how gorgeous she looks, but before I can open my mouth, she says, "I think we should get something straight."

"What's that?" I ask.

"Let's not pretend we all believe the O'Malleys or the Ivanovs are always law-abiding citizens. You all grew up in Chicago, minus Anna. You've undoubtedly heard of my family. And I think you understand from your run-in with Wes Petrov at the Cat's Meow, the Ivanovs aren't to be messed with."

We sit in silence, avoiding each other's eyes.

Nora points to me. "If you're going to play in their sandbox, don't pretend you don't understand what they are capable of and use it as an excuse to run down the road. If you do, especially with Sergey, you'll have me to deal with, so fair warning."

"I think Sergey is a big boy and can handle himself," I reply.

"Kora." Aspen shakes her head.

"What? He's a freaking animal, as alpha as they come, and I'm pretty sure emotionally unavailable. And he's made it clear he isn't into relationships."

"He said that?" Anna asks in surprise.

I shrug. "Not in those words, but two plus two is four."

I can't even touch his back. He won't tell me anything about his childhood or demons. I'm not sure how we can ever be anything more than friends with benefits.

"What does that mean?" Nora snaps.

I put my hands in the air. "Easy." Nora's six months pregnant, but I don't think it's her hormones. I've obviously struck a nerve.

She releases a big breath. "Sorry. I've known the Ivanovs and their history forever."

"What's so crazy about their history?" I ask, hoping to find out something about Sergey he won't tell me.

Anna, Aspen, and Nora exchange a glance.

"What?" I repeat.

"They didn't have it easy. It's all I'm going to say. I'm sorry. I think my hormones are messing with my pregnancy brain."

Are you kidding me? You're the one person who could give me some sort of insight, and you're going to play hush-hush, too?

It's her dress fitting. Don't be nasty to her.

I need to speak to Aspen alone. She knows their history if she's marrying Maksim.

I hesitantly smile. "No worries. But for the record, I'm not out to hurt Sergey."

"I know."

The conversation turns to what Hailee is going to do about Liam. I wince then apologize again. I do feel bad I put Hailee in this position. I like Liam, but I didn't know he served time for murder. Hailee isn't the type of girl who is going to be able to deal with that. The worst thing she deals with is kids sniffing glue in her class.

He's an O'Malley. His father is the head of the crime family. Think before you act from now on.

Nora gives Hailee a stern lecture to tell Liam and be honest. The rest of the time is awkward.

There go my invites for any future dress fittings.

When the dress fitting is over, Hailee, Skylar, Aspen, and I get in Maksim's car he reserves for Aspen. Bogden is driving and seems to have become Aspen's new bodyguard. I've met him a few times.

"Hailee, I really am sorry."

She doesn't say anything and turns toward the window.

Skylar and I exchange a guilty look.

Aspen puts her hand on Hailee's. "You like him a lot, don't you?"

Hailee stays silent and still won't look at us.

"Did you go out with him?"

She shakes her head. "No. We've only talked and texted a lot."

Aspen meets my eyes then softly asks, "And you felt a connection?"

Hailee wipes her face. "It doesn't matter."

Aspen tugs Hailee into her chest. "Maybe you should give him a chance? Go to the wedding and see?"

Hailee turns. Her eyes glisten. "I'm not like you three."

"What does that mean?" Skylar asks.

"You all have great sex, hot men, and tons of confidence. I can barely form a sentence when I'm around a man."

"You aren't having hot sex with hot men because you keep choosing to play it safe," Skylar points out.

"You have confidence. You're just more reserved than those two," Aspen says, alluding to Skylar and me and trying to make a joke.

Skylar and I don't respond. It's no secret we're the wildest out of the four of us.

"It's not funny. Liam's the only guy I've been able to talk to...well, ever."

"Then go to the wedding with him," Skylar says. "He did his time. Nora says he wouldn't ever hurt you, and I don't think he would, either."

"I'm not scared of him hurting me. Not physically."

"Then what's the problem? I don't understand," Aspen asks.

Hailee scrunches her face. "He didn't tell me. I had to find out on my own. He said he was living in southern Illinois and was happy to be home."

My chest tightens. "Was Liam in Tamms?"

"Yes. That's what the article said."

"Jesus," I mutter under my breath.

"What?" Hailee asks.

My stomach twists. "Well, he didn't lie. He was down south, and I'm sure he is happy to be home. Tamms is a supermax prison. They treat prisoners like animals. My cousin was there for a few years. Plus, I had to learn all about it during law school. I can't imagine Liam in there or the hell he went through."

Hailee bites on her lip and stares out the window again.

"Hailee, stop being a chicken and go to the wedding with him," Skylar says.

"He murdered someone," she says.

Aspen shifts in her seat. When her eyes meet mine, there's no hiding the fact she's marrying a killer, and I'm sleeping with one.

"You don't know why he did it or anything about the man he killed. Maybe he deserved it," I say.

"Kora!" Hailee says.

"She's right," Aspen says.

Hailee's eyes widen. She gapes at Aspen. She finally says, "Since when are you okay with murder?"

Aspen stays silent for a while, gathering her thoughts. She gently but firmly replies, "I don't think the world is black and white anymore. There are lots of gray areas. I think love drives people to do a lot of things. When evil pops up, it's not always a black and white choice."

"The world isn't the sunshine and rainbows you teach kids about all day long, Hailee," Skylar adds.

Hailee's face turns red, and she glares at Skylar. "You're going to minimize what I do now?"

"No. I wasn't—"

Tears well in her eyes. "Yes, you did. Well, you know what? I may not be in fashion, or a big-shot attorney, or an important person for the city, but I'm proud of what I do. I'm paid a crappy salary and underappreciated by most parents. But I love what I do. And my kids, they have enough doom and gloom and need some sunshine and rainbows." The car stops.

"Hailee, I didn't mean—"

Hailee opens the door, gets out, and shuts the door. She runs up the steps of her building.

"I'll call you later." Aspen gets out and goes after Hailee.

"Crap!" Skylar exclaims.

I sigh and roll the divider window down. "Next stop, please." I hit the button for the divider to go back up.

"You shouldn't have said that," I tell Skylar.

"She's reading into what I said."

"I know, but she's hurting right now."

Skylar groans. "I feel so bad."

I put my arm around her. "Me, too. It's been a shitshow of a day so far."

She turns. "What else happened?"

I haven't told my friends a lot about Sergey and me. Work is hectic right now. My free time involves my limbs wrapped around Sergey's. And my friends all seem to have a million things going on, too. We haven't seen each other as much as we usually do. "If I tell you something, will you keep it between us?"

"Sure."

"I've been seeing Sergey."

"Duh. We all figured you two were banging."

"Yeah, but I like him."

She turns in her seat more. "Let me guess. Emotionally unavailable, cocky as hell, ruler of O town, and you're in over your head and not sure how you're ever coming out because he's going to crush you like a bug one of these days?"

"Wow. You've thought a lot about my relationship," I tease.

Her face falls. "He's an Ivanov."

I tilt my head. "Skylar, are you okay?"

"Yeah. No. I don't know."

"So something is going on with you and Adrian?"

Tears well in her eyes. She closes them. I don't speak for several moments, giving her space to collect her thoughts.

Too much time passes without her answering me or opening her eyes. "Skylar, has Adrian hurt you?"

She shakes her head. "No. But he will."

"Why do you say that?"

"I can't resist him. He's like the oxygen I need to breathe."

That's how I feel when I'm with Sergey.

It slaps me in the face and takes me a moment to recover. "And this is bad?"

"He's not the type of guy to commit."

"He told you—"

"No! We've not talked about it."

"Why not?" I ask.

She swallows hard. "I heard his brother and him talking. Obrecht didn't know I was there."

"And?"

"Obrecht was complaining about their mom being all over them to marry and have kids. Adrian said, "Mom needs to stop living in la-la land, thinking that scenario is for either of us."

"Ouch."

"Yeah. I may date a lot, but I want to find the one and get married. I know I'm almost thirty-seven, but I still have some time, don't I?"

"Yes, of course you do."

"I'm not saying I want kids. Honestly, I don't know if I do or not. But I want someone to want me to be theirs forever. You know?"

I nod. "I do."

"I'm knowingly giving up marriage and kids if I stay with him."

"You should discuss this with him. Maybe you misheard something," I adamantly say.

Skylar squeezes her eyes shut then pins her gaze on mine. "I didn't."

"Maybe he'll change his mind about it with you."

"No, he won't. He's Adrian Ivanov. He knows who he is and what he wants. He's not going to change his viewpoints or what he wants because of me."

"Skylar, you should talk to him."

She nods and blinks hard. "Should and reality are two different things. He won't even let me into who he really is. He's not going to cave on marriage and kids."

"What do you mean he won't let you into who he really is?"

"He gets calls in the middle of the night. Then I won't see him for days until he shows up at my door."

Sergey did that.

Doesn't mean Adrian is a killer, too. He could be seeing other women.

"What happens when he does appear?"

Her face turns red. "There's an animal in his eyes. I-I don't ask questions. My body just submits to him. I-I don't understand it and can't quite explain it."

"He ties you up?"

"No. He...umm...it's like he owns my body."

I rub her back and admit, "I think I know how you feel."

"I think I'm addicted to him. It's freaking me out." The car stops. Skylar looks out the window. "This is me."

We hug. I'm worried about her, but I'm not sure what to say right now to convince her to talk to Adrian. I have my own issues with Sergey I'm not sure how to get past. "I'm here if you need to talk."

She smiles. "I know. Thanks."

I sit back in the seat on the way to my place, thinking about what Skylar admitted. I don't know about kids, but like Skylar, I want someone to want me forever, too. The entire time, all I see is Sergey's face.

I messed everything up this morning by touching his back.

There's so much I don't know about him.

Why does it matter? I agreed that knowing who he is with me was enough.

But is it?

Aspen's statement about black and white and gray replays in my mind. It's my situation with Sergey. He's not black and white. He's gray. If I'm going to be with him for the long term, I need to find peace with it.

I think back to the month I didn't see him and how much it hurt. I didn't even know him as well as I do now, and I could barely breathe some days. I had a hard time focusing on work, and any free time I had, I obsessed over him.

He's the only man who's ever made me feel alive.

I ruined everything this morning.

I don't want to lose him.

When the car pulls up to my building, I get out and walk toward the front doors. I don't notice the black car in front of us.

"Kora!" Sergey's voice calls out, and I freeze.

His arms wrap around me, and he kisses my neck. I melt into his body, feeling protected and loved. It chokes me up. He murmurs in my ear, "Lapa, I'm sorry about this morning."

I nod, but the tears flow.

He spins me into him. His hands hold my face. He wipes my tears with his thumbs, stares into my eyes, then kisses me. He pulls back, looks at me again, then kisses me some more. He repeats it over and over while people bustle all around us.

"I don't want to lose you," I admit, in a barely audible tone.

"Then don't ever let me go."

24

Sergey

"WILL YOU COME TO THE REHEARSAL DINNER AND WEDDING with me," I ask.

Kora smiles. "Like a real date in front of our friends?"

I trace her jaw. Her hazel eyes locked on mine. "Yeah."

She takes a deep breath. Her expression changes. It's a mix of worry and nerves.

"What's on your mind, my lapa?"

"Are you dating anyone else?" She bites her lip.

My pulse beats harder. "No. What makes you ask me this?"

No other man better be touching her. I'll kill him.

Stay calm. Don't be an ass.

"Are you seeing other guys?"

She shakes her head. "No. I don't want to."

I release a breath I didn't realize I was holding. I drag my fingers up her arm then hold her chin. "Kora, I don't want anyone else. I want you."

Her lips twitch. She softly says, "Good. I want to be exclusive."

I already thought she knew about my obsession with her.

My cheeks hurt from smiling.

She wants to only be with me.

"Me, too." I lean over her and roll her on her back. I cage my body around hers. "Does this mean you'll bring some of your things over and leave them here?"

She softly laughs. "You seem to be very interested in me having my things here."

I peck her on the lips then refocus on her face again. "I want you to be comfortable here...with me."

"I am." She reaches down and strokes my shaft. "I'm very comfortable."

"I'm not joking."

Her face falls. She moves her hand to my ass. "I know. I'll bring things here, and you do the same for my place."

The happiest I've ever felt might be right now, at this moment. "Done." I dip my head to her breasts and begin kissing them when my phone rings. I sink my face between her cleavage and groan. "It's Obrecht. I have to take it."

She reaches for my phone on the nightstand and hands it to me. "It's okay."

I trail my fingers on her inner thighs. "Obrecht."

She playfully tousles my hair.

"Meet me at the garage," he says in Russian.

My fingers freeze, then I sit up. I reply in Russian. "Give me fifteen." I hang up and sigh. All I want to do is hang out with Kora tonight.

"What's wrong?" she asks.

"I have to meet Obrecht."

"Right now?"

"Yes. I'm sorry."

Anxiety fills her face. "Should I be worried?"

I stroke her cheek. "No. But I'm not sure how long I'll be gone." I'm not sure why Obrecht needs to see me, but if it's the garage, it won't be only an hour.

This is one of those things she needs to accept. I'm always going to get these calls.

Unless we bury all the Petrovs in the ground.

"So I shouldn't wait up?" she asks, but her face tells me she already knows the answer.

"It might be a few days, my lapa."

She turns her head.

Great. We just took a huge step forward, only for my shit to take us back several.

I turn her chin toward me. "I only want to be here with you right now."

"I wish you would tell me things. It would make this easier for me."

"I'm sorry. I can't." The look on her face almost destroys me. "Kora, I wish I could tell you everything, but I'm not going to ever do anything to put you at risk. If you were serious about wanting me, this isn't something I can make disappear. I'm always going to have these types of situations pop up."

Her silence and worried expression send my anxiety into overdrive.

I swallow hard and ask the question I'm scared to know the answer to. "Can you not handle this? Are you regretting our earlier conversation?"

She closes her eyes and slowly exhales. When she opens them, she gets on her knees and straddles me. She pushes her fingers through my hair. "No. I want to be together."

"Good. Me, too," I reassure her.

"Should I stay here or go home?"

"Here. Come and go as you please. Have your friends over if you want, but stay here."

Her lips twitch. "Okay. I will."

I kiss her, putting everything into it, trying to show her how much she means to me. Somehow, I need to figure out how to make her okay with the fucked-up shit I'll never escape.

She's the light in my life. I don't plan on it, but I blurt out, "I love you."

My chest tightens and blood pounds between my ears. The only woman I've ever said it to before was Eloise, and she didn't return my affection. If anything, it made her run farther from me.

I realize how mistaken I was to say it to Eloise. Not because she ran but because it doesn't compare to how I feel about Kora.

Her eyes soften, and she kisses me. "I love you, too."

I blink hard, choked up from hearing the words I hadn't heard since my mother last said them to me before Zamir abducted her. I fist Kora's hair and kiss her as deeply as I can until I get a hold of my emotions.

"I have to go, and now I have a hard-on," I murmur.

She grinds on my erection and kisses me some more. "Stay."

I pull away from her. "I'm sorry, my lapa. I can't. Let me go take care of this so I can come home to you sooner."

"Will you text me while you're gone? So I'm not worried?"

"I can't, but please don't worry. Everything is in our control. Honestly."

The garage is the one place nothing can go wrong for an Ivanov. Every aspect is our choice. In the end, any evidence anything occurred, we destroy. It's even in the name of one of our relatives who lives in Russia. It's on my mother's side of the family, so the name Ivanov isn't even associated with it.

She puts on a brave smile. "I'll try not to worry then."

I kiss her again, lift her off me, then get changed. When I get to the garage, Obrecht is waiting for me, sitting behind the desk with his feet on it. He pushes the pads of his fingers together. His suit jacket is off, and he unfastened his top three buttons, displaying his chest and neck tattoos.

"Anyone else here?"

"Nope. Just you and me."

"And why did I get chosen for all the fun?"

"Two reasons."

I sit across from him. "What would those be?"

"The Polish fucks you thought were behind the steel are back there."

I briefly close my eyes, and my jaw begins to tic. "Over six years, they've worked for my brothers and me."

"They're on Bruno Zielinski's payroll."

The blood drains from my face. I already knew it, but hearing the Polish mob is officially coming after us doesn't bring me any comfort. "This happened before the O'Malleys planted the evidence on the bones. He had infiltrated us before then?"

"Yes. Are you ready to hear the second reason only you are here?"

My gut drops. "What?"

Obrecht's piercing blue eyes darken. "I finally got it out of Eloise. I thought you might want to get rid of all your wrath instead of sharing the guys back there with your brothers."

Nausea hits me. I lean on the desk to steady myself. "What did she say?"

Obrecht's face hardens. "She was your toy. Wes was paying her to fuck with your head."

My stomach twists, and I turn away from Obrecht.

How could I have not seen it?

"Sergey."

I slowly face him with my insides shaking.

"I'm sorry."

"How long?"

He swallows hard. "Everything was a setup, including how you met."

I grip the edge of the desk. Guilt, shame, and self-hatred sear through me. I don't love Eloise. I love Kora. But it doesn't stop the humiliation.

"It could have happened to any of us," Obrecht says.

"No. Only I would be a big enough idiot to stay with Eloise through all her abuse and continue to want her," I mutter then realize I said it out loud.

Heat flares through my cheeks.

"Fuck. I'm—"

"Just like any Ivanov. In love with pussy and fucked by the Petrovs," Obrecht says in an attempt to make me feel better.

"Don't."

"It's true."

I snort. "No other Ivanov would be set up like this."

"Not true."

"Bullshit," I mumble.

"I was."

I freeze, wondering if he's lying to me.

How does Obrecht get set up? He's the epitome of a GQ pretty boy in an expensive suit with bad-boy flair. He's also one of the smartest people I know.

"Remember Annika?"

"Your girlfriend when you were in your twenties?"

"Yeah."

"No way." He was going to marry her. We never knew why he called it off. Shortly after, he learned how to track and became the best one in our family.

He rises. "Get up and get changed. I spent seven years. You only spent three." He pulls clothes off the shelf, and we both put new attire on.

We spend hours with the Polish men whom I've considered family. When it's clear they were just Zielinski's pawns but don't know anything, we kill them. As much as torturing them makes me feel somewhat better for what Eloise did, my mind is messing with me.

I never think about anyone, except the thug in front of me. Tonight, I can't get Kora out of my head.

What if she's a setup?

She's not.

I have a new need. It's to get home and unravel every part of Kora and torture her with my body until she admits to me she's with me of her own free will. The obsession to know she wants me, and I'm not another pawn in a Petrov or anyone else's game, consumes me.

She said she loved me.

She does.

Does she?

Obrecht thought dealing with the thugs who stole our steel would help me deal with the truth of Eloise. It didn't. I spiral with doubt about Kora and me.

I remove my gloves and throw them in the bin. "Obrecht, I need to get out of here. Can you clean up?"

He pulls a joint out of his pocket, lights it up, and hands it to me. "Yeah. Shower though. Don't skip important steps."

I nod and inhale, but it doesn't calm the thoughts in my head.

When I get home, it's four in the morning. Kora's asleep in my bed.

This can't be fake.

What if it is?

I go into my dungeon room and pace. I look at the wall of tools. I focus on the ones I used to use on Eloise. I told Kora they weren't for her.

I hold the sharpest one in my hand. It's one Eloise used to get off on the most. I hated using it on her. It made me feel like I was on the brink of killing her.

Maybe that's what Kora needs.

What the fuck am I thinking?

Jesus.

I go into the attached bathroom and put water on my face. The man in the mirror's reflection has evil in his eyes. I take another shower. This time it's ice cold. When I get out, I see part of the man I want to be instead of the one I loathe.

I grab the bag out of the trash can and go to the wall with all the impact play toys.

These aren't fucking toys. They are torture devices.

I pick up every one I don't ever want to use with Kora and throw it in the bag.

They all need to go.

I go to the kitchen and get a black garbage bag. I toss every item in the room not bolted to the wall, including the plug I used on Kora, even though it was new and came straight out of the box.

She doesn't need black. She needs pink.

I take the sheets and pillows and toss them down the shoot with the bag.

I go online and order all new items but only ones I know Kora will enjoy and nothing that would cause severe physical pain. I get everything in different colored pinks and rhinestones. I even order new sheets in a shade of hot pink.

No more Eloise.

Why did I not do this sooner?

I shower again, trying to remove any remaining pieces of Eloise on me. It's stupid. All I did was touch things I used on her, but I feel dirty and used.

When I finally scrub my skin so much I need to stop, I go back into the bedroom and lower all the shades so it's pitch black. I turn on the fireplace and watch Kora breathing. I study every inch of her gorgeous face. Her tongue slides a hair out of her mouth and licks her pouty lips. I resist running my finger over her high, sculpted cheekbones. I gently press my lips to her smooth forehead.

She's mine.

I need to make sure.

Don't put your mental shit on her.

I need to tie her up so she can't touch my back.

No. I want her pulling my hair when she comes.

I'll restrain her hands later.

Naked, I crawl under the sheets with my face between Kora's soft, silky thighs. I slide my hands under the sides of her light-pink panties and groan. It's as if she knew how much it turns me on to see her in pink and wore them just for me. They're delicate and soft, and as much as I love them, I'm in the mood to destroy every part of her so she can't think about anything, except how good we are together.

There's a tight pull in my chest. I thought I needed Eloise. It was a lie and wrong on so many levels. I need Kora. She's the light in my darkness. And I need to know she needs me just as much.

I slowly inhale her scent, stroking her hips, and then press my mouth over her panties.

A soft whimper escapes her lips, and her eyes flutter. Her hand moves toward my shoulders and caresses my biceps.

I tug my hands away from her hips, ripping the delicate material, then tracing the curve of her inner thigh.

"Oh," she murmurs, not fully awake.

I snake through her wet folds, utilizing the tip and flat of my tongue at times, lapping her juices, as if it's water and I'm dehydrated in the Sahara.

"Oh God!" she whispers, moving her hands over my shoulders.

I move her hands to my head, and she grips my hair.

That's my girl.

I reach up and manipulate her nipple, circling the outer edge. "Please be real and love me," I mumble in Russian then begin fucking her with my tongue.

Her skin turns warmer and dewy. She pulls at my hair. An emotion-filled groan builds in my chest, and I fight letting her come, continuing to edge her.

"Sergey! Oh God! Please!" she begs. Her body quivers, and her walls clutch my tongue.

I glide up to her clit, refocusing on her bundle of swollen nerves. She shudders hard the moment I make contact.

I wrap my arm under her thigh and splay my hand on her stomach, holding her down. I tease her nipple with my middle finger.

"I missed you," she pants. It's so low, I think my mind might be playing tricks on me.

Did she miss me or only my body?

She isn't Eloise.

"Please don't be like her. Tell me I'm not your toy," I growl in Russian then circle my tongue against her inner walls.

"Sergey!" she cries out and readjusts her hands on my head.

I slow down my tongue. At the same pace, I press my thumb on her marbled clit, make a figure eight over it, and pinch her nipple.

Her back tries to arch, but my palm continues to hold her down.

"Submit to me," I grunt out.

"I already have. I'm yours," she whimpers.

She hasn't.

She has.

My cock leaks with pre-cum. I'm desperate for her in ways I've never thought were possible. It's dangerous. I feel myself spiraling, as if I might break down and lose it. If she's playing me in any way, I'm not sure what I'll do.

She's friends with Aspen.

I met her in a Petrov VIP room.

She's not one of them.

"Please," she begs.

"You're coming with me," I growl and lunge up her body, placing my legs and forearms on the mattress, caging her in.

She strokes my cheek. Her eyes bore into mine. "Thank God you're okay. I couldn't stop worrying about you."

I blink hard. An uncomfortable feeling crawls through my chest.

"I love you," she whispers, softly kissing me, then pulling back and meeting my eyes. "Tell me you're okay?"

I can't. I'm not sure if I am. I answer her by slipping my tongue back in her mouth and fucking it like I just fucked her pussy.

Every moan and caress she gives me is heaven and hell. I want it and her. If I'm her pawn and she's with the Petrovs, she'll destroy me.

I reach for the underside of her knee, push it toward the headboard, and then sink into her tight channel of warmth.

She cries out in my mouth and trembles beneath me.

I don't inch into her, giving her all of me at once. I'm in a trance of cruel emotions and thoughts I've not let myself ever fall into, and I'm not sure how to pull myself out.

I bury my face in the curve of her neck, inhaling her floral scent, licking the bead of sweat rolling down her neck.

Her hands slip to my back, and I freeze mid-thrust.

I reach to grab them, and she moves them in the middle, out of my grasp. She murmurs in my ear, "I love you, and I need all of you, Sergey. Don't hide from me."

I bury my eyes in the pillow, keeping my mouth on her neck. I'm crumbling and can't stop it.

She circles her hips toward me.

I resume my thrusts as her fingers slowly trace over my scars. The pain of that night mixes with her gentleness, destroying me further.

I am the devil. So are you. There is no escaping it. I own you, and when I call you, do not disobey. Zamir's ruthless voice fills my head.

I thrust harder and fist her hair, pulling her neck toward the ceiling. "You're mine," I growl, over and over, while she keeps crying out, "Yes! And you're mine."

"Look at me," I bark when her body shatters around mine and she closes her eyes.

She opens them, and I fixate on those hazel orbs, searching for something to show me she's capable of all that Eloise did to me. All I see is her love for me and goodness.

A violent rush of adrenaline erupts like a broken dam, seeping through every cell of my body in the most intense release I've ever had. I collapse on her, drained, and trying to pull my shit together.

My heart beats so hard, it takes several minutes for me to realize she's still stroking my back and whispering things in my ear. "I love you. You're mine. Don't hide from me."

She can't be working for a Petrov. Beauty and light don't exist among them. It's why Eloise was the perfect pawn to toy with me.

I roll off her and pull her into me, trying to take care of her instead of her taking care of me. I kiss her head. "I love you, too. Don't ever leave me."

"I won't," she promises, lifts her head, and kisses me, as if I'm her world.

I return all her affection. There isn't an ounce of me confused or unsure. She's the good part of my soul.

She's my future. Now, I need to figure out how to get rid of the past.

Kora

I HAVEN'T BEEN HOME ALL WEEK, EXCEPT TO PACK MORE clothes and other items. Every free moment, Sergey and I are together.

Something has shifted in our relationship. It goes beyond our exclusivity conversation. There's something different in his eyes when he looks at me. Sometimes it's painful. I can't put my finger on why or what is causing it. I dig with caution, but he closes up and refocuses on whatever we're doing, ignoring my inquiry to find out what is hurting him.

I step out of the closet so Sergey can zip my dress. He just stepped out of the shower. A towel wraps low around his waist. He stares at his phone. His back is toward me, displaying his beautifully inked skin.

I wrap my arms around his waist. The moment my lips touch his back, he stiffens, but he no longer tries to escape me anymore. It takes several kisses before his hand covers mine and he relaxes.

"You should go to the rehearsal dinner like this. I can brag to all the ladies about how you're mine when they get wet panties."

He spins, grinning, then looks at my pale-pink dress and groans. "Are you trying to make me think about licking your pretty pussy all night?"

I wiggle my eyebrows. "I have a hot-pink one for the wedding."

The day after he returned from wherever he went when Obrecht called him, packages arrived all day. I'm not sure when he cleaned the dungeon out, but he replaced everything with pink items. There were new floggers and paddles, handcuffs and other restraints, and tons of vibrating things. Some I had seen before and some were new to me but nothing sharp or scary looking. The hot-pink sheets and new pillows he didn't put on the dungeon bed until later in the day when two new mattresses showed up. One went in the dungeon and one in his bedroom. Pale-pink sheets and pillows replaced the black ones in his bedroom. New matching headboards and frames with pewter metal replaced the identical black ones in each room. At the same time the beds were being changed out, a few of his employees showed up. They removed the iron grate bolted to the dungeon wall and put an identical one up. On the way out, one of his employees took Sergey aside. He was quiet, but I still heard him. "Boss, can I buy the old one off you?"

"No. You can have it. Enjoy."

"Thanks, man!"

I refrained from laughing out loud and asked, "Why are you replacing everything?"

"You're pink and light, not black and evil."

I wasn't sure how to reply, but he left the room to direct the movers. That was about a week ago.

Sergey eyes my pink dress. "Naughty vixen." He gives me a chaste kiss and spins me. He moves my hair over my shoulder and kisses my neck while slowly zipping the dress.

I turn back and put my arms around his neck. "Are you going to dance with me tomorrow night?"

"Is that your way of asking if I know how?"

"No!" I say, laughing.

"You can thank Maksim for my dancing skills tomorrow night."

"What do you mean?"

He gives me a boyish grin. "When I was eighteen, he dragged my brothers, Adrian, Obrecht, and me to dance lessons."

"What kind?"

"We each had to pick. It took a year for all the lessons."

I bite my smile. "Really?"

"Yep."

"What did you pick?"

"Hip-hop."

A laugh escapes.

"What are you laughing at?"

"You know how to hip-hop dance?"

His face slightly flushes. "And tango, merengue, salsa...all the main ballroom ones."

"So, the Ivanovs can all dance?"

"I'll let you be the judge of that."

I slide my hand under his towel and palm his ass. "I'm feeling a bit intimidated."

He leans into my ear. "Dancing is all about submitting and letting my body lead yours. You'll be okay, my lapa." He pulls back, and a cocky expression appears on his handsome face.

I squeeze his ass. "Get changed, or we'll be late. And I anxiously await the Ivanov hip-hop moves tomorrow night."

"Focus on Obrecht. Give him a few shots, and he'll take over."

"Well, I wouldn't want to miss that," I say in amusement. The few times I've seen Obrecht, he's been in a tailor-made suit without a tie and a few buttons unfastened, his blue eyes laser-focused on whatever is going on, and his neck and chest tattoos on display. If Hailee weren't so against dating a bad boy, I would tell her to hop on him and find out what's underneath his panty-melting, serious exterior.

Sergey walks into his closet then comes back out in a black designer suit and maroon shirt.

"You're one sexy man," I say and straighten his collar even though it doesn't need to be. We kiss then leave and get to Boris and Nora's rehearsal dinner.

Sergey and I walk close together, with his arm around my waist, and everything feels perfect. For the first time in my life, I feel like I belong to someone. He seems to love me unconditionally, no matter my flaws. Traits I have that other men couldn't handle, he encourages, telling me how much I turn him on and praising me for my ability to take charge and fight for things I believe in or those who can't. And every day, he showers me in his love, reminding me I'm his and he's mine.

I've never walked next to a man and felt proud to be his until now.

He releases me when we get to the back of the restaurant where Maksim, Aspen, Dmitri, and Anna are. We all hug and exchange greetings then Sergey tugs me back to him.

It's the same for his brothers. There's a possessive nature they all hold with their women. And Aspen and Anna appear as happy as me to be thoroughly cherished by their men.

Adrian and Obrecht join us. I don't see Skylar, and my heart drops. I haven't talked to her since the day of the dress fitting. She's been short with her replies and hasn't answered my calls, sending messages saying she's tied up with work.

The O'Malleys are here. I spot Liam across the room, alone. Hailee has also avoided my attempts to talk. Nora invited all three of us to the wedding, so I make a mental note to call Skylar and Hailee tonight to see if they are going solo or with Adrian or Liam.

Boris and Nora come in. The room gets louder, but Boris's face has an expression I've never seen on him before. He beelines directly to us. He pulls the Ivanov men to the corner.

I glance at the front of the room. Nora looks pale, and her family is circling her. "What do you think is going on?" I ask Aspen and Anna.

They both shake their heads with worried looks on their faces.

A few minutes pass. Boris bolts to the front of the restaurant. The Ivanov men follow him. Adrian and Obrecht leave. Boris says something to Nora, and Maksim steps between Liam and Boris.

Boris leaves the restaurant. Sergey, Maksim, and Dmitri pull Aspen, Anna, and me separately aside.

Dark, cold eyes stare at me. "I have to leave. Stay and have fun then go directly to my place," Sergey instructs.

"What's happening?"

"Don't ask me questions. If I'm not back in time, go to the wedding tomorrow, and I'll meet you there."

"What?"

"Kora, tell me you'll do as I say," he barks.

"Okay."

He sighs. "I'm sorry." He pulls me into him and kisses me. "I love you."

Am I going to see him again?

"Sergey—"

He puts his finger over my lips. "Be the strong woman I know you are right now. Nora will need it."

I stand straighter and inhale deeply.

He smiles. "That's my lapa." He pecks me on the lips. "I love you." He leaves with his brothers, and Skylar walks in.

"Hey. Have you seen Adrian? Bowmen was on one of his kicks and kept me late."

"You need a different boss, but they just left."

She scrunches her face. "What do you mean left?"

I shake my head. "Boris walked in, and they all just left. Sergey said if he's not back, to meet him at the church tomorrow."

She pulls out her phone and checks it. She mumbles, "Something came up. I'll meet you at the wedding tomorrow." Her eyes widen, and she drills them into mine. "What is going on, Kora?"

"I honestly don't know."

Aspen joins us. "Skylar, you look beautiful."

"Where did they go?" Skylar demands.

Aspen shakes her head. "I don't know."

"Please tell me. I can't handle not knowing anymore."

"We honestly don't know, Skylar," I say.

"Is this normal for you? Always being in the dark?"

Aspen's eyes widen. "No. It's not an everyday occurrence. And Maksim doesn't keep me in the dark. He tells me what I need to know. The things he deems dangerous for me to know, he doesn't reveal."

"And you're okay with it?" Skylar asks.

Aspen sticks her chin out. "Yes. He would die for me. All he thinks about is how to protect and love me. So, while I worry about his safety and don't enjoy him not being here with me, I know he wouldn't have left if it weren't important. And when he returns, whatever is safe to tell me, he will."

Skylar turns to me. "And you? You feel the same?"

"Yes. I don't like it, but there isn't any other choice, except not to be with Sergey. I won't choose that option."

She closes her eyes. "What have we all gotten involved in?"

Aspen nervously glances at me. She softly asks, "Have you talked to Adrian about this?"

Skylar sarcastically laughs then she turns away and covers her face.

Aspen and I exchange a horrified glance, and I pull Skylar into me. "Hey."

"I need to go."

"Okay, let's go."

She sniffles and shakes her head. "No, you stay."

"Aspen, you're staying with Nora tonight?"

"Yes, that's always been the plan."

"Okay. We'll see you tomorrow. Skylar, you come stay with me at Sergey's tonight."

"No, really—"

"It's not up for discussion. Let's go."

We hug Aspen, sneak out the side door, and hop in a cab. We say nothing until we get inside Sergey's.

"Have you spoken to Hailee?" Skylar asks.

"No. I was going to call both of you when I got back from dinner tonight."

"So you don't know if she's going to the wedding with Liam or not?"

"No." I pull out my phone. "Let's call her."

She doesn't answer, so I text her.

Me: *Skylar and I are having a slumber party at Sergey's. Want to join us?*

Hailee: *No thanks. I can't.*

Me: *Hailee, we're sorry about the last time we saw you. Are you going to hate us forever?*

Hailee: *I never said I hated you.*

Me: *I'm calling. Answer.*

I hit dial and put it on speaker. It goes to voicemail.

"She's never held a grudge before," Skylar says.

Hailee: *I can't talk right now.*

Me: *Why not?*

Hailee: *I can't. I'll see you tomorrow.*

Me: *Hailee, why can't you come over or talk?*

Hailee: *I need to be alone and think. I'm turning my phone off now. I'll see you tomorrow.*

Me: *Okay. We love you.*

Hailee: *Love you, too. Night.*

Me: *Night.*

"Twenty bucks says she still doesn't know if she's going with Liam," Skylar says.

"Please tell me she told him by now."

Skylar shrugs. "She had to tell him something, or she would have been there tonight."

We spend the rest of the night watching rom-coms, ignoring the elephant in the room, and glancing at our phones for unsent messages.

When morning comes, we work out, eat a small breakfast, and get ready for the wedding. When it's the last minute to leave without being late, we get in a cab and go to Skylar's for her to put her dress on.

"Let's go see Nora," I say when the guys still aren't in the church. My insides are shaking. I'm past the point of worrying about Sergey. Skylar looks slightly ill, too.

I straighten up. "We need to look happy for Nora. Come on." We find the room Nora's in and step inside.

"Jesus, Mary, and Joseph! What did you do to your dress?" her auntie shrieks in horror.

Skylar and I cover our mouths. Nora had the seamstress remove the high neckline and create an off-the-shoulder look with her dress.

"I think she looks stunning," Aspen says.

"Me, too," Anna agrees.

Her auntie steps forward and gapes at her chest. "You have way too much cleavage for church."

"It could be a lot worse," I interject.

"Did you ever look at the tabloids? The women on there have much more hanging out than Nora," Skylar adds.

"What about my sleeves? They look great, don't they?" Nora asks, biting her smile.

Her auntie glances at the sleeves. "Yes, they are beautiful. Let me try and find you a shawl."

"No. She's not wearing a shawl," I firmly state.

Jesus, who does this woman think she is? Nora warned us, but jeez.

Her auntie slowly turns and throws me daggers. "Who are you, exactly?"

Here we go.

Kill her with kindness for Nora's sake.

I step farther inside and hold out my hand. "I'm sorry to be rude. I'm Kora Kilborn."

329

Her face scrunches. She takes my hand. "I'm sorry, your name sounds familiar. Have we met before?"

"No. I would remember you," I sweetly say and force a smile.

"She's Chicago's top divorce attorney," Skylar blurts out.

Her auntie's eyes widen. She snaps her fingers. "You were Mary Kelly's attorney, weren't you?"

"Sorry, I can't discuss my clients."

"You were. You took her husband to the cleaners."

I give her a tight-lipped smile.

"Did any of you see Boris?" Nora asks.

"No," her auntie says.

Skylar and I shake our heads. My stomach flips again.

Her auntie continues, "You did an excellent job. Her ex-husband is a rat. She said you found assets she didn't even know they had. He was begging for her to take him back."

"Tell me she didn't go back," Skylar says.

"Do you know Mary, too?" her auntie asks.

"No. But he sounds like an ass."

"Oh, he is."

Her auntie goes on and on, and I somehow manage to get her out of the room and away from Nora.

Twenty minutes until the wedding, and not one of the guys are here.

Where are they?

Nora's auntie is saying something. Darragh comes up and pulls her away.

"Thank God. That woman is a nightmare," Skylar mutters.

"That's an understatement. Hailee better think twice about getting with Liam. His murder wrap is nothing compared to her," I quietly add.

Skylar snickers.

I glance around, and Maksim's face catches me from the window.

I grab Skylar's arm. I see Adrian, Obrecht, and Dmitri through the window.

Where are Sergey and Boris?

Skylar sighs in relief then seems to realize I'm still waiting to see Sergey. She puts her arm around my waist. "Come on."

My voice cracks. "Where is he?"

"Let's go find out."

I put my hand on my stomach, trying to stop it from twisting. The closer we get, the sicker I feel. Sergey is nowhere.

"Where is he?" I ask, interrupting the conversation the Ivanovs are having in aggressive Russian.

Maksim hesitates.

"Tell me where he is," I demand, trying to hold in my tears.

Dmitri grabs me by the waist and leads me toward the side door. "He's in here."

"What happened to him?"

"He's unharmed. He just...he needed a minute." He guides me inside and stops outside another door. He knocks. "Sergey."

There's no answer, and my heart pounds harder.

"Dmitri, why isn't he answering?"

"Sergey," Dmitri growls, pounding on the door.

Time seems to stop. Dmitri looks up then reaches for the key above the door and unlocks it.

Dmitri and I rush in.

Sergey's naked, shaking, and staring at his back in the three-way mirror. He doesn't even flinch when we come in. It's like he's in a trance.

"Shit," Dmitri mutters and puts his arm out to stop me from getting any closer. He barks, "Sergey! It's over!"

"Get out!" I shove past him.

"Kora!"

I spin and enunciate, "Get. Out!"

He hesitates. "I'll be right outside the door." He leaves, and I bolt the lock.

I cautiously approach Sergey. I reach for his back, and he flinches. His jaw spasms faster. His breath is labored, and his eyes glisten.

I wrap my arms around his waist and put my head on his back. "Baby, come back to me."

Dmitri said he was unharmed. How is this unharmed?

I kiss his back, focusing on his scars and holding him as tightly as possible. "I love you. I need you to come back, Sergey."

He puts his trembling hand over mine and caresses me with his thumb. He squeezes his eyes. "It's over."

"What is?"

"The devil is dead."

"Who's the devil?"

"Zamir."

Zamir who?

Petrov.

Oh God! He did this to him?

Zamir is dead.

I move in front of Sergey, not releasing him. I slide my hands up his chest and onto his cheeks, forcing him to look at me.

He blinks hard, as if he's trying to figure out who I am. His eyes aren't dark or light but more lifeless.

I've never felt so scared. "It's me, baby. I miss you. Come back to me."

I slowly caress his jaw where it spasms. His shaking hands move to my ass. "I was only twelve."

Tears escape my eyes at the startling realization of what he's telling me. He was just a boy—an innocent child.

He chokes out, "Lapa."

I force a smile and push his hair off his forehead. "Yeah. It's me. I love you. Come back to me."

"It's over. He's finally dead," he barely breathes.

I tug his head toward mine then press my lips to his, looking at his eyes, trying to see the warmth I'm used to, but it's not there. I kiss him again and again until he begins to kiss me back.

His hand tugs my hair, and his other palms my ass. Slowly, he begins flicking his tongue in my mouth, taking possession of me the way he always does.

Somewhere in that kiss, he unzips my dress and turns me against the middle mirror. He picks me up, and I wrap my legs around him, submitting to him as if it's second nature.

He slides my panties to the side and enters me in one thrust. As he fucks me against the mirror, he never takes his mouth off mine.

His thrusts are fast, needy, and as hungry as his kisses ravishing my mouth. I cling to him, whimpering in his mouth as his cock and mouth devour my body.

I begin to unravel, pressed against the glass. He detonates inside me, growling like a wild animal, then burying his head in the curve of my neck.

He doesn't release me. His chest heaves against mine.

"I love you," I whisper in his ear, not sure if he's out of his trance or not but trying to find him.

"I love you, too, lapa. Don't stop loving me, please."

I can't be sure if it's hot tears on my skin or his sweat.

"Look at me," I order him.

He slowly pulls his face away from my neck. His eyes are glassy, but I see life in them again, along with pain and fear.

"I will *never* stop loving you. *Never.*"

He closes his eyes and presses his forehead against mine.

Somehow, I get him in his tux and down the aisle in time. I exchange a glance between Maksim and Dmitri, kiss him, then sit with Skylar off to the side where I can watch him. He stands between his brothers. They calmly talk to him, and to the outside world, Sergey's a demi-god in a tuxedo—a strong, gorgeous, dangerous man. But I still notice the tic in his jaw. It's not as bad as it was, but it occasionally starts to flare. And the little information he shared with me rips at my soul. I'm angry, heartbroken, and trying to piece everything together.

Boris comes out of the confessional, and the priest runs away green. A few minutes later, Father Antonio returns, and Darragh goes to get Nora.

By the time the ceremony is over, Sergey seems to be his usual self again.

"You're stunning, my lapa," he says, as if seeing me for the first time. His eyes are bright and have a smoldering look he always reserves for me.

We're around people all night. We eat, drink, and dance. Sergey laughs and holds me close to him. Or maybe it's me not leaving his side. Minus my ongoing worry about Sergey, everything is perfect, and the Ivanovs and O'Malleys all celebrate. Maksim makes a beautiful toast and ends it by saying, "To your beautiful future. Nostrovia."

We hold our glasses high in the air, and the room echoes in, "Nostrovia."

I take a sip then put my glass down.

Sergey tugs me closer to his body and leans into my ear. "You're my future, my lapa. We can have one now."

I pick my glass back up. "Nostrovia."

26

Sergey

Six Weeks Later

KORA AND I SPEND EVERY NIGHT TOGETHER. MOSTLY, IT'S AT my penthouse, but sometimes we go to her place. She's moved beyond an obsession. She's the lifeblood of my existence. Every moment I spend with her, I enjoy. She brings me happiness I didn't know could exist. And she loves me unconditionally.

Since the wedding, I've slowly been telling her everything, like how Zamir came to own us, my mother's suicide and the guilt I felt around it, and all the other toxic memories I've held inside for so long.

In return, she tells me about her childhood. One thing we have in common is we both grew up in poverty, but it ends there. My parents encouraged education and loved my brothers and me. Until my father died, there was laughter in our home. While I blocked a lot out about my past, I did have a loving family as my foundation. Kora's childhood wasn't ever rosy. She was made fun of for studying, had to deal with an environment of drugs, alcohol, and sometimes domestic abuse. Her brother died on the corner from a drive-by shooting while dealing crack with her cousins.

Kora hasn't spoken to her mother or sister since she confronted Neicy. One night, I get her to finally tell me everything they said.

"Is it wrong to cut them off?" she asks.

I stroke her cheek and refrain from telling her my exact thoughts. The truth is, I don't want her near them. But I also know it's her family, and it makes it complicated. Instead, I choose my words carefully. "Wrong, no."

"But I shouldn't, right?"

I hate the guilt she carries regarding her family. They've only used her, but I don't want to be the reason she stays away from them. Ultimately, it needs to be her choice and one she can live with forever. "You don't owe them anything. You've been beyond generous and deserve love and respect. It's up to you if you choose to have them in your life."

She closes her eyes, and I can feel her grappling with the pain. I pull her closer and kiss her head, not knowing how to help her and telling myself to keep my thoughts about her family to myself.

The more we tell each other, the closer we get. Now that Zamir is dead, something inside me has unraveled. While I haven't told Kora every detail of what I've done, nor will I ever, she knows my major scars.

"Go to sleep, my lapa. It's late." I turn her on her side and spoon her until we both fall asleep. The next morning, I meet my brothers at the gym for our daily workout.

Liam and Killian show up almost as soon as we step inside.

"There was another attack on the Rossis," Liam informs us.

Somehow, the Petrovs continue to reign. My brothers and I can't figure out who is pulling the strings, but the recruiting and destruction hasn't stopped.

"Did Darragh find out who's in charge yet?" I ask.

"No. We were hoping Obrecht found out," Liam states.

"Dead ends," I admit.

Killian stretches his shoulder. "We need to take out some Zielinskis."

My chest tightens. It isn't as bad as before when Zamir was alive, but I hate being involved in any of this, especially now that I have Kora.

"Bruno is gaining too much power," Liam states.

"We took care of Zamir. Tell Darragh we're good with the O'Malleys handling this one," Maksim orders.

Liam cracks his knuckles and looks behind his shoulder. No one is in the gym, except us. My brothers and I don't allow it this time of the morning so we can always speak freely when we work out. But I imagine when you spend years in prison, you get used to looking over your shoulder. He steps closer. "The hit on his sons is set up for tonight."

"Will it be traced to Rossi as we discussed?" Maksim asks.

Liam's eyes grow darker. "Yes. Our boys inside won't fail."

"So much for their alliance," Dmitri mutters.

"We must be prepared to take out more Petrovs. When the Italians and Poles start going at it, this war is going to escalate quickly. My father said to make sure you are ready," Liam warns.

"We are always ready."

"He's afraid you'll get lax now that Zamir is dead."

"Tell your father if he's got any worries or misgivings about the Ivanovs, then he can get his ass in here and tell me to my face," Maksim growls.

Killian chuckles. "Told you you'd irritate Maksim."

Liam throws daggers at him with his eyes. "Noted. Now, how many of you can bench more than me?"

"Let's see what you got," Boris says and racks the weights.

Liam removes his jacket. What appears to be a new tattoo is inked on his forearm. It's Celtic with two hearts. One is upside down and one right side up. The middle has a Celtic H. It's shiny.

"You just get that?"

"Yesterday."

I peer closer. "Looks good. Our guy do it?"

"Yep."

"He did a great job."

He nods and picks up a weight.

"How's the house coming?" Dmitri asks before I can ask him what the H represents.

"Great. The new floor got installed yesterday. Anna's amazing, by the way."

Dmitri beams. "Yep, my kotik knows her stuff."

"Well, she's been a real sweetheart to stop me from making crazy mistakes. I think staring at concrete for fifteen years took away my ability to put anything together. I get a bit giddy around color."

Dmitri adds some weights to the squat machine across from the bench press station. "She's happy to do it."

We all take Liam on, but no one can outlift him. The six of us mix cardio and weights and are all sweating by the time we finish. After our workout, we shower and part ways. I get in the car, and a text comes in.

Adrian: *Meet me at my house after your workout. I got it.*

Me: *On my way.*

About time.

Kora is still trying to settle Selena's divorce. Jack is getting more aggressive. Kora admitted to me he's been calling her office almost daily now. She made me promise I wouldn't

MAGGIE COLE

find him and do anything to jeopardize her case before she would tell me. It took every ounce of restraint I had, but I didn't want Kora to not trust me with these types of things in the future. She agreed to file a restraining order and let me provide her with one of our bodyguards.

Selena is on lockdown. She only goes on the roof, and all her groceries are delivered. Court dates keep getting pushed back, and Kora's maneuvering legal hoops daily.

I've been after Adrian to get me anything on Jack. I want to destroy him so Selena can settle her divorce and Kora doesn't have to deal with him anymore. Nothing has turned up until now.

What did Adrian find?

I send Kora a text.

Me: *Something came up. I need to go to Adrian's. I won't be back by the time you leave for work.*

She sends me back a selfie of her pouting.

Me: *I can think of things you can do with those lips tonight.*

She sends me a seductive pose with her finger on her lips.

It's all it takes to make my dick hard.

Me: *You're getting cuffed to the iron wall tonight.*

She sends me prayer-hand emojis.

I laugh and send her back a gif of a woman's ass being paddled.

Heart-eye emojis.

That's my naughty, sexy girl.

The car stops outside Adrian's.

Me: *Love you.*

My phone rings.

"Lapa. You okay?"

"Love you, too. What time should I expect the fun and games to begin?" she purrs.

"That depends."

"On?"

"What's your lunch schedule like?"

I can almost hear her smiling. "Thirty-minute opening at noon."

"Then you better wear your crotchless panties. Try those sparkly pink ones I just got you."

"Yes, sir."

I groan. "Don't get me harder when I have to wait over three hours to taste your pretty little pussy."

She laughs in her naughty tone. "Gotta go. Love you."

"Love you, too." I hang up, smiling, and go into Adrian's building.

When I get the door between the elevator and his penthouse, I hear Skylar's voice.

"You've kept me waiting here all night, and now you have perfume on you."

"It's not what you think!" he growls.

"You must take me for a fool, Adrian!"

"How many times do I have to tell you I'm not seeing anyone else and I don't want to?"

"Then tell me where you were."

"I told you I was working."

"Where? Doing what?"

Silence.

"Goddamnit, Adrian!"

"Skylar—"

"No! Let me go!"

"Don't leave like this."

"Then don't tell me to wait in your bed all night and arrive smelling like a whorehouse!"

"Skylar!"

"No. Don't try to kiss me, smelling like whoever you just fucked all night."

"I did not fuck anyone."

"Goodbye, Adrian."

"Skylar, don't—"

The door opens, and Skylar wipes her face.

"Morning?" I wince.

She pushes past me and leaves.

"Skylar!"

She gets in the elevator.

Adrian slams his hand against the wall. "Shit."

"I'd ask how you're doing, but..."

Adrian stomps inside, shaking his head. Perfume trails behind him.

In Russian, I say, "She's right. You reek."

"Thanks to your little assignment." He tosses an envelope at me.

"What do you mean?"

His face hardens. "I had to spend the night in an underground strip club slash whorehouse, telling multiple women to stop grinding on my cock, to get that." He points to the package.

"Why don't you just tell Skylar?"

"That I was at an underground club getting lap dances all night all in the name of Ivanov business? Yeah, that would go over real well."

"It might be better than her thinking you were screwing around on her."

He sighs. "I need a shower. I'm going to burn these pants. Your evidence is self-explanatory. Give me something better next time. Let me break someone's neck or some other assignment that doesn't involve pussy juice on my new slacks." He walks down the hall.

"You should tell her," I yell after him. "I'll tell her you aren't lying."

He slams the bathroom door, and I leave. I get in my car and open the envelope.

Oh, Jackie boy, you are going to get fried.

Jack's snorting coke off multiple strippers' bodies. In another photo, he's getting a blow job. In another, he's pounding into a woman while another woman stands behind him and gives it to him with a strap on.

Not the sort of things that are going to be forgiving when you're trying to take your company public.

I glance at my watch and tell Igor to go to Jack's house. My guess is if Adrian just got in, he's trying to pull his shit together before going into the office.

As expected, he's home. I wait until right before eleven thirty. He finally exits his building. I get out of the car and meet him near his vehicle.

"Remember me?"

His eyes widen, but he takes a step back.

I hold the envelope out. "Ah. I come in peace."

"Peace?"

I shake the package. "Take it. You don't want this getting in others' hands."

His eyes turn to slits. "What is it?" He takes it.

"It's self-explanatory. By the way, if you come near Kora or Selena, you're going to have more significant issues than this. By five o'clock, your attorney is to call Kora's office and tell her you're ready to settle. I'll text you around three with what you'll be giving Selena."

"I'm not sure who the fuck you think you are, but I'm not giving my wife anything. There will be no divorce, and she will come back to me as soon as I find her."

I'll deal with his threats after Selena gets her assets.

I step so close to him, I taste his stale, hungover breath. His eyes are still bloodshot. "When you open the package, I'm sure you'll find her terms agreeable." I pat his shoulder, and he flinches. "Five o'clock is the deadline, or I blow up your deal to go public."

I spend lunch under Kora's desk and then go to Selena's. When I get there, she doesn't answer, so I go up to the roof.

When I step out, I run into Obrecht. "What are you doing here?"

His T-shirt drips with sweat. "Working out. The turf you installed is awesome."

I forgot he bought the penthouse.

"Why are you here?" he asks.

"I need to talk to Selena."

"Who is Selena?" he raises his eyebrows.

I glance around. *Where is she?*

"There she is." I point to the corner to several concrete loungers. Selena is reading on her laptop and has head-phones in. She's wearing shorts, a long sweater, and sunglasses. Her flip-flops are next to the lounger.

Obrecht whistles. "Nice legs. How do you know her?"

"Long story, but she knows Kora, and we're friends. I need to talk to her about something."

Obrecht tears his eyes away from her and glances at his watch. "I need to get ready. See you later." He glances back at Selena then disappears.

I stroll across the roof, and when I get closer, I can hear Selena humming. I tap her shoulder, and she jumps.

I hold my hands in the air. "Sorry! It's me."

She sits up. "Oh, hey! What are you doing here?"

I sit on the lounger next to her. "I need to know something."

"What's that?"

"What do you want to get from your divorce?"

A line forms above her glasses. "What do you mean?"

"I need a list of what assets you want."

I can faintly see her eyes squinting through her glasses. "Kora has it."

"Right. But Kora isn't going to tell me your confidential information, is she?" I flash her a smile.

Her voice drops, and she glances around. "Sergey, why do you need to know this?"

"Can this stay between us?"

"I can't tell Kora?"

"I would prefer you didn't."

I don't like keeping secrets from Kora, but my gut says she won't like what I'm doing. Men like Jack need to be dealt with a different way. And I'm not oblivious to the fact that once Selena gets her assets, he might not move on. There is a time and place for everything. Kora worries my way of dealing with things will harm Selena's case. So in my eyes, there's only one way to approach this. Get her divorce settled then I can deal with him if he chooses to keep bothering her.

She hesitates then slowly nods. "Okay. I promise."

Calmness replaces the anxiety in my chest. "Thank you. Jack's attorney will call Kora before five today. He will assure her Jack is ready to settle, and whatever you want, you will get. Please tell me what you would be happy to walk away with."

"I don't want to be homeless. I don't need a lot, but I don't want to be on the street."

"Do you want your marital home?"

She shakes her head. "No. I don't want any reminders of that prison. Honestly, I would rent or buy this place off you if it's available. I like it here. I-I feel safe. I looked at what the other units similar to mine went for, and I should be able to swing it, assuming I get what Kora said I'm entitled to based on the law."

I smile. "If you want it, then it's yours. But what did Kora say you should get?"

She nods to the computer. "I have it in an email if you want to see it?"

"Please."

She types quickly then hands me the laptop. "Kora said this should be the minimum, but honestly, I don't need everything on there. I'm not sure what I would even do with all that money. The most important thing is for me never to see him again and not be on the street."

I glance at the email Kora sent. There are millions of dollars of assets and enough to last Selena a lifetime if she's smart with it. "Can I forward this to my email?"

"Sure."

I send it to my account and shut the laptop. "Is there anything else not on this list you want? Possibly something you left at the house with sentimental value?"

Her expression darkens. "No. There's nothing I want from that prison."

I pat her hand. "Okay, Selena. Can you try to act a bit surprised when Kora calls? I'm not trying to dupe her, but she won't like me interfering. She's dealing with laws, and my methods are..."

Selena's lips twitch. "Not abiding by the law?"

"Yeah," I admit.

"If you can get me out of Jack's grasp sooner rather than later, I will be nothing except grateful to you. This will stay our secret."

"Thank you." I rise and leave. As soon as I get in my car, I text the list of items to Jack from a burner cell so it isn't traceable to me. I'm not worried about Jack telling anyone, but I always cover my tracks.

Now I'll need to worry about phase two.

I pick up my phone.

Me: *Can you do me a favor?*

Obrecht: *What's that?*

Me: *The woman on the roof...can you keep your eye on her?*

Obrecht: *Want to tell me why?*

Me: *She's about to settle a divorce, and her ex isn't going to be happy.*

Obrecht: *This guy knows where she's at?*

Me: *No. I'll send you his picture. If you see him hanging around, let me know.*

Obrecht: *Done.*

I send a picture of Jack from his company website.

Obrecht: *Looks like a prick.*

Me: *Yep.*

Obrecht: *What did he do to her?*

Me: *I don't know all the details, but he hurt her.*

Obrecht: *Then I kind of hope he tries to come near her on my watch.*

Me: *Thanks. Message me if you see him.*

Obrecht: *Will do.*

I sit back in the seat, tapping my fingers on my thigh. Now I just have to patiently wait for Kora to wrap this divorce up.

One thing Zamir instilled in me was patience. But I'm about out of it with Jack. No one is going to threaten my woman.

27

Kora

"Sign here," Larry instructs Jack.

My heart beats faster as he scowls, staring at the forms. This has been the most challenging divorce case I've ever had. When Larry called me yesterday, I was surprised. I wasn't expecting him to tell me Jack was ready to settle. When he sent over the proposal, and it was everything plus ten percent higher than what Selena was legally entitled to, I was happy but suspicious.

I told Selena it might mean Jack is hiding additional assets he expects to significantly increase and wants to protect himself from giving her portion to her down the road.

"I don't care about getting more. I just want out. This is more than I ever imagined I would get," Selena replied.

She signed the paperwork earlier this morning. I wasn't going to subject her to being in a room with Jack, nor do I feel it's safe. I've not disclosed her location. I believe it's in her best interest to continue to lay low for a while until he cools off. I also advised her to hire a bodyguard once she receives her funds.

Jack grinds his molars and shakes his head, re-reading what he verbally agreed to give Selena. He slowly takes the pen from Larry and signs. He tosses the pen on the conference room table and rises then looks at me. His mouth opens then shuts. With a final glare, he leaves the room.

It shocks me. I expected a barrage of nasty comments from him. It's what I've grown used to regarding his blatant attempts to threaten me. Since I filed a restraining order, I had to get a judge to sign off on this one meeting. It happened faster than I thought it would. The security officer from our building and the bodyguard named Viktor, who Sergey insisted upon, are in the room.

Larry rises and holds out his hand. He smiles. "Well, we did it."

I groan inside, shake his hand to stay professional, and can't help but think about how Larry is a weasel. "I'll take care of filing this with the court."

He snorts. "I expected as much."

I motion to the door so he takes the hint and leaves. As soon as they are gone, I sigh in relief. The security officer and Viktor step out and close the door. I pick up my cell and dial Selena.

"Hello," she says in a nervous voice.

"It's over. He signed."

"Really?"

"Yes. Congratulations. You're officially divorced."

"I-I..." Her breathing gets heavier, and I assume she's emotional.

"Are you okay?"

"I'm free of him?"

"Yes. But I think you should still keep the security precautions we discussed."

She sniffles. "Kora... I...thank you so much."

"You're welcome. I'm happy this is over for you."

More silence.

"Sorry, I'm a little overwhelmed right now."

"It's okay. Why don't I call you tomorrow, and we can discuss what we need to do to transfer the assets into your name?"

"Sure. Ummm... I really would like you to take whatever fee you normally would out of my settlement."

"Thank you for the offer, but no. I didn't do this for the money."

"I know you didn't, but—"

"Nope. No point discussing it," I cheerfully reply. "Seeing Jack's face at the signing was priceless."

She stifles a laugh. "I bet. Well, can I at least take you and Sergey to dinner once I have my funds?"

"Sure. We'd love that. I'll call you tomorrow, okay?"

"Yes. Thank you again."

"Take care." I hang up and sit back in my chair then swivel it to stare at the Chicago skyline. Spring is on the verge of turning into summer. Lake Michigan sparkles from the sun, and the lack of wind makes the water calm, which doesn't happen very often.

Maybe we can all have peace now.

Sergey told me about how his mom turned to the Petrovs after his father's death. He explained how Zamir turned his brothers and him into torturers and killers to save their mother to pay off her debt, which Zamir claimed was theirs. He shared how devastating it was for him when she wouldn't look at him after she returned home before killing herself.

Every time he revealed something about his past, I would tell him something about mine. Compared to his, mine feels like a cakewalk. He doesn't see it that way, but I do.

Since Zamir's death, a lot of Sergey's anxiety has disappeared. I'm also trying to find acceptance regarding my family issues. I debate about going to my mother's house and asking how she could accept what Neicy has done. I don't understand why she isn't enraged about Neicy's drug habit. I'm not sure how long Neicy's smoked crack, but my mother didn't even seem fazed by it.

Did she already know?

Does she not care?

My gut says if I try to confront my mother and Neicy again, it's going to be more of the same type of conversation we had when Sergey gave me the proof of what Neicy was doing with the money she hustled from me.

I wish I could turn off the craving I have for my mother and sister to show me some sort of love. I'm not sure why my mother can't. All I want is a small ounce of motherly affection from her.

I've never gotten it. Why am I still looking for it?

At least I found Sergey.

I rise and gather the folder of signed paperwork, shoving the thoughts out of my head. Today is a good day. I'm not going to let my family dim the light on today's progress.

I pack up for the night, and Viktor leads me to the car. I slide in and go to Sergey's. He doesn't know I was meeting with Jack and Larry today. I didn't want to tell him. Larry likes to play games with me. Until the paperwork got signed, I didn't want to say anything to Sergey.

When I get in the penthouse, I call out, "Sergey?"

"In the bedroom."

I step into the suite. Sergey's speaking aggressive Russian on the phone and standing with his back to the window. He runs his hand through his hair and winks at me.

I walk over to him, move his collar over, and kiss him on the neck, then bat my eyelashes.

Gold fire blazes in his eyes. He fists my hair, speaks Russian, holds the speaker part of the phone away from his mouth, then kisses me. He continues his conversation for several minutes between torturing my mouth until I'm confident my panties are soaked.

When he hangs up, he tosses his phone on the bed and palms my ass. He tugs me into his body. A cocky grin appears. "Lapa. You're home early."

"I am. Want to know why?"

He kisses my neck and mumbles on my skin, "Tell me."

"I settled Selena's divorce."

He freezes then lifts his head. "You did?"

"Yes."

"And is Selena happy?"

"She's thrilled."

He grins. "Good." His mouth takes control of mine, and he kneads my ass cheek. It's still deliciously tender from the paddling he gave me in the dungeon the night before. Tingles race all over my spine. He pulls back. "Congratulations. Let's celebrate tonight."

"Dungeon?" I ask.

His lips twitch. "I was thinking dinner." He leans into my ear. "Somewhere I can get you off in public then we'll move on to other activities."

I softly laugh, step back, then unbutton my jacket. "I think I'll take a shower."

His mouth curves. He unbuttons his shirt. "I think I'll join you."

I toss my blazer on the bed then pull my top over my head. I drop it on the floor.

Sergey steps toward me while unbuckling his belt. He reaches for my breast and sniffs hard. A low growl forms in his chest. "This is nice."

It's become a challenge to see how many different ways I can wear pink, since it seems to turn Sergey on so much. My bra and underwear are delicate black lace, with small, barely pink, lips on them.

I innocently say, "Oh. Did you want to see the panties?"

He cocks an eyebrow.

I reach behind my skirt to unzip it when his phone rings. I pause.

He picks it up off the bed, sends it to voicemail, and puts it back down. He circles his finger at my skirt. "Continue."

I move the zipper down, and his phone rings again, but this time, it's his text message tone.

"Let me turn it off." He grabs it, looks at the screen, and the blood drains from his face. He hits a button and puts it to his ear.

My gut flips, and I instinctively pull my zipper back up.

"Leo," Sergey barks. "Tell me it isn't them."

A chill fills every nerve I have.

Sergey closes his eyes. His chest rises faster. He swallows hard and pulls me to his body. "We'll be right there."

"What's wrong?" I ask.

His eyes fill with sorrow and sympathy. "There's been a shooting."

The hairs on my neck stand up. "Who got shot?"

"Your mother and Neicy are being taken to the hospital."

My body shudders. "What?" I put my hands over my mouth and stomach. Dizziness and nausea overpower me. "Are they dead?"

He strokes my cheek. "Leo said they were going to the hospital, not the morgue. Let's get your top on so we can go."

"Sergey..." I clutch his shirt, blinking hard.

This isn't happening.

Who shot them?

Everything I felt when my brother passed comes rushing back.

Sergey pulls me into him. In a calm voice, he says, "When we get to the hospital, we can find out the details. We need to go."

Things become fuzzy as the night proceeds. Sergey helps get my top on me and guides me into the emergency room. He speaks to the staff and holds me close to him.

I can't seem to put my thoughts together to form a coherent question.

"I'm sorry, Ms. Kilborn. Your sister lost too much blood. She passed in the ambulance."

The woman in front of me becomes a blurry sea of blonde hair. I open my mouth to speak, unable to get oxygen in my lungs, and lose the ability to stand. Sergey catches me and pulls me into him as I sob.

At some point, I pull it together enough. "What about my mother?"

"She's in surgery."

I don't hear the rest. Sergey sits and pulls me onto his lap. I can't stop shaking. Someone puts a blanket over me. When I come out of shock, Aspen, Skylar, and Hailee are there. All of Sergey's brothers, Adrian, Obrecht, Anna, and Nora, are as well.

Sergey's stroking my head. I pull away. "Is my mother..." I swallow the lump in my throat, but it's hard since my mouth is so dry.

"She's still in surgery."

"How long has it been?"

"Going on four hours."

I push the heel of my hand to my forehead. I close my eyes. "What happened? Who did it?"

"I told her not to flash that money you gave her around," a familiar voice says.

I turn.

DeAndre and Terrell stand in front of me.

"What?" I barely get out, and Sergey's body stiffens. He tightens his arms around me.

DeAndre shakes his head and scowls. "I told her and your mom they were asking for trouble, making you their ATM."

Pain shoots up my arm, and my heart races. "You knew Neicy was hustling me?"

DeAndre shrugs. "The entire block knew."

Terrell looks at the floor with his leg bobbing up and down. It's the same thing he did when my brother got shot.

Skylar puts her hand over mine. Sergey's thumb strokes the curve of my waist.

Fresh tears fall. "When did you get Neicy hooked on crack? Hmm?"

"Shh! Watch how loud you are," DeAndre scolds and looks behind him.

"It's a fair question," Sergey says in a deadpan voice.

Deep lines erupt on DeAndre's forehead. "Man, I don't know why you're here, but this is family business. And this ain't your family."

"You've always been such an asshole," Skylar blurts out.

Sergey leans forward. In a menacing tone, he replies, "Kora *is* my family. *Everyone* here is her family. Maybe if you knew what that meant, we wouldn't be here."

DeAndre jumps up in front of us. The Ivanovs circle him. He glances at the five men scowling at him, their hands balled at their sides in fists, and shakes his head. He snarls at me, "You never did belong. Let's go, Terrell."

"Don't listen to him," Hailee says.

I shouldn't, but his words are valid. I never have belonged. The truth stings worse than ever before. I wish it made me not love my sister or mother or care about the current situation. It only seems to make it worse.

Sergey pulls my head toward his chest. I bury my face in the curve of his neck. Cold flows through my veins, and I shiver. He pulls the blanket over me again.

"Who did it?" I mumble.

"Her boyfriend."

I tilt my head up. "Who?"

Sergey's expression is full of worry. "Leo said it was Neicy's boyfriend. He was high and wanted money. He stormed into their apartment. The police arrested him."

He wanted the money I gave her.

"God, what did I do?" I whisper.

Sergey holds my cheek. "You didn't do anything wrong, my lapa."

"I did. I... I..." My lip quivers, and I break down in a mess of tears.

"Shhh. This isn't on you."

"Ms. Kilborn," a man calls out.

I turn and look at the doctor.

"She's right here," Sergey says.

I go to rise, but the doctor says, "It's okay. Stay seated." His blue eyes scream sympathy.

A new chill consumes me. *Don't tell me she's dead. Please.* I grip on to Sergey's thigh.

"Ms. Kilborn, I'm very sorry to tell you this, but your mother's heart couldn't handle the surgery. She didn't make it."

"No," I barely get out.

The doctor says something else, but I don't hear it.

"No!" I scream.

Sergey pulls me into him, but I don't remember anything else until the middle of the night. I'm in his bed. He has his arms wrapped tightly around me. The fireplace is on, and I slowly look at him.

"Is my mom really dead?"

He nods. "I'm sorry, my lapa."

New tears fall, and everything feels empty. It's my fault. I gave Neicy sixty thousand dollars. I should have known better.

No matter how tight Sergey holds me and tells me how much he loves me, I can't seem to stop the pain. All I hear is DeAndre telling me it's my fault. My mother's cold eyes, full of disappointment, continue to stare at me.

Take your uppity ass out of here, and don't come back, you selfish snob, the last words my mother said to me spin through my mind, creating a deeper hole in my heart.

She hated me. I'm never going to be able to change how she felt. Those will forever be her last words to me.

It doesn't matter what I attempt to alleviate the pain. The images and words never seem to leave me.

2 8

Sergey

"YOU NEED TO EAT SOMETHING, MY LAPA." I PUSH A PLATE OF Russian food she usually loves in front of her. We got back from the double funeral and wake a few hours ago. Things were tense between Kora and her extended family. I hovered over her, making sure no one got near to hurt her more. The few times I had to step away, my brothers took over.

"I'm not hungry." Her eyes have dark circles under them, and red rings the hazel. She's not slept much in the last few days since we got home from the hospital. The girls came over each day, but she sat like a zombie, barely talking. I planned the funeral with their help, since Kora kept breaking down and crying.

"You haven't eaten in days."

She turns and looks away. Her hand trembles.

I spread some jam on a blini and hold it to her mouth. "Humor me and take a bite."

She crosses her arms and snaps, "I said I wasn't hungry." Her eyes are empty of her usual warmth. Pain and grief fill them.

It cuts my soul to see her hurting. I want to take it away, but I'm unsure how. I quietly but firmly respond, "Take a bite."

She rises. "I can't do this anymore."

I put the blini down. Blood pounds between my ears. "Do what?"

Her lip quivers. She motions between us. "This."

I stand and fist her hair so her head tilts up. She inhales sharply. For a brief moment, I see the fire in her eyes return, but then it dies. Her emptiness reappears. "I know you're hurting, but I won't let you do this."

"Do what?" she seethes.

"You're not throwing us away."

"Maybe there's nothing to throw away." She defiantly glares at me, as if I'm her enemy and she's ready to take me down.

"You're not thinking clearly."

"Yes, I am."

So she's at the pissed-off stage. It happened faster than I thought it would.

"Running from me isn't going to get rid of your anger."

She pushes against my chest. "Let go of me."

I wrap her hair another time around my fist. "No. You're mine, Kora. No matter what, you're mine, and I'm not letting you go."

"I hate you," she seethes.

It's a stab to my heart, but I ignore it. She's got years of pent-up rage to get out, and if I need to be her punching bag, I will. "No, you don't."

Her lip quivers, and her nostrils flare. "I do."

"Yeah? Why do you hate me?"

"Let me go," she says and pushes my chest again.

I release her, and she spins. She practically runs into the bedroom and goes straight into the closet. She removed the overnight bag she uses to take things back and forth. She pulls random items off the hangers and throws them in the bag while red anger builds in her face.

I quietly say, "I love you, Kora. This isn't going to make you feel better."

She spins and jabs me in the chest. "You don't love me."

"I do. You know I do."

"No, you don't." The quivering in her lip grows.

"Yes, I do."

"You can't," she says and opens a drawer then tosses underwear on top of her clothes.

"Why can't I? Hmm? Tell me why."

She refuses to answer me and bends over and picks up several pairs of shoes. "I'm going home. Get out of my way."

"You're not going home. You are home. *This* is your home. *I* am your home. And I won't get out of your way. So whatever is running through your head right now, say it."

"Move!"

I block the doorway more. "No. Tell me why I can't love you."

She squeezes her eyes shut. "Why are you doing this?"

"Because I love you."

She opens her fury-filled eyes. "Stop saying that."

"No. I'm going to say it every day for the rest of our lives, so get used to it. Now tell me why I can't love you." I'm pushing her to say what I know is going through her head. She muttered it the first night we got back from the hospital. She was still in shock and kept saying it while crying. It broke my heart, and somehow, I need to find a way to make her see it's not true.

"Well, I don't love you. Now move!" she screams as tears well in her eyes.

That's it.

I pick her up and throw her over my shoulder.

She pounds on my ass. "Sergey, let me go!"

I don't say anything and march down the hall into the dungeon. I put her down on her knees in front of the spanking bench and clasp her wrists and ankles quickly.

"Get these off me," she screams wildly.

I grab my pocketknife and slice the back of her dress off.

"What are you doing? Release me now!"

"Tell me why I can't love you."

"No!"

I unclasp her bra then cut the straps and tear her panties off her with my hands.

"Sergey! What the fuck!"

"Tell me," I growl.

"Release me!"

I scan the wall, debating between a paddle and a flogger. I finally decide on a new flogger I just bought. It's black, with a silver handle with hot-pink beads. It's a more intense flogger than I've used on her in the past. But something tells me she needs the physical pain to mix with her internal pain right now.

"Sergey! Let me go," she belts out like an animal and tries to move off the bench but can't.

I crouch behind her. I kiss her cheek, and she turns her head away. "You're going to tell me why I can't love you."

She turns and looks in my eyes then snarls, "Go to hell."

I sniff hard then rise. "Let it out, Kora. When we finish, I'm taking you to bed and fucking you senseless all night."

"I'm never fucking you again."

I adjust the bench so it pops out, and her entire torso is on top of it. I run the flogger down her spine then kiss her ass cheeks.

"Don't touch me!"

"You know the safe word," I taunt her, taking a guess she isn't going to say it since she needs this. Deep down, she knows it.

"Tell me why I can't love you, Kora."

"No!"

"Wrong answer." I take the flogger and slap her back in an X mark three times. It's not hard, but it's something she hasn't felt before due to the beads on the end of the leather straps.

"Sergey!"

"Tell me why I can't love you, Kora," I repeat.

"No!"

Over and over, I ask her to tell me why, and she refuses. Each time, I mark her. Between the hits, I rub and kiss her skin and tell her how much I love her.

Her skin grows red, and tears stream down her face. She's so close to breaking and telling me what I already know.

"Tell me why I can't love you, Kora," I growl while marking the back of her thighs.

"I'm not lovable," she cries out.

"That's bullshit, Kora," I growl and smack the flogger on her ass.

She shakes her head and arches her back.

"Why are you lying to me, Kora?" I smack the other cheek.

"My own mother hated me," she screams then her body breaks into uncontrollable sobs.

I toss the flogger and rub my hands over the red marks and cage my body around hers. "Your mother was a lousy mother. She had you and never appreciated the gift she had in front of her. She had the problem, not you. You are *not* unlovable. *I* love you. Your friends love you. I'm sorry your mother is dead, but I will not let you believe this any longer. So help me God, Kora, if I have to drill this into your head every day, I will. You are mine. I am yours. There is no one I love more than you, and you will not disregard me or my love for you."

She sobs harder, and I release the cuffs and pick her up and carry her to my bedroom. I turn on the tub and stroke her hair as she continues to cry.

Her voice breaks. "Why did those have to be her last words to me?"

"I don't know, my lapa. But listen to me." I pull her chin up. The pain in her eyes just about kills me. I put my hand over her heart. "This hurt you have, it's based on cruel lies. There's no one more deserving of love than you. I know what's in here and who you are. If you forget it, I will remind you."

More tears fall. "Sergey, I'm sorry. I didn't mean—"

I stick my tongue in her mouth, flicking it in and out and taking every part of her I can. When she finally moans into my mouth, I retreat and palm her head. I hold it near my face. "I know. And I've self-destructed before. I won't let it ever happen to you or us."

She nods and sniffles.

I put her in the water, remove my clothes, and get in behind her. I gently wash her back then wrap my arms around her.

She sinks into me, and I tuck her hair behind her ear. I murmur, "You're my life, my lapa. There's nothing I won't do for you."

She turns her head. "I love you, too. I'm sorry. I—"

I kiss her. "Shhh. I know you do. You're in pain. Just relax." I kiss her forehead and slide lower in the tub.

We stay in the tub for an hour. When we get out, I dry her off, then have her lie facedown on the bed. I put lotion on her skin to help with the red marks. When it's dry, I flip her over and hover over her on my forearms. I pin my gaze on her. "I need you to come back to me, my lapa. You need us, and I need us."

She nods and cries out, "I know. I need you so much."

I kiss her, and the rest of the night, I do what I warned her I would do. I fuck her senseless, wearing her out, so she has no other option but to sleep. When she stirs, I start all over. And all night, I remind her how much I love her.

Kora

Five Weeks Later

SERGEY NEVER LETS UP. HE REMINDS ME EVERY CHANCE HE gets how much he loves me, and slowly the pain fades to where I can function. It makes no sense to me why I let my mother's lack of affection or my sister's hatred bother me so much. Rationally, I shouldn't grieve them, but I do.

My friends shower me with love as well. I saw a grief counselor Aspen recommended. She saw her when her mother died. The counselor recommended I take time off work for a month. It was something I'd never done before. After a month of weekly sessions, she told me it was time to go back.

Sergey walks me into the office and gives me a goodbye kiss. "Have a good first day back." His phone buzzes. He pulls it out, looks at the screen, then grins. "Nora's in labor."

"Should we go to the hospital?"

He shakes his head. "Boris said it might be a long time. He'll message us when it's time to go." He kisses me again and leaves.

I review my schedule. It's light, and the only appointment I have is with Selena. Most of her settlement assets were transferred into her name. My staff took care of things while I was gone. There are a few loose ends and then she should have no further reasons to ever speak with Jack. Instead of alimony, she opted for a payout so she could sever all ties. I'm glad I get to take care of this last piece with her. It's a form of closure for me.

It feels good to be back at my office, but summer is coming, and it's a nice day. I stare out of my office window and don't want to be here, so I call Selena.

"Hey, Kora!"

"Hi! Can I meet you at your place instead of you coming to the office? Maybe I can check out your roof?"

"Sure. I'm already up here. It's beautiful out today."

"Great. Okay, if I head over now?"

"Sounds great. See you soon."

I hang up, collect the paperwork I need Selena to sign, then leave. It only takes ten minutes with traffic to get to her place. Since Sergey gave me access on day one, I go directly to the roof. I spot Selena in the lounge chair with her laptop.

She rises, and we hug. Concern fills her eyes. "How are you?"

"Doing better. It feels good to be back. Thanks for the nice card and flowers you sent."

She smiles and squeezes my arm. "You look good."

"Thanks." I glance around. "This is really nice." The back of a man running sprints on the turf catches my eye. He has his shirt off, and his skin glistens. "Umm, hello, Mr. Sweaty, Ripped, and Fabulous!" I say low enough for only Selena and me to hear and wiggle my eyebrows at her. "No wonder why you love it up here if you have that eye candy. And now you're divorced, you can partake in the dessert."

She laughs, and her face turns red. "He is hot, isn't he?"

"Scorching."

The man drops to the ground then jumps back up, doing a round of burpees.

"Wow. That's impressive form. I bet he would be a good rebounder for you," I tease.

She elbows me then covers her face. She groans, "Kora!"

"What? If I weren't with Sergey, I'd go introduce—" The man turns, and I stop in dead silence. "Oh, shit."

"What?"

"That's Sergey's cousin, Obrecht."

"Well, that explains the accent."

"You've spoken with him?"

Selena's face turns almost purple. "Yeah."

I tilt my head and whisper, "Have you guys—"

"No! Kora!" Her eyes widen.

"What? It's a legit question. I mean, you're single, he's single...well, I think he is. I can find out if you want."

"No! Do not say anything about Obrecht to Sergey!"

"Why?"

She licks her lips. "It's embarrassing. He's a nice guy who helped me with my plumbing—"

"Helped you with your plumbing!" I tease.

She groans again while laughing. "Kora!"

"You just bought a brand-new condo. What broke? The Ivanovs build quality properties. If something is wrong, you should tell Sergey, and he'll fix it."

"No, it wasn't like that."

"Then how did he fix your plumbing? Or are we talking about 'your plumbing?'" I put my fingers in quotes and lower my voice. I'm enjoying teasing her since everything has always been so serious about her situation.

She puts her hands over her face and shakes her head.

I laugh. "Well? Do tell."

"I wanted to change the sink faucet. The one they had was nice, but I wanted something a bit fancier and to do something to make the place feel like mine. When Jack and I remodeled, he wouldn't let me pick anything. I fell in love with this faucet, but he wouldn't choose it. The one the Ivanovs picked was identical to the one Jack chose, and it kept reminding me of him. The delivery man accidentally sent the faucet I ordered to Obrecht's condo instead of mine. So he dropped it off, and we started talking, and he volunteered to install it for me."

"Did he do it shirtless?"

"No!" She flings her hand on my arm. "It was sweet of him to do."

"Yes, very sweet," I agree and try to keep a serious face.

"Okay, please don't tease me in front of him. He's jogging over."

We turn, and Obrecht soon joins us. "Kora. I thought that was you. How are you?"

"Doing better. Thanks. And I never got to properly thank you."

He scrunches his face. "For what?"

"Sergey told me you and Adrian kept DeAndre and Terrell away from me at my mother's wake." My chest tightens, thinking about the funeral and after.

Obrecht's ice-blue eyes pin mine. "No need to thank me. You're family now."

I blink hard, and there's an uncomfortable silence. I'm a bit choked up at his statement and smile.

He finally says, "What are you doing here?"

I recover. "I'd ask you the same thing, but it seems you live here?"

He runs his hand through his thick, sweaty hair. "Yeah. I moved in a little over a month ago. Maksim talked me into the penthouse and gave me a good deal."

"Aww. Maksim showed you his soft side, did he?"

Obrecht chuckles. "Something like that."

"Do you like it?"

"Yeah." He glances at Selena. "Hey, Selena."

She beams at him, and a small flush fills her cheeks. "Hi."

"Okay. I need to get ready for work. It was good seeing you, Kora. I'll see you later, Selena."

"Okay," she says.

"Bye."

We watch him disappear through the doorway. I turn to Selena. "When is later?"

Her face turns the color of a tomato again. "I just got divorced."

"Skylar would tell you a divorce is the number one reason to get back on the horse."

"I can see her saying that."

"Yep. Anyway, I brought the forms for you to sign. Has Jack tried to contact you?"

"No. I'm going to keep my number and address unlisted. I bought the condo under a trust. Your office recommended it when you were out. I didn't name it anything related to my name."

"Very smart." I pull the forms out.

She signs, and we talk a little more. Then I leave, go back to the office, and finish up my day around three. My counselor wanted me to ease back into work and not spend eighty to one hundred hours working anymore. Part of my therapy was starting a new journey. And now that I have Sergey, I don't want to work that much.

I decide to pick up some groceries and make Sergey dinner. I started cooking when I took the last month off and discovered I love it. Something about it feels good for my soul. There's a new recipe I wanted to try. It's called Okroshka, or Cold Summer Soup. Sergey said it's one of his favorite Russian dishes, so I secretly hope to perfect it.

By the time Sergey comes home, the soup is in the fridge cooling off. The recipe says it's better the second day, which I overlooked before I got to the bottom of the recipe.

He comes into the kitchen and kisses me. "What are you making?"

"I made Okroshka but didn't notice the disclaimer until the end."

His eyes twinkle. "You made Okroshka?"

"Yes."

He gives me a chaste kiss. "Good woman."

I laugh. "You haven't tried it yet."

"I'm sure it's going to be delicious." His phone buzzes, and he drags it out of his pocket. He grins. "It's a girl!"

Happiness fills me. "Are they ready for visitors?"

"Yes, Boris said to come."

Sergey and I go to the hospital. All of the Ivanovs and Anna and Aspen are there. We all get to hold Shannon. She has Nora's fiery red hair and green eyes, but I see Boris in her, too. "She's beautiful."

Sergey strokes her head. "Yes, she is." Something passes in his eyes I haven't seen before. I'm not sure what to make of it, but it's loving and happy mixed with something else.

When we get home, I go into the closet to change. When I come into the bedroom, the lights are off, and the fireplace is on. Sergey is staring out at the Chicago skyline. The lit buildings and streetlamps give a faint outline of Lake Michigan.

I wrap my arms around his waist.

He caresses my fingers then spins to face me. His brown eyes drill into mine. It's intense, and flutters fill my stomach.

I nervously say, "What?"

He raises my hand to his lips, kisses it, then drops to his knee.

I slide my fingers in his hair, assuming he's going to rip off my pink silk robe and do something deliciously naughty to my body, but he doesn't.

"I love you."

I smile. "I love you, too."

"I'm not good with words, sometimes."

"Since when? You always say the right things to me."

He slowly exhales. "Marry me."

My heart stops beating. "Did you—"

"Yes. Marry me. I promise to love you until the day I die. I want you to be mine forever and everyone to know you're mine and I am yours."

A tear falls down my cheek.

"Say, yes. Please."

I start laughing and wipe my cheek. I lean down and meet his lips. "Yes. Of course I'll marry you."

He kisses me. It's possessive and dominant and incites every soul-stirring emotion I have. He pulls back and holds up a pink diamond ring. It's brilliant in color, flawless, and set in platinum with another perfect clear diamond on both sides of the pink gem.

I gape at it.

He chuckles. "You should see your face right now." He slides it on my finger.

"It's..." I hold my other hand over my mouth, studying it.

"The moment I saw it, I imagined it on your finger. I've been trying to figure out how to ask you."

More tears fall, and I kneel next to him. "It's perfect. I love it, and I can't wait to marry you."

He grins. "Yeah?"

"Yes."

He kisses me then rises and picks me up. "I'm ready to get you naked in nothing but your ring."

I laugh. We spend all night wrapped up in each other. Sergey's stomach growls.

I sit up. "Let me grab something for you. We never ate dinner."

"I'm ready for your soup."

"It hasn't been a day yet."

"It only needs a few hours. It should be good by now."

"Okay. You stay here, and I'll serve you in bed."

His eyes gleam. "Is this going to be part of your wifely duties? Cooking for me and servicing me in bed?"

I stroke his balls. "If you're lucky."

He pulls me on top of him. His face turns serious. "I think you should stop taking your birth control."

My stomach flips. "I'm thirty-nine soon. What if I can't get pregnant?"

He tucks my hair behind my ear. "Then we'll deal with it and be fine. But you'll be an awesome mother."

"You think so?"

He snorts. "Without a doubt."

A smile plays on my lips. "So you want me to have your baby?"

"If it's in the cards, yes."

Sergey's baby. Another jolt of happiness sears through me. I've always wanted a family, but I really want one with him. I have no doubt Sergey will make a great father.

"Okay. I'll stop taking it."

He slaps my ass. His sexy, cocky expression appears. He teases, "Good. Now go serve me."

I give him a peck on the lips and reach for my robe.

"Nope. Naked."

I toss the silk on the floor. "Naked it is." I hold up my hand with my pink diamond and wave as I walk to the door.

"Perfection," he mumbles.

I giddily go into the kitchen and open the fridge. I reach for the bowl, and thick arms go around my waist. I get tugged back so quickly, I drop the bowl. The glass shatters everywhere. I scream, attempt to fight back, then stop moving when a knife comes to my neck.

"Kora!" Sergey yells

A musky scent overpowers me. Nausea swirls in my stomach. The knife's flat blade is cold against my throat, almost as if it's been in a freezer. A chill sweeps through me.

Sergey runs into the kitchen and freezes. Fear fills his eyes. They dart between me and whoever is holding me.

The stranger restraining me and Sergey exchange aggressive words in Russian.

My chest tightens. Oxygen becomes harder to inhale. Shivers overpower me. The man's arms tighten, and his palm moves over my breast. I scrunch my face as my skin crawls from his touch. His erection grows and digs into the bare skin on my back. He flattens the blade over my nipple, and I cry out, afraid he's going to cut it off.

Sergey screams at him, and the man laughs.

More conversing in Russian takes place. It feels like forever, but he finally stands back and slices the knife over my left bicep.

I scream in pain and fear, and he shoves me on the ground. He puts his dirty boot on my back. Blood pools on the floor.

Stay calm.

He puts more of his weight on my back, and I wince in pain. I barely scream. My lungs feel crushed.

He's going to kill me.

I can't move my head. All I see is my pink diamond, shining in front of my eyes. Sergey and he continue to talk in Russian.

Fear of death mixes with visions of Sergey's and my future. I see blood, a wedding, and a baby as the foot of the thug on top of me crushes me further.

30

Sergey

"Your debt to Zamir is a Petrov debt. I now own this debt. You will be the one to pay it off," Boyra, Zamir's brother, barks while adding more weight to Kora's back.

Blood is all over the floor, pooling near her chest where he pinned her arm under her body.

"Get off her," I growl. My pulse is pounding so fast, I can barely think. He has my lapa under him. He already hurt her. I'm not sure how to get Boyra out of here and keep her alive.

"Tomorrow night. You will meet me where I text you."

My heart thumps against my chest cavity.

"I better hear 'yes, master,'" he orders and grinds his boot into Kora's back.

I swallow all my pride. "Yes, master."

"Louder!"

I scream in Russian, "Yes, master." Sweat pops out on my skin. I avoid looking at Kora in an effort not to give him any more reason to stay here.

He finally takes his foot off her. A sinister grin erupts on his face. He crouches over Kora and pats her ass cheeks.

"Don't touch her!" I yell without thinking.

Kora sobs on the ground.

He points at me while keeping his other hand on her ass. "You are my property. If she is yours, then she is mine. Don't forget it."

I grind my molars, unsure about how to stop this nightmare. Every move I contemplate seems to have harmful consequences.

Boyra leans down and mutters something in Kora's ear. She shudders, and new tears fall on the floor. He rises and comes toward me with his knife. In Russian, he says, "How is she at sucking dick?"

I refrain from speaking and ball my fists at my sides.

He laughs. "One wrong move from you, and I'll put her in my whorehouse." He glances back at her then refocuses on me. "I bet she'd like my cock in her mouth. But her ass..." He takes a deep breath, checks out her backside, then licks his lips. His grin gets wider. "I can put that to work as well."

Rage boils my blood. I work hard at not reacting. I've only met Boyra a few times. It was years ago when I was still a boy. Everything I remember about him reminds me of Zamir. No reaction is usually the safest action to take.

He waits several moments and leans into my ear. "I heard you wailed like a baby when my brother branded you. I've always regretted not being there."

The spasm in my jaw intensifies.

He laughs and firmly swats my cheek. "Tomorrow. Don't be late." He steps back then turns and walks out.

As soon as he's gone, I lock the door and run back to Kora. I pull her into my arms. "Lapa, are you okay?"

She's breathing hard. I pick her up, grab a blanket off the couch, and wrap her in it. I keep her bloody arm on the outside and carry her to the kitchen counter. I set her on it and hold her face. "Kora, I'm sorry." I kiss her and tug her back into my chest.

"Who was he?"

I pull away and lock eyes with her. "Zamir's brother."

The color drains from her face. "What does he want?"

"Let me clean your arm."

"Sergey, what does he want?" she cries out.

"I don't know. He's going to send me a location I have to go to tomorrow night."

"What? No!"

"I don't have a choice."

"No! You aren't going."

"He'll put you in his whorehouse!" I bark.

Shit. Why did I say that?

Her eyes widen, and she shudders.

I firmly hold her face to mine. "Listen to me, Kora. I need to attend to your arm. I'm going to get the first aid kit. When I get back—"

"No! Don't leave me."

I pick her up and carry her into my bathroom. I set her on the counter, trying to keep it together but flipping out inside. I warned my brothers about this. We should have destroyed every last piece of the Petrovs and their operation. I should have fought harder or done it myself if they disagreed. Now Kora is in danger.

I clean the blood off her arm and sigh. "It's a thin cut. I'm going to put some medical glue on it."

Her voice cracks. "Sergey, what does he want from you?"

I stay silent.

"Sergey! I'm going to be your wife. Tell me. Please!"

I meet her eyes. "He says I'm paying off the debt from now on instead of Boris."

More color drains from her face. "What? What does that even mean?"

"I don't know." I put the liquid bandage on her arm and wrap my arms around her. "I'm so sorry I didn't protect you from him."

"How did he get in here?"

"I'm not sure. I need to meet with my brothers. I don't want you here until I figure out how Boyra got past security. I'm going to take you to Adrian's."

"Take me with you."

I contemplate it. "It's late. We've not slept. Let me take you to Adrian's, and you can try and sleep."

"I'm not going to sleep!"

I cup her face. "I don't know how long I'll be. You need to rest. We've been up all night. Adrian will keep you safe while I meet with my brothers. I need you to trust me about this."

"I-I'm scared."

I tighten my arms around her and stroke her hair. "I know. It's why I need you to rest at Adrian's while I meet with my brothers and figure out what to do."

She finally agrees.

I text my brothers to meet at Boris's. It's around nine in the morning, and he texted they got home from the hospital about an hour ago. I message Adrian I'm coming over with Kora, and we get dressed. I drop her off at his house. Skylar is also there. I explain what happened. "I need you to stay with Kora until I get back."

Adrian agrees, goes into the bedroom, and gets his gun.

I kiss Kora goodbye, tell her to try and rest, and head to Boris's.

I arrive first. I pace, and my anxiety grows. I can't get the visual of Kora naked with Boyra's arms wrapped around her and a knife to her throat out of my head. I'm almost dizzy with nausea and feel like I might break out in a sweat.

Nora asks, "Are you okay?"

I lie. "Yeah."

Boris eyes me over. "Nora, why don't you and Shannon go rest in the bedroom."

"Okay." She pats me on the shoulder and takes Shannon with her.

"What's going on," Boris demands in Russian.

I point in his face, pissed off he never listened to me when I insisted we needed to destroy the Petrovs quicker than what can be achieved by the war. "I told you we needed to get in the Petrov organization and destroy it piece by piece until nothing was left."

His face drains of color. He firmly asks, "What happened?"

Dmitri and Maksim walk in.

"We have a problem," I bark.

"What?" Maksim asks.

"I had a visitor in my house today." I continue to pace and pull at my hair.

Maksim steps in front of me and puts his hands on my shoulders. "What is going on?"

"Kora stayed over last night. She walked out of the bedroom to get something out of the kitchen. I heard her yell. When I got to the living room, Boyra Petrov had a knife to her throat and a hand on her naked chest."

"Boyra, Zamir's brother from Russia?" Dmitri barks.

"Shh. I have a baby in the house," Boris reminds us.

We all step closer and drop our voices.

"Is Kora okay?" Maksim asks.

I scowl. "She's shaken up. Adrian and Skylar are with her right now. He slit her arm."

"Shit. Was it deep?" Dmitri asks.

"No. But she bled, and it hurts."

Boris scrubs his face. "Why was Boyra in your home?"

My stomach pitches. "He said since his brother is dead, our debt carries over to him. And I'm the one who's going to pay it off."

"That motherfucker. Zamir and I had a deal. Anything to do with paying off our debt was through me," Boris growls.

"He threatened to put Kora in his whorehouse." The spasm in my jaw intensifies.

"Shit," Dmitri mutters.

"You're going to have to do better than 'shit.' He's going after *my wife*."

"Your wife?" Dmitri raises his eyebrows.

"Future wife. Whatever. I'm not into semantics. It doesn't matter when the wedding is. She's already my wife in my eyes, and he just terrorized her."

Through the stress of the newest events, my brothers' faces light up.

"When did you propose?" Maksim asks.

"Last night. Before Boyra shoved *my wife* on the ground and put his boot on her back after cutting her," I angrily reply.

Maksim embraces me. "I'm very happy for you. She's a good woman."

I push away from him. "Which is why we need to figure this out."

"Agreed. How did Boyra get into your penthouse?" Dmitri asks.

"I don't know. But I'm not staying there, and Kora's place doesn't have the security mine is supposed to."

"Come stay with Aspen and me until we figure this out. Boris, text Obrecht to get over here. We'll have Adrian look into your security issue once Kora's moved to my place," Maksim orders.

"Then what? We can't do what we did before to trap Zamir. Boyra will expect it."

Silence fills the air and makes my nerves worse. I can't fall back into the Petrov's grasp, and nothing can happen to Kora. The clock is ticking. Time is running out before Boyra sends for me.

"Obrecht said he'll be here in twenty," Boris states. "I'm messaging Darragh as well."

"So we can owe the O'Malleys even more?" I seethe.

Boris calmly states, "We need as much strength as we can get. The O'Malleys are part of us now. My wife and daughter carry their blood. It's time you got used to it."

"I don't want to owe Darragh and Liam."

"It's not an option. We have an alliance. We need their strength."

I tug at my hair, feeling like I may crawl out of my skin.

"Sergey, let's go out on the balcony," Maksim instructs.

I obey, not sure what else to do. I hate how weak the Petrovs make me feel. I detest myself over Kora getting hurt and Boyra threatening her safety.

How am I going to protect her?

Maksim shuts the door. "Take a hit, Sergey. You look like you're going to lose it any minute."

"He sliced her arm, fondled her breast, and stood on her," I growl.

Maksim nods. "Yes. And he's going to pay. I promise you, little brother, but I need you calm."

I close my eyes and try to steady my rapid heart rate.

Maksim pulls my pipe out of my pocket and hands it to me. "You think better when you're not full of anxiety."

I take a hit and hold the smoke in my lungs then slowly release it. "His hands were on her. He was in my house."

Maksim's piercing icy blue eyes pin mine. "Boyra will die before anything else happens. Whoever the leak in security was will pay. Kora is a part of us. Now we know Boyra is targeting her, we will increase security on her and all our women. He showed his cards. We will take advantage of it."

I inhale another large hit of smoke and close my eyes. When I open them, Maksim smiles. "When do we get to throw you and Kora a party?"

I snort. "Kill Boyra and then we'll celebrate."

"Between the O'Malleys and us, we will figure it out."

I sigh. "I hate owing Liam. He's a loose cannon."

"Maybe in the past. I'm not so sure about now. He's showing a level of maturity he didn't have before."

I grunt. "It's Liam O'Malley."

"He spent fifteen years thinking about his mistakes. So far, his decisions have illustrated strategy. Call me crazy, but my trust in him is growing."

I stare at the crashing waves on the shoreline. "Excuse me if I don't hand over my full faith in him. I can't stop thinking about how he almost got Killian and Boris arrested when they were barely in high school."

Maksim huffs. "He was a kid. We all did stupid stuff when we were kids."

"Guess I didn't have the same luxuries as Liam, knowing Zamir owned my ass."

Maksim's eyes grow colder. "He lost his freedom like we did. You know how it changes a man. Let's be cautious but hope for the best. His heart has always been in the right place."

"Fine," I grumble.

Boris knocks on the glass and motions for us to come in. Darragh, Liam, and Obrecht had arrived.

"This is easily solved," Darragh advises.

"How?"

He points to Obrecht. "You're a tracker, correct?"

"The best," I say.

"What's your point?" Obrecht asks.

A smug expression fills Darragh's face. "Boyra isn't a ghost like Zamir was. He can't help but show his face. My guess is he'll utilize his time at the Petrov's whorehouse. Anytime he arrives from Moscow, he spends time there. You confirm it, we'll take care of him."

"You make it sound easy," Dmitri states.

Darragh attempts to light up his pipe.

Boris moves his hand, holding the lighter. "You can't smoke in here. Our baby is in the other room."

A low growl of frustration comes out of Darragh.

I cross my arms. "He's calling on me tomorrow night. There isn't a lot of time before I'll be his pawn in whatever sadistic event he has planned."

Darragh has a coughing fit and pulls his handkerchief out of his pocket. When it subsides, he replies, "Don't go."

"Don't go?" I sarcastically laugh. "Are you out of your mind?"

"No. Hole up with one of your brothers. Send me the address when you get it, unless we take care of him sooner. My boys will take out some of his men. We just eliminated more of Zielinski's bastards last night. More Petrovs sliced up will be good for the balance." He addresses Obrecht. "Why are you still standing here?"

Obrecht sneers. "I don't take orders from you."

Darragh's arrogant expression says otherwise.

"He's right. Go now," Maksim says.

Obrecht's jaw clenches. He shakes his head, unhappy, but leaves.

"I want Boyra to look at me when he takes his last breath," I say.

"I said the O'Malleys are handling this."

I step in front of Darragh and growl, "He groped my woman. After he sliced her arm, he threw her on the ground and put his boot on her back while fondling her ass and threatening to put her in his whorehouse."

Darragh's eyes turn to slits. "And he will pay, but the O'Malleys will handle this."

"No. Let Sergey join us," Liam says.

Darragh slowly turns to him.

Why is Liam agreeing with me?

Now I'm going to owe him even more.

It'll be worth it to slice into Boyra for touching Kora.

"You said I needed to override your decisions when it was beneficial to the O'Malleys. This is a benefit for us."

Fuck it. I knew it.

I glance at Maksim and shake my head, trying to keep my mouth shut.

Darragh seems appeased by his admission. "Fine. Where can I smoke?"

Boris leads him to the balcony.

"Always has to be something in it for you, doesn't it, Liam?" I sneer.

He scowls. "No. I said that to get my father to agree. If anyone did to my woman what you just described, I wouldn't let anyone else kill him."

Part of me wants to believe Liam. The other part says not to trust him.

"Jesus, Sergey. When are you going to realize we're on the same side? And my father won't be here much longer to guide me. At some point, I might need your help. I hope if that time comes, you do it because you want to help me, not because you feel obligated."

Chills run up my spine. "Darragh's dying?"

Liam's face and eyes harden.

"Shit. I'm sorry."

"It is what it is. Can we get on the same side? I don't see an alliance working out if we aren't."

He seems sincere. I remember watching my father disintegrate in front of our eyes. I don't imagine it's easy at any age to watch a person you love die, especially when Liam's been locked up for fifteen years and only got to spend time with his father recently.

Liam turns away and exhales. He addresses Maksim. "I'm going to need help. I can't go back inside. My father doesn't have any advisors still alive. If I take advice from any of the O'Malleys who would be more than willing to give it, I'll destroy our clan. It's not a question of if, but when."

Maksim assesses him. "Besides this war, I don't want Ivanovs pulled into O'Malley business. I will be here for you and guide you if I can, as long as you agree to my terms. And that includes Boris."

He nods. "I have no intention of doing anything of the sort."

Maksim pats him on the back. "You come to me at any time then."

Liam's face fills with gratitude.

He's stressed over this.

I'd be freaking out, too, if I had to lead the O'Malleys.

I need to stop worrying about him. Maksim is right. He has changed.

I take a deep breath. "Tell you what, make sure I'm there to destroy Boyra, and you've got my support."

Liam's lips curl. "As long as I get to watch you take the bastard out, consider it done."

Kora

"ADRIAN, TELL ME WHAT HE WANTS FROM SERGEY."

Adrian sighs. "I'm not hiding anything from you. I don't know. Zamir's deal was with Boris, not Sergey. It doesn't make sense. But nothing the Petrovs do is rational. He's probably doing it just to show he can."

I continue pacing the family room.

Skylar comes into the room. Her hair has a towel around it. "What's wrong?"

I put my hands over my face, inhaling deeply.

"Holy...what are you wearing?"

I look up.

Skylar gapes.

I glance at my jeans and baggy sweatshirt. "What?"

She jumps up and grabs my hand. "When did you get this?"

I stare at the brilliant pink diamond Sergey gave me only hours ago. We were so happy all night.

We still are.

Nothing can happen to him.

Skylar tugs on my hand. "That's from Harry Winston."

"It is?" I don't follow fashion the way Skylar does. Of course it's her career, so it makes sense she would know.

"Yeah. It's from their summer collection. Bowmen lashed out at me last week when the manager called and said we couldn't use it in our upcoming shoot. He said the purchaser paid twenty percent more, so he didn't have to wait to get it. It was a showcase item. It's super rare."

My heart melts. Not because of what it costs but because Sergey wanted it so badly for me.

"Can I see it? Please!" Her face lights up like a kid in a candy shop.

I slide it off my finger, and she holds it to the light. "Wow. This is incredible." She spins it then looks closer. "What does this say?"

"What?"

"There's something engraved, but I think it's in Russian."

I peek at the letters on the inside of the ring. "I don't know. Sergey didn't show me or tell me about it. He slid it on my finger. This is the first time I've taken it off."

"Adrian, come read this and tell us what it says."

I grab the ring from her. "No, it's okay. I'll ask Sergey." I don't want Adrian reading it. Something about it seems intimate and private to me. I want Sergey to tell me what it means. I slide it back on my finger.

"Okay. Well, it's beautiful."

"Thank you."

"When are we going dress shopping?"

I laugh. "I'm not even sure when the wedding is."

She hugs me. "I'm happy for you."

My mind shifts back to worrying. "Thank you."

Her eyes widen. "So...why are you here? And where is Sergey?"

I look at Adrian for guidance on what to tell her when Adrian's phone rings.

He holds his finger in the air. "Yes. I'll tell her. See you soon." He shuts his phone. "Sergey said to make a list of what you want from his penthouse or your place. Until further notice, you're staying somewhere else."

"Where?"

"Not sure, but it's best if he doesn't say anything over the phone. He'll be over once he picks your stuff up."

"Is someone going to tell me what's going on?"

Adrian's face hardens. My insides quiver. I don't want to lie to Skylar, but I also don't want to tell Sergey's secrets. It's clear Adrian doesn't want her to know, either.

Her eyes turn to slits. She glares at Adrian. "Again?"

He clenches his jaw and focuses on the ceiling.

She turns to me. Hurt is in her eyes and voice. It's swirling with anger. "You're going to keep me in the dark, too?"

"Skylar—"

"We're supposed to be best friends."

"We are."

"Not if you're going to lie to me."

"Skylar, I've not lied to you. Things are complicated." It sounds weak as it flows out of my mouth.

She gives Adrian the look of death then says, "So Kora can know, and I'm assuming Aspen will know, but I'm not trustworthy enough to tell?"

"I never said that," Adrian replies. His Russian accent sounds thicker. He pins his blue eyes on her. "I've told you this isn't about trust."

She stares at him and blinks hard. It pains me. I know how she feels about Adrian. I understand how big of a deal it was for Sergey to tell me. I'm not sure what Adrian's story is, but I know he hates the Petrovs, too. Maybe it's just what Zamir put Sergey and his brothers through, but my hunch is there's something else driving his disdain.

She swallows hard. Her hands shake. In a soft voice, she says, "I'm done, Adrian."

His eyes harden further. "Stop this foolishness. We've gone through this."

"Yeah. You obviously don't listen." She spins and glares at me. In a hurt voice, she says, "I expected more from you, Kora."

"Skylar," Adrian bellows out.

"Don't, Adrian!" She opens the bedroom door and slams it.

"Shit," he growls and slams his hand on the counter.

My heart tears between going after Skylar and convincing Adrian to fess up. I decide on the latter since I know how Skylar needs to cool down when she's upset.

"You should talk to her. She won't tell anyone."

"This isn't your business, Kora."

"You're right. But when Skylar decides she's had enough of you, she isn't going to let you back in. If you completely break her trust, she'll wash her hands of you entirely. She's already past her tolerance level with you."

"What does that mean?"

I cross my arms. "Do I really need to explain this? She already thinks you're seeing other women."

"I'm not. She knows this. And I'm tired of being accused of doing things I'm not."

"Does she know it? And if you think you're tired, how do you think she feels. If you were in her shoes—"

"But I'm not, am I? She's not in mine, and neither are you. So while you think you know everything about me, you don't. So stay out of our relationship."

A relationship you're about to no longer have.

After several minutes of an intense stare-off, I decide to change the subject. "Adrian, how would Boyra have gotten into the penthouse?"

His eyes darken. "We've got a traitor on our hands. It's the only explanation."

I put my hand on my flipping gut. I'm not sure how I'm ever going to feel safe there again.

Or anywhere.

He hands me his phone. "Send him your list."

"How many days will we be gone?"

"Not sure."

I send off a short but quick list and give Adrian his phone back. Skylar walks out of the bedroom with her overnight bag.

Adrian walks over to her. "What are you doing?"

"I said I'm done." Her voice has the finality I've only heard her use a few times in her life. My chest tightens.

He needs to tell her.

"You can't leave right now."

She laughs. "You don't own me, Adrian. And you can't keep me here against my will."

"You aren't leaving this place until I tell you it's safe."

A disgusted huff comes out, and she goes toward the door.

Adrian steps in front of it. He growls, "Don't ignore me, Skylar."

"That's rich coming from you."

"I don't ignore you," he states.

"Move, Adrian."

"This isn't up for debate. It's not safe for you to leave, and you aren't going anywhere until I say," he barks.

"Skylar, you need to stay," I quickly tell her.

She spins on me. "Why, Kora? Tell me why."

Blood pounds between my ears. "I got attacked this morning."

"What?" Her face scrunches.

"Someone entered Sergey's penthouse and attacked me in the kitchen. Adrian is right. Until he says it's safe, you can't leave."

Her eyes turn to lasers. "Why would I be in danger if you got attacked?"

I look at Adrian for help.

She spins.

Adrian stares straight ahead, avoiding her eyes, his chiseled face emotionless.

"Tell me, Adrian."

He stays quiet and doesn't move.

"If my safety is at risk, I deserve to know what's going on. Look at me," she orders.

He doesn't.

She reaches up and smacks him. A red mark appears on his face. He blinks hard then slowly puts his hand over his cheek. He glances down at her with the same emotionless expression.

"I hate you," she whispers, turns, and ignores me. She walks back into the bedroom.

Adrian closes his eyes and leans against the door. Several minutes pass. He doesn't move. I knock on the bedroom door. "Skylar."

"Leave me alone, Kora," she calls out, and I can tell from her voice she's crying.

I hate I'm hurting her. I wish Adrian would tell her what is going on. I decide I'll talk to Sergey to see what he is okay with me telling her, so she isn't in the dark.

There's a pound on the door, and Adrian jumps. He looks out the peephole and opens it. Sergey walks in.

"Kora, we should go."

I open my mouth to speak then shut it. I'm not sure what to say right now.

Sergey looks between Adrian and me. "What's going on?"

"Another day in Ivanov paradise," Adrian mutters.

"What does that mean?"

"Nothing," Adrian grumbles. "If you'll excuse me, I've got a mess to clean up now. Lock up when you leave." He reaches on top of the door sill, grabs a key, and unlocks the door. He walks in and shuts the door.

A line forms between Sergey's eyes. "What happened?"

"I'll tell you later. We should go." I embrace him quickly then kiss him. "I'm so happy to see you."

He strokes my cheek. "Are you okay?"

I nod. "As long as I'm with you."

He gives me a peck on the lips, and we leave. He pulls out his keys and locks Adrian's front door then guides me to the car.

"Where are we going?" I ask.

"Maksim's. We'll stay there until we sort out who the leak in security is."

He pulls me onto his lap. "I'm so sorry you got hurt and this is happening."

"Shh. This isn't your fault."

"It is. My past—"

"Isn't your fault, either. And you're my life." I kiss him, trying to shove the feeling of Boyra's hands on my body out of my mind.

We make out for a while until Sergey pulls back. He glances out the window, and his face turns white. He attempts to put the divider window down, but it's locked. "What the fuck?"

I swallow hard when I look out the window and realize we aren't anywhere close to Maksim's. The car stops, and goose bumps pop out on my skin. "Where are we?"

Sergey moves me off his lap. He reaches under the seat, and his face falls.

"What?"

"My other gun is missing."

"Where's the first one?"

He lifts his shirt then takes out his pocket knife. He puts it in the waistband of my underwear. "If you have to use this, don't hesitate. Stab and keep stabbing."

My voice cracks. "What?"

He picks up his phone, texts, then dials Maksim. He puts his phone under the seat.

"What's happening?"

"I don't know, my lapa." He pushes the lock on my side of the car down, removes his gun, and flips the safety. He squeezes my hand. "If you get a chance to run, don't look back."

"I'm not leaving you!"

"Listen to me—"

The door flies open. Igor has a malicious expression on his face. Sergey shoots him in the head. He slumps to the ground.

I put my hand over my mouth.

Clapping echoes in my ears. My insides quiver. Four gunshots ring through the air, and loud pops sound like explosions. The car jerks lower.

Breathe.

The voice from earlier this morning yells in Russian.

"Fuck." Sergey tosses the gun out of the car. He puts his body in front of mine to shield me. He mutters, "When I say now, you give me the knife."

Boyra steps over Igor's dead body and kicks his head. He says something else in Russian. His eyes are the devil's. A fear I've never known consumes me.

Sergey

BOYRA ONLY SPEAKS IN RUSSIAN. I'M NOT EVEN SURE IF HE knows English. "Throw your gun out, or I shoot you and keep her."

My insides churn. I toss the gun out and tell Kora to give me the knife if I say the word now. I try to block Kora from the danger of whatever lies outside the car, but it's pointless.

"Both of you out of the car, now," Boyra demands.

I step out and over Igor's body, feeling betrayed my own driver would conspire with a Petrov.

How did I not see it?

I've known Igor since we were kids.

I reach in for Kora and pull her close to me. She's shaking, and I try to calm her, but it's in vain. I quickly glance around.

I know this place.

Nausea hits me. It's where Zamir branded my back when I was twelve.

Boyra laughs. "Ah. I see you realize where you are."

Only one thug? Where are the rest?

Zamir always had several men around him.

Surely Boyra has others hidden somewhere?

Where are they?

I scan the empty lot. We're on the outskirts of the city, in an abandoned parking lot. A black SUV sits behind mine. The blacked-out windows could be hiding another thug, but something in my gut says no one is in it.

"In," Boyra orders and motions for us to enter the run-down office building that sits on the property. It's a one-story, falling-apart, brick building. There are only two windows. Everything about it looks identical to when I was twelve. The feeling of déjà vu sweeps through me, and I swallow down the bile rising in my throat.

Stay calm. Kora can't afford for me to lose my shit.

The door creaks as I pull it open. Just like before, there's an open space taking up the entire building. Chains with rings hang from the ceiling and are secured to the floor by bolts.

Sweat pops out on my skin, and I tug Kora tighter.

Why hasn't he patted me down?

Boyra strolls past me. His gun is tucked in the back of his pants. He motions to the thug, who joins him by his side. He, too, isn't holding a gun.

He's cockier than Zamir.

Why didn't I keep my knife?

It's going to be more challenging to get it from Kora.

Boyra's cold eyes bore into mine. I try to ignore his lips curving in a sinister smile, the chill going down my spine, and the flashing of memories from being in this room.

"Strip," he orders.

Fuck. My heart beats faster. I hesitate.

"Now!" he screams, and Kora jumps.

I release her. I drop my pants and pull off my T-shirt.

"Tie him up," he orders his thug.

His thug pushes me toward the restraints. I avoid looking at Kora. Memories of being twelve are spinning so fast in my head, I can hardly breathe. If I look at her, I'm going to lose it.

The thug restrains my arms so I can't move then he kicks out my ankles.

I scream, stand on my tiptoes, and take shallow breaths, trying to regain my composure.

My ankles get locked down. The pain hits me from my muscles being overstretched. My toes start to go numb.

Boyra takes his finger and drags it along my back, scratching his nails along the scarred tissue. He leans into my ear. In

Russian, he says, "Did you think you could cover up the devil's mark?"

I don't respond and make the mistake of looking at Kora. Her hand is over her face, and tears fall off her cheeks.

"You're a piranha," I growl in English and lock eyes with her.

She straightens her shoulders and wipes her face.

Boyra laughs and steps in front of me. He drags his finger over my chest then pats me between the ribs. "This will do."

He spins and shouts, "Vlad."

Boyra steps over to Kora, and Vlad, the thug, moves in front of me. He takes out a knife and cuts a line down the middle of my chest.

"Argh!" I grit my teeth. It's a thin line, enough to draw blood, but not deep enough to drain me. I've done it to many men over the years. It extends the amount of time you can torture a person.

"Stop!" Kora cries out.

"Piranha!" I yell at her, trying to keep her mentally strong so she doesn't get hurt, hoping Maksim can find us in time from the text I sent him.

The tears don't stop. Boyra puts his arm around her waist, and she gasps.

"Piranha!"

Vlad mumbles the Russian word for piranha, which is similar to the English version. "Is that what you're saying?"

In English, I say, "Neither of you knows English, do you?"

"Russian!" Boyra screams.

Something snaps in me. "I killed your brother. I peeled off the skin of his back and held it in front of him to see. I dragged my knife over his raw spine over and over while he pissed himself."

"Russian!" Boyra demands again.

I start to laugh. Vlad slaps me hard in the face.

I slowly look up at him. "You're a pussy. If you're going to kill me, at least do it with some balls."

"Russian!" Boyra screams with rage.

I watch him take a step toward me. "You mother—"

Kora rips the gun from Boyra's pants, flips the safety, and shoots him in the back. He screams out in pain and collapses. She moves several steps away from Boyra. He's still alive and reaches for her, but she steps too far away. She aims the gun at Vlad.

"Untie him, now," she screams hysterically with tears falling down her cheeks.

Vlad stands paralyzed.

"Now!"

"Untie me," I order him in Russian.

He glances at Boyra, who gets on his knees and reaches again for Kora.

She moves the gun and shoots him in the chest then aims it back at Vlad. "Now!"

I repeat her demands. He releases my ankle then my wrist. He spins and looks at Kora. I regain my balance on my foot and reach for the other hand but can't get it undone.

"Untie him!" she screams again.

"Other side," I repeat in Russian.

He moves to untie me, but instead, lunges at Kora.

The gun goes off three times. He falls on her, and a pool of blood rapidly spreads under them.

"Kora!" I repeat over and over, but she never answers. I attempt to untie myself again, but I can't reach. "Kora!"

The sound of cars echo in my ears. The front door opens, and Maksim comes running in.

"Kora," I yell again.

Maksim rolls Vlad off her, but there's so much blood, and neither one is conscious. I hang from the ceiling, feeling like my entire world is sinking in around me.

Another car pulls up, and Liam and Killian come flying in. Liam picks up Kora and takes her away. Killian unties me, and I fall against him. Maksim hands me my clothes, and I grasp them as I run to the car Liam is in.

"Where was she shot?"

Blood covers Liam. "I can't find a bullet. She might have hit her head. She's breathing."

I pull her shirt off her, trying to find a wound, but I can't find anything. I press my head to hers. "Wake up, my lapa." I kiss her, stroke her cheek, and keep repeating it. We're almost to the hospital when her eyes flutter open.

She sees me, and tears well in her eyes. "Sergey," she whispers.

I pull her into my arms, blinking back my own tears. "Shh."

"You're bleeding." She presses her cold hand on my chest. Her body shakes hard.

"Shh." I wrap my body around her as much as possible. She passes out again.

We pull up to the hospital. I slide on my pants and carry her in. A team of people takes her from me and puts her on a stretcher. "She's going into shock," I hear a woman yell out.

I don't notice Maksim, Liam, or Killian by my side.

A woman with gray hair approaches me. "Sir, you need to come with us. You're bleeding."

I glance down and look at the blood drying on my chest.

"Get cleaned up," Maksim instructs.

I turn to him. "She can't..." My mouth turns dry.

"Get cleaned up," he repeats. "You can't do anything to help her right now. All we can do is wait."

A nurse stops me in the hall. "Sir, you brought the Black woman in who was unconscious and is going into shock?"

"Yes."

She hands me Kora's engagement ring. "This is too nice to be put on a table."

33

Kora

A LOUD BEEP ANNOYINGLY PULLS ME OUT OF MY SLEEP, drawing my attention to the horrible headache pounding in my skull. It's dark. There's a faint glow, but the light from the hallway is bright.

I groggily turn my head away from it and smile.

Sergey's hands are over my arm. His head is on top of them. I reach for his hair and tousle it. He slowly raises his head.

"Hey," I barely get out. My mouth is dry, and my throat feels like a crack is going through it.

His brown eyes glisten. He puts his lips on my hand and takes a few shaky breaths.

"Baby, are you okay?" I ask.

He rises and slides in bed with me. "You had me so worried."

"I'm okay. But..." I glance around. "Why am I in the hospital? And why does my head feel like a Mack truck drove into it?"

He tugs me closer to him. "Boyra's thug fell on you when you shot him. You have a concussion from hitting your head when he landed on you. You went into shock when we got to the hospital."

I stare at Sergey, and a chill runs through me. "I-I killed them both?"

He nods. "You saved us both, my little piranha."

I reach for his face. "I thought they were going to..." I swallow hard, and my body trembles. I put my hand on his chest. "How bad is the cut?"

He shakes his head. "It's not deep. I'm fine." He kisses my forehead.

I snuggle closer to him. "You're nice and warm. Can we go home?"

"They said we had to keep you here for observation due to your shock, but hopefully tomorrow we can go home." He opens his mouth then shuts it.

"What?"

"I'm sorry. I can't believe Igor was with the Petrovs. I've known him forever and..." He takes a shaky breath. "You could have been killed. Twice in one day. I...fuck."

I stroke his cheek. "Shh. I'm fine."

"I've been sitting here, wondering how I protect you from all this. If people I trust have turned against me, how do I keep you safe? I've pulled you into this world of sick, sadistic, toxic chaos, and I hate myself for it."

I roll into him further. "Don't do this."

His jaw spasms under my fingers.

"I love you. Don't try to throw me away."

He looks at the ceiling and sniffs hard. "That's the thing, Kora. I'm a selfish man. You shouldn't be around me. There's no way I'm ever escaping this life. Every time I think it's over, something else pops up. And I sat here with my mind spinning, trying to figure out how to let you go, but I can't. The thought alone makes me feel like I can't breathe. It's not right. You deserve so much better—"

I put my fingers over his lips. "If you let me go, I would die. The only person who's ever truly loved me is you. I don't take it for granted. What we have isn't replaceable. What you give me isn't something I can get from anyone else. And I would rather go through hell and back with you than be without you."

His heart beats faster against my hand.

I peck him on the lips. "You confirmed they are both dead?"

"Yes. Darragh dealt with the police. They won't be questioning you."

I stay silent, letting the power of Sergey's statement sink in.

His fingers brush my hips. "How did you know how to shoot a gun?"

My pulse quickens. "When my brother got shot, I took lessons. I went to the gun range for years, but it started to feel a bit unhealthy. I obsessed over it. So I put my gun in my safe and forgot about it."

"You were amazing. Strong. Brave. A total piranha," he says, and his lips form into a grin.

"Do you know what I thought when you first called me a piranha?"

"No. What?"

"That you would break me for fun."

A line forms between his eyes. He shakes his head. "I thought you were the sexiest woman I'd ever met. I love you're a piranha." His face turns serious. "You don't seem fazed you killed two men."

"Should I be?"

"No. I want to make sure you're okay though."

My lungs feel tighter. "They tried to hurt you. They would have done who knows what to me. The world is a better place without them."

He scans my face and nods. "I agree."

"I should have killed Boyra sooner for making me drop your soup on the floor," I joke.

He snorts. "I was looking forward to your soup."

"I'll make some this week."

"You're going to make the best wife."

I put my hand on his chest and stare at it. Panic fills me. "Oh no! I must have lost my ring."

He chuckles. "Nope. The nurse was kind enough to bring it to me." He dips his hand in his pocket and removes it. He slides it on my finger.

I sigh in relief. "Thank goodness. I love this ring."

Pride appears. "The moment I saw it, I knew it was perfect for you."

"Hey, what's the inscription mean?"

He takes my hand and holds it to his heart. *"My lapa, you are mine to love forever. Don't ever forget."*

I smile and blink my tears away. "I love it."

He holds my face and kisses me. It's raw and tender. Possessive and dominant as always. Every kiss breathes life into me. Each hungry flick of his tongue holds promises of our future. He's everything I never had and everything I've always wanted.

The city of Chicago knows me as Kora Kilborn, divorce attorney for wealthy women. The only title I crave for others to know me as is Mrs. Sergey Ivanov. I want him for life. He's the strongest, sexiest man I know.

Others tried to break him, but he never let them, even as a boy. And any remaining shattered piece of his past, I'll try to repair. It's what he does for me every day. He takes every little shard of pain or feeling of disappointment and glues it back together.

"When can we get married?" I ask.

His lips twitch. "As soon as you want."

"And how many people do we have to invite?"

"As long as you're there, I don't care about any of the details. I want you to have the wedding of your dreams."

I stroke his jawline. "It already is. I'm marrying you."

EPILOGUE

Sergey

Maksim straightens my light-pink bowtie. "It's almost time."

I can't help grinning like an idiot. I've not stopped smiling since I woke up. My cheeks hurt from the strain.

Boris passes out vodka shots and holds his in the air. "Nostrovia!"

"Nostrovia," the room of men repeat, and we all down shots of Beluga vodka.

Killian winces. "When are you going to learn to drink real alcohol?" He chases it with his flask of whiskey.

Boris pats him on the chest. "It'll put hair on your chest."

Dmitri puts his hand on my shoulder. "There's one rule to marriage you must never forget."

"Don't cheat, or she has a right to beat you to death?" Nolan calls out across the room, already slightly tipsy.

Dmitri grunts. "Happy wife, happy life."

"Nostrovia," Boris says and takes another shot.

Darragh takes a drag of his pipe and goes into a coughing fit. When his eyes are bloodshot, teary, and red marks speckle his handkerchief, he says, "Don't forget anniversaries, birthdays, or that time of the month."

"That time of the month?" Declan asks.

"Yeah. You know, when to stay out of the house. Your auntie is one hell of a nasty woman once a month. Menopause hits, and she still reserves her monthly right to gripe and nag me."

"Dad, when doesn't Mom nag?" Liam asks.

He swats his head. "Watch your tone. That's your mother."

Liam groans.

There's a knock on the door. The wedding officiant sticks his head in the room. "Ready?"

"Yep." My stomach erupts in nervous butterflies.

She's going to be my wife.

More pain from smiling hits my cheeks as happiness soars through me.

The room clears out as the other men go to take their seats. My brothers and I make our way to the chapel where we stand at the front and I wait for Kora to appear. She wanted a small wedding. It made me happy. I made sure she told me exactly what she wanted before voicing my approval over her choices, but everything she decided coordinated with what I deep down imagined.

When the music changes and the doors open, my breath is stolen.

Jesus. She wore pink.

My cock hardens, watching my soon-to-be wife glow in a pale-pink, form-fitting wedding dress. Her elegant shoulders and arms are bare. She carries a bouquet of white roses. Her hair is up, and a white veil trails past her shoulders.

Kora walks alone, confident, her eyes focused only on me. She didn't want anyone to give her away. I love her ability to do this independently.

"You're my only man. No one else has been. I don't want to pretend," she had said.

There's my piranha.

When I finally can take her hands, the nerves in my belly disappear. I inhale her floral scent and lean into her ear. "You wore pink to distract me from our vows?"

Her lips twitch.

"You look stunning. As soon as this is over, I'm getting under that dress, my lapa."

She blushes and murmurs back, "Yes, sir."

I groan inside.

This is my wife.

We say our vows, promising to always love, cherish, and respect each other until the day we die. No one else could say those words to me and have it affect me like it does when Kora says it.

"You may kiss your bride," the officiant says.

I take my wife in my arms and give her a kiss bordering indecent, until she's breathless and moans in my mouth.

"I'm pleased to introduce to you, Mr. and Mrs. Sergey Ivanov!"

The guests all cheer, and I lead my beautiful bride down the aisle and out into the beautiful summer air. I kiss her again, and our wedding party joins us, then the other guests all come to give us their congratulations.

Every moment of our day is perfect. When the night turns to the next day, we get in the car and head to the airport for our honeymoon.

"There's too much of this dress," I laugh, pulling the pink fabric up before finding her panties. I run my finger over her wet slit and grunt when I discover her crotchless panties. "You're the perfect wife."

She kisses me and slides over my erection, and we both groan, as if in relief. All night I tried to get her alone and couldn't.

I fist her hair and pull her head back. "I can't wait to lick your pretty pink pussy tonight," I murmur in her ear.

"Yes," she breathes and circles her hips faster.

The divider window cracks open. "Sir, I'm sorry to interrupt, but your brother just called. Maksim said you need to call him now." He puts the divider back up.

Kora stops moving, and goose bumps pop out on her skin. "What could be so important?"

"I don't know." I pull out my phone and hit the button. I stroke Kora's cheek.

"Sergey. You can't go," Maksim states.

"What are you talking about?"

"Meet us at the hospital. One of Zielinski's guys just shot Adrian. They don't think he's going to make it."

READ VICIOUS PROTECTOR - FREE ON KINDLE UNLIMITED

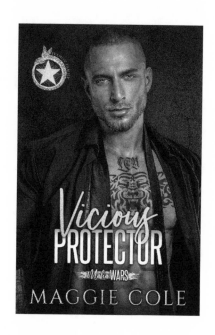

Demons so deep they destroy us...

Every part of Adrian Ivanov is pure, unable to ignore, male virility. He's arrogant. Protective. Sweet and intensely attentive. On rare occasions, outright vicious.

If only his soul weren't tortured over who he is and what he has become. It makes him hide it all from me, proclaiming the truth will ruin us. No matter how much I insist anything he confesses won't deter my heart, his ghosts won't allow him.

But they aren't apparitions. The present collides with the past in a dangerous and twisted game he doesn't even know he's a pawn in. It causes everything in our future to remain in jeopardy.

There's a choice, yet nothing hard in life comes without consequences.

He's my vicious protector...

READ VICIOUS PROTECTOR - FREE ON KINDLE UNLIMITED

SKYLAR
VICIOUS PROTECTOR PROLOGUE

Skylar Scott

FAIRY TALES AREN'T REAL. I LEARNED THIS LESSON THE HARD way. Looking back, I curse myself for ever wanting to find true love. Everything I assumed about it is wrong. It's not the amazing feeling I expected.

It's one hundred percent soul-crushing, delicious at times, painful in ways you never imagined, addicting beyond measure, all-consuming torment. Love grips and holds on to you, stabbing you any chance it gets.

Or maybe it's only like that if you love Adrian Ivanov.

Why didn't I bring a date?

Did he?

I didn't see anyone with him.

She could have been in the bathroom or talking to someone else.

Why was I even looking? We're finished.

"It's time. Everyone, please take your places," the wedding planner tells us. It's Kora and Sergey's wedding. She's been my best friend for longer than I can remember. She's so happy, she's glowing. It gives me joy and creates a jealous flare in my bones. I hate feeling envious of her happiness. Kora deserves every morsel of delight. She and Sergey have been through so much. They are perfect for each other, and you can feel their love.

I hug her again. "You look stunning."

Her beaming smile only grows. "Thank you."

I take my place behind Aspen and Hailee. I'm Kora's maid of honor. When I walk down the aisle, I try to avoid Adrian's cocky stare, eating me up, as if I'm going to be his dinner. I take controlled breaths to attempt not to blush. I can feel him checking me out with his piercing, icy-blue orbs, even though I'm avoiding him.

My insides shake. Before last night, I hadn't seen him in several months. Our last encounter was at the hospital. Kora and Sergey got abducted, and something went down. I still don't have all the details. I'm tired of asking for them. Kora and Aspen hide issues concerning the Ivanovs in a secret vault. I've fought with them so many times to tell me things, but they won't. I finally decided I needed to let it go. I already lost Adrian. I don't need to lose my friends, too.

Last night, I stayed on the opposite side of the room from Adrian. We were at a restaurant for the rehearsal dinner. My heart raced similar to what it's doing now. Somehow, I got through the night without talking to him. Earlier today, I saw him across the room when I went to the bathroom. I ignored him, and when I came out, he was gone. Disappointment and relief swirled through me.

Focus on the ceremony, not him.

The peek I allow myself only makes my pain expand. Adrian Ivanov is the epitome of sex on an average day. In a tux, he's a demigod. Adonis himself would be jealous. Fabric stretches over Adrian's hard, chiseled body, with just enough tautness to tease any female who glances his way. Assumptions about his body will make your panties melt, but firsthand knowledge is what makes everything even more unfair. Until you see and feel Adrian's naked body against yours, you assume he's ripped, no different from other fit guys.

All hypotheses of Adrian and what an experience with him is like are wrong. Other men may have good bodies, but they don't know how to use them. Adrian can dominate you in the bedroom in the smallest of ways. His eyes alone can bring you to your knees. I'm convinced no other man on the planet knows how to use his tongue or fingers, and I'm not even referring to the most intimate acts.

Sex with Adrian is filthy ecstasy. There's no boundary of how he'll please you. His smug arrogance drew me to him. Each cocky expression is well-earned. Everything he does with his hands, mouth, or eyes turns my insides to hot lava. There's masculinity about him other men don't possess, along with a thick Russian accent growling in your ear.

Focus on Kora. Focus on Kora. Focus on Kora.

He's staring at me.

Don't look at him.

My eyes dart to his sculpted features and verify my feeling

was correct. He's got his hardened, cocky expression pinned on me. Heat rushes to my cheeks. I quickly refocus on Kora.

No one is next to him.

Is his date hiding somewhere?

Why am I even thinking about this?

A pulse of paranoia creeps from my toes and crawls up my body, torturing me. When I was with Adrian, I loved how his mere presence sent my loins into overdrive. Right now, I detest how much he still affects me.

If he could only trust me enough to tell me the truth about what he does and where he goes at night, or what happened to Kora and Sergey, we could be together.

He chooses not to let me in.

I can't help myself. I gaze away from Kora and catch Adrian's eyes again. The heat on my face intensifies.

Someone should tell him it's rude to stare.

The ceremony continues. I miss what's going on. All I can think about is Adrian and how much I miss him. His ongoing arrogant poker face gives me the impression he wants to do naughty things with me. It's not helping my current predicament.

I've missed that look.

Not helping!

The officiant announces Sergey may kiss the bride. I snap out of my thoughts when the room erupts in cheers. My reaction is a mix of tears and a smile. I'm happy for Kora, but having Adrian this close, keeping his intense eyes on my body, only reminds me how I fooled myself I could have the happily ever after.

No man is ever going to match up to Adrian in any department. Not the looks, sex, or way he made me feel when I was with him. Besides all the fights about where he was and who he was with, everything about us seemed to sync. He made me laugh. I felt safe with him. We just got each other.

Most days, I feel like I can't breathe. I keep trying to convince myself it'll get better. Somehow, I'll get past Adrian.

It's a lie. How do you go from a five-star resort with luxurious amenities you never knew existed to a cheap, dingy motel?

You can't. It's impossible not to remember what you once had.

Over the last few months, I've had good-looking men from every walk of life hit on me. I attempted to date to move on. I keep thinking if I find someone else, I'll forget Adrian. It's another lie.

I couldn't get past dinner, coffee, or whatever else we were doing to get to know each other. I hoped enough time passed that I could move on. Each date only reaffirmed my suspicion. There is no getting over Adrian Ivanov.

I follow the happy couple down the aisle and go through the motions. When the photographer tells us we can all go and for Kora and Sergey to stay, I hightail it to the bathroom.

No one is inside, except me. I wash my hands with cold water and refrain from putting it on my face so I don't mess up my makeup. I give myself another pep talk to stay away from Adrian.

Straightening my shoulders, I step out of the bathroom. My gut flips. Adrian is standing against the brick wall, as if waiting for me.

Blood pounds between my ears. My heart hurts, looking at the man I love whom I can't get over. I think the pain can't get any worse, but I overestimated the ache that keeps growing. It's nothing compared to what lies ahead.

READ VICIOUS PROTECTOR - FREE ON KINDLE UNLIMITED

ALL IN BOXSET

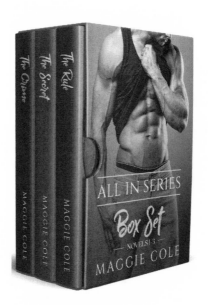

Three page-turning, interconnected stand-alone romance novels with HEA's!! Get ready to fall in love with the characters. Billionaires. Professional athletes. New York City. Twist, turns, and danger lurking everywhere. The only option for these couples is to go ALL IN...with a little help from their friends. EXTRA STEAM INCLUDED!

*Grab it now! **READ FREE IN KINDLE UNLIMITED!***

CAN I ASK YOU A HUGE FAVOR?

Would you be willing to leave me a review?

I would be forever grateful as one positive review on Amazon is like buying the book a hundred times! Reader support is the lifeblood for Indie authors and provides us the feedback we need to give readers what they want in future stories!

Your positive review means the world to me! So thank you from the bottom of my heart!

CLICK TO REVIEW

MORE BY MAGGIE COLE

Mafia Wars - A Dark Mafia Series (Series Five)

Ruthless Stranger (Maksim's Story) - Book One

Broken Fighter (Boris's Story) - Book Two

Cruel Enforcer (Sergey's Story) - Book Three

Vicious Protector (Adrian's Story) - Book Four

Savage Tracker (Obrecht's Story) - Book Five

Unchosen Ruler (Liam's Story) - Book Six

Perfect Sinner (Nolan's Story) - Book Seven

Brutal Defender (Killian's Story) - Book Eight

Behind Closed Doors (Series Four - Former Military Now International Rescue Alpha Studs)

Depths of Destruction - Book One

Marks of Rebellion - Book Two

Haze of Obedience - Book Three

Cavern of Silence - Book Four

Stains of Desire - Book Five

Risks of Temptation - Book Six

Together We Stand Series (Series Three - Family Saga)

Kiss of Redemption- Book One

Sins of Justice - Book Two

Acts of Manipulation - Book Three

Web of Betrayal - Book Four

Masks of Devotion - Book Five

Roots of Vengeance - Book Six

It's Complicated Series (Series Two - Chicago Billionaires)

Crossing the Line - Book One

Don't Forget Me - Book Two

Committed to You - Book Three

More Than Paper - Book Four

Sins of the Father - Book Five

Wrapped In Perfection - Book Six

All In Series (Series One - New York Billionaires)

The Rule - Book One

The Secret - Book Two

The Crime - Book Three

The Lie - Book Four

The Trap - Book Five

The Gamble - Book Six

STAND ALONE NOVELLA

JUDGE ME NOT - A Billionaire Single Mom Christmas Novella

ABOUT THE AUTHOR

Amazon Bestselling Author

Maggie Cole is committed to bringing her readers alphalicious book boyfriends. She's been called the "literary master of steamy romance." Her books are full of raw emotion, suspense, and will always keep you wanting more. She is a masterful storyteller of contemporary romance and loves writing about broken people who rise above the ashes.

She lives in Florida near the Gulf of Mexico with her husband, son, and dog. She loves sunshine, wine, and hanging out with friends.

Her current series were written in the order below:

- All In (Stand alones with entwined characters)
- It's Complicated (Stand alones with entwined characters)
- Together We Stand (Brooks Family Saga - read in order)
- Behind Closed Doors (Read in order)
- Mafia Wars (Coming April 1st 2021)

Maggie Cole's Newsletter
Sign up here!

Hang Out with Maggie in Her Reader Group
Maggie Cole's Romance Addicts

Follow for Giveaways
Facebook Maggie Cole

Instagram
@maggiecoleauthor

Complete Works on Amazon
Follow Maggie's Amazon Author Page

Book Trailers
Follow Maggie on YouTube

Are you a Blogger and want to join my ARC team?
Signup now!

Feedback or suggestions?
Email: authormaggiecole@gmail.com